PRAISE FOR PAUL E. HARDISTY

'A solid, meaty thriller … Hardisty is a fine writer and Straker is a great lead character' Lee Child

'A gripping, page-turning thriller that is overflowing with substance to go along with Hardisty's atmospheric prose and strong narrative style' Craig Sisterson, *Mystery Magazine*

'A stormer of a thriller – vividly written, utterly topical, totally gripping' Peter James

'Hardisty's searing third Claymore Straker thriller, a tale of racial hatred, greed, and corruption, might break the reader's heart – or tear it out. The writing can be disturbingly graphic but it also at times achieves the level of genuine poetry' *Publishers Weekly*

'The Straker novels are fast-paced, gripping and exciting … Hardisty's writing and the underlying truth of his plots sets these stories above many other thrillers' *West Australian*

'I was a big fan, in 2013, of Terry Hayes's *I Am Pilgrim* and I hadn't up to now read a conspiracy thriller which came close to it in terms of quality' Sarah Ward, author of *A Deadly Thaw*

'A compelling read and more thought-provoking than many mainstream thrillers. The writing at times is poetic, at other times filled with tension in a narrative complete with well-delineated characters and several shocks. Highly Recommended' Shots Mag

'This is a remarkably well-written, sophisticated novel in which the people and places, as well as frequent scenes of violent action, all come alive on the page … This is a really excellent debut' *Literary Review*

'The plot burns through petrol, with multiple twists and turns, some signposted, some completely unexpected' Vicky Newham, author of *Turn a Blind Eye*

'With echoes of Terry Hayes' *I Am Pilgrim*, this book just knocks it out of the park in terms of what I look for when I want to read a thriller' Bibliophile Book Club

'The story rockets along, twisting and turning amid clouds of dust from the Yemeni deserts, pausing occasionally to put aside the AK-47s and take tea amid the generosity of an Islamic culture Hardisty clearly understands and admires … exceptional' Tim Marshall, *Prisoners of Geography*

'A page-turning adventure that grabs you from the first page and won't let go' Edward Wilson

'Beautifully written, blisteringly authentic, heart-stoppingly tense and unusually moving. Definite award material' Paul Johnston

'This is an exceptional and innovative novel. And an important one. I can't praise it highly enough' Susan Moody

'The author's deep knowledge of the settings never slows down the non-stop action, with echoes of a more moral-minded Jack Reacher or Jason Bourne. A forceful first novel by a writer not afraid of weighty issues and visibly in love with the beauty of the Yemen and desert landscapes his protagonists travel through' Maxim Jakubowski, LoveReading

'A trenchant and engaging thriller that unravels this mysterious land in cool, precise sentences' Stav Sherez, *Catholic Herald*

'I'm a sucker for genuine thrillers with powerful redemptive themes, but what spoke to me more strongly than anything was the courage, integrity and passion with which this novel is written' Eve Seymour, *Cheltenham Standard*

'Smart, gripping, superbly crafted oil-industry thriller' Helen Giltrow, author of *The Distance*

'Wow. Just wow. If you need a point of reference think, John Le Carré's *A Constant Gardener*. A thriller with heart and a conscience' Michael J. Malone, author of *A Suitable Lie*

'A thriller of the highest quality, with the potential to one day stand in the company of such luminaries as Bond and Bourne … This is intelligent writing that both entertains and challenges, and it deserves a wide audience' Live Many Lives

'The sense of place, and the way that the climate, the landscape and the people all combine within a location very foreign to that which many of us live in is evocative' *Australian Crime*

'Just occasionally, a book comes along to restore your faith in a genre – and Paul Hardisty's *The Abrupt Physics of Dying* does this in spades. It's absolutely beautifully written and atmospheric – and it provides an unrivalled look at Yemen, a country few of us know much about … appreciate intelligent, quality writing' Sharon Wheeler, *The Times*

'This thrilling debut opens with a tense, utterly gripping roadside hijacking … Hardisty's prose is rich, descriptive and elegant, but break-neck pace is the king … an exhilarating, white-knuckle ride' Paddy Magrane, author of *Disorder*

'Hardisty details Yemen, the political climate and the science with an authority that's never questionable and with a delivery that's polished enough to make you wonder whether he hasn't secretly been publishing thrillers under a different name for years…' Mumbling about…

'If you enjoy a story that is well written, with a plot that twists and turns and leads you astray, then I'd recommend this. If you want a hero that is a little bit unusual, with his own issues, but is determined and so well created, then I'd recommend this. If you want a complex and intelligent thriller, then I'd really, really recommend this' Random Things through My Letterbox

'It is clear that the author's background and experience has enabled him to write a thriller that is so rich and detailed in description that you can almost feel the searing heat and visualise the vast endless desert…' My Reading Corner

'I seriously cannot remember the last time I was this gripped by a thriller … a beautiful package of really exceptional storytelling, with an authentic edge which means you honestly believe every moment of it. This is a modern thriller with a literary edge, one that could equally win the highest awards' Liz Loves Books

'A thought-provoking and heart-wrenching book, and a real page-turner with a pulse-poundingly fast pace' Steph Broadribb, author of *Deep Down Dead*

'A gritty, at times violent and gripping, eco-thriller' Trip Fiction

'The well-written, almost poetic, vivid descriptions are unusual in a book of this genre, showing how the author, Paul E. Hardisty, has a gift for detailed but fast-paced writing' Off-the-Shelf Books

'An epic reading experience that will have you yearning to know what happens next' Segnalibro

'An exciting, absorbing and provocative stormer' Kevin Freeburn

'The story is gritty, action-packed and topical … prepare to be wowed by a new kid on the block' The Library Door

'Despite its panoramic scope – personal, political and cultural – it hooks you in from the start and challenges you to try putting it down before – breathless and exhausted – you reach its shocking and satisfying conclusion' Claire Thinking

'Read this for the pleasure of an edge-of-your-seat adventure. You will be offered so much more' Never Imitate

'There is so much happening in this book that I think the phrase "action-packed" was coined especially for it!' Damp Pebbles

'Feels like James Bond at his best – a perfect distilling of contemporary fears, producing a final product which is pure action. While Bond fought Communists and nuclear annihilation, Straker's enemies are fundamentalism and environmental destruction. But Straker is a much more palatable hero for our times; a damaged man, who will inevitably lose something more of himself before the novel is over' Crime Fiction Lover

'The feelings evoked stayed with me a long time after I finished the last page and I cannot recommend it highly enough' Crime Book Junkie

'An edge-of-your-seat thriller that comes at you fast and hard' By-the-Letter Book Reviews

'A brilliant thriller, with so many twists and turns it will make you dizzy' Tracy Shephard

'Civil war, terrorism, corporate ruthlessness and corruption, and harsh global realities are examined in a thrilling, action-fuelled style that has enough authenticity and atmosphere to sink the reader into the story' Crime Thriller Hound

'The science reminds me of Patricia Cornwell's Scarpetta novels. This is a modern treatment of a centuries-old conflict between indigenous peoples and usurpers bent on exploitation' Texas Book Lover

ABSOLUTION

Absolution

PAUL E. HARDISTY

**ORENDA
BOOKS**

Orenda Books
16 Carson Road
West Dulwich
London SE21 8HU
www.orendabooks.co.uk

First published in the United Kingdom by Orenda Books 2018

ISBN 978-1-912374-13-7
eISBN 978-1-912374-14-4

Typeset in Garamond by MacGuru Ltd
Printed and bound in Denmark by Nørhaven, Viborg

For sales and distribution, please contact *info@orendabooks.co.uk*

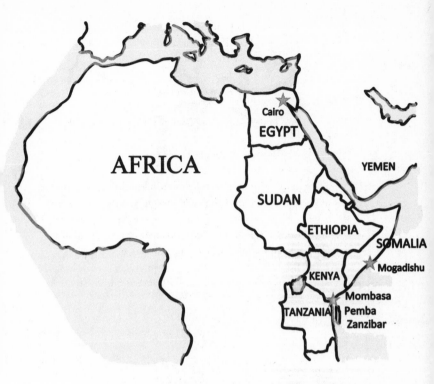

EASTERN AFRICA

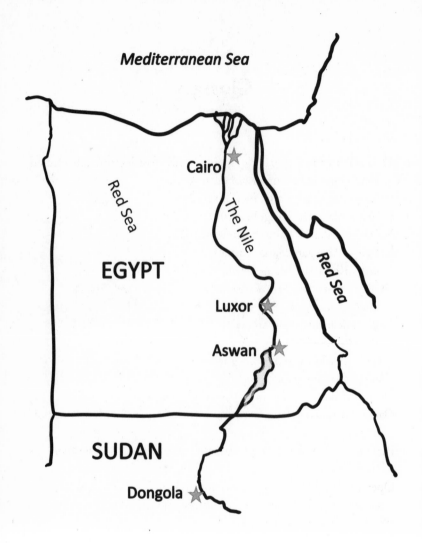

EGYPT AND SUDAN

Glossary

ANC – African National Congress; formed first legitimately elected democratic government of South Africa

Bakkie – Afrikaans slang: pick-up truck

Bokkie – Afrikaans slang: beautiful woman

Bossies – Afrikaans slang: bush dementia

Bliksem – Afrikaans slang: bastard

China – Rhodesian slang: friend

DGSE – *Direction Générale de la Sécurité Extérieure*: French intelligence agency

Doffs – Afrikaans slang: idiots.

Glide – Rhodesian slang: trip

Lekker – Afrikaans slang: nice, sweet

Okes – Afrikaans slang: guy

Oom – Afrikaans slang: uncle (word of respect)

Ooma – Afrikaans slang: aunty, old woman, grandmother (word of respect)

Parabat – Army slang: South African paratrooper; also *vliesbom* (meat bomb)

Operation COAST – Apartheid South Africa's super-secret chemical and biological weapons programme

Poppie – Afrikaans slang: doll

R4 – standard issue 5.56 mm calibre assault rifle of South African Army, the South African-made version of the Israeli Galil rifle, semi-automatic

Rofie – Afrikaans slang: new recruit

Rondfok – Afrikaans slang: literally 'circle fuck'

RV – rendezvous point

SADF – South African Defence Forces

Seun – Afrikaans: son

Sitrep – situation report

SWAPO – South West Africa People's Organisation; rebel group fighting for Namibian independence

Torch Commando – banned underground organisation of mostly white South Africans dedicated to overthrowing apartheid

TRC – South Africa's Truth and Reconciliation Commission, chaired by Desmond Tutu, started in 1996 to help heal the wounds after apartheid

Valk – Afrikaans for hawk, the designation for a platoon of South African Army paratroopers, approximately thirty men

Volkstaat – Afrikaans for the dreamed-of independent Afrikaner homeland

Vrot – Afrikaans slang: wasted, intoxicated

Zut – Rhodesian slang: nothing

For Heidi

'And God has created you, and in time will cause you to die'
Holy Qu'ran, Surah 16:70

'It would kill the past, and when that was dead, he would be free'
Oscar Wilde

Part I

25th October 1997. Paris, France. 02:50 hrs

Chéri, mon amour:
My husband has disappeared. And so has my son.

As I write this, my tears stain the page. How many have I wept onto these pages in the three and half years since you and I first met? Has it really been that long? It is as if I have known you forever, and not at all.

I am frantic. I can feel the panic churning in my breast. It has been two days since I discovered that they were gone. God, help me, please.

I wish you were here.

It was a Tuesday. A normal day. We got up, had breakfast at the usual time. I got Eugène ready for the day. Hamid left for the office as he always does, taking Eugène with him to drop him at the crèche.

I replay that morning in my mind, trying to identify something – anything – that might have been different, out of the ordinary. Something that may give me some clue. The coffee and bread on the table; Eugène in his high chair attempting to spoon puréed vegetables into his beautiful little mouth; the radio playing in the background – Radio Nationale, something about the international chemical weapons treaty coming into force. Hamid is dressed in his favourite suit with the silk tie I gave him for his birthday last year – the grey one that sets off the silver that has begun to fleck his temples. I wanted to make love with him that morning, but he was in a hurry – a big case he is working on – so he kissed me, rolled out of bed and got into the shower.

As usual on Tuesdays, I went to the bureau. I worked on my latest piece – child slavery in the Philippines. I was a little late coming home. I usually return by two o'clock so that I have plenty of time to start dinner and welcome my husband and son when they get home, which is normally at about three o'clock. That day I didn't arrive until just before three. Hamid and Eugène weren't home yet, so I started preparing the vegetables, marinating the filet. By half past three, they still had not arrived. Hamid is fastidiously punctual – always calls if he is going to be late. I waited another quarter of an hour and then tried his mobile. He did not answer. I left a voice message. At a quarter past four I tried again. Still no answer. I called his office. His executive assistant told me that he hadn't been in the office all day. I sat, stunned.

I waited, told myself that it would all be fine, that the rising panic I was feeling was ridiculous, that there was some logical explanation, and that very soon the door would open and my husband and son would be there, smiling at me.

The hours crept by. I drank cup after cup of coffee. I telephoned everyone I could think of that might know where they could be: Hamid's sister in Toulon, his law partner, our family doctor, all of the other mothers that I know from the crèche. Later that evening, I even called Hamid's mother in Beirut. No one knew anything. That night I did not sleep at all.

Yesterday, I went to the crèche first thing in the morning, as soon as it opened. The manageress confirmed that Hamid had dropped Eugène off on Tuesday morning, as usual. She showed me the registration records. Hamid's signature was there, very clearly. The time was 08:25. This is part of our arrangement, how we have decided to run our life together. Three days a week, Hamid takes Eugène to the crèche on his way to work in the morning, and then collects him again at half past two and brings him home. We eat an early supper together as a family, and then Hamid goes back to the office, or works in his study at home. This allows me to go directly to the bureau three mornings a week. I catch the bus and the metro. It means we only need one car. On Thursdays and Fridays, I work from home, and we both try to spend the weekends together, and avoid work for a time. We are a very modern Muslim family, and for that I am grateful. It means I have been able continue my career.

Our life, I thought, all considered, was good. Happy. I still cannot believe they are gone. I look around the room, smelling them both, feeling their presence in every object, expecting at any moment to hear the echo of their footsteps on the parquet floor, see their smiling faces peering around the doorframe.

I met Hamid not long after I returned from Cyprus after losing the baby. Our baby, chéri. *I was still damaged and withdrawn after everything that had happened – the time in Istanbul with you, then Cyprus and the minefield, the explosion … the miscarriage. Hamid was thoughtful and patient, sending me flowers and listening to my stories, and when he asked me to marry him we still had not slept with each other. In fact, during our three-month courtship, all he ever tried to do was kiss me. He was very respectful, a perfect gentleman. We were married in spring, in the countryside in Normandie, and Eugène was born a year later, healthy and strong and holding his head up in the first month. Every time I look at him I wonder what might have been.*

I have never told you any of this, I know. Those two letters you sent me from prison in Cyprus still lie in my bureau, read and reread … but unanswered. Only here, in these pages, have I shared my life with you. Any other way would have been too hurtful – for us both.

It has been just over two years now since Hamid and I married, and Claymore, I want you to know that he has been a good husband. He treats me well and is never disrespectful. He works long hours, and over the past year he has had to travel quite frequently for work, mostly to meet with clients he is defending. I miss him when he goes, but I have not had any reason to worry, to think he might be unfaithful. Not until recently. He is a gentle man, quietly talkative yet considered. Delicate, in a way. Everything that you are not.

Hamid is a good Muslim – better in many ways than I am. But his faith is not overt. As with everything he does, his piety is quiet and understated and thoroughly planned. He goes to the mosque on Fridays, occasionally, if he can get away from work, but otherwise I have never seen him praying at home or anywhere else. He does not smoke or drink, and I have not seen him lose his temper or raise his voice since we have been together. Above all, he is open and communicative in a way you never were, and probably never can be, wherever you are, Allah protect you.

Perhaps Hamid has taken Eugène to the country. Maybe he just needed a break, some time to himself. I know he has been under a lot of stress recently. This latest case in Egypt has been very difficult for him. He has not told me much about it – he never does, but a wife knows these things. This is what I tell myself. That I know. That everything will be alright. That, despite two days of silence, he will pick up the phone and call me. Now. Now.

Now.

He must know that I am worried beyond sickness. Yes, he would know. The only reason he hasn't called is that he cannot. Something must have happened to them on the way home. Mon Dieu, I cannot bear to think of it.

And yet, I have telephoned every hospital in Paris. No one bearing the name Hamid or Eugène Al Farouk has been registered anywhere. I called the police, of course, and completed a missing person's report, but have heard nothing back yet. It is as if they have vanished. As if they have been erased from the surface of the Earth.

I need to sleep now. I can barely see the page. I have cried myself out. And I realise that without them – without you – I have no one.

I am completely alone.

1

Guns and Money

26th October 1997
Latitude 6° 21' S; Longitude 39° 13' E,
Off the Coast of Zanzibar, East Africa

Claymore Straker drifted on the surface, stared down into the living architecture of the reef and tried not to think of her. Prisms of light crazed the many-branched and plated corals, winked rainbows from the scales of fish. Edged shadows twitched across the shoals, and for a moment dusk came, muting the colours of the sea. Floating in this new darkness, a distant echo came, hard and metallic, like the first syllables of a warning. Clay shivered, felt the cold do a random walk up his spine, seep into the big muscles across his back. He listened awhile, but as quickly as it had come, the sound was gone.

Clay blew clear his snorkel, pulled up his mask, and looked out across the rising afternoon chop, searching the horizon. Other than the weekly supply run from Stone Town, boats here were few. It was off-season and the hotel – the only establishment on the island – was closed. He could see the long arc of the island's southern point, the terrace of the little hotel where Grace worked as caretaker, the small dock where guests were welcomed from the main island, and away on the horizon, a dark wall of rain-heavy cloud, moving fast in a freshening easterly. He treaded water, scanned the distance back toward the mainland. But all he could see were the great banks of cloud racing slantwise across the channel and the sunlight strobing over the world in thick stochastic beams, everything transient and without reference.

He'd lost track of how long he'd been here now. Long enough to fashion a sturdy mooring for *Flame* from a concrete block that he'd anchored carefully on the seabed. Long enough to have snorkelled every part of the island's coastline, to know the stark difference between the life on the protected park side, and the grey sterility of the unprotected, fished-out eastern side. Sufficient time to hope that, perhaps, finally, he had disappeared.

The sun came, fell warm on the wet skin of his face and shoulders and the crown of his head. He pulled on his mask, jawed the snorkel's mouthpiece and started towards the isthmus with big overhand strokes. Months at sea had left him lean, on the edge of hunger, darkened and bleached both so that the hair on his chest and arms and shorn across the bonework of his skull stood pale against his skin. For the first time in a long time, he was without pain. He felt strong. It was as if the trade winds had somehow cleansed him, helped to heal the scars.

As he rounded the isthmus, *Flame* came into view. She lay bow to the island's western shore, straining on her mooring. He could just see the little house where Grace lived, notched into the rock on the lee side of the point, shaded by wind-bent palms and scrub acacia.

And then he heard it again.

It wasn't the storm. Nor was it the sound of the waves pounding the windward shore. Its rhythm was far too contained, focused in a way nature could never be. And it was getting louder.

A small boat had just rounded the island's southern point and was heading towards the isthmus. The craft was sleek, sat low in the water. Spray flew from its bow, shot high from its stern. It was some kind of jet boat – unusual in these waters, and moving fast. The boat made a wide arc, steering clear of the unmarked shoals that dangered the south end of the island, and then abruptly changed course. It was heading straight for *Flame*. Whoever was piloting the thing knew these waters, and was in a hell of hurry.

Clay floated low and still in the water, and watched the boat approach. It was close enough now that he could make out the craft's line, the black stripe along the yellow hull, the long, narrow bow, the raked V of the low-swept windscreen. It was closing on *Flame*, coming at speed. Two black men were aboard, one standing at the controls, the other sitting further back near the engines. The man who was piloting wore sunglasses and a red shirt with sleeves cut off at heavily muscled shoulders. The other had long dreadlocks that flew in the wind.

Twenty metres short of *Flame*, Red Shirt cut power. The boat slowed, rose up on its own wake and settled into the water. Dreadlock jumped up onto the bow with a line, grabbed *Flame*'s portside mainstay and stepped aboard.

Clay's heart rate skyed. He floated quiet in the water, his heart hammering inside his ribs and echoing back against the water. Dreadlock tied the boat alongside and stepped into *Flame*'s cockpit. He leaned forwards at the waist and put his ear to the hatch a moment, then he straightened and knocked as one would on the door of an apartment or an office. He waited a while, then looked back at the man in the jet boat and hunched his shoulders.

'Take a look,' came Red Shirt's voice, skipping along the water, the local accent clear and unmistakable.

Dreadlock pushed back the hatch – Clay never kept it locked – and disappeared below deck. Perhaps they were looking for someone else. They could be just common brigands, out for whatever they could find. All of Clay's valuables – his cash and passports – were in the priest hole. His weapons, too. It was very unlikely that the man would find it, so beautifully concealed and constructed was it. There was nothing else on board that could identify Clay in any way. Maybe they would just sniff around and leave.

Nine months ago, he'd left Mozambique and made his way north along the African coast. Well provisioned, he'd stayed well off-shore and lived off the ocean for weeks at a time – venturing into harbour towns or quiet fishing villages for water and supplies only when absolutely necessary, keeping clear of the main centres, paying cash, keeping a low profile, never staying anywhere long. He had no phone, no credit cards, and hadn't been asked to produce identification of any sort since he'd left Maputo. Then he'd come here. An isolated island off the coast of Zanzibar. He'd anchored in the little protected bay. A couple of days later Grace had rowed out in a dinghy to greet him, her eight-year-old son Joseph at the oars, her adolescent daughter in the stern, holding a basket of freshly baked bread. He decided to stay a few days. Grace offered him work doing odd jobs at the hotel – fixing a leaking pipe, repairing the planking on the dock, replacing the fuel pump on the generator. In return, she brought him meals from her kitchen, the occasional beer, cold from the fridge. He stayed a week, and then another. They became friends, and then, unintentionally, lovers. Nights he would sit in *Flame*'s darkened cockpit and look out across the water at the lamplight glowing in Grace's windows, watch her shadow moving inside the house as she put her children to bed. One by one the lights would go out, and then he'd lie under the turning stars hoping sleep would come.

After a while, he'd realised that he'd stayed too long. He'd made to leave, rowed to shore and said goodbye. Joseph had cried. Zuz just smiled. But Grace had taken him by the hand and walked him along the beach and to the rocky northern point of the island where the sea spread blue and calm back towards the main island, and she'd convinced him to stay.

But now Clay shivered, watching Dreadlock move about the sailboat. The first drops of rain met the water, a carpet of interfering distortions.

'*Hali?*' shouted Red Shirt in Swahili from the jet boat. News?

'No here,' came the other man's voice from below deck.

'Is it his?' said Red Shirt.

'Don't know.'

'It looks like his.'

'Don't know.'

'No guns? No money?'

'Me say it. Nothing.'

'Fuck.'

'What we do?'

'We find him. Let's go.'

The jet boat's engines coughed to life with a cloud of black smoke. Dreadlock untied the line, jumped back aboard and pushed off. The boat's bow dipped with his weight, then righted. Clay dived, watched from below as the craft made a wide circle around *Flame*, buffeting her with its wake, then turned for shore.

It was heading straight for Grace's house.

26th October 1997. Paris, France. 17:35 hrs

Still nothing.

Today I did something I have never done before. I went into my husband's office and looked through his things. I went through all the papers on his desk, the bookshelves, the filing cabinet in which he keeps his personal financial records, some files from past cases. I had to pry open the lock on his desk drawer with a screwdriver and a hammer. The desk belonged to Hamid's father and is made of French oak. When I hammered out the clasp, the blade of the screwdriver splintered the wood of the drawer frame and cracked one of the front panels. I must take it to be repaired before Hamid comes home. If he sees it he will know I was spying. When we were first married, we agreed to trust each other completely. I have violated that now. God knows if I ever found him going through my office; I would be more than furious.

Why am I feeling this? Under the circumstances, I am sure he would understand. It has been three days now, and still I have had no word from him.

The police have assigned a detective to the case – Assistant Detective Marchand; an agreeable young lady who seems very junior, but is undeniably bright and enthusiastic. She came to see me this morning and I gave her recent photos of both Hamid and Eugène. This afternoon she contacted me to confirm that no persons bearing their names or matching their descriptions have been admitted to any hospital in France, nor have they reported to or been brought into any police station in the country. Our silver Peugeot has not been seen anywhere. She called me just now to tell me that they have also finished checking all outgoing passenger records from all the major airports and ferry terminals in France, and have found nothing. She asked me if their passports were still in the house. She also asked me if my husband had been having an affair. I was shocked. I know I must have sounded shocked.

I found their French passports just now in the bottom drawer of Hamid's desk, along with Eugène's birth certificate and Hamid's Lebanese passport. At least I know that Hamid had not planned to leave the country when he left for the office on Tuesday morning. This is a big relief to me. It should not be.

In the same drawer, I found the deed to a life insurance policy. I knew Hamid – meticulous person that he is – had taken out policies on both of us, right after Eugène was born. The policy on my life is relatively small. His policy is significant: over a million euros in the case of death, with me as the beneficiary. I also found twelve hundred US dollars in one-hundred-dollar notes, over three thousand euros in mixed denominations, and a stack of Egyptian pounds worth about six hundred euros. If he had been planning to go somewhere for any extended period, especially if he did not want to be found, he would have taken cash. Whatever happened, it was not premeditated.

I went through all the drawers in his desk looking for any signs of an affair. There was not a hint of feminine perfume – not even mine. There were no compromising photos or letters. I went through his bank statements looking for hotel or dinner charges, purchases from florists or jewellers or lingerie shops – any of the obvious things that he is intelligent enough to have avoided if he had been trying to hide something from me. I was shocked at the cost of the beautiful necklace he bought me for our anniversary, but it has only convinced me more that an affair is unlikely. Still, you never know these things. My aunt had been married to the same man for thirty years and then caught him being unfaithful with an older woman. The affair had been going on for more than three years.

There was another thing the young inspector asked me: Did my husband or I have any enemies? She had done her research. She was aware of the columns I wrote last year about South Africa's apartheid-era chemical and biological weapons programme – the ones I based on the information you sent me from Mozambique last year; the ones that led to the arrest and indictment of the head of that programme on charges of murder, embezzlement and extortion. And she knew about my role in exposing the Medveds' corrupt operations in Yemen and Cyprus before that. She knew about all the stories that built my reputation – the ones we worked on together, chéri.

This is part of being an investigative journalist, I told her. All of us in this profession must deal with the same threats, the social media bullying, the vilification, the accusations of bias and political motivation. As for my husband, he is a human rights lawyer, I said, I now regret, rather rudely. So what do you think? I added. Sometimes, I think I have started to speak as you do, Claymore.

The inspector looked at me with a patience that belied her years. She showed no sign of being offended. I told her that Hamid had been doing this work for a long time, and while there had been verbal attacks and legal injunctions, there had never been a time when he was physically threatened. Not that he had told me about, anyway.

Is there anything else, she asked me, anything at all that seemed strange or unusual? You would be surprised at how important the most seemingly innocuous observations can be in these cases.

No, I told her. Nothing else. Even as I was saying it I knew I was lying. Because there is something else. Of course, there is.

In the hours since Inspector Marchand left I have done nothing but pull apart and upend every detail of the last three days, until the whole of it has become nothing but a churned-up morass. And now, from this reduction, only the malaise remains. I cannot yet describe it, but I can no longer deny it. It has been with me for too long.

So, for now, here are the possibilities:

1) Hamid has decided he needs some time with his son, alone, and is ensconced somewhere in the countryside, in a Norman farmhouse or a villa on the Côte d'Azur – he has always loved those weekend getaway places. Perhaps the stress of the last few months has simply become too much. If so, why has he not called me? Does he think I would not understand?

2) Hamid has run off with another woman. He has been having a secret affair and has decided that he can no longer continue our relationship. Being the Muslim man he is, he cannot bear to live without his son, and believes in his heart that he has a prior and unalienable right to custody of his male heir. But if so, would he not by now have had the courage and compassion to inform me of his decision?

3) Hamid and Eugène have been in a car accident and are still undiscovered, perhaps down a steep embankment along a wooded country road. They are trapped or in pain, and are unable to walk to help. The reason for such a trip into the country may have been for reasons (1) or (2). If so, God help them, please. All is forgiven.

4) Hamid has left the country, has taken Eugène with him, and for any combination of the reasons above is unable or unwilling to contact me. Even though the police say they have not been through any of the major airports, he is a very experienced international traveller and there are many places he might have crossed the frontier unchecked. If so, why would Hamid have left behind their passports and all that cash? This makes no sense.

5) Hamid's enemies have taken him and my son hostage, or worse. It sounds melodramatic even thinking it. But I know that his recent work has put him in direct confrontation with some powerful people in Egypt, including members of the government. He has been defending political prisoners accused of various crimes against the state, including Muslim activists. In January, he won a major victory – widely reported in the international news – which resulted in the release from prison of a high-profile environmental activist. Would the Egyptian government really resort to kidnapping a French citizen from his own home? I find this highly implausible. But if it is true, why no ransom demand? Unless of course, they have simply been murdered. God protect them and forgive me for even thinking it.

6) Hamid and Eugène have been kidnapped or killed by our enemies – yours and mine, mon chéri. I can barely bring myself to write the words. Regina and Rex Medved are dead, their empire fragmented and dispersed. Whoever has picked up the pieces should be thanking us. Chrisostomedes, the bastard, has been politically disgraced and ruined financially. He is certainly spiteful enough, and kidnapping is his style, but I simply cannot believe that he would erode his remaining resources on a vendetta against me. He has many far more dangerous enemies.

With people like him, however, you never know. The white supremacists of the South African Broederbond are a possibility. The last time I spoke to you, a little over nine months ago, you had just testified to Desmond Tutu's Truth and Reconciliation Commission, where you revealed the full horror of the atrocities committed by Operation COAST during apartheid. I remember every word of our too brief telephone conversation. You were convinced that the Broederbond were hunting you down to exact revenge for this – and because of what you knew and had not yet revealed. That is why you sent me the information – the photographs and the notebook. I promised you I would write the story, Claymore, and I did. I hope you know, wherever you are, that I kept my word.

I am just a reporter, and there are many others who have written about COAST's activities since. So it does not seem plausible or logical that they would single me out. They cannot silence us all. And if they wanted to stop me writing about them, why not just threaten me, or kill me? And I have heard nothing since Hamid and Eugène disappeared – no demands, no threats. If anything has happened to them – it hurts just to write their names – because of something I have done, I will never forgive myself.

7) Hamid knows he is in danger (from his enemies or mine), and has disappeared, perhaps to protect me. That is the kind of person he is: principled, self-sacrificing. But if this is the case, why would he take our son, and why did he not trust me to help him? He knows that I have experience and training in these matters and that I would be an asset to him. Why would he not confide in me? Together we are stronger.

None of this analysis helps in the least.

Please God, if you must take someone, take me.

21:45 hrs

Inspector Marchand has just telephoned. They have found something. She will not tell me what it is over the phone. I am to meet her at the police station tomorrow morning at eight. I have not slept for seventy-two hours. My heart is racing. I am going to take a sedative.

2

The Only Constant in Life

Of course, it was the ultimate indulgence. Friends, lovers, family, people you cared for. They tied you down, kept you dependent, made you vulnerable. And worse, they paid for their friendship with vulnerability. When someone wants to hurt you, they target those you love most.

There was no time to swim back to *Flame*. Grace's house was a good three hundred metres along the shore. The jet boat was almost there now, slowing in the shallow water of the cove. Clay turned and made a straight line for the rocks of the isthmus, swimming hard. At the water's edge, he pulled off his fins, mask and snorkel, and started barefoot through the rocks, breathing hard.

Red Shirt killed the engine and the boat drifted towards the little white beach in front of Grace's house. Clay upped his pace, sprinting now along the sand footpath that skirted the tree line. A sheet of rain swept across the island. He could hear Red Shirt and Dreadlock talking as they waded from the boat, gained the beach and started up the rock-edged pathway to the house, still apparently unaware of his presence. Red Shirt knocked on the door.

At this time of day, Grace would still be at work, the children hunched over home-school lessons in the empty restaurant. Clay decided to keep to the trees, approach the house from the landward side, try to observe the intruders from close range. Rain sluiced from the palms, sheeted across the bay. He slowed, staying hidden. Red Shirt stood at the front door, knocked again. The door opened. Little Joseph, in shorts and a Manchester United t-shirt, stood in the doorway. Clay snatched a breath, stopped dead.

He could hear Red Shirt speaking to the boy, then Joseph calling for his mother. But before she could come to the door, Red Shirt grabbed the boy by the hand, spun him around and put a knife to his neck.

Clay's heart lurched. From inside the house now, the sound of Grace screaming. Red Shirt kicked the door aside and disappeared inside. Dreadlock followed him, pulling a fighting knife from under his shirt.

Clay didn't have a choice. There was no time. He ran straight for the front door, burst in.

The place wasn't big. A sitting room at the front with a big couch and a little TV on a stand, a table by the door with an old-style rotary telephone on it – one of only two on the island. A doorway out back led to the kitchen and the children's room. Clay stood in the doorway, dripping in his swimming shorts, unarmed. Red Shirt stood with Joseph clutched to his chest, the knife's blade poised against the dark skin of the boy's throat. A drop of blood kissed the steel. Grace was kneeling on the floor, tears in her eyes, her lower lip cracked and bleeding, her hands raised in supplication. Dreadlock stood above her, hand raised.

Both men turned to face him, *what-the?* expressions on their faces.

'Looking for me, gents?' said Clay.

'It's him,' blurted Dreadlock, glancing at Clay's stump.

'*Ja*, it's me,' said Clay, raising his open hand, and stepping towards Red Shirt and the boy. 'So how about we just talk about this. No need for any trouble.'

'Oh, no trouble, *baas*,' said Red Shirt, a grin cutting his face.

'Give me the boy,' said Clay, 'and we can talk.'

'Oh, but we don't want to talk,' said Red Shirt. 'We here to deliver a message.'

Clay was within a long pace of Red Shirt and Joseph now. Dreadlock had moved away from Grace and was circling in towards Clay, crouching low, brandishing the knife in a right-handed dagger grip. Clay had a pretty good idea what the message was.

He had learned, many years before, that the only way to win is to take the initiative and keep it. Hit first, hit hard. That's what Crowbar – his platoon leader during the war in Angola – had drilled into them from the first day of jump school. Later, in prison in Cyprus, it had kept him alive. Red Shirt was closer, but Joseph was vulnerable. The slightest mistake and the boy's throat would be opened. Dreadlock was coming at Clay from the side. Red Shirt was looking at his partner, trying to communicate to him with his eyes.

Clay laughed, forced it out. 'Why don't you just tell him what you want him to do?' he said, pushing a smile across his face. 'Go ahead. I won't listen.'

The two men sent perplexed glances at each other.

It was enough. Clay pivoted and burst low and to his left, caught Dreadlock's knife arm in a vicious cross-body hammer blow, wrapping the stunned arm with his, and following a quarter-second later with a back-handed hammer fist to Dreadlock's jaw. He felt the bone go, heard Dreadlock grunt and go slack. Then he stepped left, thrust out his hip and slammed Dreadlock to the floor, holding the outstretched knife arm as a pivot. Dreadlock tried to roll away, still clutching the knife, but Clay brought his left shin down onto the man's head and leaned in, pinning him to the floor. Dreadlock grunted as his broken jaw deformed further. Then Clay slammed the back of Dreadlock's straightened arm down across his knee. Dreadlock screamed in agony as his arm broke. Clay let the shattered limb fall to the floor, grabbed the knife, and twisted back upright. As he did he brought his right boot heel down hard onto Dreadlock's outstretched knee.

It had all taken less than three seconds. Dreadlock lay whimpering on the floor. By now, Grace had managed to crawl away into the kitchen.

'Now,' said Clay, facing up to Red Shirt. 'I'll tell you what. You let the boy go, and you can deliver that message of yours. What do you say?'

Red Shirt was backing away now, towards the kitchen, his knife still at the boy's throat. He looked scared.

Clay let Dreadlock's knife clatter to the floor. 'Look,' he said, kicking it away. 'I won't hurt you. I know you're doing this for someone. Whatever he's paying you, I can pay you a lot more. I have cash, gold if you want it, out on the boat. Name your price. Please, just let the boy go.'

Red Shirt's eyes widened, considering this perhaps. 'How much?' Rain hammered the roof.

'Whatever you want,' said Clay. 'Name it. A hundred thousand?' Red Shirt's eyes widened. 'Dollars?' he said.

Clay nodded. 'American.'

'Cash?'

'If that's what you want.'

Red Shirt's mouth opened, as if he was about to speak. Just then, Grace emerged from the kitchen. Blood dripped from her chin onto her white uniform. She held a tyre iron in one hand. Before Clay could move, she stepped up behind Red Shirt and swung at him with both hands. She was a strong woman, but Red Shirt was quick, and a lot bigger. In one movement, he flung the boy away to the floor, twisted and parried the blow with a forearm to the back of her raised elbow. The iron glanced off the side of his head just as he drove his blade into her body.

Grace staggered back into the wall, the knife buried in her chest, a look of disbelief on her face. Joseph was on the floor, his hands wrapped around his neck. Blood streamed from between his fingers. A constricted gurgle emerged from his throat. Red Shirt grabbed the tire iron, charged towards the door, swinging wildly. Clay ducked, let him go, moved to the boy.

He pushed the boy's hands from the wound. The knife had gone deep, sliced through the oesophagus, the carotid artery. The opened cartilage glistened white. Blood pulsed. He'd seen wounds like this before – during the war, and since. He knew there was nothing he could do. He went to Grace. She was sitting with her back to the wall, breathing hard, holding the knife handle between her hands. Blood covered the front of her white uniform. The blade had gone in between two ribs, penetrated deep.

He had a full medical kit on *Flame*, but there wasn't time to get it. He ran to the kitchen, flung open drawers and cupboards, scattering the contents, searching for anything he could use to staunch the bleeding. Outside, the roar of the jet boat starting, backing away. He grabbed a couple of towels, ran back to Grace. She was still breathing. He wrapped the towels around the knife, left the weapon in place. He had to get her to a hospital. The nearest was in Stone Town. At full speed with *Flame*'s little diesel engine, two hours away.

She reached her hand to his face. 'Joseph,' she said, a whisper.

Clay closed his eyes.

'Why?' she said. Blood frothed from her mouth. Tears streamed from her eyes.

What answer was there? What could he tell a dying woman who'd just witnessed her own son's murder? What explanation, for any of it? Should he tell her that it was his fault, that they'd simply been caught in one of death's coincidences, those random tragedies that seemed the only constant in life. Would it help her to know, in these last few moments, that the minute she'd befriended him, she had inadvertently increased the probability of her own demise a hundredfold, a thousand, and that the longer he'd stayed, the worse her chances had become. And now that her son lay dying at her feet, was there any point in telling her how sorry he was – for being so self-indulgent, for allowing himself the luxury of a connection with another human being, for letting some warmth into his life?

'I'm sorry,' was all he could say. Tears blurred his vision. He wiped them away, secured the towels, tried to help her up. He would try to get her to hospital. Even though he knew she would be dead in minutes, he would try. What else was there? Just sit there and let her go, passive, accepting of fate? He would try. That was all life was: a futile and inevitably unsuccessful battle against death.

She moaned, hung limp in his arms. Her eyes were closed.

He swung her into his arms. 'Here we go, Grace,' he said, starting for the door.

Joseph lay open-eyed in a pool of blood, the afternoon sun slanting across the hardwood floor, across his motionless body. Dreadlock groaned nearby. Clay stopped, looked down at the man, Grace heavy in his arms. She'd stopped breathing. He lay her down, put his mouth to hers and inflated her lungs. Blood filled his mouth. He spat, tried again. Her lungs were flooded. He touched her neck, felt for a pulse. She was gone.

Clay slumped to the floor. He sat there a long time, eyes closed, his mind blank as a starless desert night.

Dreadlock's groans brought him back. The man was dragging himself towards the door, unable to stand, pushing himself along with his one good leg, his shattered arm hanging limp.

Clay stood, picked up Dreadlock's knife, crouched beside him, ran the blade across the guy's face. 'Tell me everything,' he said, 'and I won't cut your throat.'

Dreadlock stared up at him, wading through the pain.

Clay pushed the point of the blade into his neck. Blood welled up around the steel. 'Now.'

'Contract,' Dreadlock blurted. 'Some *baas* from the mainland. Give we two grand, US. Come here kill you. Two more we bring you body living.'

'How did they know I was here?'

'Me no know. He no say much.'

'Who was he? Where was he from?'

'White man. White African. No name.'

Clay swore. 'Where is he now?'

'Some rich hotel out de' Stone Town.'

'And your friend. What's his name?'

The man shook his head, closed his eyes. Clay pushed the knife in.

Dreadlock yelped. 'They call him name Big J.'

Clay pulled back the knife, wiped the blood on his shorts. As he did, he heard a gasp. It had come from behind the couch. Clay stood, listened. A moment later, another gasp, a sob.

'Zuz,' he said. 'Is that you, sweetie?'

The girl emerged from behind the couch. She stood surveying the scene, eyes strained wide, her mouth hanging open as if in mid-scream. He could see the deep red of her tongue and the white of her lower teeth and the rictus black of her throat. She was shaking.

'Zuz,' he said. 'Close your eyes, sweetheart. Don't look.'

The girl did as she was told.

Clay crouched back down next to Dreadlock, looked into the man's eyes. He placed the point of the knife's blade over the man's heart. Rain thundered on the sheet-metal roof.

Dreadlock stared up at him, shaking his head from side to side. 'Please,' he gasped. 'I never hurt no one.'

I spent all morning with Inspector Marchand. She took me to an indus-
trial estate on the outskirts of the city, near Crétail. We sat in her car and
looked out through the rain-blurred windows at the charred remains of
an automobile. It had been driven into the yard at night and set alight.
She said that the engine block registration plate had been filed clean and
the number plates removed. Everything inside the car had been inciner-
ated. It was, I already knew, a professional job.

Then she passed me something. It was a piece of paper, a grocery-store
receipt. Read it, she said. I did. Where did you find this? I asked her.
And what does this have to do with the car? But I already knew. She
had found it yesterday, not far from the car. Two litres of milk, a kilo of
coffee beans, some asparagus, yoghurt. It was from our local store and was
dated five days ago. It was my receipt. And that, out there, was what was
left of our silver Peugeot 406.

There were no bodies in the car, she said. But not far away we found
this. She passed me a sealed plastic evidence bag. Do you recognise it?
I turned the bag over and over in my hands, not believing what I was
seeing. It was one of Eugène's t-shirts, the one with the little Canadian
beavers on the front. Hamid brought it back from Montreal for him last
year. I could not speak. I just sat there staring at the shirt, at the brown
stains across the neck and sleeve. That is blood, she said.

And there was this, not far away, she said, handing me another evi-
dence bag. It was the jacket from Hamid's blue suit. It was torn at the
shoulder and chest, stained with dirt and blood. We are going to test the
blood from both items, she said. DNA evidence can be very useful in
these cases.

We drove back to the police station in silence. When we arrived, we

went to a small café nearby and had a coffee together. Inspector March-
and was suitably respectful and sympathetic, treating me as a friend
would in such a situation. Then she started asking me about Hamid and
our relationship. She was very adept, but I cannot help feeling that she
knows more than she appears to. Does she know about my past, about the
person I once was? Perhaps she is testing me. The questions came.

Had Hamid and I been having problems?

Everyone has problems, I replied, letting my irritation show, knowing
where she was taking this.

Had we fought recently, argued – about Eugène perhaps?

No, I replied. No more than usual.

And then sharply, did I own a gun?

No, I said. I do not. I hate guns.

Have you been trained in the use of guns or other weapons? she asked.

No, I replied.

It was only partially a lie. I was trained, but as you know, Claymore,
I was never very good with weapons, and I always despised them. The
only time I was ordered to kill someone, in Yemen in 1994, I failed.
You were there. You saw it. And in the end, of course, I was glad that I
failed. I was an observer, a researcher, an analyst, not a field agent. The
Directorate was never the right place for me. I know that now. Leaving
and becoming a proper journalist (not just using it as a cover) was one
of the best things I ever did.

One of them.

Inspector Marchand ruminated on this a while, sipped her coffee,
glanced out into the street one too many times. Then finally, she came
out with it.

We haven't found any bodies, she said, but we are treating this as
a murder investigation. Where was I on the day Hamid and Eugène
disappeared?

23:45 hrs

I went back to the crèche this afternoon. Something I had glimpsed there, on my earlier visit, stuck in my mind. I spoke again to the manageress, explained that Hamid and Eugène were missing. She was very sympathetic. I asked to look at the sign-in book again. And there it was. Why had I not noticed it before? On the day they disappeared, Hamid returned to collect Eugène at 13:05, well over an hour before the normal time. Looking back through the record, there were a number of similar early pick-ups, and yet Hamid had never mentioned any of this to me, nor had they returned home early. I asked the manageress if she could confirm this. She excused herself a moment, and then returned with one of the young women who works with the children. Her name was, coincidentally, Eugenie. Yes, she said. She remembered seeing Hamid strap Eugène into the back of a silver Peugeot and drive away a little after one o'clock that day. And then she looked at me in a strange way, almost in pity. But Madame, she said. Do you not remember? I stood, nonplussed, staring at her. You were there, she said, sitting in the car. You looked at me and waved. I told the same thing to the police.

3

What It Meant To Be Alive

Clay rowed the bodies out to *Flame*.

The rain had stopped. One by one he lifted Grace and Joseph aboard, then carried them below and laid each on a berth. He stood in the gangway and looked at the corpses. He'd wrapped them in bedsheets and tied their ankles and around their arms and chests with rope, and now they lay, pale and still, in the rising moonlight. He looked at them for a long time – queen and prince in their floating sarcophagus, ready for their final journey into eternity.

Then he rowed back to the house. Zuz was waiting on the beach as he'd instructed, her little travel case packed and clutched to her chest. She had a mobile phone in her hand. As Clay approached she held it out for him.

'Where did you get this?' he asked. Grace didn't have a mobile. The mobile system was still very new in Zanzibar, and only the most well off had their own phones.

Zuz pointed at the house.

'One of the men?'

Zuz blanched, nodded.

Clay pocketed the phone. He rowed her out to the boat and sat her in the cockpit, where she couldn't see the bodies of her brother and her mother. And then he went back for Dreadlock.

By the time they reached Stone Town, the sky was lightening over the Indian Ocean. Cloud billowed in the distance, dark anvils of cumulonimbus – more rain coming. Clay dropped anchor in five fathoms of water, south of the gardens and the white façade and clock tower of the House of Wonders and the old fort, away from the pier and the little notched fishing harbour. He shut down the engine, let *Flame* swing on the breeze.

Clay left Dreadlock in the cockpit, tied, as he'd been all night, to the starboard main cleat, and went forward to check on Zuz. He opened the forward hatch and peered down into the berth. She was still asleep, snuggled under the blankets. He closed the hatch, went below and made a pot of coffee.

'Here's the deal,' Clay said, freeing Dreadlock's good hand and passing him a mug of steaming coffee. 'You help me find your friend, Big J, and the guy who hired you, and in return I'll let you live.'

Dreadlock mumbled into the tape covering his mouth.

'Just nod if you understand.'

Dreadlock nodded vigorously.

Clay took the Glock G21 from the pocket of his jacket and balanced it on his knee so the other man could see it. 'Cross me, that arm will be the last thing you'll be worrying about. Understand?'

More nodding, eyes wider now.

Clay yanked the tape from Dreadlock's mouth. Dreadlock winced in pain, but managed not to spill any of the coffee. They drank.

When Dreadlock had finished his coffee, Clay pulled a sling from its package and started positioning it around the man's broken arm. 'Help me,' he said, 'and I won't turn you in to the police. Do it well, and I'll give you ten grand.'

Dreadlock grunted as Clay tightened the sling. 'US dollars?' he said, trying to keep his jaw still.

Clay pulled a wad of US one-hundred-dollar notes from his pocket and riffled the bills with his stump.

Dreadlock stared at the money a moment, mouth open, then looked up at Clay. 'Kill him, then,' he said, trying not to move his jaw. 'If me help you and you no kill him, me dead.'

Clay nodded, peeled off ten notes, pushed them into the man's good hand. Then he pulled out the mobile phone Zuz had found. 'This yours?'

Dreadlock shook his head. 'Big J.'

'Can you unlock it?'

Dreadlock nodded.

'Good. Can you find the guy who hired you – the white African?'

'Yes.'

'Do it. Tell him that you have my body, that you brought it over on my boat. Tell him you want to meet on the shore, over there.' Clay raised his stump and pointed to a clutch of palms near a small beach beyond the point.

'If he still here, Big J already tell him what de fuck happened.' Dreadlock raised his hand to his jaw, worked the broken hinge, winced.

Clay put his British passport on the cockpit seat. 'Tell him you found this. Read him my passport number. Tell him I brought you back to the boat, but you managed to grab my gun and shoot me. Tell him your buddy Big J ran when the fight started, that now you want the money for yourself.'

Dreadlock sat staring at the money in his hands; in this part of the world, a year's wages – ten. 'Him kill me,' he said after a time. He moved his head from side to side. 'No. Him kill me.'

Clay raised the G21, chambered a round. 'That's fine, then. I'll do it myself.' He started to depress the trigger.

'Wait,' said Dreadlock, sweat blooming in the big pores ranked across the bridge of his nose.

'Decide.'

Dreadlock dropped his head. 'Okay.'

'Tell him one hour. On the beach.' Clay put his passport on the cockpit seat.

Dreadlock fumbled with the phone, thumbed the keypad, raised it to his ear.

'English,' said Clay, pointing the gun at Dreadlock's forehead.

Dreadlock closed his eyes, nodded.

Clay heard the phone ring, click. A conversation ensued.

Dreadlock killed the call, dialled another number. It rang, connected. A voice on the other end, a distinctive Free State accent

– South African. Dreadlock nodded to Clay, spoke, stuck to the script. After a moment, he picked up Clay's passport, opened it to the picture page, read out the passport number, listened a moment and then killed the line.

'He come one hour,' said Dreadlock.

Clay retied Dreadlock and went forward to check on Zuz. When he opened the hatch, she looked up at him.

'I'm going into town for a while,' he said. 'I need you to stay here. Don't leave this cabin. Do you understand?'

She nodded, blinking in the light streaming into the little cabin.

They rowed to shore, pulled the dinghy up onto the sand, walked into a palm thicket. From here they could see along the beach towards the docks and the town, but were well hidden.

Clay handed Dreadlock a 9 mm Beretta.

The look of surprise on Dreadlock's face was almost comical.

'There's one round in the magazine,' said Clay. 'If you decide to use it, make it count.' Clay pulled the G21 from his jacket pocket to emphasise the point.

Dreadlock took the weapon, examined it a moment, looked up at Clay. Possibilities whirled in the dark spaces behind his retinae.

'Don't think about it too much,' said Clay. 'You'll hurt yourself. Now go and sit out there, where he can see you, and wait.'

Dreadlock hunched his shoulders, trudged out to the beach and sat on the dinghy's gunwale.

Clay didn't have a plan, not really. Ever since fleeing South Africa – again, for the second time in his life – he'd been operating on impulse. Part of it, by now, was simply instinct, the inbuilt impetus to survive, to kill when necessary, to adapt, to run. After losing any hope of ever being with Rania again, there had been no guiding objective, no deeper meaning. Each dawn was simply another sunrise, every gloaming just the start of another sleepless night.

Until Zuz had emerged from behind the couch, he'd been set on driving the knife into Dreadlock's heart. Then, in the channel, still an hour out of Stone Town, he'd readied the Glock and was about to put a bullet into the bastard's head when he'd heard Zuz calling him from the forward berth, where he'd locked her so she couldn't get into the main cabin and see the bodies. He'd had a vague idea about making sure Grace and Joseph got a proper burial, that Zuz should be seen safely to her grandmother's care. That, somehow, justice be done. That had been about it.

'Shit.' Dreadlock stood, pushed the Beretta into his waistband.

Clay looked down the beach. Two men were approaching. One was tall, fair, built like a rugby forward. The other was Red Shirt – Big J.

'They kill me,' whispered Dreadlock.

'No, they won't,' said Clay.

'What I do?' Dreadlock's voice wavered, cracked. It sounded like he was going to piss himself.

'Just wait,' said Clay. 'Let them get close. Tell them you've got my body out on the boat. Show them my gun.'

Dreadlock shuffled his feet in the sand, raised his good arm, waved.

Clay moved deeper into the trees, crouched low, screwed a silencer onto the G21.

Big J and the white man stopped ten metres from the dinghy.

'Where is he?' said the white man. He had a big voice, a strong Boer accent. The bridge of his nose had been pushed sharply to one side of his face, as if the last time it had been broken he hadn't bothered to recentre it.

Dreadlock pointed to *Flame*.

'Why didn't you bring him in?' said Big J.

'You run,' said Dreadlock. 'Leave me there.'

'I thought you were dead,' said Big J, glancing at the Boer. 'I did.'

Dreadlock hunched his shoulders, pulled out the Beretta. 'He broke my arm. But I got his gun.'

'Well done,' said the Boer. 'Is that his boat?'

Dreadlock looked towards *Flame*, nodded. 'My money?'

'Our money,' said Big J.

'You'll get it when I see him,' said the Boer.

'Why him get money?' said Dreadlock. 'Him no do fuck all.'

'My boat,' said Big J. 'My contract. You work for me, idiot.'

'You leave me die.'

'Shut up, both of you,' said the Boer.

'What the fuck?' said Big J, pointing at *Flame*.

'What?' said the Boer.

'Look at that,' said Big J.

Clay's insides lurched, tumbled.

Zuz was up on deck, walking towards the cockpit, her nightdress fluttering in the rising sea breeze.

4

All It Took

It was the best reason not to have plans. They never came off the way you intended. Something always jarred them from their path, and almost invariably the destabilising element was human.

Clay checked his watch. If they hadn't dismissed his call as a crank, the cops should have been here by now. He would have to do this himself.

'What the fuck you bring her for?' said Big J, puffing out his cheeks.

'Who is she?' said the Boer.

'She de daughter.' Dreadlock pointed at Big J. 'Him kill de mother and son. De one Straker take up with.'

The Boer grabbed Big J by the neck. 'I told you monkeys, keep it clean.' He pushed Big J to the sand. '*Fokken* amateurs,' he muttered, shaking his head.

Big J glared up at Dreadlock. 'You dead, brother.'

'You leave me there,' spat Dreadlock, pulling out the Beretta. 'You run. Leave for him kill me.'

'Shut the *fok* up, both of you,' said the Boer, looking back down the beach towards town. He grabbed the dinghy's bow line and started pulling it towards the water.

'You dead,' repeated Big J, standing and brushing sand from his arms.

'You want de money for you own self,' shouted Dreadlock. 'You leave me die.'

Big J pulled a knife and lunged at Dreadlock. They fell to the sand, Big J thrashing wildly with the knife.

The Boer paid them no attention, kept pulling the dinghy down the beach. He was almost to the water when a single shot pierced the morning.

Big J slumped to the sand, blood welling from a hole in his back.

Dreadlock was pushing his way from under Big J's body when the Boer let the dinghy's rope fall from his hand. Four uniformed policemen were running along the beach towards them.

'*Kak*,' said the Boer as he walked past Dreadlock and into the trees. He stood a moment under the palms, very close to where Clay crouched, hidden behind a clutch of closely spaced palms, G21 ready. Then he checked his watch and started running.

Clay stayed hidden. He watched two of the cops half walk, half carry Dreadlock, bleeding from several stab wounds to his abdomen, to a waiting police Land Rover. The other pair lugged Big J's lifeless body along the beach and swung it into the back of the vehicle. One of the cops closed the rear door and the Land Rover pulled away, lights flashing.

Clay stayed put long after the cops had left, hoping that the Boer might return. He waited out the afternoon cloud bursts and watched the steam rise from the ground as the sun reappeared. The sky darkened and the first stars appeared, strobing on the horizon like time itself. He thought of Grace and little Joseph, robbed of this twilight, their dying screams echoing inside him still. He thought of Rania, married with a child, living her life. There was now no longer any doubt in his mind. He weighed the Glock in his hand, the sure dependability of the thing. The simplicity. So many times he had come so close, fractions of moments away, but each time something had pulled him back from the edge. Now he was sure. And if, as Rania believed, there was *something* afterwards, he would tell them all – everyone he'd murdered and caused to be killed – if he could, when he met them, how sorry he was for depriving them of the small treasure of years that had been their only wealth.

But before that time came, there was something he had to do.

❨

He rowed back to *Flame* in darkness, the lights of the town refracting across the quiet water of the harbour. Zuz was asleep in the forward berth. He fired up the stove, dumped some tinned stew into a pan, boiled water for tea, opened a tin of peaches. When everything was ready, he woke her and helped her up through the hatch and into the cockpit and sat her down to eat. Clay watched as she ate. He imagined this was what Grace would have looked like at fourteen – the same eyes, the same delicate nose, the smooth copper skin.

These people he had been taught to think of as not quite human.

After she had finished eating, she asked him for a napkin. They were the first words he'd heard her utter since the killings.

'Sorry,' said Clay, 'don't have any.'

She gave him a sidelong look and then wiped her lips with her thumb and index finger. 'The bodies are starting to smell,' she said.

Clay stared at her in the near-darkness.

'You didn't lock the main hatch,' she said.

'I'm sorry,' said Clay.

'You say that a lot.' She looked down at her hands, ran the palps of her fingers back and forth across her opposite palm, switching between left and right. 'Who were those men?' she asked.

'They came for me.'

'Why?'

'Someone paid them to kill me,' he said.

The girl sat a long while, looking down at her hands. After a time, she whispered: 'Why do they want to kill you?'

'A lot of reasons.' Because he'd refused to cower, refused to be silenced; because, in the end, he'd decided to act, to do what was right. And now he knew that he would never be able to escape. That they would hunt him wherever he went, that there could only be one end to it.

'It wasn't you,' she said.

'Yes, it was.'

'No,' she said, looking right at him now. 'It was me.'

'It's okay, sweetie. I know it's hard,' he said.

'No,' she said again. 'It was my fault. I was angry. I was jealous of you. I missed my daddy.'

Clay said nothing, let her cry.

'I told him,' she said. 'Mummy told me not to tell anyone, but I did.'

'Who?' said Clay. 'Who did you tell?'

'Francis. When I went back, that one time, for my last exam, a few days after you first arrived. I told him that you were staying with us on the island. A white man with…' She looked at his stump. 'With one hand.'

'Francis?' said Clay.

'A boy from school.'

There it was. One conversation between teenagers in a schoolyard on an island in the middle of nowhere. Six weeks. That was all it took.

28th October 1997. Paris, France. 05:00 hrs

Chéri:

The thought that my husband and son might have been killed plunges me into a state of torpor. Nothing matters. I can neither move nor think. The smallest tasks seem impossible. I stayed in bed all morning. Allah, most merciful, protect them, bring them home to me.

'Do not lose heart or fall into despair. You shall triumph if you are believers.'

I reread these words ten times, more, tracing the script across the page of my father's Koran – the one I lost in Istanbul; the one you found and returned to me. I must not despair. I will not despair. Hamid needs me. Eugène needs me.

The police have not charged me, but the implication was clear: I am a suspect. How could they think I was responsible? I know they must investigate all reasonable possibilities, but it wounds me deeply. The young woman in the crèche must have been mistaken. Occasionally Hamid collects me from work in the car and together we go to the crèche for Hamid. The last time was the week before last. She has simply mixed up the days. Nevertheless, I know now I must take matters into my own hands, while I still can.

I've spent all afternoon and deep into the night going through Hamid's study. I've gone through every business card in his catalogue, every paper in every file I can find. I've rummaged through boxes of warranty papers and expired passports, letters from an old flame (he told me about her before he proposed), envelopes full of faded photographs of his family holidaying on the beach in Lebanon, stacks of notebooks from his university days. I've done this as much because I miss them, as to find some clue to their disappearance. Just being here, surrounded by all of it, somehow makes me feel closer to them, wherever they may be.

I've tried getting into Hamid's computer. I've tried every password I can think he might have used, without success. He has left me no choice. Earlier this evening, I telephoned an old friend. We did our training together, became close. I know he was in love with me. He even came close to telling me once or twice, but I managed to deflect him from something we would both have regretted. We were both very young, then. He is still there, at the Directorate, and is based here in Paris, working as a senior analyst and IT specialist. I haven't spoken to him for years, since before I met you. He is on his way here, now, as I write this. He should arrive any minute. God bless him, he is a wonderful man.

The last big case Hamid was working on took him to Cairo at least a dozen times over the past year and a half. Some of the trips were short – a few days only – but several lasted longer than a month. I missed him terribly. I am a woman who needs a man in her life. I know it is not fashionable to admit this. But you will understand. It was always one of the things I loved about you, Claymore – your complete disdain for what one is supposed to think and say.

Hamid mentioned the case to me several times; never in any detail, just fragments. The defendant was an Egyptian engineer from a good family who had been studying Cairo's chronic air pollution. He and a colleague were accused of treason, and ended up in jail and were being held without charge. Yusuf Al-Gambal was his name; he is the son of a respected High Court judge. He had been in prison for over a year when Hamid managed to bring the case to trial, and, spectacularly, won some sort of reprieve. I do not know any of the details.

I remember the day Hamid arrived home after the acquittal – if that is what it was. He was exhausted, as usual, but also different somehow – changed. At the time, it seemed perfectly natural to me. Intense experiences of that kind take a toll, sometimes in ways you are not even aware of. I know. That was four months ago.

Thinking back, the changes were subtle, and started long before the acquittal. We fought more, usually about the same old things, the simmering frictions about housework, about money (he thinks I spend too much on clothes and shoes), about his smoking. But new points of discord surfaced. Talk of moving to Lebanon so Eugène could be close to his grandparents (all of my family are dead, as you know). Arguments about Eugène's education and future – Hamid seemed to have developed a deep distrust for the national educational system, and expressed concern over what he saw as increasing intolerance in France, particularly towards Muslims. I do not necessarily disagree with the validity of his concerns, and certainly as parents we should be thinking about them, but his tone had become increasingly strident. He began to dictate rather than discuss, something he had never done before. It did not happen often, a few times only that I can remember. But it was a definite shift. I can see that now. And it all started with that case. Something happened to him over there.

Something else changed, too. Hamid's interest in Eugène started to grow. He wanted to know what food he ate, and how to prepare it. He had always tried to be there for bath time in the evenings, but now instead of going off to his study and leaving me to put Eugène to bed and read the bedtime stories, he would sit with us and watch. I was pleased, so I paid it no particular attention at the time. I just put it down to a father's naturally increasing connection as the infant became a child. Hamid struggled when Eugène was a baby. I know he felt cut off from us, particularly with work taking him away so much. So, as Eugène began to walk and talk and become a little person, of course it was natural that Hamid should pay more attention, want to engage more. Was this all a precursor to what has happened? Am I reaching – reading significance into normal events? I need an alternative. I cannot accept that they are dead.

It is early morning. From the window I can see the sky paling over the city, the lights along the Seine. My friend has just left. He looks older than I remember. He is probably thinking the same about me. He got into Hamid's computer easily, but the hard drive was full of encrypted files that my friend could not access. I suppose encryption must be standard practice in law firms dealing with confidential matters that may affect people's lives. But still, it surprised me. Everything was encrypted. Everything. My friend has taken the hard drive with him and will work on it at the Directorate. He is taking a big chance, doing this for me. I am very grateful. And I know I can trust him.

Dawn comes. Lights go out. The city is shrouded in drifting smoke. I should go to the office, but I am very tired. Self-pity wells up inside me. I try to push it down but it comes nevertheless, thick, black, traitorous bile. I hate it, hate feeling it within myself, this weakness, this self-indulgence. This is not who I am.

But denial of the truth is an even greater sin. So yes, I admit this is exactly who I am. I am weak and I am alone and the tears come unabated. My husband and son have disappeared. They may be dead. Yet I am thinking about you, Claymore.

I try not to but I cannot help myself. I can only describe it as an emptiness, a void inside me that I can neither fill nor banish. My wickedness knows no limits. I dream of you, wake in my bed wet and panting. If you should ever see these words! I gasp at my shame.

I ask Allah to forgive me. How could He, so powerful and all knowing, have created such a weak creature, so lustful and deceitful, so full of self-pity and doubt? For more than two years now I have made love to my husband, and each time I have imagined that it was you, Claymore, who was inside me, kissing me, devouring me. God forgive me. Even on my wedding night, it was you I was with, in my mind. It was as if I could feel your big rough hands – hand, now, if you are even still alive – on my skin, your powerful arms enveloping me. After that first time, I was so shocked by the images my mind had conjured, that I promised myself I would stop. I would banish you from my thoughts and dreams, from my waking fantasies. For a time, I was successful. I blanked myself out. Hamid noticed immediately. I had become cold and distant. My husband told me he felt guilty coming unless I had also reached orgasm, and so he stopped, too. After a while we stopped having sex altogether. But I knew he was upset and hurt by it. I wanted to please him, to be a good wife. So, I let you back in. It was the only way I could reach orgasm.

I want to obliterate myself. I could never have imagined myself capable of such depravity. And now I know, deep down, that I am paying for my wickedness, for my betrayal. I have been unfaithful, I have debased *myself, and in doing so have shown my disrespect for my God. And as punishment, Allah, most merciful, has taken Hamid and Eugène from me.*

I pray to God, most humbly, to protect them. Please do not make them pay for my sins.

5

If You Could Live

Later that night they weighed anchor and slipped out to sea.

Soon the lights of Stone Town were nothing more than a glow on the horizon. Stars appeared. So many they could not count. Galaxies swam the dark waters, swarmed in the shallows. Nebulae swirled above them. And as they rounded the northern tip of the island and headed out to sea, it was as if they had tumbled off the surface of the Earth into some other, deeper ocean.

They had discussed it, Clay and Zuz, and they'd decided it was too risky to stay. By now, the Boer had probably learned that Clay was still alive. If so, he was still on the island, still hunting Clay. The local cops must have seen the Boer on the beach with Dreadlock and Red Shirt, and they would be searching for him – he wasn't hard to miss. He may have decided to get to the mainland, but if he'd stayed on Zanzibar, he would be looking for *Flame*.

Zuz had also made the decision, on behalf of her mother and brother, that the bodies should be buried at sea. She'd seen a movie once where they'd done that – wrapped and weighted the bodies. And she remembered her mother saying that it would be a fine way to be put to rest – the ocean so big and deep and wide; to think that part of you might one day end up in Alaska or Europe as part of a fish or whale. Much better, she'd said, than to be held so tight and close in the same ground where you'd spent all your living days.

And so, with the stars bright and land gone over the horizon, they tied Grace and Joseph together and shackled the big spare CQR anchor to them and wrapped three fathoms of chain around their legs and positioned the bodies on the stern. Then Zuz spoke some words of her own choosing, and Clay promised Grace and Joseph that he would look after Zuz, and they let them pass over the side.

Clay and Zuz stood a long time, watching the phosphorescent wake stream down into the depths, the wind pushing them gradually further away until the glowing scar healed and was gone. After, Clay opened a bottle of whisky and poured two glasses, adding water to one. He sat with Zuz in the cockpit under a following breeze and drank the whisky as the stars disappeared and day came.

'She loved you,' said Zuz, trying the whisky and putting her glass on the cockpit seat.

Clay said nothing. If he had been stronger, he would have left weeks ago. Then none of this would have happened. But he wasn't, and he didn't, and it had.

'She told me about you,' said Zuz.

Clay faced the girl, asked the question with his gaze.

'She said she was curing you.'

'Curing me?'

'She said you had a disease – a bad spirit inside you. That you were too weak to fight it and that she was pulling it from you. She said it was difficult and would take a long time.'

Clay stared at the girl, the perfect reflections of her mother there in the dark irises.

'She said that after it was gone, you would be free.'

Grace had never mentioned any of this.

'I know what you and my mummy did together. I saw you.'

Clay looked away, said nothing.

'Did you love her?'

'Yes,' he lied.

'She wanted to have a baby with you.'

'Zuz.'

'She told me.'

'Zuz, stop.'

'Joseph worshipped you.' She pulled her knees to her chest,

wrapped her arms around her shins. Tears bloomed in her eyes. 'I hated you at first. Now I don't.'

'I'm going to take you to your grandmother,' said Clay, checking the mainsail trim. 'She can look after you.'

'You said you were going to look after me.'

'I will.'

'How?'

'By taking you to your grandmother's.'

'I want to come with you.'

'She lives in Nungwi, at the top of the island, doesn't she?'

'I said, I want to come with you. I don't want to live with my grandmother.'

'You can't come with me,' said Clay.

'Why not?'

Clay stood at the helm, unable to speak.

'In a year, I can be your wife.' The starlight caught her eyes. 'We can have a baby together.'

'No,' said Clay. 'Absolutely not.'

'You don't love me,' she whispered. 'It was my fault those men came, and now my mother and brother are dead, and you don't love me, and I am all alone.' The words came as sobs, wrenched from somewhere deep inside. Tears poured down her face, each a crystalline tragedy.

'It wasn't because of you, Zuz.'

She buried her face between her knees.

'And you're not alone,' he said. 'You have your grandmother.'

Clay let her cry, checked the compass, listened to the sound the hull made through the water.

After a time, she looked up, wiped her face with her hands. 'Where are you going to go?' she said.

'I don't know. Away from here.'

'And those men, will they follow you?'

'Yes.'

'And try to kill you?'

'Yes. That's why you can't come with me.'

'Why do they want to kill you?'

He looked her straight in the eyes. 'Because, Zuz, I am not afraid.'

She gazed back at him. 'They want you to be afraid, though?'

Clay nodded. 'They want everyone to be afraid.'

'I'm like you,' she said. 'I am not afraid.'

'I know you're not.'

'When I'm with you, I feel brave. That's why I want to come with you.'

'You're going to your grandmother's, Zuz. We're on the way now. That's the way it has to be. You're going to have to be brave by yourself.'

☾

By first light, *Flame* was lying at anchor just outside the reef edge on the north-western coast of Zanzibar.

Zuz had argued the whole way, as day edged night from the sky and the land breeze brought the scents of the island: cloves, cinnamon, the deep inhalations of wood smoke and cardamom. This was the chemistry of her home, the land of her ancestors. This was where she belonged. But the girl, who was in the process of becoming a woman, would not relent. If he sent her back, she said, the men who had come to kill him would come after her. One was dead, but the other was not. And the white man was still there, she was sure. If Clay left her with her grandmother, they would soon find her. They probably had already, and were waiting there for them even now. No, she said. She had seen their faces, seen what they had done. She was a witness to murder. They would kill her, as they had her mother and brother. And if he went with her, to protect her, they would kill him too. It was stupid to go back, dangerous. She loved him and she didn't want to put him in danger again. This wasn't about fear, she said. She wasn't afraid. But it was stupid to die if you could live.

Finally, though, she'd relented. Not from the force of any

arguments Clay had offered. He had remained mute, guiding *Flame* through the night, following the edge of the broad reef system that fringed the island's northern shore. It was exhaustion took her. Now she lay curled under a blanket in the same berth that only hours before had been occupied by her mother's corpse.

Clay checked the anchor, paid out more chain, glassed the shore with the binoculars.

Of course, he knew that all she'd said was true. It was always this way. Faced with two bad options, there was no choice at all. He'd tried running, and this was where it had led him. If he'd stayed in South Africa, Grace and Joseph would still be alive, and Zuz would have had before her the prospect of a normal life – or as normal as an economically disadvantaged fourteen-year-old African-Arab girl could expect to have in 1997 in East Africa, or anywhere else for that matter. A few more years of school, then an early marriage, to a decent husband perhaps; five or six children before she was thirty, a few years of happiness maybe. And if he ran again – ran now? Took Zuz with him as she wanted? It might work for a while. They could keep to the smallest towns, come ashore only when they absolutely had to. He could keep her out of sight. But sooner, not later, questions would be asked. They would be too conspicuous – a thirty-seven-year old white man with an already-beautiful black teenage girl. She without a passport, he without any proof of guardianship. And conspicuous meant vulnerable.

No. Never again would he allow someone else to be hurt because of him.

29th October 1997. Paris, France. 23:40 hrs

Assistant Inspector Marchand came by again this morning, early, before I left for work. She said that they have had dog teams searching the area near where our car was found, but so far, nothing else has turned up. They have now spoken to eyewitnesses, who have confirmed that our car entered the main gate of the industrial park during the evening of 23rd October. The witnesses have provided sworn statements that the car was occupied by one man, a woman, and a child in a car seat.

She asked me if they could collect DNA samples. I signed a consent form, and then her people took a blood sample from me, and hair and skin samples from Hamid's hairbrush and Eugène's pillow.

I still have not heard back from my friend at the Directorate. I am afraid to call him lest I rouse suspicions. All the calls are monitored. I went to the office today, not because I thought I would get some work done, but simply to get out of the apartment. Everyone at the bureau knows about Hamid's disappearance. They were all very sympathetic and my editor was supportive as usual, telling me to take whatever time I needed and pledging the agency's resources to help in the search.

I cannot help feeling that I am being steadily boxed in. As the days go by and the reality of what has happened crystallises inside me, every-thing makes less and less sense. There seems no logic to it. Hamid picks Eugène up from the crèche that day, an hour or so early, and then is seen entering an industrial park (of all places!) in eastern Paris nearly eight hours later, with a strange woman. What happened in those intervening hours? Where did they go? I know the police think it was me in the car. My editor told me they were at the office yesterday interviewing colleagues about my whereabouts that day. I left a bit later than I usually do, and did some shopping on the way, but then went straight to our flat. I did not phone in the missing person's report until the next day. So I have no alibi for the time of the supposed murders. I know that the police think I killed them, that I hid the bodies and burned the car. I have read and written enough about the horrific things that family members do to each other to understand why the police believe this.

No bodies have been found. Is that why they haven't charged me yet? Are there no other suspects? And who is this other woman?

Are they really dead? No, I cannot believe it. No. Anything but that. Anything. My mind spins like a leaf in a hurricane.

Tonight, I called Hope in Cyprus. I took the metro to my favourite restaurant, sat alone, picked at my food, and then called her from a phone box on the street. I have no doubt that the police have wire-tapped the line to our flat and are monitoring my mobile. Hope is doing well. Little Kypros – she and Jean-Marie call him Kip – is growing fast. He'll be big and healthy like his father. Her work on the new national park in Agamas is going well, despite the continual frustrations of dealing with government. Jean-Marie (I still, after all this time, cannot bring myself to call him Crowbar) left suddenly two days ago on a job. He did not tell her where he was going, or for what. He never does. Hope says that he is planning to get out soon – once he finishes up a couple of key projects he is working on. That is what he calls them – 'projects'. They do not need the money, not after everything that happened in Cyprus. I know she worries. She knows that he loves what he does, and that I do not approve, but we both owe him our lives, and I know she loves him and he her. Some of the most improbable couples seem to have the best relationships. Some, not all.

Then I told Hope everything. I suppose I just needed someone to talk to. She has become a very close friend. We have been through a lot together. She offered to help, as I knew she would. I had to stop her from flying out here straightaway. It is good to have a few friends in this world upon whom one can depend utterly.

I asked her if she had heard from you. I thought perhaps you might have checked in with her, knowing about the two of you and what you share, but she had heard nothing, not since Maputo. No one has. Not even Crowbar. That was more than nine months ago. It was, she said, as if you had decided to renounce man- and womankind. That was how she said it, Claymore: man- and womankind. After the way I have treated you, I do not blame you.

Wherever you are, I pray to Allah to protect you and help you to forgive yourself, and forgive me.

I need your help, Claymore. That was the last thing I said to Hope: When you speak to Jean-Marie, tell him I am in trouble and that I need Claymore's help.

6

Thunder in the Distance

'Pack your case, Zuz. Don't leave anything behind.'

Clay opened the priest hole and pulled out the Glock, two extra magazines and a roll of US one-hundred-dollar bills. Then he secured all the portholes, turned off the gas, disconnected the battery and padlocked the sail locker. He went above deck and secured the boom, tightened the vang and set a kedge to the anchor to keep the chain low on the seabed.

He waited in the cockpit until Zuz emerged, blinking in the morning sun, her little case tucked under one arm. She had brushed her hair back into a ponytail and put on eyeshadow and lipstick.

'Aren't you a little young for makeup?' said Clay.

Zuz sent him a sidelong glance, the edges of her mouth turned down, her eyes narrowed.

Clay closed the main hatchway, double locked it. He sat in the cockpit and turned on the mobile phone, unlocking it using the code he'd seen Dreadlock punch in. The battery was almost dead.

'What are you doing?' said Zuz.

'Giving us an edge,' he said. 'What is the emergency number here?'

She told him. He dialled the number. A woman answered. He asked for the police. The woman asked him to wait. Clouds drifted overhead. The line clicked. The battery was almost gone. A man answered. Police, he said. Clay spoke: I am the person who called in the murders on Chumbe Island two days ago, and who alerted you to the meeting of the culprits on the beach yesterday. You have two local men in custody, one shot through the chest, the other suffering from stab wounds. They are the killers. The other witness, the daughter of the woman killed, will come forward. But there is a third man responsible. White South African, tall, well built, fair, nose pushed to one side of his face. Sunburn. Not a tourist. He is trying to kill me. He is trying to kill her.

The phone died. Clay tossed it into the sea.

'As soon as I leave you with your grandmother, go to the police station with her. Tell them everything.'

'What about you?'

'I am going to help the police. I will make sure you are safe, Zuz. I promise.'

She smiled a little half-smile. 'And then?'

'And then I'm going to buy as much food as I can carry and I'm going to sail far away.'

'Where?'

'India,' he lied. 'Australia maybe. As far as there is.'

Zuz dropped her head. 'And I will never see you again.'

Clay pulled the dinghy alongside. 'Let's go, sweetie.'

They rowed to the beach, tied the dinghy to the trunk of a palm well past the high-water mark and started inland through low reef-rock scrub.

Zuz reached for his hand, took it in hers. 'You are going to kill them, aren't you?' said Zuz. 'I saw what you did to that man at our house.'

Clay pulled his hand away, kept walking.

They reached a road, started walking north through scrub fields and smallhold farms, plots of yam and cassava, then, as they neared the outskirts of Nungwi, roadside stalls piled with fruit, makeshift garages wedged between the trunks of coconut palms and thick-waisted baobab, their owners peering out at them from under the shade of palm-frond shelters.

'Everyone is looking at us,' said Zuz, trudging along the frayed and crumbling tarmac at the road's edge.

'That's why this is the only way,' said Clay.

Zuz shook her head, kept walking.

After a while a *dala-dala* came along. Clay waved it down and they climbed into the back with the other half-dozen passengers – women with kids. The smaller children smiled at Clay, reached out to touch him, but Zuz scolded them away.

Soon they were in Nungwi proper. Clay paid the fare, a few shillings, and they continued on foot, Zuz leading him through the narrow stone streets of the old fishing village, now rashed over with the new, plastic fluorescence of tourism.

They stopped outside a small bakery. The street was lined with two-storey grey reef-rock buildings, shuttered and strung with wires and vines. Zuz pointed to a second-floor balcony on the other side of the street, four doors down.

'There,' she said. 'That's her house. She lives upstairs. That's her shop underneath.'

Clay looked her in the eyes. 'Stay here,' he said.

'Where are you going?'

'Stay here. If you hear anything, run.'

'Anything like what?'

'Screaming, gunshots.'

Her mouth opened so that he could see the red underside of her bottom lip.

'I'll only be a minute. If it's clear, I'll wave from the balcony. Come straight up. If we get separated, meet me at the place the *dala-dala* dropped us. Understand?'

This time she nodded, stayed quiet.

Clay set off down the street.

'Wait.'

Clay turned back to face her.

'Her name is Geraldine. My mother's mother.'

Clay kept going. He reached the shop, found the stairway and started up the rough stone steps, breathing in the cool air, the odours of tropic mould and the warm, turgid transpirations of close living. Halfway up the stairs he stopped, pulled the G21 from his waistband, checked the mag and chambered a round. He stood a moment, back against the sweating pores of the wall. He felt his chest expand against the stone as he tried to steady his breathing.

He wasn't sure what he was expecting, but he wasn't going to take any chances. The door was locked. From inside, the sound of a radio playing, the twittering of birds. He followed the hallway to the back of the building. An unlocked door led to a fire escape. Narrow wooden balconies shaded by a slouching pergola of rusting corrugated sheet metal. Pots of geraniums and herbs edged the railing. Clay clambered across to the balcony, palmed the Glock. He was outside the flat now, pressed up against the wall. He could hear the radio, the birds. And now, wood creaking, footsteps approaching.

Clay pushed open the door, stepped inside, pistol raised.

An old woman stood facing him. She was dressed in a long, patterned nightdress and wore thick-rimmed spectacles. In her right hand was a birdcage. Three yellow-and-green budgerigars twittered on the perch. The woman stared at Clay, at the gun. For a moment Clay thought she was going to scream, but she supressed it, gathered herself.

'That is quite unnecessary, young man,' she said. 'My money is in the sitting room, in the roll-top desk.' She placed the cage on the table, moved to the stove, lit the gas, put a kettle over the flames. 'Tea?' she asked.

Clay moved past her without answering, scanned the front room, the small bedroom. She was alone. There was no phone that he could see in the flat. He pushed the G21 into the waistband of his trousers at the small of his back, opened the door that led to the front balcony.

'Geraldine,' he called. 'Can you come here, please, ma'am?'

The old woman appeared, stood in the kitchen doorway, one hand clutching the frame. 'In the desk,' she said, pointing. 'There.'

'Come here, please. I don't want your money.'

She hesitated.

'Don't worry,' Clay said. 'I won't hurt you. I'm a friend.'

'Friends normally use the front door,' she said.

Clay held out his hand. 'Please. There is something I need you to see. Outside.'

The woman shuffled towards him, clearly wary. Clay stood back to let her pass. She walked out onto the balcony.

'On the street to your left, outside the bakery.'

The woman stepped to the railing and peered down into the street. Grey cloud scuttled across a blue sky. Thunder rumbled in the distance.

'Is there anything in particular I should be looking for, young man?'

'Your granddaughter, ma'am.'

'You must have mistaken me for someone else. I know how difficult it is for you white folk.'

Clay stepped out onto the balcony, looked down into the street.

Zuz was gone.

30th October 1997. Paris, France. 03:30 hrs

I met my friend from the Directorate tonight. He was waiting for me in a car in the parking area outside the Gare du Nord. As I got in out of the rain, he ran one hand through his hair and lit a cigarette with the other, and I thought that one of the men I love is not able to do such a simple thing.

My friend told me that the encryption on Hamid's computer is very sophisticated, much more so than he would have expected. Almost military grade, he said. He had not managed to get into the main files, but he did get into the email account, at least for the last two weeks or so. He apologised for calling so late – he is like that, very polite and considerate – but he thought I would want to know right away. Tomorrow might be too late, he said. He looked very stressed, as if he had not slept any more than I have in the past few days.

I didn't print them, he said. He reached into his pocket, unfolded a paper. I've written some of it down, he said, resting his smoking Gitane in the car's ashtray. 14th October, he began: an email from an Egyptian IP address, someone calling himself simply J, warning Hamid that the authorities would take action if he didn't abandon the case. That was all it said, just 'the case'. No reply. Then, two days later, an email from a Yusuf Al-Gambal, saying that 'the situation was worsening appreciably' – that is a direct quote – and that he was being watched and he feared that he would soon be made to disappear. Hamid replies by giving him a contact name and an address. (He pointed to the paper.) Then again, two days later, another email from Al-Gambal; same thing, more urgency, desperation also. Hamid tells him there is nothing more he can do. Then, over the next twenty-four hours, a flurry of emails from Al-Gambal. It is as if he is up all night, sending out emails, pleading for help, for forgiveness. And then the tone becomes increasingly accusatory: You are abandoning me; you promised you would help me; I trusted you – that kind of thing. They all go unanswered. The next day there is an attachment from the same address – a spreadsheet full of numbers that I can't make sense of. A few latitude-longitude coordinates, it looks like, a bunch of other stuff. That was it, no more communications between them.

My friend handed me a stack of papers as thick as my finger. He swallowed then lit another cigarette. He took his time doing it. And then this, he said, pointing to the page with a nicotine-stained finger. On the 19th of October, Hamid writes to this email address, indicating he thinks that someone is planning to murder him. Someone close to him. My friend fell silent, looked at me. His face was washed blue and fluid from the lights on the street and the rain on the windscreen. Have you checked your own email? he said.

Then he handed me the hard drive and the papers. I've done all I can, he said. I'm sorry, he said.

I told him that I understood – and I do, fully.

What are you going to do with it? he asked.

I don't know, I said.

I got out of the car. Rain leapt from the pavement, angled across the yellow cones of light strung along the boulevard. It was cold. He drove away and I walked back to the station. As I turned to wave, I realised that I hadn't thanked him.

At home, I went straight to my office and turned on my computer. I went through every incoming email for the last four months, and found nothing at all out of the ordinary. Then I looked through the papers my friend had given me. There were stacks of emails to and from Hamid's Cairo office concerning details of the various cases they were working on – pdfs of Egyptian legal statutes, all in Arabic, of course; legal procedural advice from a local consultant; and various research documents, including saved web pages from news agencies – AFP, Reuters, Al-Jazeera – dating back almost two years. There were stories about Cairo's worsening air pollution, a BBC article on Egypt's burgeoning tourism industry and the rapid development on the Red Sea coast, and several pieces about the re-emergence of an Egyptian extremist organisation – Al-Gama'a al-Islamiyya – and its new leader, the shadow who goes by the nom-de-guerre *of The Lion, and his anti-regime agenda. There were even a couple of articles about the case itself, with Hamid mentioned by name.*

Throughout, one name kept coming up: Yusuf Al-Gambal, one of the men Hamid was defending. The spreadsheet that Al-Gambal sent Hamid and the cryptic warnings in his emails clearly suggest that whatever trouble he was in was not over, and in fact may have deepened. Thinking back now to one of the few times that Hamid did discuss the case with me, I recall him mentioning that he'd made a deal to win a form of reprieve for Al-Gambal. He did not tell me what the deal involved. He then went into some detail about the Egyptian legal system, so I didn't pay much attention.

I need to know more about the case. Tomorrow, I will go to the bureau and do some more research on this. Guilt grips me: I am already thinking about the story this could become. What does that say about me, about the person I am, the person I have become? One word burns in my mind: selfish.

'Whenever misfortune touches him, he is filled with self-pity.

And whenever good fortune comes to him, he selfishly withholds it from others.'

It is the nature of man. We were put on this earth to rise above it.

09:50 hrs

Assistant Inspector Marchand called.

The police found a high-temperature industrial incinerator on the property where our Peugeot was abandoned. Inside they found residue of a mass and chemical composition consistent with what would be expected from the incineration of two human bodies. The temperature and duration of incineration meant that even the two sets of teeth were largely reduced to ash, but they did find five small, deformed lumps of metal that were clearly fillings, and an almost intact titanium plate about five centimetres long. There were also the molten remains of what appears to be a wedding ring. She asked if any of this sounded familiar.

I stood speechless for a long time. She repeated: Madame Al Farouk, are you there?

Hamid, I believe, has five fillings, although I never asked him or checked myself. Who, however close, knows the number of fillings her spouse carries in his head? Some details are entirely beyond intimacy. But I do know that Hamid broke his leg several years ago, before I met him, skiing in Lebanon, and had a titanium plate inserted in his right tibia. He wears a wedding ring. At least, he did.

Finally, I recovered, although I have no idea how long I stood there, mute, blank. It probably was not more than a few seconds, but I cannot be sure. I replied yes, I was still on the line. I told her about Hamid's leg.

There is more, she said. The DNA testing on the clothing found at the site has come back, and I can confirm that the blood on the t-shirt is your son's and the blood on the jacket is your husband's. Your DNA, Madame Al Farouk, was on both. Do you do the laundry in your household, Madame Al Farouk? Assistant Inspector Marchand's new formality sent a shiver running against my growing despair, like the waves that reflect back off a winter beach and collide in an explosion of spray and foam with the incoming breakers.

Yes, I said, trying to think. Yes, I do the laundry.

That would explain it, then, she said. I thought she sounded disappointed.

Assistant Inspector Marchand wants me to come to the station this afternoon. There are a number of additional questions she and her colleagues would like to ask me.

So, they are dead.

Allah has taken them to his eternal grace and protection. Surely, if any souls have ever deserved paradise, it is my husband and my beautiful, innocent little son. And yet I weep. I scream. I grind the pencil deep into the paper, tear the pages, pull at my hair.

I stare out across the city, every window a life, a story, dreams and fears and hopes and sorrows contained in each. Suddenly I am strangled by panic. Fear chokes me, bewilderment at the chaos in which we spin, powerless, deluded into a sense of control and order by all that we have

*built to give our lives solidity and meaning – the buildings and institu-
tions and conventions; the streaming red-and-white highways and these
clothes I wear to cover my nakedness, to hide my true self from the world
and from my own introspection.*

'And God has created you, and in time will cause you to die.'

And so, they are dead.

10:15 hrs

*My friend from the Directorate has just called me. My cover has been
blown. Someone in the Directorate has informed the police that I – the
person they know as Lise Al Farouk, née Moulinbecq,* journaliste *for
Agence France Presse – am actually Rania LaTour, one-time operative
for the DGSE Groupe Action. He does not know who did it, or why. But
the timing is clear. I am capable of murder; indeed, I have been trained
in its art, and the other subtler techniques of concealment and misdirection, surveillance and coercion.*

*The police are about to charge me with murder. And somewhere out
there are the devils who took the lives of my husband and my son. This
is not the work of amateurs, of some jealous woman. Professionals did
this. Every detail was planned, slowly, meticulously. I am being framed.*

*I have not heard back from Hope. Wherever Crowbar is, clearly she
has not been able to contact him. And Claymore, wherever you are, I
know that you have your* quarin *to deal with – your own personal Satan.
So, I am on my own. And I am running out of time.*

7

Courses of Action, Various and Consequential

Clay scanned the street both ways. There was no sign of Zuz. He took the stairs four at a time, burst out onto the street. He ran to the bakery, walked inside, through into the back-room darkness and the heat of the wood-fired ovens.

A heavy-set man in an apron glanced at his stump, brushed flour from his arms. His skin shone red with sweat. 'You look for a girl?' he said.

Clay nodded, relief pouring through him.

'A man take her. White man.' The baker raised a floured hand to his face and twisted his nose to one side. 'He say you meet him at the boat.'

Relief congealed into dread. He shouldn't have left her. The Boer must have been following them, watching them, just like Zuz had said.

'Did he say anything else?'

'Just this. Meet him at the boat.'

A kilometre and a half into town. Four and a half down the road, another kilometre and a half through the scrubland to the beach. Full-out run: twenty-six minutes. Too long. Winded after.

'Do you have a car?'

The baker looked him up and down.

'I can pay.'

'A motorcycle.'

Soon they were flying along the coast road, south towards Stone Town, Clay riding pillion, clouds darkening the sky. The temperature had dropped. Rain was coming. Flour streamed from the baker's arms and hair. At the giant baobab garage, Clay tapped the baker on the shoulder. He slowed and pulled to the side of the road. Clay pushed a fifty-dollar note into his hand.

'Geraldine's daughter's little one?' he said.

Clay nodded.

'I thought.' He pushed back the note. 'I should have…'

Clay fended away the baker's hand and started towards the coast at a run. As he reached the trees the first raindrops touched his face, pattered against the leaves. He kept going. Moments later, the clouds opened. Rain lashed his eyes, soaked his clothes, poured from the tips of his fingers. He'd been stupid. He was stupid. He'd always been stupid. At every point in his life, when choices had been offered, where courses of action, various and consequential, had been available, somehow he'd managed to pick the wrong one. Zuz had been right. They'd been waiting. And he'd obliged, come right to them. And he knew, as he ran through the scrub towards the beach, the wind and rain coming harder now, ripping through the palm fronds, shredding a hail of husk and leaf and branch from the canopy, that Zuz was of little importance to these people, and that if she wasn't already dead, she would be soon. And even before he'd completed the thought he had already started to reproach himself for it; in its very nascence he could see the proof of his callousness and he hated himself for it.

As the sea appeared through the trees, he slowed. *Flame* was there, beyond the reef, where he'd left her, just visible through the downpour. She'd swung around to landward, head to the storm coming in from the ocean, across the island. As he neared the beach, he could see the dinghy, still where he'd left it, tied to the same tree. He crouched behind the trunk of a palm and pulled the binoculars from his pack, focused out across the rain-swept water.

The first thing he noticed was the boom, swung abeam as if in a following wind so that the leach end hung out over the water. Suspended from it, hanging from a rope, was a dark bundle. Clay wiped the lenses, refocused through the slanting rain. The bundle was tied and appeared to be weighted with chain and anchor. As the rain relented a little, details appeared. Arms. A face. A swinging ponytail. Clay's heart valves tripped. It was Zuz.

Clay lowered the binoculars, scanned the beach left and right, tried to breathe. The coast appeared deserted. *Flame* swung at anchor as the storm passed over, Zuz hanging there over the water. Then, slowly, as *Flame*'s bow came around, the nose of another craft appeared. Clay raised the binoculars. The other boat had been tied alongside, and the two craft spun across the rain-pelted surface together, thunder exploding in the distance. As more of the boat came into view, he could see the stripe along its hull, the v-shaped windscreen. It was the jet boat Big J and Dreadlock had used before. Two black men huddled under a tarpaulin in the open cockpit. Clay shook the rain from his hair, tried again to wipe the lenses, scanned *Flame* bow to stern. The Boer was nowhere to be seen.

Suddenly, the wind veered hard, gusted. *Flame* jerked on her rode, swung hard so that Zuz dipped momentarily and the anchor touched the water, dragging her feet down into the water in a white wake. Then *Flame* righted and she was jerked clear of the surface. The jet boat was now in full view, tied amidships. The rain was coming hard again, pelting across *Flame*'s deck, ripping through the palms all around him. He had to go.

He replaced the binoculars in his pack, checked the G21, thrust it into his waistband and started towards the dinghy. They wanted him. That was the message. If he gave himself up, she might yet live.

He was a few steps from the beach when, above the screaming barrage of the storm, he heard a shout. He crouched, reached for the Glock, spun towards the sound, narrowed his eyes in the rain.

Again, a voice raised above the storm. 'Straker. Stay where you are.'

Clay raised his weapon. 'Let her go,' he shouted into the rain.

'Lower you weapon, Straker.'

'Tell them to let her go. Then we talk.'

A figure emerged from the scrub. 'It's me, Straker. For Christ's sake, put that thing away.'

Clay peered through the rain.

The figure moved closer. A big man, the shoulders broad and powerful, arms like hawsepipe.

It was Crowbar.

30th October 1997. Somewhere over the Mediterranean.
22:30 hrs

Chéri, *you of all people know that the training never leaves you.*

After Yemen, when the Directorate faked my death and provided me with a new identity, I took my own precautions. They trained us to think this way.

It was therefore not difficult for me to get out of France. It is amazing how a woman can alter her appearance completely, simply by changing her hair and clothes and demeanour. Some makeup and a pair of spectacles help, too. I drove to Switzerland, left the car, walked over the border – just another hiker out for the day – and then took a train to the airport in Geneva. I know the country well, as you know. I grew up there.

Leaving your life behind is not so hard, if those who define and give purpose to that life are gone.

The Egypt Air first-class cabin is cold. I pull the blanket up around my shoulders, and stare at my passport. The photograph is of me. But the name, the history is someone else's: Veronique Deschamps, thirty-two, Swiss, born in Geneva. In fact, she died at the age of three, along with her parents, in a car crash. In the bag at my feet are enough cash to last me a year, my father's Koran, and every bit of information I have been able to gather about Hamid and Eugène's murder. Just writing their names sends sorrow and anger shooting through me.

I put away the passport and open my laptop. I start searching through my email. I go through every email I have sent, starting with the most recent and going back in time. In my main account, six and a half months of replies and requests and routine administrative rubbish – nothing unusual. So much irrelevance, pages and pages of it. My eyes start to close. I am tired.

And then, on the edge of sleep, I see it – in the outbox of my secondary account. An email sent on 18th October to an address I do not recognise. The subject line: Call Me.

Dearest Hope:
I tried calling you but you were out, probably taking Kip to daycare. I need to talk about what we discussed earlier. I think Hamid is having an affair. I think he is planning to take Eugène away from me. I am not going to let that happen.
R.

I almost choke on my drink. I can hear myself pleading: I did not write that email. It was not me. And yet here it is, in my account, apparently addressed to my closest friend, and signed R. Hope is one of the very few people who knows me by my original name, Rania. Am I going insane? I read the words again, double-check the date, the time the email was sent, the address. How is this possible?

My finger hovers over the delete button. But it is obvious, as I knew it was as soon as I read the words. Someone has accessed my email account and sent an email as me. What better way to provide me with a motive for murder than a cri-de-coeur *to my best friend?*

I go back further in time. On 4th October, another email, again to the same unfamiliar Hotmail account:

Dearest Hope:
Hamid has started to behave strangely. He is becoming increasingly paranoid, ranting about how I have betrayed him, that I was not a fit mother. Yesterday, for the first time in our marriage, he struck me. I am frightened. What should I do?
R.

There is one more, on 29th September:

Dearest Hope:
I live in fear. Not only for myself, but for my son, his very soul.

Yesterday Hamid accused me of apostasy. He called me a whore. He has become radicalised, the worst incarnation of Islam. I know he is planning to leave me, to take my son away. I am not going to let that happen. To think of my son being brought up that way – intolerant, misogynistic, brutal, vile and backward. I would rather he be dead than become such a person. Hope, why don't you answer me?

R.

I sit and stare at the seatback in front of me. The pattern is abstract, like the eddies in a stream, hues of saxe and heliotrope no doubt designed to soothe, to reassure. My heart is pounding. I cannot breathe. The words I am trying to write come out as scrawls. Just as well. I look back at the screen. There it is: a perfect ternion of growing suspicion and desperation. Paranoia and fear ooze from every word. Whether or not the police have managed to access my email accounts – by now they will have initiated a full-scale search for me – I delete the emails from the sent box and from the trash file. Of course, it makes no difference. I must proceed as if the emails have been sent – they are out there. The moment I try to access my accounts, I am traceable.

I must assume that my motive for murder has now been firmly established. They have placed me at the scene of the crime. My DNA is on everything. No bullets were found with the remains of the bodies in the incinerator, which means they were killed by other means, most likely with a knife. That would explain the blood-stained clothes. My ability to plan and execute such a murder has been established. And now, I have fled the country, reinforcing my guilt.

And yet, as attempts to implicate me in the murders, these emails are beyond clumsy. How could any mother kill her own child? Before I have finished the thought, I realise my error. Of course, it happens all the time. Every day, children are murdered, abandoned, violated by their own flesh and blood. God help us all.

Claymore, Majnun – my tortured soul, where are you? If ever I needed you, I need you now.

8

The High-Blown White and Blue Aftermath

His eyes were timeless. Reminders of so much that he wanted to forget, of what he could not live without. Glacier-blue mirrors that revealed his own weakness, replayed his betrayals, and in their icy depths, made him acutely aware of how fucking scared he was.

Crowbar smiled, looked at Clay's Glock.

Clay lowered the weapon. 'What are you doing here?' was all he could say.

'Came as soon as I could.'

'How did you find me?'

'Same way everybody else did.'

'What is that supposed to mean?'

Crowbar glanced out towards *Flame*. 'How about we deal with this first?'

'She's only fourteen,' Clay said, choking on it. 'An innocent.'

'They always are.'

The rain was still coming down, hard and heavy now, the clouds and all of the land and the sea beneath darkened, the sun eclipsed by the storm. *Flame* had swung almost stern to shore now. A lone figure emerged from below deck and stood in the cockpit. It was the Boer.

'*Moeder van God*,' said Crowbar. 'What the *fok* is he doing here?'

'You know the bastard?'

'*Ja*, you could say that.'

Clay stared at the man who had led him through the maelstrom of war, taught him how to kill when he was young enough to learn it well, showed him how to love it. 'Who is he?'

Crowbar waved his question away. 'We need to go now,' he said. 'While this storm lasts.'

'It's me they want,' said Clay. 'I'm going out there.'

Crowbar nodded. 'Leave the two blacks in the speeder to me. Can you take Manheim?'

'That his name?'

'Still got that habit of asking stupid questions.'

And then, without even knowing it, he was back there, in the war. He stiffened. 'Sorry, my *Luitenant*,' he said. 'Yes. I can take him.'

Crowbar inclined his head. 'Wait for me to hit. Then take out Manheim. Don't kill him. Just neutralise him. He and I, we need to talk. Get going.' Crowbar disappeared into the scrubland.

Clay dragged the dinghy to the water's edge, pushed off, started rowing. He'd adapted the left oar with an extension he could hook his elbow into, but even so, progress into the wind was slow. A determined chop had risen, and the dinghy's bow ploughed through the water, raising puffs of spray. By now, Manheim was standing in the cockpit, watching him. The two blacks in the jet boat were standing too. He had everyone's attention.

A hundred metres off *Flame*'s port stern, Clay pulled up, drifted just inside the reef. Rain pelted the dark surface of the water.

Manheim stood, raised a shotgun, pumped the action and levelled it at Clay. 'Come on in,' he shouted. 'Try anything, you get a new ventilation system.'

One of the black men laughed. Across the water, with the wind, it sounded like he was right there in the dinghy with Clay.

Clay nodded, dug in the oars. As he got closer, he could see that they had trussed Zuz with one of the extra jib sheets from the forward locker, tied her hands behind her back and bound her ankles up against the backs of her legs with all the extra chain they had been able to find. There was tape over her mouth, and the big spare Danforth hung from her knees. She swung from the boom, suspended by a single line that ran back to the cockpit. If the line was released, she would sink to the bottom as surely and quickly as her mother and brother had.

Ten metres away now, and Clay could feel the big twenty-four-gram Foster slug loaded atop forty-five grains of powder, imagine the hole the projectile and its 4,200 joules of energy would blast through his body. And it would all happen before he'd even heard the shot.

'Stop there,' Manheim said. 'Whatever you're carrying, toss it here.'

Clay pulled the G21 from his waistband, held it a moment then underhanded it up into *Flame*'s cockpit.

Manheim jerked the shottie. 'Now, come along side, Straker.'

Clay sculled nearer, grabbed for *Flame*'s toe rail and cleated the dinghy's bow line.

Manheim stood back in the cockpit, the shotgun levelled. Clay climbed aboard.

Manheim motioned for him to sit. 'Now we wait,' he said, sitting facing Clay.

'Let her go,' said Clay.

Manheim laughed. 'So attached to your *kaffir* friends, aren't you, Straker?'

'I'm here. You've got what you want. Let her go, asshole.'

Manheim smiled. 'You're stupider than they said you were.'

Clay said nothing. By now Zuz had registered his presence, and was staring at him wide-eyed. He didn't acknowledge her.

'I don't give a shit about you,' Manheim continued. 'Or her. You're just the lure, Straker. Shame, really, when you consider it, no? That you and your little *kaffir* whore are going to die like bait on a hook. Serves you right. Both of you.'

Manheim reached for the line holding Zuz, uncleated it, held it in one hand. Her weight was now borne by two wraps on the starboard winch, nothing more.

'Come to think of it,' he said, 'we don't need her anymore, do we?'

'Please,' said Clay. 'Don't. She is nothing, like you said. I'll do anything you want. Just let her go.' Whatever Crowbar was planning, he had better do it soon.

Manheim smiled. The bastard was enjoying this. 'Not a very

appealing proposition, Straker. You've already done everything I wanted. You've cooperated very nicely, in fact. Just a little longer, and it will all be over.' He let the line slide through his hand. It spun through the winch. Zuz started to fall.

'No!' shouted Clay, springing forwards, reaching out for the line.

Manheim smashed the shotgun's stock into Clay's shoulder, knocking him to the cockpit floor. Manheim grabbed the line. It jerked and went taut. Zuz let out a muffled scream. She swayed from the boom, her knees touching the surface, the forty kilos of steel that hung from her legs dragging in the chop.

Clay pushed himself to his knees, worked his shoulder.

'Try that again, and I'll use the other end,' said Manheim. 'Sit down.'

Clay sat. Zuz was staring at him through the rain. He could see her nostrils flaring and closing, pumping air as adrenaline cascaded through her system.

Manheim glanced at Zuz, cleated the line, and started winching her back up again, keeping one hand on the shotgun's pistol grip. 'See that? Stupid little bitch shit herself,' he said, laughing through the words.

Clay said nothing.

'Now that stinks,' said Manheim, pinching his nose with his free hand. 'Nothing stinks worse than *kaffir* shit.'

As he said it, a geyser of water erupted just off *Flame*'s port side where the jet boat was rafted up. There was a shout, a muffled cry, and then, in rapid succession, three silenced gunshots: *Tfk, tfk, tfk.*

Manheim jumped up, peered across the coach roof towards the jet boat, raising the shotgun. As he did, he let go of Zuz's line. The rope spun through the winch and Zuz hit the water. Manheim's twelve gauge erupted just as Clay dove over the side.

By the time Clay reached her, Zuz was on the bottom, struggling against her ropes. The anchor's crown was half buried in the sand. He could see that she had already expended most of her oxygen. Her eyes were stretched wide in adrenaline-fuelled terror. Bubbles poured from her nostrils, her muffled screams ringing through the water like so many nightmares.

With the anchor and chain, she weighed almost as much as he did. There was no way he could propel her to the surface on his own. Clay reached under his shirt, unsheathed his neck knife. Then he steadied the girl between his legs and started cutting the loops of rope that secured the anchor to the lines around her knees. He severed one loop, pulled free the line, then the other. The anchor's shank fell to the seabed. He grabbed at the chain, but it was tied to her body. She was out of time. She was going to let go, take that deep breath her body so desperately wanted. Clay steadied her, ripped the tape from her mouth, and, just as she opened her mouth, put his mouth to hers and exhaled, filling her lungs. He held her there a moment, staring into her eyes so she would know he was there, so she might calm herself. She stared back. He nodded, pointed to the surface. She nodded.

With three kicks, Clay was at the surface, gasping in air. He took two deep breaths and plunged back down. He cut away more rope, pulled off about a fathom of chain, not nearly enough. Zuz remained weighted to the seabed. He knew that she was almost at the end of her reserves, that the little air he'd been able to give her wasn't nearly enough. In her state of agitation, she was burning through her oxygen five times faster than normal. Seconds remained. Once more he steadied her, filled her lungs with whatever remained in his, looked her in the eyes, and kicked towards the light.

As he broke surface, the concussion of Manheim's twelve-gauge pierced the air. He looked up, surprised to be alive, but saw nothing. He sucked in air, purged his lungs, filled them again, and dove. As he reached Zuz, he heard the rumble of the jet boat's engine starting up, and then the roar as it accelerated and sped away. He cut away the last of the chain, gathered her in his arms, and kicked towards the surface.

☾

Clay cut away Zuz's ropes, stripped off her clothes and let the sea wash her. She was shivering, going into shock. He held her close, rubbed her back and arms a while, then he got her aboard. He wrapped her in a blanket, carried her below and laid her in the starboard berth.

The storm had passed and the sun had returned. Steam rose from *Flame*'s teak decking. He found Crowbar draped across the foredeck. His platoon commander was unconscious, bleeding from the head and shoulder, but alive. Clay made him comfortable on the foredeck, propping his head under a pillow from the main cabin. The gash in Crowbar's head was nasty and would need stiches, but wasn't life-threatening. He'd taken what appeared to be a partial load of shot in his right shoulder, most of it in the big fleshy deltoid. Some of the pellets were badly deformed and several had penetrated a few millimetres beneath the skin. Clay picked out what he could and bandaged the wound, but it was messy. He would need to get him to a doctor soon.

Clay scanned the horizon, but there was just the dark ridgeline of storm cloud moving off towards the mainland and the high-blown white-and-blue aftermath above and the darker blue of the channel below.

Clay went below and grabbed a bottle of whisky and the medical kit. When he returned topside, Crowbar was sitting up, his back against the mast.

'That for me?' said Crowbar, pain in his voice, relief.

Clay clambered forward, handed Crowbar the bottle, checked his wounds.

'It's not bad,' said Crowbar, raising the bottle to his mouth. 'I was behind the mast.'

'You need a doctor.'

Crowbar tried to move his shoulder, winced. 'It's *lekker*.'

'Manheim?'

'*Bliksem* took off in the speeder,' said Crowbar. 'The other two are shark food.'

Clay nodded. 'What are you doing here, *Koevoet*?'

'Came to warn you.'

Clay applied a compress, tied it in place. 'You came a little late.'

'Did my best, *ja*.'

'How did you know?'

Crowbar closed his eyes a moment, opened them.

'You're not going to tell me, are you?' said Clay.

Crowbar shook his head.

'Manheim told me that I was bait. What the hell does that mean?'

Crowbar's eyes narrowed. It was almost imperceptible, but for him it was tantamount to an exclamation mark. 'What did he say?'

'He said he didn't give a shit about me or Zuz. That we were just the lure.'

'*Kak*.'

'What's going on, *Koevoet*?'

Crowbar pushed himself up with his good arm, crouched, got to his feet. 'Follow me,' said Crowbar, stepping carefully towards the cockpit.

Clay followed him below into the main cabin. Zuz was there, curled up under the blanket, shivering.

Crowbar walked past her, opened the forward port wet locker, crouched and reached inside.

'What the hell are you doing, *Koevoet*?'

Crowbar withdrew his hand, held it up for Clay to see. A small disc about the diameter of a tin of tuna and as thick again nestled in his palm. On one side was an opening – a USB port.

'What is it?' said Clay.

Crowbar handed it to him. 'Transmitter. There's a line that runs up the mast.'

The implications of this ripped through Clay like hot shrapnel. They'd been tracking him. Probably for a long time. 'Jesus,' he managed. 'How long?'

'Since Maputo. They went in and did it when you were testifying to the Truth and Reconciliation Commission in Johannesburg. I didn't know until a few days ago.'

Clay slumped onto the starboard berth, put his head in his hands. Jesus Christ. 'Who is "they", *Koevoet*?'

'Who do you think, Straker?'

'The Broederbond.'

Crowbar nodded. 'Question is, how did Manheim know?'

Clay looked at the object in his hand. 'If I was the bait, who was the prey?'

Crowbar grabbed the transmitter from Clay's hand, walked to the main hatch, and threw the thing overboard. 'God damn it, Straker,' said Crowbar. 'Isn't it obvious? He was after me.'

Part II

2nd November 1997. Cairo, Egypt. 09:35 hrs

I stand on the balcony and look out across the buildings of Ma'adi towards the Nile. This is one of the city's older neighbourhoods and there are still big trees shading the streets and the walled gardens. The greenery attenuates the din of traffic along the corniche and cools the cement. A brume cloaks the city, hangs in the streets, drifts among the buildings. The colour is hard to describe, an admixture of wood smoke and eye-shadow. And the smell betrays its provenance. Above, the sky is clear and blue. The sun is already high and it is hot. If I lean over the railing I can glimpse the Nile, and beyond, through the haze, the washed-out green of papyrus growing on the banks of one of the islands.

Each morning since I have arrived here, the reality of my situation walks into the room and sits down facing me. It comes in the form of a dour Islamic matron. Her black headscarf is pulled severely around her face. Not a wisp of hair shows. Her skin is the colour of a dust-covered olive withering on the branch in one of the stony groves of my childhood. Black down shadows her upper lip. She informs me in my mother tongue that I am now a widow, childless and a fugitive. She knows there is vengeance in my heart. Repent, she says, in a whisper. Repent.

But penitence is for after.

Who was the woman in the car with Hamid and Eugène, the day they were killed? I ask her. What were they doing, presumably together, from the time Hamid collected Eugène from the crèche that day until their fateful arrival at the waste management plant in Crétail? Apparently, she looks like me, this woman. Enough to pass for me at a distance, anyway. Was this all part of the plan to frame me? Was this woman the assassin?

The only thread I have is Yusuf Al-Gambal. Something happened to Hamid here in Egypt in the months leading up to and after his trial, and I need to know what it was. If only for the sake of my sanity. I know I cannot bring them back, that they are in paradise now, but my life has been ripped apart, and I need to know why. And if I am to continue on, somehow, I need to prove my innocence, at least of these crimes. The thought that this woman is out there, somewhere, tortures me. She knows what happened, and she knows why. I must find her.

I have rented this small room in one of the old houses in Ma'adi. Even the smallest hotel was too conspicuous. A woman alone, even today in supposedly modern Egypt, is subject to constant and intense scrutiny. After a while you get tired of men assuming you are a prostitute, approaching you in that way they do when they think that you are for sale. I have lost track of how many times in the last few days I have uttered the words 'I am waiting for my husband.' After the second day, I bought a hijab and disappeared behind my veil. I can now move about the city unmolested, and relatively inconspicuously. Conform and survive.

I have been here three days and have made no progress. My calls go unanswered, my enquiries are politely brushed off. The moment I open my mouth, everyone here knows I am a foreigner. My Arabic is perfect, but it is the formal classical Arabic of school and government and academia, not the accented dialect of the Cairo streets, with its extensive slang. But I am learning quickly. A few more days of practice on coffee-shop attendants and ladies in the markets and I will be speaking like a Cairenian.

How everything can change from one week to the next. It is not as if I am a stranger to sudden convulsions, to abrupt changes in the direction of events, but one forgets. Happiness weakens you. The sense of loss grows within me and at times becomes overwhelming. I cry for hours at a time, usually at night, here alone in this dusty room so far from my home. My home. Not our home any longer.

I think of our flat in Paris, of our possessions, the furniture and clothes, the photographs and books, the paintings and trinkets, all the things that we surround ourselves with, the things that somehow are supposed to express our individuality within the constrained conventions of society. I imagine our apartment block in Paris, all of the people who live there – the Randous next door; Madame Lechenault two down;

Monsieur Tryphon across; the Blernier family along the hall with their two children – stripped of the adornments and coverings they use to claim a degree of differentiation. The whole block, the entire street, the city, all of us as we arrived and as we will depart: naked, frail, vulnerable, with our breasts and genitals and arses there for all to see, come face to face with our God. The image makes me gasp. We are animals.

One person was killed today and four more injured in the Egyptian resort of Taba, on the Red Sea. A bomb went off in a café frequented by tourists. All those killed and injured were members of staff – four Egyptians and one Syrian, preparing for morning opening. The detonation appears to have been timed to ensure that no tourists were killed. It was in all the Cairo newspapers this morning. The Islamic splinter group called Al Gama'a al Islamiyya has claimed responsibility. In a pre-recorded statement, The Lion regretted the loss of life, but warned that the restraint they have shown in protecting foreign tourists has limits. He claims that government repression and corruption defy the teachings of Islam and impoverish the people.

These people are fanatics, wilfully misrepresenting the words of God for their own purposes, tarnishing all of Islam. The government has announced a curfew in the area and has arrested suspects. Tourism is now such a big part of the Egyptian economy that such incidents are considered a major threat to the national interest. The president himself has condemned the attack.

The world is a lunatic asylum, and we are all inmates.

And now I am going to walk along the Nile and then I am going to make some calls.

23:10 hrs

Finally, some progress…

I went to the main post and telephone office in the centre of the city and I left another message on Yusuf Al-Gambal's answering machine. Then I called Hope. She was home. It was wonderful just to hear her voice, like a breath of jasmine from the climber that grew outside my window in Algiers when I was a girl. But right away I could tell that something was wrong. She was flustered and upset. Kip was crying in the background, and I could hear her dog barking. She was packing for a trip, she said, but she would not tell me where, only that Jean-Marie was in trouble and had told her to get out of Cyprus. I could hear the strain in her voice, the worry. Claymore is with him, she said, I passed on your message.

The sound of your name sent a fizz through me, and then a bolt of dread. If Crowbar of all people feels threatened enough to worry about the safety of his family, then I know that you, too, are in danger. The dread echoes within me still. It is as if the world is spinning out of control, as if everything has let go all at once.

Can I call you in a few days? she asked. I gave her the number for my room. Egypt, she said, I understand. Night-time is best, I said, but be careful. And Hope, I said, it is Veronique.

I made a few other calls, but nothing came of them. I wandered the centre of town for a while, sleepwalked through the Egyptian Museum, seeing but not seeing. I returned to my room before nightfall, fixed myself something to eat. My appetite has gone. I left most of it. I tried to read, cried, dozed a while.

And then, just now, the telephone in my flat rang for the first time. A voice introduced himself as Yusuf Al-Gambal. I had almost given up on hearing back from him, so many messages had I left. On the voicemails, I had identified myself simply as a colleague of Hamid Al-Farouk. As we spoke I maintained this vague identity. He was guarded, as was I. We talked only briefly. He had heard about Hamid's murder in Paris and expressed his condolences. He has agreed to meet me tomorrow, God willing.

9

This True and Constant Force

3rd November 1997
Latitude 4° 26' S; Longitude 39° 48' E,
Off the Coast of Kenya, East Africa

Clay trimmed the mainsail, checked the compass. They were making good time in a following wind, the lights of Pemba now gone under the southern horizon.

Crowbar took a swig of whisky. 'Don't worry,' he said, passing the bottle to Clay. 'They'll be fine, *ja.*'

Clay drank, felt the alcohol burn into the uncertainty. 'Definitely.'

Before leaving Unguja, Zanzibar's main island, Crowbar had gone ashore to find a doctor. Clay had gone back into town for Zuz's grandmother. He'd taken Zuz with him, shattered though she was. Together, they'd convinced the old lady to leave the island and that both she and her granddaughter were in danger, real danger. The kind where you are killed quickly and without pity.

Zuz's grandmother had a sister on Pemba, the northernmost island of the Zanzibar archipelago, remote and little visited. Later that night, Crowbar had returned, patched up and drunk, and they'd slipped anchor – Clay, Crowbar, Zuz and her grandmother – and set sail.

By morning, they'd reached Pemba, eighty nautical miles north. Clay accompanied Zuz and her grandmother to the sister's village just outside Chake-Chake. He told them not to worry. Crowbar had learned that both Big J and Dreadlocks had died of their wounds, and that the police had dropped the case. Clay gave Zuz's grand-mother twenty thousand dollars in cash. He told her there was more for Zuz's education, when she needed it. The girl was bright. If she studied hard she could go to university, learn medicine, languages, engineering, philosophy. He'd once had a friend who wanted to be a philosopher, he told them.

They'd promised to stay put, to be careful, not to be conspicu-ous with the money; never to mention any of what had happened. And then he told Zuz he would come back one day, when he'd done what he needed to do. Zuz had cried, and held him for a long time, her arms wrapped around his waist. And then he kissed the hooped wire piled on the top of her head and walked away and did not look back.

'She's a pretty little *bokkie*,' said Crowbar. He lifted the bottle to his mouth and took two big gulps. Clay could see his throat working in the wan and fractured starlight reflecting from the dark surface of the water.

'Smart, too.'

'What happened?'

Clay reached for the bottle, drank hard. 'I happened.'

Crowbar sat for a long time, saying nothing.

Clay passed him the bottle. 'They'll never stop, will they?'

'No.'

'I'm going to kill him,' said Clay. Then it would be over. One way or another. The mainland was only half a day away, less if the winds freshened. 'I don't give a shit what they do after that.'

Crowbar tilted back the bottle, drained the last. 'I spoke to Hope,' he said, tossing the empty bottle over the side. 'Called her when you took the *bokkie* and her *ooma* ashore.'

Clay waited for him to continue.

'Told her to take Kip and get the hell out of Cyprus. Go to her mother's place in California.'

'Shit.'

'*Fokkers* touch either of them…' Crowbar trailed off into silence, stared out to sea, mouth set hard, eyes narrowed. Clay had seen that look before.

'They'll be good, *oom*,' said Clay. 'Hope's smart.'

'As they come, Straker. Definitely. But she couldn't fight her way out of a baby shower with a Parabellum.'

Clay clipped back the early edge of a smile. 'Mombasa is less than six hours away. Get on a plane. Go to her.'

Crowbar looked at him hard, didn't let go.

'What?'

'There's something else.'

'Jesus, *Koevoet*. Just tell me.'

'Hope spoke to Rania.'

Kinetic energy surged through Clay's spine, fizzed in his extremities.

'She's in Egypt,' said Crowbar. 'And she's in trouble.'

Clay looked out across the star-lit horizon, felt the water humming against the rudder, flowing across the hull, tried to process this.

'She needs your help, *seun*.'

Clay stared at his friend, his mentor, his commanding officer once, in another life – and in so many ways, still.

'That's what she told Hope. She needs you.'

The human brain is a chemical reactor. Dopamines light up pleasure centres. Hormones regulate mood and desire. The amygdala sends bursts of proteins triggering flight and fear in ways that bypass deductive processes. It was as if all of it had ignited inside him at once, a simultaneous cascade of fear and desire and the deep, pure drive to kill.

'We get to the airport in Mombasa, get out fast,' said Clay.

'They'll be watching the airports.'

'Good.' The sooner he could get to Manheim the better.

'Think it through, Straker. What's more important? Get to Rania. Leave Manheim to me.'

Crowbar was right. 'Overland?'

'Too far, too risky.'

More than two thousand miles separated the port city of Mombasa from Egypt's southern border. It would take them at least ten days, probably more, over some of the worst roads on the continent – through Kenya, Ethiopia and war-torn Sudan. But *Flame* was too slow. The journey by sea up around the Horn of Africa and through the Red Sea would take at least a month; time they, Hope, and Rania, did not have.

'I know someone in Mombasa who might be able to get us a small plane. We could fly out of a private airstrip. Much less chance of being detected.' Crowbar adjusted the sling that supported his right arm. 'We could be in Cairo in four days.'

'We?'

'I'm coming with you, *seun*.'

'What about Hope?'

'Either way, we both have to get out of Kenya. Then I can deal with Manheim. We get you to Cairo, I go on to America. It's the only way.'

Clay nodded. 'We need to find somewhere on the coast where we can leave the boat.'

Crowbar went below deck, returned a moment later holding the chart. 'Here,' he said. 'Up the river at Funzi. About a hundred clicks south of Mombasa. A big estuary. Quiet. No villages.'

Clay nodded, pushed the tiller. Stars spun, Rigel notching a few more degrees to starboard, big and close to the horizon. He watched the compass dial swing behind the needle, this true and constant force in the world, this reliable magnetism. Zuz would be alright. Now, it was time to get to Rania.

Suddenly, four days seemed a lifetime.

3rd November 1997. Cairo, Egypt. 13:00 hrs

This morning I met Yusuf Al-Gambal. He was not at all what I had expected.

We met in a small café near the Ibis hotel in Ma'adi. I arrived early. I had removed my hijab and was dressed in a blue business suit, jacket and knee-length skirt and just-high-enough heels. As a Muslim gentleman, Hamid would have considered it highly inappropriate to show a photograph of his wife to a male colleague, so the risk that Al-Gambal might recognise me as his lawyer's wife was low. But I kept my headscarf on nonetheless and wore my oversized sunglasses. As I waited, I realised that something had changed within me. Now that my husband is gone, it is as if I never really knew him.

Al-Gambal arrived on time, to the minute. I had pictured him as a professional protester, of the type one sees on the television news in Europe – bearded and dreadlocked, dressed as if he had just emerged from the forest after two months chained to a tree. But he wore a suit and tie, was clean-shaven. He smelled nice – an airport duty-free cologne; Hermes perhaps – and his hair was impeccably combed. His shoes were Italian, leather, expensive, well polished. It was as if he was there for a job interview or a date. He was a lot younger than I had expected too, mid-twenties I guessed. His English was excellent, almost perfect. I suppose the son of a High Court judge can either rebel or conform. It seems he has done both.

Yusuf ordered tea for us. I thanked him for seeing me and explained that I was following up on some aspects of the case on which Monsieur Al-Farouk represented him.

I have spoken with the senior partner at Hamid's firm, said Yusuf. There is no person with the name Veronique Deschamps in their employ.

My heart jumped in my chest. I do not work for the firm, I replied. I am Mr Al-Farouk's private assistant.

He never mentioned you.

I smiled. Good, I said.

This seemed to fluster him. He called to the waiter and ordered more tea.

Then I hit him with it. What is this? I said, putting the spreadsheet file on the table between us, the one my friend at the Directorate had printed for me.

His reaction was quick and strong. I could see the fear in his eyes. Where did you get this? he whispered, placing a newspaper on top of the document and leaning back in his chair, as if to put as much distance as possible between himself and the offending object.

I told you, I am – I was – Monsieur Al-Farouk's private assistant. I handled all of his correspondence and did research for him.

This is … He stumbled … This is confidential. It is one of the terms of my acquittal that information from the case not be divulged – to anyone. Hamid knew that.

Yusuf looked around the café. I could tell he was getting ready to leave, to run. I had to keep him engaged, or I would lose him.

I leaned in towards him. Let my blouse fall open. He didn't even glance.

Please, I said. Monsieur Al-Farouk has been killed. His son also. The police have accused his wife of murder. I know Monsieur Al-Farouk cared for you very much. He often spoke to me of you. I know you cared for him too.

That seemed to hold him. I continued: Monsieur Al-Farouk never explained what was contained in this file. And of course, I did not ask.

I paused, hoping he might respond. He did not.

Something happened to him, I went on. Here in Egypt, while he was defending you. Something that might explain why he was killed and bring the real culprits to justice. Please, I said, dropping my head, I need your help.

I gathered myself, let him process this.

He sat a while in silence. The tea came, and cooled untouched. Then he looked at me. I could see the conflict in his eyes.

I am very sorry about what has happened, he said. Hamid was a good man. But this is the time we live in. Everywhere, good is silenced. I am sorry, he said. I cannot help you. There was something very sad about him, a deep resignation. Please do not try to contact me again, he said. Then he placed some money on the table – enough for the tea and a small tip – and stood. He reached to shake my hand. Perhaps this will help, he said. Then he turned and walked away.

I sit here now, back in my room, and look at the card he slipped into my palm. It is an ordinary business card for a Mr Sayed Amadallah, Operations Manager, Fabrika el Hamra Company, in the Hadayek-el Koba district of Cairo. Phone and fax numbers. An address. And on the back, in a neat hand in blue ink, a name – Mehmet – and a telephone number.

I am now sure that we were being watched. Everything about Yusuf's demeanour spoke of caution, paranoia even. Whatever he was mixed up in, his acquittal in the courts clearly has not been the end of it. I do not know if he believed my story.

18:45 hrs

Chéri*:*

My fears are confirmed. This evening I was visited by the police.

They were plainclothes detectives of some sort, two of them. I had no sense that they knew who I was. I asked them for identification, which surprised them. A woman does not challenge authority in that way. They asked to see my passport, pored over it for a while, kept glancing up at my face. The taller one asked me a few questions one can only describe as routine – if one lives in a police state. What is the reason for your visit to Egypt? Tourism, I answered. How long are you planning to stay in Egypt? A month. But they quickly became more specific.

Your Arabic is very good for a foreigner, said the shorter one, who in my mind I was starting to call Moonface – his face was broad and round, and his skin bore the scars of vicious teenage acne. My mother is (was) Algerian, I said; my father, Swiss – which is the truth, as you know. The other detective, the taller one with the moustache, asked if I enjoyed sight-seeing. They both had that practised, slightly off-hand demeanour that I have always so detested in men who believe they are in a position of power, as if they can't quite be bothered. But I knew where his questions were going, and so pre-empted him with something about being a town planner at home in Switzerland, and being interested in the transitional zones between industrial and residential land uses. He looked nonplussed.

And you are travelling alone, said the shorter one. It was not a question, but its mere utterance triggered a lurch deep within me, the reignition of the simmering conflict between what I have come to see as the two poles of my being: the conservative, Muslim, conventional, maternal side; and the progressive, Western, secular, rebellious paternal part. Travelling alone I invite harassment, danger, ridicule. It is improper, immodest. This is something that you, mon amour, a man, can never understand – the undercurrent of fear that never leaves me. Of course, I have as much right to travel alone as anyone. And yet, as this debate raged inside me, I recognised that more than anything, I wanted you here with me to stare down these bullies, to walk with me, to make me whole. I know I can do the same for you, mon amour. I can make you stronger, surer of life.

I lowered my gaze and told the detectives that I am a widow. That seemed to mollify them slightly. Islam offers special protection to widows.

The shorter one, Moonface – did I only imagine that he was slightly embarrassed? – looked at his notebook. Do you have friends here? he asked.

Professional acquaintances, yes, I replied.

He looked at me a long time, a withering gaze that I held at first, staring back hard, unflinching, challenging. I would like to say that my defiance persisted, but in truth it was not more than a fraction of a second. I quickly provided the response that these men expected – a respectful and demure lowering of the eyes. Defiance is not the way to be invisible. It was the first thing they taught us in the Directorate. Conform in every way, blend in, be silent, anonymous.

Enjoy Egypt, said the taller one. *The pyramids are very nice. Finally, they left.*

The implications are clear. Yusuf Al-Gambal is being watched by the police. When they observed him meeting with a strange woman in a café – someone they had not registered previously – they followed me to my flat. It was a warning. Stay away. Be a tourist. Thank God I spent some time going through the Egyptian Museum and walking along the Nile.

10

Diverse and Cruel Motivations

Dawn came. Low cloud misted over a becalmed and leaden sea. Clay doused the sails, started the motor. They chugged along, the coastline materialising in the distance. He wondered about the rhythm of meetings and partings, of the people he'd known for periods shorter and longer, of lives suddenly and brutally ended, as if the savage chemistry of existence was predicated on this eternal cycle of beginnings and endings, with such scant and difficult territory in between.

Crowbar fixed breakfast and handed Clay a mug of coffee. They sat in the cockpit and ate. Clay sipped, holding the tiller in the crook of his left elbow.

After a time he ended the silence of hours. 'Did Manheim see you, *Koevoet*, back on Zanzibar?'

'*Ja*, definitely. I'd just capped those two black *fokkers*, and was about to climb aboard. He looked right at me.'

'That's when he let Zuz go.'

'*Ja*, and tried to shoot me.' Crowbar raised his hand, pointed forward. 'Slug's still there in the *fokken* mast. You said you were going to take care of him, Straker.'

Clay shrugged.

'*Fokken* leave me to do everything.'

Clay said nothing. You just had to let Crowbar go through it.

'While you were hiding on the bottom of the ocean, Manheim was trying to take off my shoulder.' Crowbar winced as if to prove the point. 'Good thing he'd alternated slug and shot, or I'd be a cripple now, just like you, Straker. Or dead. Most of it ended up in the boom and the mast.'

'Finished?'

Crowbar smiled. 'What's your hurry, Straker. I'm enjoying this.'

'*Fok jou, Koevoet.*'

'That's better, *seun*. We've got a long way to go.'

'Why is Manheim trying to kill you, *oom*?'

'Kill both of us, *ja.*'

'Me, I can understand, after what I told the Truth and Reconciliation Commission. But you? You said you knew him.'

Crowbar did not answer for a long time, sat sipping his coffee, staring out at the brown smudge of the coast. 'We were friends, once.'

'Serious?'

'It was a long time ago. We did some Special Forces ops together in Angola, back in the seventies. But we fell out, years back.'

'Is he with the Company?' 'The Company' was the independent security firm that Crowbar had started with two ex-SADF colleagues after the election of Nelson Mandela's ANC in South Africa in 1994. No longer wanted by their country, they were putting their skills and experience to use, fighting other people's wars across Africa. Angola, ironically, was their latest and most lucrative contract.

Crowbar shook his head. 'The last time I saw him, back in the eighties, he'd joined the AWB – Afrikaner Weerstands Bewring.' Crowbar hesitated a moment, thought it through. 'He'd changed.'

'Changed how?'

'He'd gotten meaner. More ideological. Always on about *fokken* God, People, fatherland, all that *kak* about an independent Boer homeland.' Crowbar spat across the lee scupper. 'After that I lost track of him. Last I heard he was doing contract security work for one of the big mining companies in the Transvaal.'

'Well, whatever happened to him, he's working for the Broeder-bond now.'

'Looks as.' Crowbar tossed the dregs of his coffee over the side. '*Fokken* good fighter, though. Once saw him take out a whole SWAPO squad single-handed. Just charged in chucking frags like *fokken* John Wayne. Never seen anything like it.'

'So why is the Broederbond after you, *Koevoet*?'

Crowbar shrugged. 'Must have given Manheim a hell of shock, seeing me on your boat.'

Clay waited for Crowbar to elaborate, but he didn't.

'I hope that slug I put into him is keeping him awake at night, ungrateful bastard.'

'What aren't you telling me, *oom*?'

Crowbar waved this away.

'Goddam it, *Koevoet*.'

Crowbar didn't move.

'For once, can you just tell me the truth? What the hell is going on?'

Crowbar spun around and faced him, the crags of his face and his pale eyes cast in the grey morning light. 'Don't you *fokken* talk to me like that, *soutpiele*. Ever. You hear me?'

Clay stared back at him. 'God damn it, *Koevoet*. I'm not a fucking *rofie* anymore. Rania's in trouble, and I need to know what you know.'

Crowbar sat for a moment, staring back. But the expected counter-attack did not come. Instead, he hung his head. 'What the *fok* do you know about anything, Straker?' His voice sounded far away, resigned. 'You and all those other cowards. Just *fokken* upped and ran – left the rest of us to do the fighting.'

Clay breathed in, let it go. 'I don't know if you've figured it out yet, old man, but the war's over. We're not in the army anymore.'

Crowbar rubbed the stubble of his beard. After a while he got to his feet and disappeared below deck.

Clay stood tiller in hand and ran his gaze along the horizon. He'd fled South Africa in 1981 as a twenty-year-old combat veteran and deserter – with Crowbar's help. He hadn't returned until 1996, to testify to Desmond Tutu's Truth and Reconciliation Commission. Crowbar had warned him not to go, that it would end badly. He'd been right.

There was a lot Clay had missed. Thirteen years of pain and

upheaval, rebellion and useless sacrifice. The death of a system, the rise of a nation. And all that time, Crowbar had stayed, lived it, right until the end.

Sometime later, Crowbar reappeared and clambered into the cockpit. He handed Clay a hip flask. 'The Broederbond isn't what you think, *seun*. It's changed.'

Clay put the flask to his lips, let the liquid flow into him. He handed it back. You couldn't push Crowbar, you just had to let him come to things in his own time.

Crowbar sat, lit a smoke. 'Started back in the eighties. Apartheid was doomed, and they knew it. How do you hold on to power when your system is crumbling?'

'But the Broederbond *was* the government,' said Clay. 'Controlled it anyway. Apartheid was their idea, for Christ's sake.'

'Exactly. But they knew black rule was inevitable. So, in the eighties, they secretly started repositioning. By ninety-three, when it was clear that apartheid was finished, they renamed themselves the AB – the Afrikaner Broederbond. Then they did a deal with the ANC and declared their support for a democratic South Africa.'

'Jesus. Even while we were fighting…'

'*Ja*, even then.'

Clay felt as if he was being swallowed up, as if a huge hole had opened up in the sea. 'Fuck me,' he said, trying to steady himself. 'Eben, Bluey, Cooper, all of them…'

Crowbar closed his eyes, opened them again.

'For nothing.'

'Don't, Straker. You can't.'

Clay took a deep breath, tried to hold it all back. 'And what about Manheim?'

'When the AB did the deal with ANC, the shit flew. About a third of their members – the die-hard white supremacists, including Manheim – quit and joined the AWB. The AWB had fifty thousand SADF troops loyal to the Afrikaner cause ready to crush the ANC. We were a telephone call away from civil war.'

'So how the hell did Manheim end up working for the AB?'

'That's what I don't understand. The AB doesn't give a shit about the Boers, or a white African homeland, or any of the things that Manheim believes in, or used to believe in. The AB is a business, Straker, a huge conglomerate of dozens of businesses – everything from agriculture to mining to telecoms, operating across Africa, from the Med to Cape Town. In reality, nothing's changed. Not a goddam thing. They still run everything. Just in a different way.'

'So, it was never about the *volkstaat*.'

'Not since before you were a *rofie*, *ja*.' Crowbar shifted in the cockpit, burned down his cigarette and flicked the smouldering end overboard.

Mombasa was now a distant smudge on the horizon. Clay checked the compass, judged speed through the water. A sea breeze was coming up. They could put up sail. 'Should be there in about three hours,' he said.

Crowbar nodded. 'The AB did a deal with the ANC because it was a way to make money. A lot more money than they had ever before imagined was possible. Billions.'

'So the same people who thought up COAST are running food and telephone companies now?'

'Pharmaceuticals, metals, engineering, oil, lumber, diamonds, water, tourism … everything.'

Clay pondered this for a time, the variables and possibilities, the diverse and cruel motivations. 'But why come after you now, *Koevoet*? They've had months, years.'

'Who the *fok* knows? All I know is that now they've started, they're not going to stop. That's how they work.' Crowbar levelled his eyes at Clay, held his gaze, meaning burning in his retinae. 'The AB is very patient, very methodical.'

'And Manheim?'

Crowbar shook his head, drank from the flask, secured the cap. 'I've got to talk to him.'

'And I've got to kill him,' said Clay, looking away. He tried to assimilate it all, piece together the fragments, but there was too much void and far too few pieces.

After a while he said: 'Did Hope say anything about why Rania's in Egypt?'

'Just that her husband and son were murdered back in France, and the cops think she did it.'

'Jesus Christ.'

'And you thought you had problems, Straker.'

Yesterday evening, after dark, I slipped out through the back garden and walked to the metro. I knew immediately I was being followed. It was the two policemen – if that is what they are – who came to my flat earlier that day. They were hanging back, moving on opposite sides of the street. I walked on, stayed calm. As I neared the station, the crowds built. I went inside, bought a ticket, walked to the platform. I had to push my way between the waiting passengers. The policemen had followed me in. I could see them approaching the ticket barrier. I turned, sank deeper into the crowd.

The train arrived. I got on. I saw them push onto a carriage three or four back. The tall one gazed out over the bobbing heads of the passengers, searching for me. They were moving up the carriages, checking each as they went. At each station, Moonface, the shorter one, jumped off and stood by the open doors, scanning the platform. I moved forwards, trying to keep some distance between us. A group of tall young men in blue track suits were standing at the far end of the carriage. I went and stood among them. Shielded from view, I pulled off my burqa, shook out my hair. A couple of the boys looked at me in my black tracksuit and training shoes and smiled to each other, then at me. I smiled back.

The two policemen had by now moved up and were in the next carriage back. At the next stop, the boys started out the door. I went with them, stayed close as they moved along the platform towards the exit tunnel. By now, the boys were glancing at me and at each other as they walked. One of them said something that I could not make out and a few of them laughed. I kept with them. By the time we reached the ticket hall, I was reasonably sure that I was no longer being followed.

I peeled away from the boys and started back towards the southbound platform. As I moved away I heard one of the boys say: Where are you going, sister?

I kept going, jumped on the next train, doubled back. Finally I emerged into the night outside Al-Zahraa station. The streets were full of evening shoppers. I lost myself in the crowd, sure now that I was no longer being followed. Back in my burqa, I hailed a taxi and told the driver to take me to the Hadayek-el-Koba district.

The traffic churned. We crossed the Nile, the lights of the big hotels dulled by a fog of exhaust. The streets were choked with cars, the air thick with diesel and the smoke from burning rubbish. I could see the taxi driver glancing at me in the rear-view mirror. I flashed a scowl at him. He held my gaze a moment and looked away.

Hadayek-el-Koba is an industrial area, ventured the driver after a time.

I ignored him, remained silent. He drove on.

As we neared the district, the air grew thicker. You could see it, a brown miasma, skulking through the backstreets like a thief. The lights of the city dimmed behind us. The driver looked back at me again, but I silenced him with my gaze before he could say a word. He shrugged, kept going.

After a while, he found the address that was on the card – a gated entranceway attended by two armed guards. I told the taxi driver not to stop. He looked back at me again, questioning. Drive, I snapped. He kept going.

At the far end of the fenceline I told him to turn right and follow the perimeter road. It was a factory of some sort, one of many in the area: a series of windowless brick buildings set in a floodlit compound surrounded by a chain-link fence topped with razor wire. Yellow-lit smoke belched from two big chimney stacks, merged with the plumes from dozens of others and settled into the valley like a well-fed cat curling into its sleeping basket. Equipment, crates and used pallets choked the fenceline, spread along the walls of the buildings. Huge piles of what looked like black stone covered the back part of the compound. The smell was overwhelming. It reminded me oddly of the garage in Algiers where my father would take our Citroën for service when I was a little girl. My memories, my girlhood fantasies and nightmares, are of big, hairy men *with blackened faces and oil-stained clothes, blank, staring eyes, and these same odours: carbon and abrasives and hot metal.*

After we had gone three-quarters of the way around – the complex must have covered at least ten hectares – I told the driver to stop. I had seen no other entrances or guards. I paid the driver and made to get out.

He asked me if I wanted him to wait. I said no.

Are you sure? he said. You should not be here alone, after dark, he said. Where is your husband?

I got out and slammed the door. He shrugged his shoulders and drove away, the red tail lights dematerialising in the smoke.

The streets were dark and deserted. In my black burqa, I felt almost invisible. I moved quickly along the rough ground outside the fence, keeping to the darkness between the streetlights.

It did not take me long to find the place I had noticed from the car: a crumbling mud-brick building – once a dwelling of some sort – that defied the fenceline like a protester refusing to retreat as the police cordon bends around her. As I entered the structure, I could see that the fenceline had been notched inward to detour around the house. I imagined some resolute family matriarch refusing to be moved from her home as the factory was built around her, succumbing eventually to age and poor health, alone and with no one to continue her fight.

I moved under a fallen archway, clambered over a pile of slumped brick, a few stars showing through the bare roof timbers. The fence skirted a small, overgrown garden, a wilderness of untended vines and collapsing trellises. Beyond, the back lot of the factory, dominated by a huge pile of the black stone and two big pits filled with dark liquid. The smell here was even stronger, and it was difficult to breathe.

The garden afforded me complete cover. I watched the factory for a while, and seeing no one, and no evidence of cameras, I set to work on the fence. Using the wire cutters on the multi-tool I always carry in my purse, I cut a flap in the fence, wrapped my scarf closer around my nose and mouth and was soon inside, moving quickly between the two ponds.

I had no idea what I might find.

I gained the rear wall of the main building and followed it along to a loading area of some kind. Crates were stacked along the wall, four, five high in some places. I clambered up and pried open the wooden lid of one of the crates with my multi-tool. It was too dark to see what was inside, but I did not want to use my torch. I reached in. My fingers brushed rough-cut wooden slats, then slippery metal. Ingots, ranked side-by side, a dozen perhaps on this layer. I pushed my thumbnail into the metal, felt it sink in. Lead.

I replaced the lid, slid to the ground. I continued along the wall until I found a doorway. It was unlocked. I pushed it open, looked inside. A blast of hot air nearly pushed me over. It was a stairwell, dimly lit. I went inside. My heart was beating so hard that I could barely hear my own footsteps. I climbed two flights, three. Another doorway, again unlocked. I pushed it open. A piercing yellow light blinded me, and for a moment I stood there, immobilised. As my vision returned I looked out across a broad factory floor. I saw first the big crucibles, giant ladles pouring bright orange streams of molten metal into hissing ingots. And then the creaking conveyers, the towering belching furnaces tended by dark, helmeted servants, the whites of their eyes staring out from blackened, industrial faces.

I scanned the elevated walkway left and right. It appeared to be empty. I stepped out onto the grated platform and started moving towards what appeared to be the quenching area. Clouds of steam billowed among vessels and pipework. For a moment I was engulfed. I kept walking. When I emerged, I found myself standing face to face with a uniformed worker. I do not know who was more surprised.

We stood a moment looking at each other, he soot-faced, stubble-jawed, with a fall of greying hair pushing from under his ill-fitting hard hat; me encased in my burqa, only my eyes showing, sexual dimorphism at its most extreme.

I turned and ran. I was already out the back door and across the open ground between the pits and to the back fence by the time he opened the door. I found the flap in the wire and was back inside the garden when a second man appeared in the doorway. Alarm bells were ringing now and

I could hear dogs barking in the distance. The second man switched on a torch, swung the beam across the silvery surface of the pits. I crouched low, watched as more men arrived, guards with dogs on leashes, some brandishing weapons. They were coming towards me.

I fled across the perimeter road and into the warren of run-down apartment blocks and crumbling houses that abutted the industrial district – the dwellings of workers and their families. I moved quickly, keeping to the darkness whenever I could, heading east, back towards the centre of Cairo. My heart was pounding. Inside the burqa I was covered in sweat. Police sirens blared in the distance. I kept going.

After a while the sounds of the chase subsided. In the darkened recess of an old foyer, I peeled off my burqa and threw it into a rubbish container. An hour later I was stepping out of a taxi, back at my apartment in Ma'adi.

It had seemed the most ordinary of industrial operations, indistinguishable from the others in the area and like so many I have seen over my career. A lead smelter. Why had Al-Gambal directed me there?

This morning I telephoned the number on the back of the card. The conversation went something like this:

Isis be blessed.

Ezeykh'a. (My Egyptian slang: 'hello'.)

And to you, good lady.

May I speak to Mehmet, please?

You are, good lady.

Yusuf Al-Gambal gave me your number.

I see. (Silence.)

He said you might be able to help me.

If your soul is willing and pure, I can.

I do not know about the latter. (I cannot believe I said this.)

Lady.

Please.

It is the work of Set.

Pardon me?

Set. The fallen one, the god of nothingness, the one who murdered his brother.

Please. What can you tell me about Yusuf's trial? What was he accused of?

He was accused of telling the truth.

Pardon me?

The Ma'at has long since departed from the Two Kingdoms. Corruption rules here now.

I am sorry, I do not understand. What is the Ma'at?

The Ma'at, good lady, is truth, justice, order. It is that which is right.

What was the truth he told?

Osiris walks the Earth! (He shouted so loud I had to move the phone away from my ear). Many know this. But Yusuf had the courage to speak of it openly. This was his crime. Good lady, the children of Isis are being sacrificed to ugliness, cruelty and greed.

I am sorry. Mehmet, I do not understand.

Please, call me Amenhotep.

Amenhotep, then. (I was shaking my head by this stage. Had Yusuf played a nice little trick on me, sending me traipsing around nondescript industrial sites, putting me in touch with a Kemetist quack?) Why would Yusuf send me to a smelter in the Hadayek-el Koba district?

The Two Kingdoms are being destroyed, good lady.

Please, call me Veronique.

Of course, thank you, Madame Veronique. As I said, the ancient birthplaces of the greatest civilisation the world has ever known are being laid waste.

By whom?

By the consortium.

What is that? Is it an organisation? A company? Is it connected to the smelter? I do not understand.

I cannot tell you more. Not now.

Can we meet?

You must understand, Madame Veronique, that you must be very careful. Call me in two days. From a different phone.

And that was it. He hung up.

11

Incentive

They double-anchored *Flame* in a low-tide tributary of the main estuary where the mangroves grew thick along both banks, shielding the boat from view. Clay left the MP5 and its spare magazines in the priest hole, along with a dozen Krugerrands. Everything else – his passports, the money, the rest of the gold, extra ammunition for the G21 – he took. As they rowed away he thought that she looked very small, very lonely here, this vessel that had carried him safely over so many miles.

They left the dinghy hidden among the mangroves and walked inland. An hour and a half later they reached the coast road and hitched a ride north in the back of a farmer's truck. The outskirts of Mombasa loomed and then thickened, red laterite and corrugated iron replacing grassland and scrub acacia. They continued by taxi into the centre of town. Crowbar paid the driver and they started into the market-day chaos of old Mombasa.

'Who is this friend of yours who can get us a plane?' said Clay, pushing past a donkey cart piled with freshly dug cassava.

'Rhodesian,' said Crowbar. 'Does contract work for me occasionally. Logistics is his thing. He's no fighter, but if it exists in Africa, he can find it.'

'You trust him?'

'I've known G a long time. He was a quartermaster in the Rhodesian Army. He used to help me out sometimes, back then.'

'I asked if you trusted him, *oom*.'

'I trust him to get a plane for us. Beyond that, no.'

Walking the streets of another African port city, Cairo seemed as far away as it was. Clay wondered what had driven Rania to Egypt, if she was safe. Nine months ago he'd asked for her help, and she'd given it. Now she was asking for his.

'I need to call her, *Koevoet*.'

'Be quick.'

They found a telephone kiosk off the main street. Crowbar took one booth, Clay the other. He dialled the number Hope had given Crowbar. The line clicked, gurgled, rang. No answer. He tried again.

'Ready?' said Crowbar, tapping him on the shoulder.

Clay shook his head. 'I'll try a few more times.'

'I'll be at the bar. Turn right, about a hundred metres. The Violet.'

Clay nodded, put down the phone, watched Crowbar disappear into the street. Kenya was in the same time zone as Egypt. Just gone four in the afternoon. He imagined her there, gliding over the pavement in some traffic-filled street, everything about her veiled and inscrutable, and despite everything they'd shared and lost, he realised that he'd never really known her, and probably never would.

He reached for the receiver, started dialling the number. Halfway through he stopped, killed the line. What was he doing? The Broederbond, the AB, was set on killing him. Manheim was close. Clay could *feel* him. Assuming they could get to Cairo, how long until the AB tracked them down? It would only compound Rania's problems. No. He needed to stay away.

He tried her number again, with the same result, a hollow ring echoing through an empty room somewhere in Cairo, with no one to hear it.

He trudged out of the kiosk, turned right, pushed his way through the crowds towards the port. The Indian Ocean shed blades of ultra-violet light that hurt his eyes. Sweat ran from his temples, guttered in the hollow of his solar plexus. The last time he'd seen her, back in Cyprus almost two years ago, she'd been in intensive care, holding on to life – hers and their unborn daughter's – by the faintest echo. Since then, he'd travelled the world without her, an outcast, unable to understand what had made her do the things she'd done, lost within the raging gales of his own regret. They were all so close to him now, these people, these dark eyes and darker faces, jostling him, calling out to him in languages he could not understand. And then he realised. They were all dead.

Clay closed his eyes. Unburied corpses stiffen and bloat quickly in the tropic sun. Decomposition begins, and the carrion eaters do fast work. Vultures are often the first to appear. Then the hyenas come, and the jackals. During the war, he'd seen the dead stripped of flesh and bones crushed to powder within hours, and he'd seen the yet-living plummet through the atmosphere towards a seemingly endless sea. And he knew, now, that if he willed it so, he could open his eyes and see them as they were: living, breathing, whole. It was progress, of sorts, this ability to recover.

Clay swayed, cycled oxygen through his lungs, forced the air into the deepest part of himself. He narrowed his eyes, kept going.

Crowbar was in the Violet, seated at a back table with a flaxen-haired, sunburnt white man and two glistening black whores.

'Any luck?' Crowbar said as Clay approached.

Clay shook his head and sat.

'You look like *kak*,' said Crowbar.

'*Dankie*.'

Crowbar pushed a glass of beer across the table towards Clay. 'This miscreant is G,' he said. 'And his friends.'

Clay nodded to the man, then to the whores.

'Welcome to Kenya,' said G. He was pale. Sweat covered his face. He looked as if he was fighting a bout of malaria.

The women smiled at him, big lipstick and blue eyeshadow, the stains of some cheap skin whitener.

'We're all set,' said Crowbar. 'Leave tomorrow.'

G said something in Arabic and one of the whores got up and went to the bar. G drained his beer. 'Where you *okes* headed?'

'South,' said Clay.

The whore returned with a beer, placed it on the table, sat back down.

G wiped his forehead with a greying handkerchief, lanced a cigarette between his lips. 'Catch me a glow, would ya?'

Crowbar pulled out his lighter and set the flame to the tip of G's
smoke.

G leaned back and took a long pull on the cigarette. 'South, eh?'
he said, exhaling towards the ceiling. 'I'm surprised.'

'I'm happy for you,' said Clay.

G drank. 'You *okes* in a bit of trouble?'

'And *howzit* with you, *broer*?' said Crowbar. 'Not too good, I hear.'

G put his arm around the whore on his left. His hand hovered
over one of her substantial breasts. 'I make do.'

'Of course you do.' Crowbar stood. 'Tomorrow, then.'

'Aren't you forgetting something?' said G.

Crowbar stared down at him.

'The *kite*, *china*. The money.'

'Tomorrow.' Crowbar turned and walked away.

'You the main *manne* what counts, *Koevoet*,' G shouted after him.

Clay stayed seated, finished his beer. 'Thanks, *broer*.'

G raised his half-empty glass. 'Check you, *china*.'

Clay followed Crowbar out onto the street.

'Friend?' said Clay, catching up to Crowbar.

'Like I said.'

'"Check you, *china*"?'

Crowbar smiled. 'Rhoddie slang: "See you, friend."'

Clay nodded. 'What's the bet he's on the phone to Manheim right
now?'

'*Vyftig-vyftig.*'

'Good odds.'

'I've given him a little incentive.'

'Down payment?'

'If the bastard screws us, I'll kill him.'

☾

They walked back to the kiosk. While Crowbar waited outside, Clay tried Rania again. This time, she answered first ring.

'Hello beautiful.' He couldn't help it. She was.

'*Mon Dieu. C'est toi.*' She sounded as if she'd just run up three flights of stairs.

'I got your message. I can't come.'

The line hissed.

'Did you hear me?'

'I need you.'

'They tried to kill me, Ra. I can't lead them to you.'

'I am all alone.' She was crying now, but trying to hide it. 'The police are watching me.'

Clay cut his breath short. 'I don't want to make it worse.'

'*Mon Dieu, mais ce n'est pas vrai,*' she said, anger replacing tears. 'My husband and son are dead. I am being accused of murder. How could it be worse?'

'I'm sorry, Ra, for what happened to them.'

He could hear her breathing, trying to steady herself.

'*Chéri*, if you love me, you will come to me now.' She paused. He started to answer but she cut him off before he could get past the intake of breath. 'I know,' she said. 'Don't say it. I know you think that you cannot love. I have never believed that.'

'That isn't the point, Ra. It's not about that, and you know it.'

'Why does the idea frighten you so? Do you think it a weakness, a frailty?'

'I don't know what it is.' He'd tried to explain this to her before, in Istanbul.

She sighed.

He could feel the frustration rising, his inability to express himself in a way that she would understand. 'It changes nothing.'

'Stupid man. It changes everything.'

Clay said nothing, let the line burn between them. And he knew she was right – about the forces that had kept them apart; about the need to act for positives rather than against negatives; about everything.

'Come to me, *chéri*.' Tears drowned her words. 'Please. I am afraid.'

Clay took the receiver away from his ear, pushed it down hard against the tabletop, stared at the veins in the back of his hand, the calloused welts of his knuckles. It was as if she was reconfiguring his DNA using nothing but her voice.

He lifted the receiver to his ear. 'How can I find you?'

'How long will it take you?' Her voice brightening.

'I'm not sure. A few days.'

The sound of commotion in the background, scraping, a door closing in the distance. Then a pause, a long one. 'Wait a moment,' she said, stress in her voice.

'What is it, Ra?'

'*Mon Dieu*,' she gasped. 'Someone is coming.'

'Who is it?'

'I don't have time to explain. Call me when you get here.' She read out a string of numbers. 'Ask for Veronique.'

'Be careful, Ra. Please.'

'Yes, *mon amour*. You also.'

Her words pulsed inside him. 'Where will you be?' he started to ask.

But before he could finish, she was gone.

12

All the Rest of His Life

They left the taxi five kilometres from the airstrip and walked in under a vault of stars. By the time they reached the strip, the sky was ash above them.

They crouched among the sickle wood and cassia and watched the sky lighten. From their position, they could see the whole of the runway and back along the cut road that led to the red-dirt clearing that served as the apron. Two aircraft – single-engine high-winged Cessnas – stood next to a small corrugated-steel shack, a fuel bowser nearby. A ragged windsock hung limp from its post at the far side of the strip.

'There it is,' said Crowbar. 'The larger of the two. Cessna 172. Cruises at about one hundred and ten knots. Range about nine hundred nautical miles.' He handed Clay a pair of binoculars. 'Glass the perimeter, *ja*.'

Clay tracked the tree line, looking for anything that might signal that they were being watched. He shivered despite the heat. She was being hunted. He could still hear the terror in her voice. Two thousand, five hundred miles separated them. That meant at least three refuelling stops on the way, four to be safe. Assuming twelve hours of flying a day, they could be in Cairo in three and a half days. But this was Africa. He doubled it, immediately crushed the calculation. All you could do was take each mile as it came, each day. Anything else was a prescription for failure, for pain.

Crowbar pulled out a handgun, checked the magazine, pulled back the slide. He looked at Clay. 'Jericho 941, up-chambered to forty-five cal, *ja*. We get a lot of our stuff from the Israelis these days.' Crowbar had spent almost a decade sourcing weapons and equipment for the SADF during the late eighties and nineties, when apartheid South Africa was under economic sanction. Back then, Israel had been a key supplier – indirectly, of course. 'Anything?' he asked.

'Looks clear.'

'Check again.'

The sky was lightening quickly now. Clay swung the glasses back over the same ground, looking for any indication of concealment, of linear geometry among the fractal chaos of the bush, but could see none. He set the binoculars on the ground, gazed out across the airstrip to the low, dark hills beyond and the red edge of the world as dawn came.

'Will he show?' Clay said.

'*Ja*, definitely. G wouldn't miss a chance to make this kind of money.'

Clay picked up the binoculars, scanned the tree line again.

He was halfway through when Crowbar nudged him. 'Here they come.'

A solitary vehicle was speeding toward the airfield, trailing a cloud of red dust. An old Land Rover stopped next to the shack and three men got out: G, another white man dressed in coveralls and a blue cap, and a black man. The man in coveralls and the black man started wheeling the hand-pump bowser towards the larger of the two Cessnas while G unlocked the shed.

'The *kaffir* is carrying,' whispered Crowbar.

Clay could see the bulge under the black man's shirt front, hear the men's voices across the fifty metres or so of open ground. A giraffe wandered out from the bush, strode past the aircraft and disappeared into the trees at the far side of the airstrip. The men paid it no attention.

G had re-emerged from the shed and was opening the plane's engine cowling. The other white man was up onto the underwing strut and was holding the fuel nozzle in the overhead tank opening as the black man pumped.

'Your friend's carrying too,' said Clay.

'If it all goes to *kak*, you take the *kaffir*,' said Crowbar.

Clay nodded, checked his G21. 'Is the other one the pilot?'

'Hell no,' said Crowbar.

'Who then? G?'

Crowbar grinned.

Clay shook his head. 'Didn't know you could fly.'

'I learned in the service. Flew Bosboks for a while, coordinating with the parabats. After about a year I realised I wanted to be on the ground where the fighting was. I'm better at it. Haven't flown for years.'

'How's your navigation?' said Clay, searching the tree line again. 'It's a hell of a long way.'

'Was counting on you for that, *seun*.'

Clay handed Crowbar the binoculars. 'Should have brought my sextant,' he said. 'All clear.'

Crowbar stood, pushed the Jericho into his waistband. 'Here we go, *seun*. Follow my lead.'

So many times had he followed this man into danger, that this – here, now – seemed nothing more than a continuation, as if he had never done anything else, as if all of the rest of his life had been nothing but preparation for these moments. And as he followed Crowbar across the coarse stubble towards the aircraft, the lower terminus of the sun's disc separating from the surface of earth, the Glock's barrel pushed up against his spine, he realised that this was what he was meant to do. Rania was right. His fate, and those of the people he cared for, and of all those he did not, was governed by forces completely beyond his control. He could just as easily stop the sun from rising before him as change what he had become. And the future, as much of it as he might have left, was being hungrily gobbled up by the present and shit out as the past.

As they approached G turned to face them, raised his hand. '*Lekker*, eh?' he called out, indicating the plane as if it were a television game show prize.

'Depends,' said Crowbar.

'You got the *kite*?' said G, wiping his hands on his trousers.

'Start it up,' said Crowbar.

G frowned, climbed up into the cockpit. The four-cyclinder Lycoming coughed, turned over, roared to life. Crowbar stood there a moment, let the motor run then signalled G to shut it down.

Crowbar handed G an envelope. 'Count it.'

G peered inside and started flicking through the notes. Satisfied, he stashed the envelope in his jacket then produced a plastic file folder and handed it to Crowbar. 'Manifest, ownership deeds, Kenyan pilot's licence, registration, charts. Everything's there.'

Crowbar took the documents and stashed them in his pack 'Long-range tanks?'

'Forty-eight US gallons useable,' said the man in the coveralls. 'Should get you about eight hundred miles. More in the jerry cans.'

Crowbar nodded. 'I owe you.'

'You sure as hell do, *china*. Manheim came to see me yesterday.'

Clay's pulse quickened.

'How's he feeling?' said Crowbar.

'Sore.'

'I hope so.'

'He was asking about you,' said G. 'You and Straker.'

Crowbar nodded.

'He's offering a lot of money.'

'How much?' said Crowbar.

'Fifty grand US. Each.'

Crowbar stood hand on hips. 'How about I just kill you now?'

G shrank back. 'Shit, Crowbar, no need to get like that, man. I didn't tell him anything. I'm just saying, he's offering a lot of money.'

'What did your *ma* always tell you, G? Money isn't everything.'

The black man laughed.

Crowbar hefted his pack and pushed it into the back seat of the 172.

G kicked the dirt. His boot sent a puff of laterite dust spiralling into the air. 'He had a message for you. Both of you. In case I saw you.'

'And I've got one for him,' said Crowbar. 'In case you see him. Tell him he still has a choice. He owes me, and I'm not going to forget it.'

'What was his message?' said Clay.

G switched his gaze to Clay. 'Have fun. That's what he said. Have fun in Cairo.' G smiled his gap-toothed grin. 'You *okes* have a *lekker* glide.'

5th November 1997. Cairo, Egypt. 23:10 hrs

When you called yesterday, it was the first time since Maputo that I had heard your voice. That was almost a year ago. Mon amour, *you sounded so far away! Not the miles, but the reticence. You do not trust me. Should that surprise me? So many times I have allowed you to come close, and each time I have crushed you. My behaviour towards you has been unforgiveable. I look inside myself and see again the hateful poles at work.*

In Istanbul you opened yourself to me. I know it is very difficult for you to do this. You have seen and done terrible things. You are not a talkative man. And yet you tried. You told me things you have not told anyone else. I know you were trying to be as honest with me and with yourself as you could. And for a few days we were close, so close. I felt closer to you then than I have to anyone before or since.

Why did I turn you away? Was it losing the child – our baby? You wrote to me twice from prison in Cyprus, and not once did I answer. Your letters sat on my bureau for months, calling out to me, but I steadfastly, stubbornly ignored them, with all the discipline and self-abnegation a good Muslim woman could summon. Was it guilt? An illicit affair with a kafir *is a mortal sin. God punished me by destroying the fruit of my transgression.*

And now I am calling you back again. Can you forgive me? Will you come?

Yesterday, when we were speaking on the phone, I saw a car pull up across the street. Two men jumped out and started towards my flat. It was the two policemen who questioned me the day before – Moonface and the tall one. I could tell right away that this time, they had not come to talk. I knew that I needed to run.

The Directorate trained me well, Claymore, as you have seen. I had already worked out alternative escape routes. My bag was packed and ready to go. I was out on the rear balcony and over the railing and down into the back garden before the policemen were halfway up the front stairs. By the time I heard the crash of my door being broken down, I was already in the back alley and making my way to the metro station.

Where are you now, chéri? *Are you thinking of me, I wonder? Hurry to me, please.*

أكبر الله.

13

Eons in Minutes

Crowbar leaned off the fuel mixture control and trimmed up the little four-seater for level flight.

The take-off had been rough, Crowbar yawing the Cessna left and right across the airstrip as she gained speed and rotated into a light crosswind. Once airborne, he put the plane into a gentle climb and started a broad right-hand turn to the south. Clay looked back down at the airstrip; G and his men were already speeding away, their Land Rover just a toy throwing up a thin tendril of iron-oxide dust.

Not long later, Crowbar banked the Cessna sharply and ticked her through 180 degrees. Clay had already plotted a course that took them north towards the border with Ethiopia. Cruising at eight thousand feet, the Cessna's manual estimated a range of well over eight hundred miles. The charts showed an airstrip with fuelling facilities in Marsabit, about ninety nautical miles south of the border. There they would refuel, and push north to Addis Ababa, then the Sudan border another four hundred miles north, and Khartoum as far again. From there, Cairo would be less than a day's flying away.

Kilimanjaro's dark, glacier-capped bulk loomed on their starboard wing, sixty kilometres away. And yet, in the rarefied troposphere, it seemed to tower over them. Clay could see the extinct volcano's wide caldera and the broad horseshoe ridge, the filaments of ice dripping down its dolerite flanks. He thought of the book his father had given him one Christmas, Hemingway's short stories.

'I always wanted to climb it,' said Clay. 'Never got the chance.'

'Take your son, when he's older.'

'How is he?' Clay had never seen him.

Crowbar smiled, adjusted the headphones, pulled the mike closer to his mouth. 'Poor little bastard looks like you. Thank God he seems to have got his mother's brains.'

Clay smiled, couldn't help himself. 'Kypros,' he said. 'I like it.' Clay thought it would be good if he could walk among these places with his son, one day. But he quickly pushed it away.

'I don't. Hope insisted.'

'She's the boss.'

Crowbar smiled again. His mouth opened very wide and his lips stretched back to reveal strong teeth as white as the mountain's far-off spire. His eyes flashed high-altitude blue. '*Ja, ja*. And the boss is pregnant.'

Clay slapped Crowbar on the thick hump of ox muscle that was the man's trapezoid. 'That's great, *oom*. Fantastic.'

'*Ja, ja*.' Crowbar beamed. 'And this time, I get to name him.'

Clay smiled too, shot it out across the Serengeti.

Hours passed. Africa slipped away beneath them. Rift volcanoes, dormant and active, marked out deep scars in the earth's crust. Herds of wildebeest and buffalo wandered the plains, congregated at drying waterholes, flowing pinpoints of cantor dust held to the slowly diverging plates.

But the worry was always there. Someone had come to her door. What had happened? Why had she given him a different number? And how in hell did Manheim know they were headed for Cairo?

By mid-afternoon they were approaching the airstrip at Marsabit. Crowbar throttled back into a slow descent. The airstrip was quiet, no other aircraft in the circuit. He lined the Cessna up for final approach.

'Been a while since I've done this,' said Crowbar, fighting to keep the aircraft on course in a strong crosswind.

Clay grabbed the edge of his seat, held tight as the dirt strip loomed in the windscreen. As they crossed the threshold, Crowbar cut power and flared, but instead of settling, the Cessna floated above the runway, ballooning in ground effect. They were chewing up runway fast, the scrub and trees at the far end racing towards them.

'Hold on,' said Crowbar, pushing down hard on the steering column.

The Cessna bounced once, hard, and then twice before sticking. Crowbar applied the brakes in a spray of gravel. They slid to a stop only a few feet from the end of the runway.

Crowbar took a deep breath, threw open his side window and taxied the aircraft over the red dirt towards a cluster of small buildings set at the midpoint of the runway. Heat poured from the hard-baked ground in shimmering updrafts.

'Good landing,' said Clay.

'Like riding an elephant.' Crowbar grinned. 'I'll check the landing gear once we stop.'

As they neared the small red-dirt apron they could see a couple of other aircraft set under a makeshift hangar – a turbo Pilates and what looked like a very old Piper Cub. Crowbar shut down the engine, ripped off his headphones, flung the door open, jumped to the ground and started pissing on the undercarriage.

Clay stepped to the ground, felt the solidity through his bones. He scanned the length of the runway, the apron, the low scrub beyond. The place appeared to be deserted. He couldn't see any fuelling facilities.

Crowbar zipped up, checked his .45, pushed it into his belt, flipped his shirt over to cover the weapon. 'I'm going to see if I can find any fuel in this shithole. Stay here. Keep alert.'

'Yes, my *Liutenant*,' Clay said before he could catch himself. It was an old habit, yet unbroken.

He stood in the dust and watched Crowbar trudge off across the apron and disappear behind the hangar. The plane's engine ticked in the heat. A kite turned in the sky above. Clay could see its raptor head moving as it scanned the ground for prey. The biogeochemistry of the rift lands came to him, thick on the breeze: the burning grasses, the freshly extruded basalts, the fossilised, powdered bones of the oldest hominids. Nightfall was still four hours away. Enough time to cross over into Ethiopia. More than enough for a drowning, a murder, the slaughter of innocents. For things such as these, he knew, there was always time, eons even in minutes.

Crowbar returned about an hour later carrying two cold tins of Tusker lager and a plastic shopping bag. 'No avgas,' he said, tossing Clay a beer, 'but at least they had something to drink in town.' He pushed a wisp of titanium hair from his forehead and drank down half the tin.

They finished their beers then refuelled the Cessna using the jerry cans. Crowbar checked the engine oil, cleaned the windshield with a rag and some of the water.

'Manheim knows we're going to Cairo,' said Clay, opening a second beer. He'd been turning it over in his head ever since leaving the airstrip.

'Apparently.'

'How the hell could he have known, *oom*? Until yesterday, *I* didn't even know we were going to Cairo.'

'He knows. The question is, what do we do about it?'

Clay crushed one of the empty beer tins under his boot. 'If you were Manheim, what would you do?'

'I'd go to the best surgeon I could find and get a nose job,' said Crowbar. That big smile again.

Clay let it go. 'Does he go straight to Cairo, intercept us there?'

'I know the *poes*,' said Crowbar. 'He's not going to wait to see if we might show up three thousand clicks away.'

'Then it's got to be Addis,' said Clay, kicking a furrow into the crushed and powdered stone of the apron's surface. 'G probably told him what kind of aircraft we have, so he'll know the range. It's one of the only places in the whole country where we can be guaranteed of finding fuel.'

'It doesn't matter,' said Crowbar, retrieving another beer from the plastic bag. 'We're not going to wait to find out. We're going to intercept *him*.'

'How the hell are we going to do that?'

Crowbar tipped back his beer, drained it. 'I made some calls from town,' he said.

'And?'

'It's all set up.'

'Where?'

'Sudan.'

'Jesus.'

Crowbar opened the cockpit door. 'Let's go.'

Clay reached out, held the door closed. 'Tell me, *Koevoet*. How did Manheim know that we were going to Cairo?'

Crowbar grabbed Clay's arm, tried to push it away from the door. Clay held firm.

'Let it go, Straker.'

'Tell me, God damn it.'

'You're not going to like it, *soutpiele*.'

Something welled up inside him, fear and impatience and longing and a hundred things, bilious and forlorn beyond his ability to describe. 'We're not going anywhere until you tell me.'

'I need you functioning, Straker. I can't have you distracted. We have a job to do. Now *fokken* get out of the way.'

'You think I can't handle myself? *Fok jou, Koevoet*.'

'I *know* you can't handle yourself, *soutpiele*. I've always known it.'

Clay took a half-step back, let go the door and drove his forearm up under Crowbar's neck, slamming him into the side of the aircraft's fuselage. Crowbar's beer fell to the ground, spilling foam.

'I don't need you to look after me,' Clay shouted. 'You hear me, old man? We get to Cairo, you *fok* off and leave me alone. For good. I never want to see—'

But before he could finish, Crowbar cut his legs out with a vicious ankle reap, sending him toppling to the ground in a cloud of dust.

Crowbar kicked the near-empty beer can, sent it spinning across the dirt. 'What the *fok*, Straker. Think I'm the *fokken* enemy?'

Clay spat the silt from his mouth. 'I don't know, old man. You tell me.'

Crowbar straightened, looked down at Clay. 'Manheim knows we're going to Cairo,' he said, 'because the AB knows Rania is there. And they know we know.'

The words knocked the breath from Clay's lungs. He slumped back to the ground.

'That's why we have to get Manheim,' said Crowbar. 'Before he gets to Rania. The AB doesn't like her any more than they do you.' He smoothed his hair back. 'After that, you can *fok* the hell off, Straker. But until then, you're mine.' Crowbar opened the door and climbed into the cockpit.

Suddenly, Egypt seemed a lot farther away.

5th November 1997, Cairo, Egypt. 20:15 hrs

Dearest Claymore:

Chéri, *I write to you now, in the event that I never see you again.*

I have decided to disappear. And how better to disappear than in plain sight? I have become one of the thousands of faceless, ignored, homeless wretches who wander Cairo's slums and alleys, who pick over the piles of rubbish that choke every empty plot of ground and work the corniche and the other thoroughfares, holding out withered underfed hands to passing motorists, hoping for a few worthless coins. I have never felt so completely invisible, so alone. We are the actively ignored. People literally will us away.

I have found a corner in an empty lot where several other unfortunates have fashioned shelters from old sheets of asbestos roofing, cardboard and discarded plastic tarpaulin. We are all clustered up against the brick wall of a low-rent apartment building in old Giza. My shelter is strangely cosy already, and my neighbours are surprisingly, well, human – friendly and good-humoured and, despite all their various afflictions, as helpful as they can be. What had I expected? A snarling community of animals, devoid of compassion or feeling?

Today, my immediate neighbour, a woman in her mid-thirties with two children under the age of ten, seeing that I was struggling with the roof of my shelter, took the time to help me. I thanked her, and after, we spoke. She spends her days with the Zabbaleen, the garbage pickers of Cairo, scraping out a living for her family. Her name is Samira. She is a widow, like me. And like me, she has known better times.

The canal nearby serves as both latrine and water supply, and the smell is something I cannot describe. I try to stay away. I have three big bottles of good drinking water here in my shelter, and some tinned and packaged food. For a bed, I have three layers of cardboard and an old blanket. It is comfortable enough.

There was another bombing here yesterday, Claymore. This time in Alexandria. I read about it in a newspaper that someone discarded on the street. El Assad, The Lion, claimed responsibility on behalf of Al-Gama'a al-Islamiyya, the same group who perpetrated the attack in Taba a few days ago. Again, the target was a tourist resort. They blew a hotel reception area to pieces, injuring five workers. Again, no tourists were harmed – they appear to have planned it for very early morning.

The Lion released a statement, condemning the wealthy families who control the nation's businesses and the government, plunder the country's wealth, and maintain the majority in a constant state of poverty and illness. How can people do such things, Claymore, however just they believe their cause to be? These terrorists are not Muslims. For them, Islam is nothing but a convenient camouflage. They are political extremists, nothing more. These cowards debase themselves and our religion. I burned the newspaper in my evening fire.

Claymore, as I lie here and write this, the flame of my candle flickering on its wick, I think of that first time we were together, in Yemen. It seems so very long ago now, almost a dream, even though it is only three and a half years. Oh, chéri, I cannot describe the conflict that explodes inside me whenever I think of you. And while I know that you will never see this, it helps me to write it, to think that perhaps one day I will understand what is happening to me. I am alone, childless now after two attempts to bring a life into the world. Guilt crushes me, from the inside out. Now that Hamid is gone, I know that I did not love him. I think, now, that I loved the idea of him, a good Muslim husband who nevertheless aspired to the secular and modern, who would let me be my own person, have a career. Please do not misunderstand me, Claymore. I do not mean to imply that you would have sought, if we had married, to domineer me in any way, quite the opposite. Sometimes, back then, when I would contemplate what it might be like if we were to be married – and I did, often – I imagined that as a husband you might actually be too malleable for me, too easily manipulated. I need somebody strong. My father was strong.

Thinking back, I am not sure what it was that kept making me push you away every time you got close. In part, I think, it was that I simply could not imagine a life – the kind of life I wanted, stable and gentle and happy – with you. Your violence frightens me, Claymore, that volatile, unpredictable core that seems to burn so close to your surface. I have seen what you can do, the brutality you are capable of. I know it frightens you too. And yet, how gentle you can be! There are times I have felt as if I could crush you in one hand, like the most fragile of shells. And when, in Istanbul, you told me that you were incapable of love, something inside me let go. I did not believe that it was true, and still do not, as I told you on the phone a few days ago. But the very fact that you believed it made me understand that you were not ready – might never be ready – for me, or for anyone.

Oh, chéri, I hope that going back to South Africa to testify has helped to exorcise some of the terror you carry within yourself. What I do know now, very truly and clearly, is that you are the only man I have ever truly loved. And if God sees fit to bless me with one more day with you, that is what I will tell you.

And if not, if Allah makes it my destiny to wander this earth alone until he chooses to take me to his Grace, I will thank him for the time we have spent together, and for the gift of knowing, if only for a few days, the grace of being truly loved. دمحلا هلل

Goodnight, my tortured soul, wherever you are.

Yours always, Rania. أحبك

14

The One Who'd Taught Him

They crossed the border into Ethiopia later that day, flew on as the sun set big and red over the highlands. Before the light faded, Crowbar found a strip of lonely dirt road that cut, long and straight, through the scrub. He brought the Cessna down low, lowered the flaps to their full forty degrees and put the plane down. This time the wheels kissed the gravel.

'Welcome to Ethiopia,' said Crowbar. They were the first words he'd spoken since leaving Marsabit.

Crowbar shut down the engine. They jumped out and pushed the Cessna off onto the shoulder and then into a small clearing surrounded by dry acacia and spreading juniper, where it would be well hidden from the road. Under a spreading iridium sky, they lit a fire and unrolled their blankets.

Soon the coals were glowing. Crowbar adjusted the stones of the fire ring into an even square and balanced a grill over the coals. Then he unwrapped four big pork chops from the paper he'd bought them in and laid them carefully on the grill. The fat sizzled and dripped. Orange flame burst and flared, lit Crowbar's face and the bladed phyllodes of the trees and reflected from the aluminium skin of the plane. They drank the last of the beer as stars filled the sky.

Crowbar turned the meat. 'Hope and Kip should be in California by now,' he said. It was as if their earlier confrontation had never happened.

'That's good,' said Clay. 'They'll be safe there.'

'She wants me to join her.'

'She's right,' said Clay. 'Get out.'

'I don't know if I can leave this place,' said Crowbar, looking up into the night sky.

Back again in the land of his birth, this land of spirits, Clay knew exactly what Crowbar meant. Africa, it reached down inside you and attached itself, became part of you. You could no more detach it than pull out your own heart.

'You said it yourself, *Koevoet* – they won't stop looking for you, not as long as you're on the continent.'

Crowbar stared into the fire, said nothing.

'I'm going to kill Manheim.' said Clay. A hunger opened up deep inside him, Neolithic, old as the extruded rift-rock on which they lay, as undeniable. Time stalled. Precession reversed. Lost equinoctial markers reappeared. Ancient gods and spirits, long dormant, threw off their slumber of centuries. It was all there, above them, writ in the constellations.

'*We're* going to kill him,' said Crowbar.

Clay nodded. 'Okay. We. How?'

'I called my business partner, told him I was flying to Cairo, that I was planning to stop in Sudan, close to the Egyptian border. We have connections there, have been doing some business. I told him to leak it to the AB.'

'Your business partner has links to the AB?'

Crowbar nodded but didn't elaborate.

Clay left this alone. 'Can you trust him, *Koevoet*?'

'We've been partners since ninety-four. We were in the DCC together.'

'That wasn't my question.'

'Who the *fok* knows? Can you trust anyone, Straker?'

'Where in Sudan?'

'I didn't tell him.'

'Then how will they know?'

'Don't worry, they will.'

Clay said nothing.

'I'm going to put you down about a hundred miles south of the rendezvous point. You're going to go in by road. They'll be waiting for me, but they won't be expecting you.'

Clay let this settle, looked up at the stars. 'What if they don't bite down on it?'

'They will.'

Clay's pulse quickened. Still two days away, then, this killing. He could feel the anticipation simmering within him. It felt like lust. 'Good,' he said.

'But if not, we go on as planned.'

'And after, no matter what happens, you get out, go to Hope.' He regretted his earlier outburst, but he wasn't going to say anything about it.

'*Fokken soutpiele*, giving *me* orders again.' That big grin, impossible to resist.

'Promise me, *oom*. We get to Cairo, you get out. I'll find Rania.'

Crowbar nodded, speared a chop with a sharpened branch, handed it to Clay. 'Okay, Straker. Okay. But one condition: we kill every last one of the bastards.'

Clay nodded. 'You said before that Manheim owed you. What happened, *oom*?'

Crowbar crushed his beer can under his palm. 'Like I said, we were friends once. Close friends. A couple of months after an op inside Angola, a bad one, we went on pass together to his family's farm near Bloemfontein. Beautiful place. He introduced me to his parents and his younger sister.'

Clay waited for him to continue.

'We had fun. His sister was *lekker*, a real knockout. We hit it off. Hanneleen – that was her name. We exchanged addresses. She wrote me a couple of times. Not long after Manheim got transferred to the Recces.' Crowbar tore off a chunk of meat, chewed. 'Next time I got a pass, a few months later, I went back there, on my own. Didn't tell Manheim. The family welcomed me like I was one of their own.' Crowbar closed his eyes, filled his lungs. 'One night I was banging Hanneleen out in the back, when three *kaffirs* broke into the house.

They shot Manheim's father, cut his mother up pretty bad before I could get there. I killed all three of the bastards.'

'Jesus,' muttered Clay.

'His mother died in hospital a few days later. The next time I saw him, a couple of years later, he'd changed. That was when he joined the AWB. I never saw him again until a few days ago.'

Clay speared a second chop from the grill. 'A thinker? You're joking.'

'Don't underestimate him, *seun*. Manheim is one of the most intelligent people I've ever met. In his own *fokked*-up way.'

'You saw what the bastard did to Zuz,' said Clay. 'Grace and Joseph are dead because of him.'

'Like I said, he changed.'

Clay filled his lungs, held it, exhaled. 'Leave the bastard to me.'

Crowbar looked up at him. Firelight lit his face, flickered across his retinae.

'When I kill him, I want him to know it's me,' Clay said.

Crowbar closed his eyes a moment, opened them again, stared hard at Clay. 'It's just business, *seun*. That's the way you've got to do it. The minute you forget that, the wrong people get hurt. We are going to do a job. That's all.'

Clay stared back, hearing, understanding. Despite what he'd heard, hate burned inside him, plasma hot, and he was unable to govern it or separate its effect from its origin.

'Straker?'

Clay nodded. 'That's why you chose Sudan.'

'*Ja*. A few extra bodies in a place like that, who the *fok* is going to notice?'

☾

Early the next morning they pushed the plane back out to the road and roared off towards Sudan under a monochrome sky. The weather in the highlands had grown unsettled, and all day they dodged

thunderheads and the swept-back anvil tops of towering cumulonimbus. Bands of rain slanted across the green hills, darkened the
landscape for a time then vanished, ghostlike. Lightning flashed in
the distance.

By late afternoon they'd refuelled and were approaching Sudanese airspace, halfway through a bottle of Johnny Walker Red that
Crowbar had produced from his pack. Clay watched Africa slide away
below him like a dream. Once more he was flying into a country at
war – a place he had never seen – to kill. He could still remember
a time, very soon after he'd been sent to the war in Angola, when
he was young, when killing was an abstract, unknown quantity,
made unreal by its sanctioned legality and the brute, industrialised
indifference with which it was carried out. But then, as the corpses
multiplied, the shocking waste and cruelty of the war had permeated
his soul. He was poisoned, infected, lost. And he'd never recovered.
And then, later, after being badly wounded, witnessing firsthand
the horrors of his country's chemical and biological weapons programme, he'd deserted, fled over the border into Mozambique. It
was 1982. He was twenty-two. Still badly injured, exhausted and out
of water, he'd been taken in by a family of itinerant farmers. An old
healer had sewn his wounds, nursed him back to health. The generosity of these simple people had stunned him. It was with him still,
locked away like a precious talisman. And yet the old healer's words
continued to haunt him.

Clay depressed the talk button on the headphone mike. It was the
first time he'd done so in hours. 'Do you believe in spirits, *Koevoet*?'

Crowbar looked over at him. 'What, like the Holy Ghost?'

'No, not that. The evil kind.'

Crowbar passed him the bottle. 'Witchery?'

Clay nodded.

'Me, no. But I've seen people die, just drop dead, after being
cursed by the local witch doctor. Belief is a powerful thing.'

Clay drank, felt the alcohol cut into him. 'An old healer I met in
Mozambique, in eighty-two, he said I had an evil spirit inside me.'

Crowbar laughed. 'That would explain a lot, *ja*.'

'I'm serious, *oom*. He said it would never leave me. That I'd have to live with it until I died.'

'*Fok*, Straker. We all have one of those.' Crowbar grabbed the bottle, drank.

'He said it was strong. That it wanted to kill.'

'Good. Get it ready.'

'That's the problem, *oom*. It's always ready.'

Crowbar raised the bottle. It was three-quarters gone. 'Good thing to have in this life, a spirit like that.'

'I've tried to live with it. I can't.'

Crowbar drank, one hand on the wheel, wiped his mouth with the wrist of his drinking hand. 'Here's what you do, *seun*. When you're ready – I mean, *really* ready – go and get some village *juju* man to incant it away. As long as you believe it's gone, it will be. It's all in your head, *seun*.'

'Are we paying for what we've done, *Koevoet*?'

Crowbar's eyes narrowed behind his aviator's Ray-Bans. 'Don't talk *kak*, Straker. We all do what we have to. You, me, even *fokken* Manheim. Stay alive. Do your best. That's all you can do.'

'It's you, isn't it?' said Clay. He could feel the alcohol blurring his thoughts now, its folding, looping distortions. And yet, suddenly, it all made sense.

'What are you talking about, Straker?'

Clay swallowed another mouthful of the whisky. Everything was clear, clear as the rarefied ten-thousand-foot atmosphere, as the rumpled topography spooling out beneath him like a carpet he could step out and walk on. It had always been Crowbar, ever since his first kill, just after his nineteenth birthday on that hot, dry day in Angola. It had been Crowbar who'd put him on point that morning, and when they flushed that *terr*, he'd told the rest of the platoon to hold their fire so that Clay could take the shot. And after, standing over the body of the boy who'd been not much older than Clay, Crowbar had clapped him on the back. Good kill, he'd said.

It was Crowbar who'd taught him the art, in all its beautiful variety, who'd been there to congratulate him every time he'd torn an enemy's stomach open with the high-velocity 5.56 millimetre rounds from his R4, every time he'd blown apart someone's skull or severed a spine. And it had been Crowbar who had told him to forget the other things – the killing of innocents, of children – as if it were simply part of the process. Which of course, it was. Crowbar had taught him that too. It was all just a business. And for people like Crowbar and his erstwhile employers, a horrifyingly lucrative one. Even now, flying towards another killing, the taste of it already sweet in his mouth, Crowbar was here, guiding him, preparing, planning, marshalling his resolve.

'It's you,' Clay said again. 'God damn it. Fuck. Of course. How could I have been so stupid? It's you. That's what the old guy was trying to tell me. It's been you all along.'

Crowbar reached over, grabbed the bottle from Clay's hand. 'What the *fok* are you ranting about, Straker? Calm down, for *fok*'s sake.'

Clay ripped off the headphones, threw them into the backseat.

'What's wrong, *seun*?' shouted Crowbar.

'It's you,' said Clay, mouthing over the noise of the engine and the air rushing past the open windows. 'You're the spirit. It's you. It's always been you, god damn it.'

Crowbar shook his head, pointed to his headset, spoke something into his mike.

But Clay did not answer, just stared out across the mountains and plains to the future.

6th November 1997. Cairo, Egypt. 22:40 hrs

I write this from my shelter in Giza. I am still shaking.

Tonight, Samira and her children shared their evening meal with me. She had had a successful day, she told us as she stirred the pot over the fire. Under a pile of rotting vegetables she had found a small trove of almost-new electronics: a tape deck, amplifiers, a personal computer. The Coptic Zabbaleen she works for was very pleased. He took her finds back to his shop in Moquattam, above the City of the Dead, and will burn out the plastic, recovering the precious metals: gold, copper, perhaps titanium.

With the money Samira bought a bag of chickpea flour, a bottle of canola oil and four oranges. She wet the flour and rolled it into falafel, which she cooked in the hot oil. The smell was wonderful and the taste better than any I have enjoyed before. We ate in silence, even the children, all focused on this delicacy. After, we all shared an orange, two succulent sections each. Samira put her children to bed and blew out the candle and we sat in the half-lit city darkness and had tea.

That some people are so wealthy they can afford to throw away such things, she said, shaking her head. Of course, I did not tell her that until very recently, I too had regularly disposed of perfectly good mattresses and shoes, and occasionally phones and televisions, and every other kind of implement and device, to make room for newer, more functional, more exciting models. We threw away perfectly edible food, disposed of once-worn clothes, and even – I gasp now, thinking of it – books. And the worst part of it is that I never even thought about it. And yet, because of such profligacy, Samira and her children and I eat. Is this the real definition of trickle-down economics? Tomorrow night I will claim a similar windfall, and I will treat Samira and her children to a feast.

This afternoon, I met Mehmet.

I was very careful this time. I am sure no one followed me, or was watching me. He gave me his address over the phone – I used a public telephone – and then I watched his building for more than six hours before entering. I picked through the rubbish in the vacant lot opposite and along the flanks of the alleys, just another poor, homeless wretch, invisible, all the time watching for any signs of surveillance. I entered the building by the back stairway and climbed the four flights to his flat.

It was quite a humble place for the second pharaoh of the eighteenth dynasty, and I told him so, unable to help myself. He looked me up and down, at my filthy hands and unkempt hair and already ragged clothes – it is amazing how quickly one can descend. And then he pointed out that he had taken the name Amenhotep out of respect, and in actuality, he was only a grand vizier of the lawful descendants of the last Egyptian pharaoh, Nectanebo the Second, who died in 343 BC, before the corruptions of the Persian rule of Egypt.

He certainly looked the part. He had a long, flowing beard and was dressed in a floor-length white robe. In his right hand, he held an ankh ♀ – the symbol for life and the unity of matter and spirit, he told me. We sat on cushions in the middle of the floor. Shutters dimmed the afternoon light. He offered me tea. I asked if I could use his bathroom. It had been three days since I had used a proper toilet or washed myself in clean water.

Please, he said, standing. Feel free to shower, if you like. He led me to the bathroom and opened the door. There are towels, soap and hot water, he said.

I thanked him and closed the door behind me, searched for a lock but could not find one. Any hesitation I had disappeared as the shower beckoned. I could not resist. I turned on the hot water, stripped off my filthy clothes and jumped in. Allah forgive me, but this must be what heaven is like. I stayed under the water for far too long, knowing he would be listening, wondering what he would be thinking. I soaped myself raw, used his shampoo, washed my hair out twice, bundled myself into clean towels. At that point, there was a knock on the door.

I froze, remembering where I was – in a strange man's house, naked but for a towel. His voice came through the door, asking me if I would like clean clothes. Perhaps he was married? I had seen no signs of a feminine presence.

What do you have? I asked him, staring at my stinking rags piled on the floor. A moment later he handed me in a clean dress. It was very plain with a high neck and low hem. It hung off me like a sack, but it was clean and smelled as if it had been freshly laundered. Had he anticipated the state I would be in?

Almost half an hour after entering the bathroom, I emerged, realising how badly I must have smelled when I had first arrived. To his credit, he said nothing, just smiled, poured me tea and offered me a plate of sweets, which I devoured.

Thank you, I said.

He nodded, smiled. It is my great pleasure, lady, he said.

Please, tell me about Yusuf Al-Gambal, I said. Why are the police watching him?

He is a very dangerous man, Amenhotep said.

He does not look dangerous, I said.

No. It is always thus, said Mehmet. He spoke a very formal, traditional Arabic, quite unlike the street, slang-ridden dialect I have already begun to emulate. Clearly he is an educated man.

Tell me, please.

His danger comes from what he knows. And to your second question, madame, the police simply enforce the will of those in power.

What is it that he knows? I asked. Is it something about the Consortium, the ones you spoke of before? I was sure he could hear the desperation in my voice.

This Hamid Al-Farouk must have been very important to you, he said, piercing me with his gaze.

I looked away. Yes, I said. He was.

I understand, he said, watching me very carefully.

Then please help me.

He considered this for what felt like a long time. I sat and watched the candle flame burn on its wick, the wax drip slowly to its base.

Then you will also know that Yusuf Al-Gambal and Mr Al-Farouk were very close. But something happened. At some point during the trial, there was an argument. Threats were exchanged. I do not know what precipitated it or what it concerned. I was not present. But whatever happened, they never spoke again.

What is your relationship with Yusuf Al-Gambal? I sounded like the analyst I was, the reporter I am.

We are… He hesitated …Allies.

Fighting a common enemy? The Consortium? The ones you said were violating the Ma'at, destroying the Two Kingdoms, Upper and Lower Egypt?

He nodded.

Who are they, this Consortium?

They are the godless ones. Those whose souls Set has poisoned.

Please, I said. I know he could sense my impatience.

I do not know who they are, madame. Only what they are. Then he stood and offered me his hand. I took it. He looked at me. Perhaps, madame, we too can become allies, in time?

I smiled. I know its power. Inshallah, I said, pulling away from him.

He stood looking me up and down, and then said: If Isis wills it.

Of course.

He placed his hand on the small of my back, escorted me to the door, something a Muslim gentleman would never do – touch a woman not his wife without permission. He clasped the door knob, started turning. But then he stopped. He leaned in close to me. His lips brushed my ear. I could feel his hot breath on my neck.

We can help each other, he whispered, sliding his hand lower.

I pushed him away, pulled open the door.

Call me in two days, he said. Perhaps I will have more information for you then.

I stopped, stared at him.

But I will need something in return, he said.

I have money, I said.

He laughed at this. Money is not for allies, good lady. He leaned close again. You must understand, he whispered. Your enemy is our enemy.

I looked into his eyes, my pulse doing hummingbird wings. Who is my enemy? I said.

Those who murdered your husband and son, my dear lady.

And upon You, Peace

With the sun low in the sky, they set down on a deserted stretch of road about ten kilometres north-east of Al Dabbah, a small town on the wide green sweep of the Blue Nile. The country here was very dry. Since leaving the green and fertile highlands of Ethiopia, the land had become increasingly barren and featureless and there were few signs of human habitation. The big herds, so clearly visible from the air in Kenya, were long since gone, and now, for as far as they could see, there was desolation.

This was a country at war with itself. The signs of the long descent into chaos were everywhere. Villages raised, charred, empty. Shot-up tanks and columns of burned-out vehicles shimmering in the heat. Sometimes Crowbar would descend to get a closer look, and they could make out the close-spaced hummocks of shallow graves, rows of them, as if planted in the hope that crops might grow instead of hate. Not far from Khartoum they overflew a refugee camp, a city of white plastic and canvas that seemed to go on forever. It was like seeing London from the air for the first time, and then realising that every building was a makeshift shelter, every monument a tent, each street an open sewer.

They had agreed that Clay would set out immediately, find transport and try to reach Dongola, about 180 kilometres north, that night. Crowbar would aim to land at the Dongola airfield at seven the next morning. He wasn't sure who was going to show up to meet them, or when. He'd dangled the lure. They would just have to wait and see if anyone bit. And if they did, they would have to play it as it came.

Crowbar reached into the plane's rear storage compartment, pulled out one of the bags he'd been toting around since Zanzibar and handed it to Clay. 'You may need this,' he said.

Clay opened the bag, looked inside, caught a breath. 'Jesus, *Koevoet*.' It was a scoped Galil MAR assault rifle with a folding stock – a smaller, lightweight version of the R4 he'd used in Angola. It was a beautiful weapon.

The corners of Crowbar's mouth flipped up into a grin. 'Nice scope on it, too, *seun*, but a shorter barrel. You get there early, find a good place, close enough in, and cover me. I'm depending on you, *ja*. Use that spirit of yours one more time.'

Clay stood a moment, weighing the Galil in his hand. 'I'm sorry, *oom*, I…'

Crowbar put his hand on Clay's shoulder. 'Who knows,' he said. 'That old *juju* man may just have been right.'

Clay replaced the weapon, zipped the bag closed and stashed it in his backpack, along with three extra thirty-five-round magazines. Crowbar also handed him two M27 frags and one smoke cannister.

'Got enough cash?' said Crowbar.

'Plenty.'

'Then get going. See you tomorrow morning.'

They shook hands and Clay started off towards town, the last of the day's light throwing long shadows across the sand.

Soon it was dark. And with the darkness came the cold. Stars appeared: Aldebaran, blood red, lost as an equinoctial marker here almost five thousand years ago; Sirius, destined to burn on as the brightest star in the sky long after our own sun was gone; so many others he could not name.

Trudging through this ruined country he could feel the uncertainty burning away his patience, and he knew that these killings – those done and yet to come – were just parts of a whole, a seemingly endless firmament of death. And in this detachment, he began to see a possibility that perhaps, one day, he might exorcise the murderous spirit that had taken hold inside him and live in peace. One day. If he could get to Cairo. If he could find Rania. If he could convince her to leave with him. If they could escape. If they could find a place where they might be free of the past. If.

Hope was a dangerous thing.

After two hours of walking, Clay reached Al-Dabbah. He found the main road through town and struck north. Time was running on. He needed to find transport to have any hope of reaching the airfield in time. It wasn't until he was nearing the outskirts of town that he came upon what appeared to be a garage. Vehicles in various states of disrepair hulked in the sand, their punctured bodies painted orange by the flamelight from a glowing brazier. The owner of the place, a dark-skinned and suspicious local, showed him an old Enfield motorbike. It was banged up, but the engine ran and the tyres looked reasonable. Clay haggled a price, paid cash and started north, the way lit only by stars and the wavering yellow cone of light from the bike's headlamp. The road was unpaved, shot through with potholes, cut by ruts and washouts. After a while, the moon rose, a shimmering, waning half.

His progress was slow. By midnight, he was still some forty kilometres from Dongola. He continued north, the bike rattling over the dusty washboard, the Blue Nile warm and fragrant on his right. Stars beckoned, the town's far-off glow staining the horizon. Not long after, he hit the first roadblock.

Clay slowed and cut his lights as the barrier came into view. It had been placed where the road skirted the river's narrow floodplain of fertile ground. Old car wheel rims had been arranged across the tarmac to stop traffic. Two soldiers stood warming themselves beside a steel drum set back on the shoulder. Orange flame jumped from the mouth of the drum and lit the faces of the men, glinted on the barrels of their rifles. Clay could smell the smoke, hear the men's voices. He could try to talk or bribe his way through. But given what he had come here to do and what he was carrying, the risks were too great. He would have to detour around, approach the airfield from the west. He turned the bike around and started back the way he'd come.

After about five kilometres he left the main road and followed a small dirt track that led west towards the hills. Fifteen minutes in he turned north again, Polaris showing the way. Cross-country, in the near-dark, the going was slow. Riding with one hand was hard enough on a half-decent road, but now the bike bumped and lurched over the hard, uneven ground, powered out in swales of soft sand. The inside of his left forearm was bruised and sore from working the clutch lever. Twice he went over the handlebars, picked himself up, righted the bike and kept going. He was running out of time.

Then, with the sky lightening in the east, the rear tyre blew.

He stopped and inspected the damage. The sidewall had ruptured, spilling a big flap of fibre belting and rubber. He tried to continue, but with each revolution the tyre disintegrated further, tearing itself to pieces. Soon there was nothing left, and the bike was churning along on an almost bare rim. There was no point in going on.

Clay dismounted and scanned the horizon with the binoculars. He could just make out the low mud-brick and concrete jumble of Dongola town, and beyond, the darker thread of vegetation along the river. The airfield was still at least ten kilometres away. Less than an hour until Crowbar was scheduled to land. Clay filled his lungs, hefted his pack, secured the chest and waist straps, tightened it all down and started to run.

As the sun broke the horizon, he reached a rise and looked down across the sweep of desert towards the Nile. The airstrip cut a grey scar on the outskirts of the dawn-lit town. At four minutes per kilometre he would arrive at the airstrip just as Crowbar was landing. He upped his pace, pushing hard, watching the sun's fiery rebirth, his feet skimming across the rocky ground.

As he neared the airstrip, he began searching the sky. The sun was up and the heat was coming. He wasn't going to make it in time. Crowbar would land, expecting him to be there, expecting cover. He would be walking into an ambush. Clay bit down, kept going. Sweat poured from his temples, soaked his shirt. Less than a kilometre to go and still he hadn't seen or heard a plane approaching.

Clay glanced at his watch. Just gone seven. Not like Crowbar to be late. Could he have arrived early?

As he neared the airstrip he could make out a cluster of small buildings on the town side, an elevated fuel bowser, the wind sock hanging limp from its post. No sign of people, no aircraft on the ground that he could see. Relief poured through him. He plotted a course around the far end of the strip and towards a sandy ridge that ran parallel to the landing strip, just beyond the apron.

Twenty-five minutes later, Clay lay tucked behind the crest of the ridge on the eastern edge of the airfield, watching the sky. It was now almost an hour since the agreed arrival time had come and gone, and still no sign of Crowbar's little Cessna.

And whoever Crowbar was expecting, there was no sign of them, either. Where were the people that ran this place, dishevelled though it was? Why was it unattended? When he'd first arrived, he'd assumed that guards or attendants might be sleeping in one of the buildings, or would arrive at daybreak. But he'd seen no movement, no indication of occupation. Now, as the sun rose in the sky, he knew something was wrong.

Clay checked his watch again. Crowbar was more than an hour late. Had there been engine trouble? They had plenty of fuel, so it couldn't be that. Had he perhaps run foul of local militia? Had Crowbar abandoned him, even – set him up, left him to die? No, that was crazy thinking. The heat was getting to him, he was dehydrated. Anything could have delayed Crowbar. There was no point speculating. None of it was in his control anyway. He was here. He would wait. He shut it all away, focused on the job.

From where he lay, Clay had a commanding view of the buildings and the access road that led to the main road and town. He arranged some brush to provide himself a bit of camouflage, dialled in the scope, and, using the ragged windsock that now fluttered near the hut, estimated windage. He scanned the airstrip through the scope, focused on the fuel bowser, picked a target at the base of the elevated platform. At two hundred metres, with the MAR's shorter barrel, it would probably take him a few shots to hit centre.

And then he heard it. A faint hum at first, coming on the breeze. He lifted his head, scanned the horizon. There it was: a small plane approaching from the south, descending towards the field. Clay watched the aircraft parallel the runway, then turn and line up for final approach. It was Crowbar.

Clay watched the Cessna float in over the runway, touch down with a puff of dust and then taxi to the ramp and stop beside the fuel bowser. Crowbar shut down the engine and jumped to the ground, wiping the sweat from his forehead with the back of his arm. He stood a moment, surveying the deserted airstrip. Then he walked to the fuel dispenser and unhooked the nozzle. A moment later he clambered up the steel frame to the single rusting tank and rapped on the side. Bone rang on hollow steel. But there was depth to the sound, the sway of fuel. Crowbar jumped down, grabbed the nozzle, clambered up onto the wing strut and started to fill the tanks.

That was when they came.

Two vehicles, speeding towards the airfield, red dust spiralling into the by-now blue morning sky. Crowbar had seen them, too. Clay watched him reach for his .45, work the action, replace it in its concealed shoulder holster and continue pumping. Clay filled his lungs, steadied himself, tracked the lead vehicle with the Galil's scope.

The vehicles pulled up side by side, just short of the Cessna – a white Toyota Hilux and what looked to be a retired taxi. The Toyota's passenger door opened. A tall Nubian in a white *jelabia* emerged from the vehicle and stepped forwards. He appeared unarmed. Clay tracked the man as he walked towards the plane, cross hairs set between his shoulder blades.

Crowbar jumped to the ground, set the nozzle down and wiped his hands on his trousers. He and the Nubian faced each other a few metres apart. Words were exchanged. After a moment, the two men closed the distance and shook hands.

It made sense. Crowbar wouldn't have leaked information about a rendezvous to the AB without having ensured that someone was actually coming to meet them. He knew the AB would seek to confirm the story. This was the Sudanese contact Crowbar had spoken of. Whether he, too, had been compromised by the AB, and was here to finish what Manheim had started, there was no way of telling. Not yet. Clay exhaled, moved his head away from the scope a moment, rolled his neck, stretched his shoulders, went back to it.

Crowbar walked to the plane, opened the rear cargo compartment, reached inside. Clay scanned the Nubian's loose-fitting *jelabia* through the scope, looking for any sign of a concealed weapon, but saw none. He shifted left and scoped the Hilux. The driver was sitting with both hands on the wheel. There were two other black men in the taxi. The one in the front passenger seat was holding something. Clay increased magnification. The distinctive muzzle and foresight of an AK-47 came into focus. Despite the weapon's ubiquity here, Clay's pulse jumped.

Crowbar closed the Cessna's rear storage door and started back towards the Nubian. He was carrying something, a package about the size of a shoe box. He handed it to the Nubian. The African opened the top, looked inside, closed it again, nodded and walked back to the Hilux.

Just then, another vehicle appeared on the access road. It was coming in fast, riding a tornado of dust. The Nubian stood and watched it come. Crowbar reached for his gun. Clay brought the Galil around, cross haired the windscreen of the approaching vehicle. The taxi's doors opened and two Sudanese jumped out and swung their AK-47s around towards the approaching vehicle, which seemed to have gained speed. It was big, black, some kind of four-wheel-drive truck – a Ford; the kind of thing the American government liked to use abroad. The vehicle sped past the empty guard shack and careened to halt in a shower of gravel a few metres from the other two vehicles.

Dust billowed and for a moment Clay's view was obscured. He heard car doors open, and then, almost immediately, the sound of automatic weapons firing, rounds crashing into metal, shattering glass, puncturing flesh. Then the screams of men, an AK barking in reply and falling silent. Clay looked on, unable to distinguish a target.

Slowly the dust cleared. The Hilux and the taxi had been reduced to smoking wrecks. The two Sudanese lay sprawled in the dust, leaking blood. Crowbar and the Nubian were nowhere to be seen.

Three men emerged from the Ford, two black, one white. One of the black men was carrying a belt-fed machine gun, the other an Uzi. Clay trained the Galil's scope on the white man. He was facing away, giving orders, waving a pistol in one hand, pointing with the other. The two black men started moving towards the plane, weapons at the ready. They had just cleared the taxi's smoking hulk when Clay heard the *pop-pop* of Crowbar's .45 Jericho. One of the black men spun to the ground, his Uzi pitching into the dust. The other dove behind the Hilux.

Clay set the Galil's cross hairs in the middle of the white man's back, flipped the fire selector switch to R – semi-automatic – and placed the palp of his finger on the trigger. It could only be one man. Clay filled his lungs, began a slow exhale.

'Pull that trigger and you're a dead man.'

Adrenaline arced through Clay's brain, crashed through the wall of dopamine that had already begun building within him in anticipation of the kill – this revenge to which he had set himself. The voice had come from behind. Clay moved his finger away from the trigger, pushed it trembling onto the Galil's receiver cover.

'Now let go of the weapon and stand up. Put your hands on you head.' The voice was familiar, the accent distinctive. From the airfield, more firing, the hammering of the machine gun, Crowbar's Jericho answering.

Clay stood, raised his hands.

'Turn around.'

The Uzi's barrel gaped. Manheim sneered. It pushed his nose even further across his face.

'Sloppy, Straker,' he said, shaking his head as he raised the Uzi.

7th November 1997. Cairo, Egypt. 06:40 hrs

I awoke this morning from a nightmare, and realised I was in another.

No matter how bizarre, I can always trace the genesis of my dreams. A few nights ago, I dreamt I was back in the Algeria of my childhood. It was a place I have been before, but only in recurring dreams in the years since my father was killed. The place is not real. I know that now. Nonetheless it retains elements of the real: the sweep of the terrain, the stony ground, the olive grove and rows of cypress trees, the quality of the light. But the route I take, which is always the same and passes houses that exist only in my dreams, leads to a place I have never seen with my eyes. My father was there. He was alive. He had grown old. His hair was grey. I wanted to ask him how it was that he was still alive, but dared not, lest it not be true. And then they came, the men with guns. I woke, as always, breathless and sweating, before the past could catapult into the present.

Last night it was different. The place was real, recognisable in every detail. Our flat in Paris. My favourite print on the back of the bathroom door. Hamid's study, usually so tidy, strewn with papers as if it had been ransacked by burglars. Hamid and Eugène are there, sitting at the breakfast table. They look at me as if I am a crazy woman. There is a pile of old computers stacked on the floor, Eugène is sitting among the screens, peeling open motherboards, playing with live wires and glass.

I shriek, run to my son, pick him up. His fingers are bleeding. I start to scream at Hamid for his irresponsibility, but he has vanished and I am standing ankle deep in sewage and my son lies cold in my arms.

I shudder at the dark violence of my own psyche. How can my subconscious conjure such things? Are these the kinds of nightmares you have so often, my love? How terrible they are. My own wickedness assails me, makes me double over in pain. I vomit up my meagre breakfast. I am getting sick. My body is not used to the germs, the insufficiency and poor quality of food, the unsanitary conditions, the cold at night, the dense, sulphurous air. To think how many people live their entire lives like this, Claymore.

I shudder to think how close I came yesterday to whoring myself.

I need to find Yusuf, to speak with him. If that lecherous Kemetic knows who I am, then I can only assume that Yusuf does also. But how could they know? And do they really know who killed Hamid and Eugène?

Just writing their names sends me into a paroxysm of grief. How could I have thought that I did not love Hamid? I am sorry, Claymore, but I did love him. I do love him. I am his wife, his widow. He is – was – the father of my son. Nothing can change that. I must do it for them. I must learn the truth. Justice, or vengeance, must be satisfied.

I do not trust the Kemetic, but I do trust Yusuf. There was something vulnerable and tragic about him that I cannot place. And yet he seems to trust the Kemetic. What is the basis of their relationship, I wonder? Is Yusuf also a member of that dead religion? Are they related somehow? Or, as he claims, are they simply allies in the fight against a common enemy, this group they call the Consortium?

Did the Consortium, whatever and whoever it is, kill my husband and son?

I have no choice. I realise this now. I must use every weapon available to me. Not to do so would be to put my own honour above the memory of my son and husband. To keep faith with them, I must debase myself even further than I already have. Only then might I find redemption.

In this that I am about to do, may Allah protect and guide me.

12:30 hrs

This morning, I went to the main post and telegraph office in the city. I placed a call to France, to my friend in the Directorate. I called him at his house. We followed our protocol. He called me back a few minutes later.

Any news? I asked.

He was silent a moment, then said: I am running facial recognition algorithms on all the airport CCTV records. I could hear the stress in his voice. We're looking for you, he said.

It was not a surprise really. But I still felt myself go cold.

Where can I reach you? he said.

I will check in.

You must be careful, he said. The Egyptian police have asked for the Directorate's assistance in finding you. It is very unusual.

Will the Directorate cooperate?

I don't know. It's a political decision.

Of course. Are you sure the enquiry came from the police?

No one knows for certain. It came through the embassy.

It could be anyone.

As always.

I thanked him and he wished me good luck.

Then I tried Yusuf's number. Despite his warnings, I felt compelled to try. I need to convince him to talk to me, to open up. I had decided to be honest with him, to tell him that I am Hamid's wife, despite the danger. It is the only way. I need to offer him my vulnerability to inspire his confidence.

I waited as the line engaged, practising my speech. I was connected. A recorded voice played, different from the one before. His number had been cut off.

Now I have no choice.

The First and Only Certainty

Death is prescribed the day you are born. It is the first and only certainty.

Of it he had learned much. Random in its dispensation, mortally cruel in method, it was, in his experience, by turns callously just and brutally unfair. It came to him in nightmares, sometimes as drowning, but more often by instruments blunt and bladed, a mindless butchering that left him gasping. And in each cold aftermath, he would contemplate his own end, by whose hand it might be accomplished, and why, after so many years and opportunities, it had not yet come.

The sounds and smells of the fight came to him now, more as vague impressions than any specific punctuation: the buzz of the rapid-fire Uzi and the industrial crack of the last AK shifting on the cordite breeze, and then, suddenly, the clean metallic tang of blood.

Time slowed, then stalled.

Cadence and interval stretched.

Time measured now in the spaces between detonations, those frozen eternities.

He thought of Rania, alone and frightened, far away. Of Grace and little Joseph, rotting on the seabed. He closed his eyes. Other faces came to him, moments that filled time to bursting: His best friend, Eben, striding towards the C-130, his face lit red by the flares, determined to do what was right; Abdulkader at the wheel of the Landcruiser, hurtling through the Masila night towards the Omani border; Vivian dying in his arms as he fled to Mozambique. He stifled a groan, let it all echo through the empty space inside him.

He opened his eyes. He had to try.

Manheim was only three long steps away, his Uzi levelled at Clay's chest. It would come at any time. He was surprised Manheim hadn't done it already.

Manheim checked the Uzi. 'Before I kill you,' he said, 'tell me something.'

Clay opened his arms. His G21 was in his front jacket pocket, loaded, ready to fire. 'I'm just the bait, remember?' Keep him talking.

Manheim twisted his mouth into a smile. 'Maybe, Straker. But you were a traitor then, and you're still one now.'

Crowbar's handgun cracked again in the distance, followed by the clatter of an Uzi.

Manheim's eyes widened. 'Crowbar,' he said. 'Did he tell you?'

'Tell me what?'

'About why…' Manheim paused, seemed to reconsider whatever it was he was going to ask.

'He's down there,' said Clay. 'Why don't you ask him yourself?'

But before Manheim could answer, a loud explosion ripped the air – one of Crowbar's grenades. Manheim's eyes snapped towards the sound.

It was the moment Clay had been waiting for. He charged.

He'd closed most of the distance separating them, had rotated his torso to make himself a smaller target and had just begun to parry the Uzi aside with his forearm, when Manheim fired.

Something slammed into Clay's side. It felt as if he'd been hit with a bat. The force of the blow wrenched him around so that his forward momentum sent the point of his shoulder smashing into Manheim's groin. The Uzi spun away as Clay wrapped his arms around Manheim's legs and drove him to the ground. They landed hard, Clay on top. Manheim twisted, pushed a knee into Clay's ribs and exploded back, kicking out with his other foot. Manheim's boot caught Clay in the chest, sent him reeling back, blinded by pain.

Then Manheim was up, scrambling across the sand towards the Uzi. He'd reached the weapon and had dropped to all fours, was about to swing himself around for a shot when Clay reached into his pocket, pulled out the Glock and fired. The .45 calibre bullet hit Manheim in the side of the face. He toppled back and slid headfirst down the slope.

The sound of the battle raged in the distance. Clay looked down at his right side. His jacket was torn, high up, under his arm. Blood oozed from the frayed opening. He steadied himself, crawled back to where the Galil lay, dropped to the prone position, scoped the ramp.

Crowbar was pinned down behind the taxi. The white man was behind the Ford, sending short bursts from his Uzi over the hood as he hunched behind the front wheel. The black guy was trying to flank Crowbar, work his way around the Hilux to Crowbar's left. Clay shuddered the cross hairs onto the white man's back, high up, on the spine. His hand was shaking from the adrenaline, from the pain exploding in his side. He took a deep breath, let it go, squeezed the trigger. That familiar bark, so much like the R4 he'd carried for over a year through Angola, and then the little puff to the man's right as the bullet snapped into the car's door. He watched the man flinch, hunch lower. Clay adjusted right, fired again. The round clipped the man's shoulder, pitched him over. The man scrambled in the dirt, looked behind him, realising now what was happening. He was bringing his weapon around when Clay fired again. This time the 5.56 mm high-velocity bullet hit him in the sternum, blew apart his chest. He slumped to the ground. Clay scanned right. The black man had heard the shots and rolled away under the Hilux.

Clay switched the selector to B, sent a three-round burst into the Hilux. Crowbar was up now, limping towards the truck. His left arm was clutched around his midriff. Clay sent another burst into the Hilux. The guy underneath would be pissing himself. Crowbar was closing in. Clay flicked to auto, put out a burst of ten rounds, shredding the Hilux. The guy underneath, if he wasn't already hit, wouldn't be paying any attention to Crowbar. Crowbar was close now, alongside the taxi. Clay watched him kneel, go prone, take aim. Clay emptied the rest of the magazine into the vehicle as Crowbar fired. It was over.

Samira's eldest daughter, Eleana, has developed a bad cold and has been running a fever. Her chest shudders out deep, bronchial hacks. The mucus she brings up is thick and green, the colour of the scum on our canal, tinged with flecks of carbon. Nursing her has curtailed Samira's garbage picking, and she has made almost nothing over the last few days. I have offered to look after Eleana tomorrow, at least until early afternoon, so that Samira can work. Work! This is what we call it. Samira gratefully accepted.

Some days, Samira takes the children with her, and they pick through the garbage together. A few days a week, however, she goes alone and Eleana looks after her younger sibling. The girls clean the shelter, collect wood for the fire and scavenge whatever else that they might find that may be of use. Then Eleana teaches her sister to read and write.

At first, I found the idea of two young girls alone in such a place profoundly disturbing. Now I simply marvel at the courage and resilience of these children. Perspective is everything.

This morning I called the Kemetic. We agreed that I will go to his apartment tomorrow evening.

And yet I am no nearer my goal. Every day that passes buries the truth just a little deeper, as if in a boy-king's tomb lost to the ages. Tuthenkhamun's golden death mask haunts me. I saw it for the first time when I visited the Egyptian Museum a few days ago. It was only a glance, so distracted was I, but ever since a vision of that perfect face has held on in a little corner of my mind. He was only nineteen when he died.

In all that has happened, there is one clear thread that can be traced. The more I consider it, the more convinced I have become. Yusuf Al-Gambal was accused of treason and brought to trial by the attorney general. The police have been watching him ever since the acquittal – if that is what it can be called – and now they are following me. And now I learn that the Egyptian embassy has asked the Directorate for assistance in finding me. What is the thread? There can only be one answer: the Egyptian government, or someone very powerful within it, wants me, and everyone else connected with this case, silenced.

A Distant and Erratic Echo

By the time Clay reached the vehicles, Crowbar had already started the Cessna and had taxied it away.

The plane now stood, engine running, at the edge of the runway. Clay could see Crowbar waving to him from the cockpit. Fuel vapours hung thick in the air, spilling from shot-up cars and the holed avgas bowser. Torn bodies hulked in the dust among scattered weapons and empty shell casings. The Nubian was there too, leaning up against the side of the main building, the front of his white *jelabia* stained with blood. Clay walked to the base of the bowser, pushed his boot into the fuel-soaked sand. Then he reached into his pocket, pulled out his lighter, took three steps back, sparked the flame and dropped it to the ground.

By the time Clay had covered the fifty metres to the plane, the flames had reached the vehicles. Clay threw the Galil and his pack onto the back seat and jumped into the front next to Crowbar. The Perspex windscreen on the co-pilot's side was shattered. Bullets had pierced the door in three places. There were more holes along Crowbar's side, and at least two of the flight instruments had been smashed, the recesses in the panel spilling torn wiring and ruptured circuitry. Despite the damage, the engine seemed to be running smoothly.

As Crowbar taxied the Cessna to the far end of the runway, the Hilux went up. A ball of orange flame burst skyward. Crowbar gunned the engine and rolled into the take-off run, ammunition detonating among the burning vehicles and scattered bodies as they lifted off.

Soon they were heading north towards the border, the airfield just a column of black smoke receding in the distance.

'You're hit,' said Crowbar, clutching his mid-section. Blood covered his hand, wicked from the hairs on his arm.

'You too.'

'Just a clip,' said Crowbar. Sweat beaded on his forehead, across his broad cheekbones.

'Let me have a look,' said Clay, reaching back for the aid kit in his pack.

Crowbar waved this away. 'Look after yourself first.'

Clay pulled off his jacket, tossed it in the back, ripped open his shirt. The 9 mm bullets from Manheim's Uzi had glanced off his third and fourth ribs, leaving two neat horizontal furrows about a centimetre apart. He'd been lucky.

Clay doused the wound with disinfectant, opened a compress, held it in place with his stump. Then he handed Crowbar a length of gauze.

'*Fokken* cripple,' said Crowbar, steadying the wheel with his knees. He helped Clay make two quick turns with the gauze and tie the compress in place.

'Let me look,' said Clay, reaching for Crowbar's midriff.

'Manheim?' asked Crowbar, pushing Clay's hand away.

'Dead. Headshot.'

'Good.'

But it didn't feel good. It never did. The anticipation was always better than the act. The adrenaline was gone, the dopamine too. He felt empty, hollowed out. Ashamed. 'Every cop and soldier on both sides of the border will be looking for us now.'

Crowbar tried a smile. It emerged as a grimace. 'No chance, *seun*. That was just another battle between rival factions. We were never there.'

'I hope so.'

'Just a normal day here.'

Clay considered this, nodded. He'd seen just how commonplace brutality could be in civil war. 'What was that you gave the Nubian?'

'Doesn't matter anymore, does it?'

They continued north, the Blue Nile to their right, an unfurling thread of life in the otherwise barren and increasingly featureless desert. Finally, Crowbar relented and let Clay tend his wound.

The bullet had entered Crowbar's torso, just above the hip, and exited through his lower back. The bullet had missed the femoral artery, but the blood that oozed from the exit wound was dark and anoxic. Clay irrigated and disinfected the wounds, pressed compresses onto both and bound them in place as Crowbar continued to pilot the Cessna. By the time they reached the border and crossed over into Egyptian airspace, Crowbar was weakening.

'We've got to get you to a hospital,' said Clay. 'I think the bullet might have hit your liver.'

'Definitely, *ja*. I can *fokken* smell it.' Crowbar's voice was weak, far away.

'Next town, we put her down.'

'*Ja*, okay. How far?'

Clay searched the chart, spread bloody fingerprints across the paper. 'Aswan. A hundred and twenty miles. About an hour away. Luxor's bigger, has a proper airport, but it's another eighty miles or so. Steer 020.'

Crowbar adjusted course, throttled up, added ten knots to the airspeed. After a time, he said: 'Took your time giving me cover, Straker.'

'Sorry, *oom*. Manheim surprised me.'

'Sloppy.'

'That's what he said. He could have killed me right there. Wonder why he didn't.'

'Wanted me,' said Crowbar.

'He was about to ask me something, *oom*. Something about you.'

Crowbar grunted, closed his eyes.

'What was this all about, *oom*?'

Crowbar reached into his breast pocket and handed Clay a wallet-sized folder.

'Look inside.'

It was a small photograph album, the kind with clear plastic sleeves. Clay thumbed through the pages, stared at each black-and-white face. Dozens of them, anonymous, staring blankly out into the day. Most of the photographs were scarred by a diagonal line drawn from top right to bottom left. Clay looked up at this man who for so long had been the nearest thing to a father he'd had, not wanting to believe what he was seeing.

'Keep going,' said Crowbar.

Clay turned the pages. And there it was. A young face, clean shaven, pale, as yet free of scars. Hair cut military short. No diagonal line.

'Jesus, *Koevoet*.'

'Most of them were assholes anyway,' Crowbar said, snatching a shallow breath. 'Probably deserved it.'

'All this time.' Clay shook his head.

Crowbar closed his eyes.

'That's how you found me in Maputo in eighty-two,' said Clay.

Crowbar grunted.

'And again last year, before I went back to testify to the TRC. And on Zanzibar.'

Crowbar coughed. 'We've been tracking you, Straker.'

We. Clay shivered. He felt naked, stripped, lashed by the wind. 'And because you helped me, they started to realise they had a leak.'

'*Ja.*' Crowbar breathed. 'So they…'

'…Floated the order to take me out, and waited to see who would turn up to warn me. And Manheim took the job.'

Crowbar nodded slowly.

'But why, *Koevoet*? Why?' Clay had known since 1982 that Crowbar was somehow linked to the Broederbond. But never in his darkest imaginings could he have conceived of this. Crowbar, all this time, an AB assassin.

'*Fok* me.' Crowbar closed his eyes, opened them again. And then he said: 'I'm not going to make it, *seun*.'

At first, Clay thought he'd misheard.

'I'm bleeding inside.' Crowbar's face was ash. A tremor had started in his right leg, and the plane yawed back and forth as his foot pulsed on the rudder pedal.

Clay felt something inside him go. Never in his life had he heard Crowbar admit defeat. Always he'd been there for them – the younger less experienced soldiers – guiding them through the maelstrom. So often they'd seen him injured, and each time he'd shrugged it off, kept going, recovered. After surviving so much, so many firefights, so many years, Clay had come to think of him as invulnerable, immortal even.

'Look after Hope and Kip for me.' Crowbar's voice was barely audible.

'You can do it yourself.'

'My son, too. Promise me, Straker.'

'Hold on, *oom*. I'm going to run you an IV.' Clay reached behind his seat, started rifling through his pack for the giver set.

'No time,' whispered Crowbar. 'I'm going to have to put her down.' His eyelids were flickering. 'I can't…' His voice tailed off. His eyes started to close. He slumped forwards against the steering column. The plane's nose dropped and they started to dive.

Clay grabbed Crowbar's shoulder, tried to shake him awake. '*Koevoet*,' he shouted into the headset. 'Wake up, God damn it.' The ground filled the windscreen.

Crowbar jerked his head up, opened his eyes, pulled back on the stick. Slowly, the Cessna levelled out. They'd lost more than a thousand feet in those few seconds. Crowbar trimmed up for a slow descent. 'You'll have to do it,' he whispered.

'For *fok*'s sake, *Koevoet*, I've never touched an airplane's controls before.'

'*Fokken* pussy. Take the controls.'

At least Crowbar was talking. Clay put his hand on the grip of the co-pilot's wheel, reached his feet to the rudder pedals. He scanned the instrument panel. Altitude: 3,200 feet. Vertical speed: descending at 200 feet per minute, about a metre per second. But they were still travelling at more than 110 knots, far too fast to land.

Crowbar's head slumped forward. Clay reached out with his stump and pushed Crowbar's chest back into his seat. 'What do I do, *Koevoet*? He shouted into the headset. 'How do I slow us down for landing?'

Crowbar grunted. 'Trim up. Sixty-five knots.' His eyes were closed.

'How, *oom*? How do I do it?' The desert loomed closer.

'Throttle back,' said Crowbar, his voice barely a whisper now above the din of the engine. 'Black knob.'

The throttle was in the centre of the console. Clay steadied the wheel with his stump, reached across his body with his right hand and eased out the throttle. The Cessna started slowing, losing altitude.

'Now ease back on the column, nose up, bleed off more speed, keep descending. Easy.'

Clay did as he was told. The plane's nose lurched up. The little plane shuddered.

'Too much,' said Crowbar, eyes wide open now. He reached between the seats, spun the trim wheel. The Cessna settled into a gentle descent, airspeed now seventy-five knots. The ground was coming up fast.

'I can't see anywhere to land,' said Clay. 'No roads, nothing.' Desert stretched away as far as he could see in every direction.

'Just ... put her down.' Crowbar's voice was very far off now, barely audible.

Clay tightened up on Crowbar's harness, made sure the shoulder straps were secure, then tightened himself in.

'Flaps,' said Crowbar. 'Too fast.' He reached for the red toggle, pushed down with a bloody hand. 'Push,' he gasped.

As the flaps came down, the aircraft's nose pitched up. Speed bled off. Clay pushed down on the column, forcing the Cessna's nose down, counteracting the flaps. Crowbar added power. 'Again,' he said, lowering the flaps.

Clay pushed the nose down. They were now descending steeply, nose down, slowed by the flaps. The ground filled the windscreen. They were very close, a few hundred feet, but settling slowly, airspeed down to just over sixty knots.

'Just before … level off, keep the nose straight, kill the power…' Crowbar tailed off, slumped over against the door.

Clay gripped the wheel, pushed the rudders left and right, felt the Cessna yaw. The ground loomed. Rocks, sheets of sand, pebble rivulets. Clay started pulling back on the column, raising the nose. They were going too fast. One-handed, he couldn't reach the throttle without letting go of the wheel. The plane ballooned above the surface, settled. Crowbar reached out and pulled back on the throttle. They hit the ground.

☾

When Clay came to, he was hanging head to ground in his harness. A dull ache spread from his right side into his shoulders and neck. His right knee was jammed up under the lip of the instrument panel. His head felt as if it was about to explode. The smell of aviation fuel filled the air. Crowbar was hanging there beside him, covered over in dust. His head hung limp in the harness. Blood ran in rivulets along his neck and across the fractured contours of his face, dripped to the cabin roof.

Clay reached over, put index and second fingers to Crowbar's neck, felt a pulse. Faint, but there.

Avgas bubbled from a hole in the wing tank, flowed over the crumpled aluminium skin of the wing's underside and pooled in the crushed bowl of the cabin's roof, inches from Clay's head. He could feel the fumes taking hold of him, collapsing his vision. He braced himself against the roof with his stump, unclasped his harness and eased himself down into the pool of fuel. The semi-volatile liquid soaked into his shirt and the back of his trousers, wicked into his hair. He gagged, rolled onto his back and kicked open what was left of the right-hand door.

He crawled from the wreckage, slid across the fuel-streaked wing to the ground, staggered away from the wreck. A gust of hot wind flashed fuel from his arms and face and neck. He shivered from the cooling, gulped in clean air.

The Cessna was on its back, wings folded up around the cabin in a crooked embrace. The left-hand wing was blocking Crowbar's door. The undercarriage was gone, shorn away. The tail section had broken off and lay a few metres away, monocoque ribs showing through peeled-back skin. Small dark stones ridged up against the torn mouth of the fuselage.

Clay stripped off his shirt and flung it to the sand, bladed fuel from his torso with the edge of his hand. He stood staring at the wreck, at Crowbar hanging there in his harness, blood streaming across his face, all of it transduced by a shimmering haze of evaporating fuel, as if the whole of it were nothing but an apparition, born of desert sun and the warped imaginings of his own mind, set to explode with the slightest spark.

Clay took a deep breath of clean air and started back toward the plane.

The cabin was less than half its normal size. He pushed himself through the mangled doorway and twisted onto his side so he could reach Crowbar's harness with his right hand. Fuel soaked into his bandage, seared the raw flesh of his gun wound. The pain was there, but he didn't feel it. Not really. It was as an echo, some distant and incomplete message come from another life.

He unbuckled Crowbar, eased him to the cabin roof. He was still unconscious, still breathing. His torso was slick with blood. Clay hooked his arms under Crowbar's shoulders and started pulling him free of the wreck. He strained against the big man's bulk, wedged him through the mangled doorway, lowered him to the sand. His side looked bad, the compresses saturated with blood, frosted over with sand and dust. Clay needed to get an IV into him, replace some of the blood he'd lost.

He dragged Crowbar away from the wreck, lay him on his back

at a safe distance then stumbled back towards the plane. He ripped open the rear door, pulled out his pack and the medical kit.

By the time he'd pushed the catheter into Crowbar's forearm and started the flow of saline, his friend's pulse was nothing more than a distant and erratic echo. He cleaned and disinfected the wounds, changed the dressings, tried to make him comfortable. There was no way to get him to a hospital.

Clay went back to the wreck, pulled out the Galil and the rest of Crowbar's stuff.

Then he sat next to his friend and watched him die.

Part III

8th November 1997. Cairo, Egypt. 04:50 hrs

Chéri:
I lie here in my shelter and watch the sky slowly shade from black to grey.
Four days it has been since you called me from Mombasa. God knows
where you are, what has become of you. When I spoke to him briefly
yesterday, the Kemetic did not mention a message for me. Have you tried
to call me, mon amour, using the number I gave you? Is the Kemetic
hiding it from me?

What I can only describe as a void is opening inside me, a deep emp-
tiness. With each day that passes, this feeling of desolation, of futility,
grows within me. I try to fight against it, to stay positive, but it is like
swimming against a strong current. I am exhausting myself, being pulled
out into deep water.

I pray now, four and sometimes five times a day – something I have
not done since I was a young girl. My mother always insisted that I
observe prayer as strictly as she did, and until my father died, I complied,
enjoyed it even. It made me feel grown-up, going to the mosque with my
mother, praying with her and the other women. I was never closer to her
than when we prayed together.

I have been now a few times to the Mustafa Mahmoud mosque here
in Giza, to listen to the imam, or just to pray in the quiet coolness. I sit at
the back, behind the screens with the other women, faceless and invisible,
just as I wish to be. The feeling of being erased, of being consumed from
inside and out, is palpable, and it frightens me more than I can admit.

Yesterday I went into the market and bought bread and fruit, beans
and eggplant, a piece of fish, a small jar of honey, a few other delicacies.
In the evening I invited Samira and her younger daughter to eat with
me. Eleana, poor thing, is still too ill to leave her little bed. Samira
was amazed at what I had managed to obtain. This kind of bounty is

unusual among the abandoned. I told her that I had had a good day, as she had recently. I did not elaborate, and she did not press me.

As we ate we spoke of the man everyone is calling The Lion. He had been in the newspapers again. Samira showed me a copy of Al-Ahram she found on the street. The Lion had announced that all tourists coming to Egypt were henceforth considered by his organisation as legitimate targets. Tourism now accounts for over half of Egypt's foreign currency revenues, and without it, the country would be crippled economically. The terrorist claims that tourists who choose to spend their money in Egypt are directly supporting a corrupt system, which enriches a powerful few and exploits millions. A group representing the tourism sector has demanded that the government and the security forces take immediate action to eliminate the terrorists by any means necessary.

As I read, I was aware of Samira watching me. She was very quiet, and I could hear the laboured rasp of her breathing. The smog from the vehicles that choke the highway and smoke from the fires that smoulder continuously in the garbage fields irritates her lungs, and even in the last few days I have noticed she has become worse. Her children, too, seem to cough continuously. It is starting to affect me now, also, although I have been here among them only a short time.

I finished reading the article and gave her back the paper. She folded it over carefully and placed it in a small carboard shoebox that she keeps on the ground by the side of her bed.

This man is a hero to me, she said, her face lit by the wavering candlelight.

I was surprised by the emotion in her voice. Surely not, I said. He kills innocent people, while claiming to be acting in the name of Islam.

He is very brave, to fight these people, said Samira, surprised, I think, by my outburst.

The tourism operators? I said. I had never thought of these people as anything but benign.

The ones who own the hotels also own everything else, she said.

But surely, I began, and then stopped. Samira was crying. I reached out and put my arms around her. She let her head fall to my shoulder.

I held her for a long time as she cried. Later, after the candle stub had burned down, she told me something of her past.

Before she was widowed, Samira and her husband spent time working in one of the big tourist hotels in Cairo. She was a chambermaid, he a cleaner. They lived in a small apartment provided by the hotel company, for which they paid approximately a half of their low combined wage. Their boss also withheld one in every five pounds they earned as an 'employment security fee'. There was barely enough left over to buy food and medicine for her eldest daughter, who since birth has been plagued by poor health. She and her husband took turns caring for their two small daughters. He worked nights, she long days. Occasionally one of the workers would complain about the poor wages and the dirty, cramped accommodation, the long hours. The response was always swift. The offending worker would be taken away by armed security guards, usually at night. By morning, replacements had arrived – there was no shortage of people waiting to fill vacant positions.

Samira and her husband worked hard as their daughter's health worsened, doing extra hours so they could pay for doctors and medicine. And then one day, after she had finished a long shift, Samira's boss asked her to meet him in his office. He knew about her daughter's illness and said he could help by increasing her salary. She couldn't believe her luck. The raise he proposed was not big, but it would have made a real difference. Her husband would be pleased.

Samira lowered her eyes, fell silent.

I asked her to continue.

She was crying now. No, she said to me. It is too shameful.

I held her a while. Nothing is shameful, I said. Look at us. Despite all of this, you survive, you worship Allah. You are true of heart.

Samira nodded, looked at me for a long time then continued.

Happy about her pay increase, she smiled and thanked her boss. He was not so bad after all. He looked at her with a strange expression, almost as if he were sad, or disappointed somehow. Confused, she asked him what was wrong.

He reached for her hand, took it in his. Oh, Samira, he said.

She pulled her hand away, made to leave. But he grabbed her wrist, held her. She struggled, but he was a big man and very strong.

That was when he told me, she said: no one gets something for nothing. Her face was hidden in darkness. He tried to touch me, she whispered. But I scratched him with my free hand and pushed him away. He touched his face and his fingers came away with blood. He hit me and I fell to the floor. He stood above me, cursing, and for a moment I thought he would hit me again. But then he pulled me to my feet, walked me to the door and told me to get out.

I waited for Samira to continue, for I knew there was more. Outside, somewhere close by, two of the men who share our vacant, rubbish-strewn plot were arguing about something, their voices strained and rough. We huddled together in the darkness of her little shelter and listened to the anger and frustration in those voices, the raw aggression, until finally they moved off, and the din of the traffic on the corniche descended upon us again like a lullaby.

Samira told me the rest of her story. The night of the incident with her boss, she had tried to cover up the bruise on her face with some makeup that she had borrowed from one of the single women, but her husband noticed it immediately. She told him that she had been reaching up into one of the cleaning cupboards and a tin of polish had fallen and hit her.

The next day, when she reported for work as usual, she had expected to be dismissed immediately. But her boss said nothing. Days went by in the normal routine, and the few times she ran into her boss he acted as if nothing had happened. The raise she had been promised did not materialise though. She stayed quiet, did her work.

And then one day, about two weeks after the incident, midway through her shift, her boss cornered her in the storeroom. He followed her, closed the door behind him, and pushed her back against one of the supply shelves. This time he was rougher. As he hit her he told her that he loved her, that she was beautiful and that he could not stop thinking about her. In desperation, she reached out behind her. Her hand closed around a plastic bottle of cleaning solution. She swung it at his face as hard as she could. The cheap plastic bottle exploded, showering them both with bleach. Her boss screamed, staggered back, clawing at his eyes. She ran.

By the time she returned home, her husband had already left for the night shift. The next morning, he was found floating in the Nile. A terrible accident, the authorities called it. He had slipped and hit his head as he walked home in the dark, they said, fallen into the water and drowned. As a widow with two children to care for, she was immediately dismissed. She went to the police and told them her story. They laughed at her, sent her away. Soon her meagre savings were gone and she was forced onto the street. That was fifteen months ago.

Yes, she said, I support The Lion. He is a good Muslim. I believe this in my heart. He speaks the truth in a country of lies. Is this not what the prophet commands? He cares for the people when those who rule are concerned only with their own wealth and power. He does not seek to hurt people, only to destroy the property of those who commit sacrilege. Is this not what Allah, blessed is his name, wishes?

I am a journalist. There are always many sides to every story, and nothing is ever as clear as it seems. But, as my mother used to say, another wrong does not right the first. I did not say this to Samira. I bid my neighbour goodnight and returned to my shelter, as I do every night, to write to you and pray for Allah's guidance.

I cannot allow myself to become subsumed in the misery of others. I need to stay focused on my task. And yet, as each day goes by, I feel my sense of purpose draining away. Eugène and Hamid are gone, God care for their souls. Nothing I do can change this. And while the truth of how and why is important, surely the suffering of others – of those still living – is of greater importance. Is revenge, the search for justice, more important to me than compassion for those who must live in fear and want? Do I want you here, Claymore, simply so I can use you as an instrument of vengeance? These are the questions posed by my rational self. But that part of me cannot compete with my heart. I will find these people who took my husband and my son from me, and, God help me, I will have my revenge.

This evening, I will meet the Kemetic.

The Means to Absolution

Welcome to Egypt, he says to the desert wind.

This land of dead pharaohs and kings.

Clay brushes the sand from his hand, blades the sweat from his temples and brow with the knuckle of his right thumb. He drops the folding shovel to the ground, looks up into the sky, blue like those eyes. Dust swirls in the distance. He'd always enjoyed digging, even in the army. The physical act of excavation, the slow but steady progress of the work. But not the graves. There had been far too many of those, filled by friends and enemies alike. And now, with one hand, it is so much harder.

He drags Crowbar's body across the sand and lets it slump into the hole. His friend, his mentor, the man who taught him everything he knows about killing, about life, lies face to the sky, eyes open, blank as the heavens. Clay kneels beside the hole, reaches down and pulls the wallet from Crowbar's pocket. He flips through the pages, finds his SADF file photograph, the one taken shortly after his nineteenth birthday, before jump school, before Angola, before Crowbar, before everything. He slides the photograph from its plastic sleeve, looks at it a moment, and slips it into his pocket. Then he replaces the wallet, lays the Galil on Crowbar's chest and folds his friend's hands across the weapon. He places the frags beside him, the extra mags for the Galil, his ancient, stained copy of *War and Peace*, the pages held together by an elastic band. Then he stands and starts covering him over, pushing the sand and stone into the hole with his boots. The sand films Crowbar's eyes, covers his forehead, and then he is gone.

Clay looks down at the mound, considers speaking a few words, thinks about all the times this man has saved his life, has been there to guide him. That everything has now changed, he is certain. He heels a furrow in the sand.

'Hit first, hit hard,' he says aloud, only the distance to hear him.

And then he hoists his pack onto his shoulders, wraps the end of his *keffiyeh* around his face, and starts walking towards where he knows the river will be.

Soon, the wreck of the Cessna has disappeared behind him, folded into the landscape of low ridges and broad washes of stone and shale. He imagines the place in a few years, the sand drifted over everything, all trace of Crowbar's grave and the plane that carried them here gone. The sun flares and burns above him, melts the land spread before him into shimmering lakes of metal. He walks on, letting the pain in his side flow through him, using it as energy. He is good at walking.

Cairo is still eight hundred kilometres away. There is only one highway, one river, north. That is where they will be watching for him. Unless they think Clay and Crowbar are still travelling by plane. Travelling overland, away from the main road, or on the river, will take too long. He must gain the highway, and start north. And he must do it quickly.

He thinks of Rania, alone, somewhere in that huge city of chaos. And while he knows she is capable and smart, and has been trained in evasion and survival, his anxiety swells. All he has is a telephone number, the one she gave him five days ago. Whose number is it? Will she be there when he can get to a phone and call? And why is she in Cairo anyway? She loses her husband and child, thinks she is being framed for their murder, skips the country and ends up in Egypt with the AB after her. It makes as much sense to him as so many of the other things she has done since he's known her. He thinks, not for the first time, that she is the most enigmatic person he has ever met. Guided by forces he does not understand, her deductions are as mysterious to him as the nature of chance and the currents of time. And he realises, trudging through this country of empty horizons, that for as long as he might live, he will never know her as he wishes to. No man can ever truly know another. How can he hope to know a woman such as her?

He walks out the day and through the night, pausing only to drink and eat, moving steadily east. His excretions are minimal, his body and the elements taking everything. The pain in his side ebbs away and then blooms again. Dawn comes. Stars fade, then disappear. The sun warms his face, pushes away the cold that has taken harbour inside him during the night.

An hour before noon, he comes over a rise. An empty road stretches out before him, both horizons obscured in a haze of wind-blown dust. He can smell water. It makes the air heavier, thicker. He starts down the slope, stepping over the exposed strata of jutting siltstone, the darker fraying shales, the wind-polished ironstone. The rock crumbles under his boots, follows him down the slope. His eyes are on the thread of road. He knows from the charts that it will lead him to Aswan, and that there, he will be able to find a telephone.

He quickens his pace. The road is there, a ribbon now. And to the south, a pair of yellow eyes shine through the heat haze. Headlights emerge, gleaming along the belt strap of tarmac. Clay breaks into a run, the long-strided lope that reminds him of the war, of the urgent days-long escapes from Angola, outnumbered and outgunned, moving steadily, the weight of their weapons and equipment pounding their shoulders and jarring their knees, hour after hour without respite, on through the night, Crowbar urging them on.

But Crowbar isn't here anymore. And never again will he be there to guide him, to give him reprieve, or praise for murder, or the means to absolution. From now, he will have to run and fight for himself. He alone will be responsible. And as the yards and the years fly beneath him, he knows that with Crowbar gone, his life might again be restored to whatever trajectory may originally have been intended. Just maybe.

He reaches the road berm just as the vehicle approaches. It's coming at speed, the headlights strobing across the tarmac. Clay clambers up to the verge, pulls the *keffiyeh* away from his face, and motions with his hand, up and down, the African way. The vehicle slows, flashes its headlights. It is an old *bakkie*, a Toyota by the looks of it, its bed loaded with sacks and logs. The man behind the wheel is wearing a white turban, Sudanese style. His skin is very dark. Clay can see him staring out through the open side window, the slipstream buffeting his perched sleeve. As he nears, his eyes widen, big and white in their sockets. And then the engine guns and the old pick-up gains speed again and flashes past him in a cloud of dust.

Clay stands by the roadside and watches the vehicle disaggregate in the heat ghost shimmering up from the tarmac. He stands a moment, contemplates the nature of fear, the warnings born of self-preservation, the prejudices built from years of childhood urgings and adolescent scarring. He starts walking north. Towards Aswan. Towards Cairo.

Hours pass. He covers at least fifteen kilometres along the road without seeing another vehicle. The sun burns heavy above him, its crazed, billion-year-old photons hammering his shoulders and the crown of his skull, burning the skin around his eyes, melting the tarmac under his feet. He wonders: when was the last time a stranger looked at him without that same fear, that same hollowed-out grin? It is as if they are sending x-rays through him, revealing not only spine and ribs and skull, but the tubercular shadow of the spirit that lives within him, that fast-twitch killing thing. The man in the *bakkie* saw it. And it terrified him.

The sun is low in the sky when he hears another vehicle approaching. He stops, turns, looks back along the road. A big truck is approaching, wheels and body seemingly disconnected, floating on the heat. Clay stands, watches the twenty-two-wheeler take shape. As it nears, he pulls the *keffiyeh* from his head, throws it over his left shoulder to hide his arm, runs his hand through his hair, drops his pack, puts out his hand. He tries to smile. Tries to hide what is inside him.

The truck slows, gears down, rolls to a stop a couple of car lengths away. Clay picks up his pack, walks towards it. The driver leans his head out of the side window. A big smile blooms under a greying moustache, wide cheekbones, ruffled dark hair.

'*Ezey'eka,*' says Clay, peering up at the driver. Hello. Egyptian slang.

'*Selam aleikum,*' says the driver. His voice is deep and rolling, like a rockfall.

Clay gives the customary Arabic reply: And upon you, peace.

'Aswan?' says the driver.

Clay smiles, gives a thumbs-up.

The driver signals for him to climb in.

They drive on in silence. After a while the driver reaches under his seat and produces a bottle, twists off the cap, and passes it to Clay.

Clay takes it, reaches across his body with his right hand, looks at the label.

'*Jayid,*' says the driver, noticing. Good.

Clay takes a swig, feels the harsh local liquor burn inside him. He winces a smile and passes it back. The driver takes a long drink, smiles that broad smile, and passes it back to Clay.

His name is Mahmoud. He lives with his wife and four children on the outskirts of Luxor. He and his brother own this truck, and two others besides, and use them to run goods along the Nile and as far as Hurghada on the Red Sea, sometimes even down into Sudan, if the price is right. 'Tourist?' he asks.

'*Muhendis,*' says Clay. Engineer.

The driver nods, does not ask the obvious question. 'English?'

'South African.' He surprises himself, saying this, after all that has happened.

Mahmoud glances down at Clay's stump, at his left side still covered over with the *keffiyeh*, wipes his mouth with the back of his wrist, seems to think about this a while. 'Everywhere in Africa there are problems,' he says.

'Everywhere,' says Clay. In his halting, ten-year-old's Arabic, Clay thanks him for stopping, and asks if he is going farther north, perhaps up to Cairo.

Mahmoud recaps the bottle and slides it back into its place on the floor. 'Tonight, Luxor,' he says. 'The day after tomorrow, Cairo. We have a shipment of dates.'

'Please,' says Clay. 'If you can take me to Cairo, I have money.'

Mahmoud smiles, waves his gear-shift hand at Clay. 'No money, my South African friend. You will stay with my family in Luxor. We will eat, and drink together, and I will introduce you to my brother and my wife and my sons. You will rest a day, and then we will go to Cairo together.'

Clay thanks the man and sits a long time contemplating this kindness as dark comes and the land of tombs falls into obscurity. After a while, his eyes close, and for a moment there is only the sound of the engine and the buffeting of the wind through the window.

☾

Clay jolts awake. The truck is slowing, air-braking towards some kind of roadblock. He realises that his *keffiyeh* has fallen away from his shoulder and arm, and that his bloody bandaged side is clearly visible.

Mahmoud looks over at him, his face lit up red and blue. 'Police,' he says.

Clay scans the ground on both sides. Two police cars are drawn up on each side of the road, stopping traffic in both directions. It looks routine, but he's been through enough of these over the years to know that you can never tell. If the police see him, there will be questions. He has few good answers, and if they examine the contents of his bag, what they will find will be enough to put him in jail while they seek more credible ones.

'Stop here, please, Mahmoud,' he says. 'I don't want to cause you trouble.'

Mahmoud stretches back his shoulders, then reaches his gear-shift hand behind his seat and flips a latch. 'In there,' he says. 'Quickly.'

The roadblock is still a few car lengths away. Clay looks back. It is some sort of sleeping compartment. 'Are you sure?'

'*Yallah*,' he says. Go.

Clay clambers over the seat, pushes himself into the space, pulls his bag in after him. Mahmoud closes the compartment door and there is darkness.

8th November 1997, Cairo, Egypt. 23:50 hrs

Samira went to work today, and, as agreed, I looked after her children.

But today Eleana was worse. Much worse. Not long after Samira left, her breathing became laboured. Then she started coughing, a deep, violent, insistent hack that grew worse and worse. I tried everything I could – heating water and adding sugar and juice from the last orange, giving her two of my remaining aspirin, turning her on her side and sitting her up – but nothing would quell it. By midday, she started coughing up blood, flecks of it in the thick green mucus. Sweat covered her body. She was burning to the touch, feverish, muttering nonsense.

I knew that without antibiotics, the infection in Eleana's lungs could be fatal. I had no choice. I went to my shelter, dug up my money and identification, and wrote a note for Samira. I tidied myself up as best I could, threw on my burqa, and went next door (next door!) for the children.

Soon we were standing on the road, Eleana in my arms, almost too heavy for me to carry, and the little one holding on to a fold of my burqa. The traffic, as usual, was horrendous – a honking, crawling, fuming mass. It took me almost half an hour to wave down a taxi. Finally a driver took pity on us and stopped. I asked him to take us to a good private medical clinic. He asked if I had money. I threw a hundred-pound note on the seat next to him. After that he was very helpful and friendly. We carved through the backstreets, and when we arrived at the clinic he even opened the door for us.

Inside the clinic we were treated no differently to how we are treated on the street. We looked as if we could not pay, and so they ignored us, shunted us to the back of the queue. Eleana was getting worse, and by then lay listless in my arms, rasping shallow breaths. It did not take long for me to lose my patience. I stormed to the front and laid down three fifty-euro notes and demanded to see a doctor.

Eleana is still at the clinic, resting now. The doctor told me that if I had waited much longer to bring her in for treatment, she may well have died. She has severe pneumonia in both lungs and is now on a powerful cocktail of intravenous antibiotics. I was forced to give the clinic my name and passport details – Veronique's – and the only telephone number I possess: the Kemetic's. This is not the way to disappear.

When I returned to the shelter with Ghada, the little one, Samira was beside herself. She had had a fruitless day, and the Copts weren't much interested in anything her subcontracting efforts had yielded. She had seen my note and feared the worst. And now she knows that I am not who I appeared to be. I am not a fellow outcast, a penniless refugee from society, as she is. I am an impostor, hiding from the law. We spoke long into the night, until just now in fact. I told her everything.

I had a choice, of course. I did not need to tell her anything. I could simply have paid for her daughter's care and then moved on, found some other dark corner of this crumbling city of alleys and doorways and rubbish-choked streets in which to hide. But I need a friend. She had shared her story with me, and so I told her mine.

I did not tell her about my life before marrying Hamid, though, and I did not tell her about you, Claymore. But of everything that has happened since, I was as complete as I could be. And as we spoke, I could see the kindness in her face, and the gratitude she felt for my help. We are both in need of an ally, a friend, and as she told me, we are stronger together.

But now, lying here, unable to sleep, I realise that I have been selfish. I succumbed to the need for friendship, the need to share my fears and travails, and now I have endangered Samira and her daughters. Whoever killed Eugène and Hamid, whoever is watching Yusuf and ensuring his silence, is protecting a powerful secret. If the Kemetic is right, and it is this group he will only refer to as 'the Consortium', the danger could be closer than I would like to believe.

Tomorrow I will take Samira to the clinic and we will check on Eleana's progress. I will pay for whatever additional treatment is required – I still have plenty of cash – and then I will try again to see the Kemetic. Whatever is required, I must know what he knows.

The Debased and the Faithful

For a long time he had thought of time as a destroyer. Of lives and hopes, of civilisations and suns. That was what he'd seen during the war, and since. A person you cared for, loved even, alive one moment, all of the future before them, and then dead in a moment's glance. Gone. Ended. The decomposition already begun. And then, later, when he came to understand more about the laws of physics, he began to see time's companion, entropy, as the unmaker of all.

But now he knew that time was not the enemy. It was the gift – the great and only commodity in life. Watching that barren, ancient land sweeping past the window of this north-bound freight truck, he realised that this short treasure of time that each of us is provided can only be used in the present. For it is the present that converts the infinite possibility and potential of the future into a single, definitive past. Eben had taught him that part, about the past always being there. But he'd never told him that the present feeds on the potential of the future, consumes it and fixes it for ever. Every moment, every breath, every ∞ converted into a 1 – this was the only reality.

☾

They reached Aswan a few hours later.

There had been no more roadblocks, and Clay had dozed in the seat with his head rattling against the doorframe as the miles sped by, fragments of dreams folding into reality until one became indistinguishable from the other. Now, as they trundled through the dusty outskirts of the city, the pain in Clay's side had blown out into a near and shining star.

Mahmoud geared down, turned the big truck off the main road and started down into the river valley, the dark Nile water flowing smooth and calm through the once churning cataracts downstream of the dam. 'We will stop here. I must unload this cargo,' he said in Arabic, the first words he'd spoken since the roadblock.

'I need to find a telephone,' said Clay.

'I do not have my own mobile phone. Not yet. But there is a PTT office in the town.'

Clay nodded.

'I will take you there now,' said Mahmoud, swinging the rig around a sharp bend, heading towards a cluster of whitewashed buildings near the river. Sandstone bluffs towered in the background.

'You do not look well,' said Mahmoud, rolling the truck to a stop. 'You need a doctor.'

'I'll be okay,' Clay said, wincing as he swung open the door. 'Where shall I meet you?'

'Here.' Mahmoud checked his watch. 'In an hour and a half. Luxor is four and a half hours away.'

'See you then,' said Clay, reaching for his pack. As he did, a spike of pain drove through his side. He groaned involuntarily.

'Are you sure you do not need a doctor?' said Mahmoud, staring at Clay. 'Perhaps it is not wise to enter the PTT as you are. There may be police. There is a phone at my house. Perhaps better to call from there.'

Clay looked down at his side. Blood had soaked through the bandage and had stained his shirt and jacket. Mahmoud was right. He wasn't thinking straight.

Mahmoud reached behind him and pulled out a dark jacket. 'Take this,' he said. Clay nodded and threaded on the jacket.

'And leave your bag.'

Clay replaced the bag containing his gold, Crowbar's Jericho, three extra clips for the G21, and two M27 fragmentation grenades on the floor of the rear compartment. He was taking a big chance, leaving all of this with a stranger, going into this highly public, official place. Perhaps he should wait, telephone from Luxor, from the security and privacy of Mahmoud's home. Clay trusted the guy, but you never could tell. Sometimes the ones you thought would stick hard were gone at the first sign of trouble, and the guys you'd swear would run ended up staying until the end. Four and a half hours away, that was all. He'd waited days already, months. A few hours more was nothing, a twitch. But then again, maybe Mahmoud would take the opportunity to call ahead, have the police waiting for him in Luxor. Here and now though, with the anvil sky pressing in on him, the thought of even a minute longer without hearing her voice was impossible to bear.

'See you here in an hour and a half,' said Clay. 'And thanks, Mahmoud. *Shukran.*'

The driver smiled and nodded.

Clay clambered to the ground, pushed the door closed. The truck pulled away. Clay pulled his cap low over his eyes, thrust his stump into the jacket's pocket, hunched to make himself smaller and trudged towards the post-office entrance. The *adhan* rose above the town, echoing back from a dozen minarets along the valley, calling the debased and the faithful alike to come to God and repent.

Twenty minutes later, he stood in the telephone cabinet and picked up the receiver. Soon he might create a different past from the one that so far had been set out for him. And it would start here, now. With Rania.

The line clicked, connected.

'*Merhaba?*' a man's voice.

Clay said nothing, held his breath.

'*Merhaba?*'

Clay steadied himself. 'I am looking for Veronique,' he said in Arabic.

'Ah, yes. Madame Veronique.'

'Is she there?'

'At the moment, no.' The voice was deep, resonant.

'How can I reach her?'

'That depends.'

Clay clenched his jaw, pushed the end of his stump into the wood panelling. 'On what?'

'That depends on who you are, sir, and what your business is.'

'Look, I am a friend. It's important.'

'Yes. She mentioned to me that someone might call.'

'Are you expecting her anytime soon?' Clay held back, not wanting to sound desperate.

'She was supposed to meet me yesterday evening, but she did not come. I am worried that something has happened to her.'

'Is she in danger?'

'The Consortium…' he began, but did not finish.

'The Consortium? Is that who is threatening her?'

'I am sorry. I cannot say more.'

Clay swallowed down the fear pushing up through his chest. 'Can you pass a message to her, if you see her?'

'Of course.'

'Tell her I will be in Cairo the day after tomorrow. Tuesday. Tell her to meet me at the Groppi Cafe, on Talaat Harb Square. I'll be waiting for her there at noon.'

The sound of scribbling, a pencil on paper.

'Tell her it's Declan.' The name he'd used as an alias for a while in Cyprus when they were together for those few days, more than two years ago now.

'It is better if you come here first,' said the man. 'We can meet. Then we can come to an arrangement.'

'Arrangement.'

'Yes. That's right.'

Clay swallowed. 'What do you want?'

'I only wish to keep Madame Veronique safe. She is very vulnerable.'

Vulnerable. Jesus Christ. 'How much do you want?'

A pause, and then: 'A thousand dollars would do well. American. Cash.'

Clay could already see the guy, on the ground, whimpering from a broken jaw. 'No worries at all, *bru*,' he said, working hard to keep the venom out of his voice. 'Tell you what. Let's make it two thousand. How about that? Where can I find you?'

The man hesitated. 'Come to fourteen Othman Road, apartment sixty-one. Just south of the Ring Road in Giza.'

'See you Tuesday.'

'Bring cash.'

'Definitely.' Clay set down the receiver, his hand shaking. The receiver was wet. Sweat soaked his shirt, covered his forearms and face. The bastard, whoever he was, was holding Rania to ransom. That was clear. Was he part of this 'consortium' Rania had mentioned when they last spoke? Had the AB already got to her? Were they using her as bait, trying to lure him in, to finish what they'd started in Zanzibar and fucked up in Somalia? His mind spun through the possibilities, each darker than the next. Was she even still alive?

Clay emerged blinking into the afternoon sun and drifted towards the place where he'd agreed to meet Mahmoud. The ground shifted beneath his feet, the horizon acute, unstable. He stopped, bent at the waist, tried to breathe. Then he dropped to one knee, reached out for the ground, felt his hand sink through the void, the hard surface he knew was there as yet unreached. And then it was as if he was tumbling in a dark well where gravity acted only on the undeserving, and the righteous flew unperturbed in the clear sky above.

'My friend.'

Clay opened his eyes, looked up towards the voice.

A hand reached behind his head. 'My friend, come, please.'

Clay's vision cleared. It was the truck driver, Mahmoud.

'Come my friend. People will be watching. I must get you to a doctor.'

9th November 1997. Cairo, Egypt. 12:15 hrs

Samira and I and little Ghada went to the clinic this morning, and despite the disapproving looks of the stern woman at reception, were taken through to see the doctor who is attending Eleana. He was a nice man, mid-sixties or so, with grey hair and a fatherly demeanour. His Arabic was beautiful, and he complimented me on mine.

Eleana is out of danger and should make a complete recovery. Allah be praised. She will need at least two more days in hospital, he said, before taking us in to see her. She was sleeping when we arrived. She is still very weak and is fighting the infection. After a moment, she opened her eyes. And then she smiled. Samira wept at her bedside.

After our visit, I paid for two more days of care, and the doctor agreed that we could come to see Eleana every morning. If after two days she is still weak, she may have to stay longer. I told the doctor this would not be a problem. As we left I could see the receptionist whispering with another matronly attendant. It will not be long before the story of a couple of destitute street women, haggard and dirty, paying hard currency for treatment at one of the best clinics in the district, spreads across the city. It is the type of thing people love to gossip about.

I attached my veil and left Samira and Ghada to find their way home. Then I went to the telephone office and called the Kemetic.

He was very excited. He said that he had been worried when I did not keep our appointment yesterday evening. Worried that perhaps the Consortium had taken me. You must be very careful, he said. Do not draw attention to yourself. I did not tell him, of course, about Samira and her daughter and the clinic, that I had violated every rule I had been taught about how to disappear.

Did you think about what we talked about, last time? he asked. His voice was deeper than usual, thickened. I am a good man, he said, almost in a whisper. A lonely man. And you are a beautiful woman. Very beautiful. Your image has burned inside me since we first met.

I let the line run quiet for a long time, my heart beating hard in my chest. I am not an innocent. I know the ways of men, the lust that can consume them. But the thought of that man touching me sends shivers of disgust running through me even now.

Before I could answer, though, he came to the point. I have something you need, he said. We can help each other.

How can you ask such a thing? I asked. Have you no shame?

Please, Madame Veronique. It is not such a great thing that I ask. I will help you. I will tell you what you need to know about your husband and son, about Yusuf. Grant me this one beautiful thing.

I cannot reproduce here the rest of his pitiful pleading. It continued for some time. I resisted. And then:

If you come to me this evening, I will assume that you have agreed to my terms.

And if I do not?

Then I will be unable to help you.

I can be very persuasive.

That is what I am hoping, dear lady. Persuade me, please.

I cannot do what you ask.

Perhaps you will change your mind. I have had a telephone call. Someone asking for you.

I gasped. I know he heard me. I could almost hear his face stretching into a leer.

Who was it?

Tonight, dear lady. Six o'clock. He disconnected.

I gave the Kemetic's number to only one person. If the wretch is not lying to lead me on, it could only have been you, Claymore. You are alive.

Allah, please have it be so.

I know what I must do. I am prepared. Forgive me, my love. And God forgive my soul.

Carry My Fate with Yours

The wound, it turned out, wasn't that bad. Manheim's two bullets had glanced off the hard curve of his ribs without damaging the intercostal muscles, leaving two parallel tears. He was in pain, but he could work his arm almost normally.

After finding Clay on the pavement outside the post and telegraph office, Mahmoud had helped him to the truck and taken him immediately to a doctor he knew in Aswan. Clay had been in no shape to argue. The doctor disinfected and sewed his wounds, bandaged him and ran him an IV. He was, the doctor explained, more dehydrated than anything else. Soon they were heading north along the Western Desert Road, the truck's cargo trailer empty.

Desert air flowed over him, hot and centuries dry. Clay blinked away the dust, felt the truck's wheels rumbling over the cracked and fraying tarmac beneath him, and looked out across the jagged aeolian horizon, miles and miles of it, the everchanging constancy of sand and wind and sun.

'Thank you for all you have done,' said Clay, in Arabic.

Mahmoud grabbed the steering wheel with his gear-shift hand, reached for the bottle, unscrewed the cap, took a swig, smiled wide and passed the bottle across.

Clay drank. 'I must get to Cairo tomorrow, Mahmoud. The day after is too late. Please drop me in the town and I will hire a car and a driver.'

'Did you place your telephone call?'

Clay nodded and passed back the bottle.

'Trouble?'

'Yes.'

'It is very important?'

'Very. A good friend. She in danger.'

Mahmoud thought on this a while, shifting in his seat. 'Then we will go together,' he said. 'Tonight, by car. My brother can drive the truck with the dates.'

'I cannot ask this of you, Mahmoud.'

Mahmoud touched Clay on the shoulder. 'Please, my friend. Allah asks this of me. He has put you in my path, and now it is my duty.'

Clay pointed to his bandage. 'You know what this was from, yes?'

Mahmoud nodded. 'Yes.'

'It is not your duty to put yourself in danger.'

The big truck driver turned in his seat and stared at him a long time, the wheel wedged stable against his hip. 'Duty is not changing with risk,' he said.

'My best friend was a…' Clay stumbled, stopped, unable to find the Arabic word. He pointed to his head. 'One who thinks.'

'*Filsw'uf*,' said Mahmoud, smiling. Philosopher.

Clay repeated the word. 'This is not the time for being a philosopher.'

Mahmoud faced the road. 'Your friend is a good man, yes?'

'Was.'

'I am sorry.'

'No need. Yes, he was good.' Clay realised it had been a while since he'd thought of Eben. 'It was philosophy killed him, Mahmoud. Philosophy and me.'

'You cannot claim this power, my friend.' Mahmoud pointed skywards. 'Only Allah.'

'The woman who is in danger, in Cairo. She tells me this also.'

'She is very wise.'

'Yes.'

'She is Muslim?'

Clay nodded. 'Very.'

Mahmoud smiled, shifted gears, pushed the truck faster. 'Then it is clear what must be done, and why.'

They drove on in silence for a long time, through Al Kajuj and then Edfu, the sun moving through the sky above them, the rare shadows of road signs and distant mesas lengthening, the heat shimmering like sky on the road ahead, always out of reach. Mahmoud did not ask how he had come to emerge from the desert, alone and cut by bullets. He did not ask the nature of his friend's danger in Cairo, nor of the reasons for Clay's fear of the police. He sat behind the wheel of his truck and hummed verses from the Koran, swigging his cheap local booze, and drove towards whatever destiny Allah had ordained for him.

By the time they reached Luxor, the first planets had appeared in the blush over the Nile – Venus cool and bright, Mars low in the sky, their positions not much changed since the time of the pharaohs. Mahmoud's family home was set in the fertile west valley of the Nile, just outside town, a place of green fields, thickets of reed and palm, and clustered mud-brick buildings rendered in alabaster and shaded by cascades of bougainvillea and wreaths of oleander. Surely, green was the colour of paradise.

Mahmoud parked the truck and turned off the engine. They sat a moment, staring ahead, silent, listening to the sounds of evening.

'Come,' Mahmoud said. 'I will speak to my brother. Then we will take the car and start for Cairo. Your friend needs us.'

☾

They left for Cairo not long after, driving through the night.

Mahmoud had given Clay a southern *keffiyeh,* which he wound around his head in the style of the Nubians. At the police checkpoint near the highway interchange at Asyut, they were waved on without stopping. A few hours later, at Minya, Clay feigned sleep as a policeman played the beam of a hand torch across the inside of the car. He heard Mahmoud exchange greetings with him. There was laughter, familiarity in their tone. They drove on.

Three hours later, they were navigating through the early-morning haze of Cairo's southern reaches, the traffic still quiet. Mahmoud pulled the car into a side street just off King Faisal Street in Giza and turned off the engine.

Clay pulled his pack from the back seat and opened the door. 'You are a good man,' he said, reaching out his hand. He thought of offering money, but decided not to risk offending him.

Mahmoud took his hand, squeezed hard and smiled. 'Find your friend,' he said. 'Protect her now and always.' Then he handed him a business card. 'If you ever need anything, please call.'

Clay smiled at the man's words. '*Inshallah.*'

'Whatever you must do, do in God's name, my friend. You carry my fate with yours now.'

'Please,' said Clay. 'I do not deserve such a responsibility.'

Mahmoud pushed his chin to his chest. 'Still, it is the truth.'

Clay took a deep breath. 'Live well. Mahmoud. I will do my best.'

'God willing,' said Mahmoud, 'we must all.' And then he was gone, swallowed up in the morning traffic. Another random meeting, plucked from the infinite and made real by fate or chance or determinism – who knew.

It didn't take Clay long to find the place. Number fourteen was a half-completed, half-decayed edifice of brick and cement and searching rebar covered over in a film of brown silt, wedged in like an afterthought between two larger, older structures. Here, the lanes between the buildings were narrow and steep, like the canyons of fraying wadis, choked with half-degraded plastic bags and discarded drink tins, torn through by speeding auto-rickshaws and lumbering, fenderless *bakkies*. He circled the place once, noted entrances and first-floor window alignments, scanned for rooftop joinings and overhangs, and then went in the front door.

If the guy was home, he would not be expecting him. If he wasn't, Clay would look around, settle himself in and wait, Crowbar style. If Rania was there, he'd do whatever he had to to get her out. Either way, he'd have the advantage. Hit first.

The stairway was dark, stank of piss and vaguely of incense and cat. He took the stairs two at a time, moving quietly, counting off the flights. At the sixth floor he emerged into a dimly lit corridor. Same smells, but with something else there now, something familiar. He scanned the Arabic numerals on the wooden doors. Apartment ٦٦ was halfway along the corridor. Clay stopped, looked both ways, listened. The corridor was deserted. He reached out to knock on the door, but stopped, his knuckles inches from the wood. The door was ajar.

Clay filled his lungs, steadied his pulse, reached for his Glock and pushed open the door.

It was the smell hit him first. A swirling miasma of heat and decay. Memories came flooding back, rolled over him. He staggered, steadied himself, followed the lurking reek through the relic-strewn sitting room, past the filthy kitchen to the bedroom.

The guy was lying on his back, his big hairy belly bulging towards the ceiling, his penis lying snaked in its den of wire. The full-length kaftan he was wearing was bunched up around his chest. His eyes were open; his mouth agape. Clay could see the guy's big upper canines, the gold fillings in the molars. His chin sprouted a dark beard that had been waxed into a long, thin curve. The sheets beneath him were stained dark, arterial red. Clay counted three wounds in the guy's fleshy neck, all in the left side.

Clay stood a moment, his eyes still adjusting to the gloom. On the floor beside the bed, a lamp lay on its side, the shade dented and crushed. Bits of glass scattered the hardwood. He reached out, touched the body. It was cold. He turned over the man's hands. Abrasions across his right knuckles and cuts across his left forearm where he'd tried to protect himself from a knife. Whoever he was, he'd fought back.

Clay moved through the rest of the apartment, checking every door and cupboard. Except for the corpse, the place was empty. He went back to the sitting room. Near the door was an old mahogany table strewn with papers. Sheets of hand-drawn hieroglyphs, utility bills in Arabic addressed to Mehmet Al Sami. Was this the guy he'd spoken to from Aswan? Clay flipped through a stack of bills, found the phone company invoice and checked the number. It wasn't the one Rania had given him. But this was the address. The invoice confirmed it. He must have another number. Perhaps another place, an office perhaps.

On the phone, the guy had mentioned the Consortium. Had they got to him? Had they got her, too? Was it the AB? He shook his head, tried to push the thought away. He had to hope that this Mehmet had passed on his message, and that Rania would meet him tomorrow at the café.

Clay took a last look around the flat, closed the door behind him and left the building through the back door, emerging into the noonday heat and stink of Cairo.

Everything That Had Defined His Life

Clay was halfway down the alley behind the building when he realised his mistake.

No more than a few hours ago, someone had gone into the man's apartment and murdered him. As far as he could tell, no one had yet discovered the body. But it was only a matter of time. Soon the police would be all over the place, looking for evidence. He'd touched the door handles, inside and out. If they dusted for fingerprints, they might be able to link him to the murder, even accuse him of it. Worse, if they found the note the dead guy had scribbled during their telephone conversation – where and when Rania should meet him, his decidedly Western alias – and if Rania had received his message, she could be going straight to them.

This was no coincidence. None of it was. Clay knew that now. The world didn't work that way – not with these things. But the causality behind it he could not see. One thing was sure: whatever Rania was mixed up in, whatever she was here trying to uncover, was worth killing for. Her husband and son were already dead, the police were after her for those murders. And now the one person she'd trusted enough for him to contact was dead.

Clay stopped in the strip of shadow against the mud-brick wall and looked down the alley. To the east, the Giza market, busy now. To the west, an empty lot choked with smoking rubbish, boys playing football in the dust. Even dressed in Mahmoud's Upper Egypt clothes, his beard now long and full but fair, he felt like a lighthouse beacon. He knew he needed to go back, and do it now, before the cops arrived – scour the flat for anything that he, or the police, could use to find Rania. He pulled the end of his turban down around his face, hunched low, leaned on his walking stick to disguise his height, kept his eyes and face directed groundwards, and started back towards the building.

Clay pushed the steel door open and stepped into the gloom of the rear stairwell. He waited a moment, listened then started up the stairs. As he neared the sixth floor, that same smell smothered him, stronger now: blood and death and decomposition pushing through the background of shit and urine and yesterday's dinner. He stood outside apartment sixty-one. The corridor was empty. He pushed open the door, stepped inside, closed the door behind him and bolted it closed.

He stood a moment, scanning the room. The place looked more like a shrine than a place for living. Against one wall was a man-sized statue of Horus, its hawk head perched on the body of a chiselled athlete. All around were offerings, garlands of dead, browned flowers, burned-down candles, smaller sculptures of ancient Egyptian deities and demigods that Clay could neither recognise nor name. He continued through the flat, scanning the piles of books ranged up along the outside wall.

A high-pitched scream cut the silence.

It had come from outside, down in the street.

Clay nudged the shutter lever with his stump, looked out through the louvres. Two boys were running away, down the lane. He took a deep breath, closed the shutters, continued his search.

In the middle of the room: some pillows scattered over a carpet, a small, low table, a couple of rolled-up scrolls. More candleholders with charred wicks and cascading with rivulets of wax. And there, on the floor next to the one of the cushions, a glint of metal. It was small, about half the size of his small fingernail. He turned it over in his fingers. It was a button of some kind, a half-sphere of faux mother of pearl with a small hook on the back. A clutch of torn thread and a flap of cloth hung from the hook. It was a pretty thing, delicate, not something the big brute lying on the bed in the other room would wear. It had been ripped away from whatever it had adorned. Clay raised the button to his lips. The faintest odour came to him, a distant chemistry. Then it was gone.

Clay pocketed the button and walked into the bedroom. The corpse lay as it had before, eyes open, arms splayed at its sides. The telephone was set on an old wooden dresser. Beside it was a journal of some sort, spiral bound, and nearby, a pencil, its wooden end crushed and marked with the imprints of teeth. Clay flicked through the pad, scanning the impenetrable Arabic scratchings, the scattered hieroglyphs, the cursive hieratic. He pushed the journal into the deep pocket of his robe. Then he moved to the bed and surveyed the knife wounds again. On the bed, half-hidden under a fold of the sheet, was a small pocket camera – one of the new digital models with a small screen on the back. Clay picked it up and turned it on. As the screen lit up, a picture came into view. He stood, silent, staring at the image.

It was a woman. She was standing in the shower, naked. Her hands were under her breasts. Her hair flowed over her shoulders and across the pale skin of her chest in dark tresses. Her head was lowered, the face obscured. He scrolled back. Another photo: the same woman, turned away from the lens, her back and buttocks glistening and wet. Another photo, and another. The woman undressing, opening her brassiere, letting her breasts spill out, bending over to step out of her dress, undoing the shiny pearl-white buttons down the front, the tear and the missing second button clearly visible – the one in Clay's pocket. Dozens of photographs. In many of them, the face was clear, and utterly, devastatingly recognisable. That stratospheric fusion of Berber and Breton. The date stamp glowed digital orange in the lower right corner. Yesterday.

Clay exhaled long, steadied himself. It was Rania. Beautiful, powerful, delicate, tragic Rania. He turned off the camera and dropped it into his pocket, realisation thudding though his brain. He pushed through it, walked to the bathroom, searched the floor, the toilet, the shower stall. It didn't take him long to find the opening, given the single perspective of all the photographs. One of the tiles had been replaced with a mirror-like panel, about the size of a postage stamp. Clay went back into the bedroom, opened the closet on the wall facing the bathroom. He pushed aside a rack of hanging clothes. The back panelling of the closet had been cut away and a layer of brick removed, creating a small, darkened space. A hole had been hurriedly hacked through the brick. Crumbled masonry and powdered mortar still covered the floor. A half-empty tube of lubricant lay shrivelled and leaking on a makeshift shelf cut into the wall. The air was dense with dust and the smell of musk and sweat. Clay recoiled, stepped back out into the dead man's room, breathing hard. Jesus Christ. What the hell had she got herself mixed up in? And how had she come to trust this guy?

That was as far into contemplation as he got.

A loud bang burst through his wondering. Someone was hammering on the door. A male voice shouting in Arabic: 'Open the door.' And then: '*Sort'ah.*' Police.

Clay froze, held his breath.

A pause, voices outside, some sort of conversation in Arabic. Then more hammering, the edge of a fist pounding the wood. The same voice, raised higher now: 'Open the door. This is the police.'

Clay moved towards the bedroom window and pulled aside the curtains. The wood casement was old, the varnish peeled and faded. He swung back the latch, pulled the window open, looked outside. The building's outer wall was rendered cinderblock, with a six-storey fall to the alleyway. The flat, brick-strewn roof of the facing building was a couple of stories lower. There was no way to get across. It was too far to jump, even with a running start. Clay closed the window, wiped the latch with his sleeve.

More hammering now, the voice telling the resident of flat sixty-one that this was his last warning. Clay moved into the hallway, turned left, away from the front door, and entered some kind of office. Stacks of books and papers covered every surface, tottered in dusty piles against the walls. In the middle of the room a large desk, with what appeared to be the carved stone legs of a lion, hulked under a mountain of journals. Clay moved toward the outside wall, pushed aside the heavy curtain and opened the window. Behind him, a crash, the splintering of wood as the doorframe gave way, the sound of footsteps heavy on the hardwood floor. Clay's heart stilled. He breathed, looked outside. He was on the other side of the building now, around the corner from the bedroom. The outside wall here, at the back of the building, was unrendered, the brickwork bare, the mortar weeping between the bricks in hardened cornices, in some places absent. Just to the right was some kind of utility conduit, a pair of vertical bricked-in columns about a metre square that ran from ground level to the roof. If he could make his way across, he could wedge himself in the channel between the uprights and chimney his way either down to the street, or up to the roof.

The sound of footsteps now, the low murmur of voices. For the thousandth time since waking up in the hospital in Oman, he cursed his missing hand, then levered himself up and out.

❨

He waited, tucked behind a water tank. From where he crouched, he could see through the skirting of perforated brickwork down to the street. He watched as the crowds outside the building grew. At any moment he expected the police to emerge from the stairway onto the roof. They would surely have seen the open window, surmised that the killer had escaped that way.

There was only one way out. There were no adjoining buildings and no rear stairs. The Glock was cradled in his lap, ready. He was prepared to fight if he had to. Soon, another police car arrived, and not long after, an ambulance. Time crept by, thick and viscous, tomorrow's appointed meeting with Rania decades distant.

He'd been on the roof just under half an hour when he saw the paramedics emerge onto the street carrying a stretcher. They loaded the body into the back of the ambulance, closed the rear door and stood chatting to a pair of cops. The crowd was packed in close, and as the ambulance moved away the people parted and reformed behind it like water in a river.

Perhaps because of what the police saw, the condition of the body, or the time since death, which was obviously considerable, no one appeared on the roof. After a time, the last police car left. Slowly, the crowds on the street dispersed. Dusk came. The sun sank red into the edge of the city, lit the brume that smothered the buildings. After a while even the great pyramids were only faint rumours of evening.

Finally, gone seven, Clay emerged from his hide, wrapped his *keffiyeh* around his face so that he too was veiled, and started down the stairwell.

He walked slowly, bent at the waist and using his stick, as an old man would, drifting through the streets as if in a morphine-induced coma.

What had happened at the flat? Rania had been there while the pervert was still alive. The photographs proved that. But then something had gone wrong. There had been a struggle. Rania's dress had been torn. Had she been there when the Egyptian was killed? Or had she witnessed the whole thing, been taken hostage by the killers – the Consortium perhaps, the AB, or those acting for them? Or maybe she had left before the killer or killers arrived. And if she had, had the pervert conveyed Clay's message to her before he was killed? Would she be there, tomorrow, waiting on the square outside Groppi's? There were a thousand possibilities, each more opaque than the last.

Soon he was pushing through the evening crowds in the Giza market, through streets runneling blood and sewage. He kept walking and at last found himself on the west bank of the Nile. He turned north, followed the river walkway towards Zamalek, where he looked out across the dark water at the smog-blurred lights of the big towers, the red-and-white streams of traffic across Cairo University Bridge. She was out there, somewhere in this city of twenty million souls. Somewhere. Perhaps hers was the spirit to guide him, now that everything and everyone that had defined his life was gone.

Maybe. But first, he had to find her. And then they had to get out.

It was at that point in his philosophising that he realised he was being followed. A dark figure, fifty metres back on the other side of the road, was matching his movements, stopping when he stopped, accelerating when he did. Clay came to a place where the river walk was well lit. He stopped, leaned back against the railing, faced the road, glanced at the figure then looked way. The figure had stopped also, was standing under a tree, behind a parked car, in the shadows, face obscured. Clay reached into his pocket, checked the Glock, put his stick under his left arm and started towards the figure.

Clay didn't run. But the old-man guise was gone. His pace was determined, quick. At first the figure held its ground. Clay crossed the road on the oblique, closing straight on the target. He was to the median when the figure took a couple of steps backwards, stumbled over a loose paver and moved momentarily out of the shadows. Clay jumped back as a car blared past. Egyptian invective spun in the slipstream. The figure turned and ran. By the time Clay reached the other side of the road, the figure had disappeared into the Cairo night.

10th November 1997. Cairo, Egypt. 08:40 hrs

This morning I took Samira and her daughter to the clinic to visit Eleana again. She is much better, and the doctors say she can be discharged tomorrow. أشاد الله

I sit in my shelter now, staring out across the rubbish-strewn ground at the neighbouring buildings. Yesterday evening I went to see the Kemetic.

He was waiting for me in the same long white robe he had been wearing before. He had tidied the place a bit. He'd lit incense and a few candles. The place looked more like a shrine to Horus than ever. When I arrived, I hung my burqa on the hook at the front door. Underneath I was wearing the most fetching of the dresses that I have kept – a simple cotton shift that flatters my figure. I could see he liked it.

He made us tea, very dark and sweet. We sat in the main room and drank. After a while I asked him about the call he had received.

Ah yes, he said.

Did he give a name? I asked.

It seems you are very popular, good lady. He smoothed his robe across his knees. I can understand why.

I lowered my eyes, smiled. This works well with certain types of men. Thank you.

Ra has made you this way, he said, starting with the ancient Egyptian rubbish again. The sun and the stars and all the gods have created the world and everything in it, and you are yet another example of their perfection.

I tried again, attempting to forestall what I knew was coming. The man who called, what did he say?

Not one, he said.

Pardon? I didn't understand. He could see this.

Three different men called for you.

I gasped, just a little, giving away my surprise. Three? I asked. Are you sure it was not the same man calling?

Yes. I am very sure. Three different men.

Please, I said, tell me who they were. Did they leave names? What did they say? You know my situation. You have seen. It is very important. Please help me. I must have sounded very desperate, speaking this way, very quickly and out of breath. I could feel the colour coming to my face.

He tugged on that little waxed beard of his, stroking it from chin to tip with his fingers, very slowly and deliberately as he had done before when I had seen him. I could see he was enjoying having put me in such a state of excitement.

Yes, he said, of course. But first, perhaps you would again like to use my shower? You have worn a becoming dress for me, but still, you smell of the street.

I blushed, even more than I already had, and he noticed. No woman likes to be told that she smells, no matter what the circumstances. No, thank you, I said in my best formal Arabic.

He crossed his arms – crook and flail – and stared at me. Please, he said. Wash. And then we can talk.

I knew where this would lead. Of course, I did. I would be lying to you, my love, if I wrote anything else. I had known since before I went there. And yet I had to keep going. There were other ways, of course. But you know I abhor violence. No descent is deeper, no fate worse. How you live with yourself, I cannot imagine. I have other powers even more compelling, and I had already decided I would use them. So I stood, smiled and walked to the bathroom. I disrobed, as before, stood naked looking at myself in the mirror, this other person preparing herself – the other side of me, perhaps. I knew he was out there, thinking about me, about what I was doing, inflaming himself. I knew. And yet I continued. I got into the shower, ran the warm water across my body, soaped myself, washed my hair, rid myself of the filth. It felt good. I took a long time. I thought of you, Claymore. I did not want to come out.

When I emerged, he smiled and asked me to sit. His face was flushed, as if he'd run downstairs for something and back up while I was in the shower. We drank more tea. Then he stood and moved to the cushion next to me. He sat close.

Please, he said, his voice thicker than before, almost a whisper. Let me. He reached his hand towards the front of my dress, the buttons down the front.

I pulled away. Who called for me? Did they leave a name?

He was staring at my chest now, all pretence gone. One of them called from France.

I straightened in surprise, pulled away. Are you sure? I said.

Yes, from Paris.

He reached up again. This time, I did not move away. My mind was spinning. He sighed, undid the top button of my dress, then the next. Cold seized me, despite the heat. I pushed him away. As I did, the button he was manipulating came away, tearing the fabric of my dress.

What was his name? I said, holding him at arm's length. Was this fool lying about everything – making up these calls to lure me in? Perhaps there had been no calls.

He did not say, the Kemetic breathed. He reached for my dress. I will tell you everything. Please. Lower your arm. For just a moment.

I let my hand fall into my lap. He slid my dress from my shoulders, breathed something I could not understand. He reached up and touched the underside of my bra, ran his fingers across the silk. Heat poured from his body. His arousal was clear and substantial.

Beautiful, he whispered. The most beautiful of the gods' creations.

Before he could go further I grabbed his hand and turned it into the beginnings of a wristlock. Jiujitsu was compulsory in the Directorate, and even though I barely passed the course, a few techniques have stayed with me. But I have learned, as I have gained experience of life, and of myself, that Allah did not put me here to cause pain, but to deliver those less fortunate from it.

His wrist was thick, his forearm big, and I had to use all my strength to get the lock to come on. He looked up at me in surprise – that something he considered so beautiful and delicate could wield such power, perhaps. Or perhaps it was just the pain he was starting to feel.

Tell me, I said, continuing to apply as much pressure as I could.

The Kemetic gasped. He said to tell you that you should call him immediately. That he had news.

I released his hand. He rubbed the wrist.

Did he leave a name? I said, hoping that the pain he was feeling might act as a warning. A telephone number perhaps?

No. Only this. A friend. No name. From Paris. He said you would know.

And the others? I asked, beginning to doubt everything he said. The first call could have been from my friend from the Directorate, but how would he have obtained the Kemetic's number? And besides, I had stated clearly that I would contact him. We were trained never to break protocol. No. It could not be him. The Kemetic knew I was from France. Paris would be a good guess. He was playing with me, keeping me interested so he could indulge his lecherous fantasies.

Amenhotep looked down at my chest. Please, he said. I have told you. Now you must allow me.

I let go of his hand and pulled my dress back up over my shoulders. No, I snapped. You are fabricating all of this, I said. There have been no calls.

Please, he said again, as if shocked that I would accuse him of such a thing. It is the truth. We are allies. We fight a common enemy.

Convince me, I said.

He glanced at my chest, pure lust pouring from him. One of the others, he gave a name. It is a name I do not know. A strange name.

What was it? Tell me.

Nteclom. Yes. Nteclom.

His pronunciation so mangled the name that at first I did not recognise it. Declan? I said, at last, my voice giving away my excitement. Was it Delcan?

He nodded, reached his hand again towards my breasts.

I sighed, reached behind my back, unclasped my bra, let it fall away. He stared at my breasts for a long time, as if wanting to prolong the moment.

He whispered something I could not understand and raised his hand.

I sat, allowed him his pleasure. He squeezed and caressed both of my breasts, and I sat, shamefully passive, my hands at my sides. I felt no pleasure. Only sadness, and a strange sense of pity for us both.

After a short time, I moved away, broke his rapture. Declan, I said. What did he say? Tell me now.

I shall, I shall, he said, standing. Come with me, he offered me his hand.

I stood and made to pull my dress back up over my shoulders.

No, he said. Leave it, please.

I covered myself up.

I have written it down, he said. It was a long message. With an address. For you to meet him. He pointed towards the bedroom. In there.

Of course I knew what this meant. The bedroom. The consummation of our arrangement. If I wanted to know what was in the message, I would have to give myself. I suppose, upon reflection, that I could have tried to overpower him. He was much bigger than I, easily twice my weight, and much taller, much stronger. I know some techniques, but I have not practised them for a long time and the difference in size and strength would have made my chances of success low. I decided instead to lure him in, and if needed, dissipate him with my hand, or as a last resort, my mouth.

Please, do not be shocked, Claymore.

He stood aside, let me enter the bedroom. I turned and faced him, the bed behind me. He closed the door and stood staring at me, breathing hard.

The message, I said. The address. Tell me and I will do anything you want.

His eyes widened and gleamed. He will meet you tomorrow at noon, here in Cairo. At Groppi's on Talaat Harb square. As he said it, he stepped close, enveloped me in his arms and pushed me to the bed.

I had not expected him to move so quickly. I struggled, but he pinned my arms over my head with one of his big hands and started pulling up my dress with the other. He was very strong. I thrashed my legs, searching for his groin with my knee, but he was too heavy. His weight crushed the air from my lungs. He ripped away my underpants, began positioning himself for entry. I screamed, lashed out with my head and caught him a glancing blow to the chin, which hurt me more than it did him.

Please, he whispered. Do not fight. This small thing, he kept repeating. This small thing. I gave you the message. We can be friends. All the time like this, talking as he placed himself against me and began his violation.

It was then that I stopped struggling. I let the tension go from my body, opened myself for him, lay back, closed my eyes.

Good, he breathed. Good, yes. He was very big.

He released my hands, reached for my breasts.

As soon as he did, I reached my right hand inside my dress and pulled my blade from its sheath around my waist. And then I did something I have never done before, in all my years.

This was a few hours ago. My hand shakes as I write this. Already I know the horror that you have lived with for more than a decade. For no matter the justification, taking another's life remains the most heinous of sins. I am twice debased, and for these transgressions, I shall never be forgiven.

I curse myself. I curse life. All is sin. And evil is everywhere

In a few short hours I will see you again.

But how can I face you now, my love?

Always So Much To Lose

After crossing the bridge to the western bank of Zamalek, Clay slipped down the embankment into the narrow strip of vegetation that grew along the water's edge. He moved along the packed silt, through little makeshift gardens and riots of untended bougainvillea and papyrus, the streets above suddenly quietened. Here the Nile was as it had always been, and he could see the lights from the opposite bank breaking apart on the water's surface, rupturing through the dark leaves and hanging vines. He found a place under the cocooning branches of a young sycamore where the ground was dry, halfway between the embankment wall and the water. He dropped his pack, sat, leaned back against the tree's trunk, closed his eyes and let the sounds of the river and the city flow over him.

He'd scared off whoever had been trailing him on the corniche. Had it been a policeman, following him from the murdered man's building? Had it been a local resident, perhaps, a nosy individual who'd seen him on the roof or leaving by the back stairs and decided to follow him, be a hero? Whoever it was, he was inexpert, and sufficiently unsure to run when challenged. Just one more variable, among so many, that Clay could neither control nor define. All he could do was keep going.

He pulled the dead man's camera from his pocket, switched it on and started scrolling through the photographs. More than three dozen of Rania in that bathroom in various states of undress. Despite himself, Clay could feel his heart accelerate, the blood pump through his extremities. That old ache beset him, would not leave. He took a deep breath, shook his head and kept moving through the images.

There were a few of her fully clothed, back turned to the lens, gazing into the mirror. From the angle the photo was taken, her face was partly visible on the mirror's surface. Clay zoomed in, stared at the image.

Tears glisten on her cheeks. Her eyes are puffy and red. Her jaw, so delicate, is set hard. Her eyes are dark. There is sadness there. And there is menace.

He scrolled further back. Faces he did not recognise, men in turbans and long beards, a few of the sun at various stages of setting behind the pyramids, photos of the inside of an apartment, more faces, the usual crap people took. He kept flicking. And then, date-stamped March of that year, a series of very different photographs: wire-enclosed industrial compounds and factories with smokestacks belching dark clouds into the sky, armed guards hovering over heavy vehicles, and, where the memory ended, a last photograph of three men and a woman standing outside a public building of some sort. There was a sign displaying Arabic characters on the building. One of the men was quite young – Egyptian, handsome, dressed in a dark suit and tie. The other was slightly older, early forties perhaps. His skin was pale, sallow. There were dark stains under his eyes as if he had been working eighteen-hour days for a month, under stress. He too was well dressed, with a clean, white, open-necked shirt and dark suit. The woman's face was partially veiled and she was looking away, as if she did not want to be photographed. The third man was dressed in a long white robe.

It was the dead man in the flat.

Clay turned off the camera, replaced it in his pocket and closed his eyes. Fatigue pushed up against him, tried to force its way inside. A deep emptiness flooded him, poured through the cracks in his defences. And despite the flickering imagery pulsing in his head – faces and breasts and bloody bedsheets – he felt himself slipping away onto that dark voyage, the foretaste of death.

☾

When he awoke, dawn was just a promise on the eastern horizon. The city was quiet. Clay clambered back up onto the corniche and started towards the Zamalek Sporting Club. He knew what he had to do. Whatever had happened after the dead man had taken the photographs of Rania, Clay had to assume that he had already passed on the message and that she would do her best to make her way to the specified rendezvous at Talaat Harb Square at noon. And if she wasn't there today, then she would be tomorrow. And if not then, he would try the day after. As long as it took. And between now and then, he needed to decipher the contents of the dead man's journal and the Arabic signs in the photographs.

Whoever the dead man was, he had been close enough to Rania that she had trusted him, at least partially. And in that journal and those photographs there had to be something he could use. He had money, he could pay someone to translate it. Find a student at the university. Anyone. But there was no way he could share any of this with a stranger. He needed a friend. Someone on whom he could depend.

Atef's flat was a few blocks from the Sporting Club, the home of the big Egyptian's beloved Zamalek White Knights football team. He lived in one of the big, old, crumbling Cairo apartment blocks that dotted the city like anthills. He and Atef had become friends while working together in Yemen – Clay as an engineer, Atef as cook and manager of the oil company guesthouse in Aden. Clay had come to Cairo a few times back then, when they'd both been off rotation, and they'd spent some time together, walking along the Nile, taking in a couple of practice sessions and even a match. It had been almost three years since Clay had seen him last. At the time, fleeing into the Aden night, with no one else to go to, he'd entrusted Atef with the documents that eventually allowed Rania to expose the Medveds' corrupt and murderous oil operations in Yemen. Three years that seemed to fill the space of thirty.

Clay stood in the dark of the corridor and raised his hand to knock on the heavy wooden door. The smell of baking filled the air. Friends. He didn't have many. Most of the best ones he'd had were dead. His fist hovered an inch from the surface of the door. For days now he'd fought against this. Was this what friends did? Expose each other to danger? Pull each other into decaying orbits of death, spirals of loss? In his experience, the answer was yes. Definitely, yes. Who else could you call on when the shit was definitely and comprehensively flying? It was, after all, the only test of the thing.

He knocked, waited.

After a moment, the door opened. Atef stood before him, a little stouter, the same big, open face peering out at him, half a smile edged as always on that generous mouth.

Atef tilted his head to one side. 'Do I know you, sir?' he said, the Cairo thick in his Arabic. 'It is very early.'

Clay unwound his turban, put out his right hand. 'Atef, it's me,' he said in the man's own language. 'Clay Straker.'

Atef took a step closer and gazed into Clay's eyes. A big smile opened up across his face, big ivory teeth everywhere. 'Mr Clay,' he began, taking Clay's hand and pulling him inside.

'Just Clay. Please, Atef.'

Atef smiled. It was a conversation they'd had many times before. 'Mr Clay is better,' he said. And then his expression changed. 'I thought…' he stumbled, went quiet a moment. 'Allah be praised. You are alive.'

Clay smiled. '*Al hamdillulah*,' he said. '*Ja*, no, definitely.'

Atef showed him into the flat, sat him in the kitchen and started heating water. 'I have fresh croissants in the oven now. They should be ready in a few minutes. Would you like coffee?'

Clay sat. '*Mumtaz*,' he said. Excellent.

Atef busied himself around the kitchen then started kneading some dough. 'The newspapers said you died in Yemen,' he said at last in a half-whisper, without looking up. 'Three years ago. 1994.'

Clay nodded.

'And then, after the stories about Medved in the newspapers, the company was closed down. We were all sent home.'

'I'm sorry,' said Clay.

'It was a bad operation,' said Atef. 'I knew this.' He handed Clay a steaming cup of coffee. 'Did you get the things I posted to Cyprus, as you had asked?'

'I did. Thank you Atef. Without you, we would never have been able to stop Medved. People were dying out there.'

Atef kept kneading. 'We knew something was wrong,' he said, his voice lowered again. 'Many of us did. But we did nothing. We wanted our jobs. They paid well.'

Clay sipped his coffee. He had learned, late, not to judge.

'Whenever I have thought about those days, thinking you were dead, I felt shame,' he said. 'We knew it was wrong. But we did nothing.' He bowed his head.

'No, Atef. You did something. Thank you.'

After a time, Atef pulled the croissants from the oven, put two on a plate and handed them to Clay, glancing at his stump. 'How did this happen, Mr Clay?'

'In Yemen. They didn't kill me, but they took this.'

Atef nodded. 'It is honourable.'

Clay ate, deciding not to contemplate this. Not here, not now. After he'd finished the croissants and drained his coffee he said: 'I need your help again, Atef.'

Atef nodded, walked across the room and closed a door. 'My wife and son are still asleep,' he said, sitting across from Clay.

'What is the Consortium, Atef?'

Atef shifted in his chair, glancing back towards the door. He leaned across the table, arms folded. 'Please do not tell me that you have made such an enemy, Mr Clay.'

'I can leave now, if you wish, Atef. It will not change our friendship.'

Atef ran his hand over his face, leaving a smear of flour on his cheeks. 'My family,' he said.

'I understand.' Clay stood. 'Thanks for the coffee, Atef. It's been good to see you again.'

Atef stood and reached out his hand. 'Wait,' he said. 'Please, sit.'

'It's alright, Atef. I shouldn't have come.' Clay started for the door.

Atef followed him, wiping his hands across his apron. 'Please, Mr Clay. This is not what I meant. Please, stay.'

Clay stopped, turned to face his friend.

'Sit. Finish your breakfast.'

Clay sat. There was always so much to lose.

'This is why you are dressed as an Upper Egyptian,' said Atef. 'It is a time like before, is it not?'

'It is.'

'It is very important?'

'My friend is in danger.'

'From the Consortium?'

'I think so, yes.'

Atef stood, walked to the kitchen, returned with the coffee pot, poured out two cups, added sugar. 'Everyone is in danger,' he said.

'I don't understand.'

'The Consortium is a group of very powerful and wealthy men. They control most of the government, most of our big industries, much of the police. They run this country. Those who threaten their control always lose.'

Clay let this trace across his nerve endings. Rania had always known how to pick her enemies. 'Jesus Christ,' he muttered.

'Him, too, so they say.'

Clay let the beginning of a smile die. 'How far does it go?'

Atef leaned back in his chair. 'All the way.'

'To Mubarak? The president?'

'That is what people say. They are all ex-army, you see. Ever since King Farouk was deposed in 1952, it has been these men, all linked through the army, who control Egypt. The Consortium works in the shadows, but everyone knows that this is where the power lies.'

'All I need, Atef, is help translating a few things.' Clay put the camera and the journal on the table. 'My Arabic isn't good enough.'

Atef reached for the journal, flipped through the pages a moment then looked up. 'Only some of this is Arabic.'

'Yes, I know. It looks like ancient Egyptian.'

'Where did you get this?'

'It's better if you don't know.'

Atef nodded. 'Yes, of course.'

Clay turned on the camera and scrolled to the last photograph. 'What does this sign say, in the background?' He handed the camera to Atef.

'It is the central courthouse, here in Cairo. The sign says the Ministry of Internal Affairs and the Ministry of Justice.' Atef stared at the image. 'I know one of these men. I have seen his face before.'

'Which one?'

'The young one in the suit and tie. He was in the news, a year ago or so. Something about a study funded by the Canadian government. He is a scientist, I believe.' Atef handed the camera back to Clay.

'Are you sure?'

'I think so. I have a good memory for faces.'

'What's his name?'

'Names not so much. I am sorry.'

Clay scrolled further back, to the images of the industrial facilities. 'And these?' he said. 'Are any of them familiar?'

Atef flicked through the images, stopping occasionally to study them more closely. 'Some of these places are here in Cairo. Some are very close, just upriver. Some north of here. One of the signs says Fabrika el Hamra Company, with an address in the Hadayek-el Koba district.'

'Do you know what they make there?'

Atef put the camera on the table. 'I have not heard of this place. I do not know.'

Clay looked at his watch. Already nine-thirty. 'Thank you, my friend. I need to go now.' He pocketed the camera, tapped his finger on the journal. 'Can I leave this with you to have a look at?'

Atef nodded, looking at the leather-bound journal as if it had teeth. 'I will do what I can.'

Clay stood. 'I will be back later this evening.'

'Do you have a place to stay, Mr Clay?'

'I'll take a room in a hotel.'

'It is not safe. The Consortium owns many of the hotels. You must stay with us. We have an extra room. It is a big flat.'

Clay nodded, thanking his friend formally.

☾

Half an hour later Clay was making his way through Tahir Square, dodging cars and motorcycles across the crazed turmoil that passed as a roundabout. Soon he was approaching Talaat Harb Square. He bent over his stick, lowered his head and shuffled along the crowded, late-morning pavement. Up ahead, he could see the statue of Talaat Pasha Harb surrounded by traffic, hounded by blaring horns and gassed with exhaust. When he reached the Egypt Air office he stopped. A group of European tourists passed him, making their way towards the square. From here he had a relatively clear view of Groppi's once-grand façade and the few tables and chairs spread café style on the street before the big glass windows. A few patrons sat sipping coffee, indulging in the celebrated chocolates.

As midday neared the streets began to fill. Soon the pavements were choked with people, and he could no longer see the front of the café. Clay pushed his way closer to the square, sliding along with a group of Western tourists. By the time he reached the street lights it was almost noon. He'd been watching the pavement outside Groppi's continuously, but so far had seen no one who looked remotely like Rania. She was trained though. He'd seen her evade pursuers before – change her hair, her clothes, transform herself into a wholly different person. So what exactly he was looking for now, he didn't know. He just had to hope that she would be looking for him.

By the time he'd installed himself within the notched entranceway to one of the big, old buildings that faced the café across the square, it was a few minutes after noon. Groppi's was filling up. Customers milled in front of the counters inside, and all the outside tables were now occupied. A couple of older gentlemen, portly Egyptian businessmen in suits and open collared shirts, sipped tea. A woman in a grey coverup and brown headscarf sat haranguing a young woman in jeans – her daughter perhaps. The girl's dark hair was uncovered and spilled over her shoulders and her expensively embroidered jacket. She bowed her head, covered her face with her hands. Inside the shop, a group of young men in rip-off jeans and t-shirts passed around paper cups; matrons in flowing hijabs reached across the counter for boxes of sweets tied with string; white-uniformed attendants moved between tables. A woman entered through the shop's side door and disappeared in the crowd of patrons. A moment later she re-emerged, made her way to the front of the café and stood just inside the front window, like a mannequin on display – a solitary figure shrouded in black, her face veiled.

Clay's pulse jumped. The woman was gazing out into the square. Clay took a step forwards, emerging into the sunshine. She was looking right at him across the swirling traffic. He started walking towards the café. She was right there, looking in his direction. Surely she'd seen him. Yes, she was still looking. He saw her glance left, then catch his gaze again. She tapped her left wrist with her right index finger, very deliberately, then opened up two fingers, held them there against her chest for a second, less, then brought up her left palm and opened it up against her right, her thumbs extended and meeting, her fingertips touching. He was almost at the streetlights now, the traffic flooding past, the walk light still red. He glanced right, looking for an opening. When he looked back at the café, she was gone.

Clay jumped into the traffic. A car screamed by, horn blaring. Its wing mirror clipped his hip, folded back, the driver's curses lost in the cacophony as soon as they were uttered. He pushed open the front door of the café and scanned the interior. Faces stared up at him, none of them her. He looked at his watch. Ten past twelve. It had been her. It must have been.

He pushed his way through to the back of the café, out the side door she'd come in through and looked back towards the square, down the side street. If it was her, she'd vanished. She had looked right at him, he at her. Surely she'd recognised him, even dressed as he was. It had to have been her. Who else could it have been? Why had she run? Something, or someone, must have spooked her.

Clay started down the side street, taking a guess that she would move away from the square, move off into the narrow warren of dark lanes that spread north and west between here and the river. It was more an impulse than any hope of finding her that drove him. He knew from experience that if she wanted to disappear, she would.

Traffic fumed past, clogged the narrow street. Clay came to the first intersection. A narrow lane tunnelled through the buildings in the direction of the river. As he rounded the corner he was jostled from behind. Two men pushed past him, then sprinted down the lane. One was tall and lanky, the other stout with thinning hair. Clay followed, doubling his pace and watched the pair stop at the next cross street. They looked both ways, hands on hips. The broad one reached into his pocket and, producing a mobile phone, put it to his ear. The tall one lit a cigarette, offered one to his partner.

Clay tucked himself behind a parked van and watched the men talking. One pointed down the lane and the other replied, indicating the left. After a time, the broad one flicked away his cigarette and they continued down the alley, walking now. Clay watched them go, dread bubbling up inside him. Whoever was after Rania, they were closing in. And in trying to make contact with him, she was exposing herself to a degree she would normally never allow.

His admiration for this woman, already finely developed, surged. Admiration was, he thought, a poor word for it. It was that, yes, but it was much more. And he knew, standing at that street corner, staring out into the blur of the city, that however long he might live, he would never be able to describe it, to himself or others. He could feel it now, a physical ache that had taken root inside him three years ago, housed within whatever fucked-up consciousness he still maintained. But to qualify it, to attribute it to any specific emotion, was impossible. And in this realisation, he knew, was the beginning of something. Maybe. Just maybe. If he had the time.

11th November 1997. Cairo, Egypt. 21:15 hrs

Samira went to the clinic late this afternoon to see her daughter. She left the little one with me and returned with Eleana not long after. All she has done since returning is weep. Every time I try to speak to her she breaks into tears. I can only conclude that the stress of the last few days, of seeing her daughter so ill, has affected her deeply. And yet I know we will be friends for as long as we live. There is no bond greater than that of shared suffering. I feel as if we are somehow sisters now, and I aunt to her daughters, but I miss my own son more than I can express in words. The tears falling onto this paper will have to suffice.

I saw you today, Claymore! Praise God!

You were dressed as a local and your beard has grown long, but it was you. I would recognise those shoulders, that tilt of the head, those eyes, among thousands, millions … all who ever lived. And from the way you emerged from that building and started across the street, I know you recognised me. Please, God, make it thus.

God help me, standing there looking at you, I could so easily have run to you and thrown myself into your embrace. I could have abandoned myself utterly. But I had to remain strong. You were being watched. It was a white man, poorly dressed, ragged and pale, with a ravaged, diseased face. When I saw him I shivered, despite the heat. He followed you all the way along Talaat Harb Street from as far as the metro station at Tahir Square, and I am sure you were not aware of it – you were never good at knowing when you were being followed. I think it is because you are always too intent on wherever you are going, too focused on what you are doing.

When I saw the man there, lurking in the doorway one down from where you were standing, I knew I had to leave. You are in danger. When I spoke to Hope last, she made that very clear. I saw no sign of Jean-Marie, though. God, most merciful, protect you both.

I must tell Samira, tonight, that I am leaving. The longer I stay, the more I expose her and her children to danger. This must be the last night I spend here. It is past time to move on. But I need her help, one last time. I wish it were not so, that I did not have to involve her, but there is no one else I can trust. And please, God, it is not that she now owes me a debt. In my heart, there is no debt whatsoever. I pray that when I ask her, she does not think this of me, that I have coerced her somehow. God help me, my guilt is swallowing me. I know I should leave now and not wait until tomorrow, but I am weak. Without her help, I will not be able to find you, Claymore, not without exposing you to your enemies, and me to mine. Perhaps I should accept my fate and go to you openly. At least we will be together, whatever happens.

But you will want to run. I know you. You will want to take me away from here, protect me. I am not leaving. Not until I know what happened here. If it means facing trial for murder, I am ready. I will plead guilty. But not before I prove my innocence in the killings of my beloved son and husband. I will learn the truth. This is all that matters to me now, all I have. The truth.

I am a murderer. I can feel this truth *eroding me into nothingness, like sand from the beach in Brittany we used to visit in summer when I was very young. I remember two big rocks the colour of honey, a swath of chamomile sand protected from the wind and waves, the sea so blue and the water lapping my legs, and my father, God rest his soul, digging in the sand with me in the sunlight. We built a wonderful castle. There was a moat and three smooth-sided towers we made by filling my little plastic bucket with sand and tipping it over. I put gull feathers atop the towers for flags. And then the tide came in. I held my father's hand and cried as the castle was washed away. It is an old memory.*

They are watching me. They were there today, at the square. The two policemen from Ma'adi – Moonface and the tall one. I am certain they did not follow me there. But when I arrived, there they were, waiting, in the shop across the street, pretending to be customers. Somehow they knew about the rendezvous, the time and place.

I can only suspect that foul Kemetic, may Allah forgive his soul. He was the only one besides you, Claymore, who knew we were to meet. And yet, if anything he said can be believed, there was a third man calling for me. Who could he have been?

This afternoon, after leaving the square and having made very sure that no one could possibly have followed me, I went to the telephone and telegraph office in Ma'adi, and I called my friend in Paris. It might have been him, although I cannot understand how he might have obtained the Kemetic's number. He was not in, and I did not leave a message.

Tomorrow, I will try again.

I hope you understood my signal. I must do it in a different way next time. And then, perhaps, afterwards, I can repay all those who I must put in danger, and perhaps God can find it in his wisdom to forgive me for what I have done, and for what I must do.

Symbiosis

Clay wandered the city until night fell then backtracked along the Nile, took the metro a few stops and wandered towards Zamalek.

Time was running out. He had to find Rania and get her away – out of Cairo, out of Egypt. Whatever had happened that afternoon at the square, he was now sure that the men following her were cops. They had that look, that air. Her signal back at the square was clear now. For he was now sure it had been a signal: Two o'clock, at the pyramids, Giza. It was a big place, teeming with tourists. They would be far less conspicuous there than on a Cairo street corner.

Clay had just reached the western abutment of the 26th July Bridge, and had stopped to check the traffic before crossing to the downstream side of the bridge, when he saw him. And this time, he had no doubt. It was the same figure – the one who had followed him the day before on the corniche. The man was standing in the darkness between streetlights, bracketed by a couple of parked cars. He was wearing a baseball cap and talking into a mobile phone. His face was obscured.

Clay reversed direction, and before the man had a chance to look up, he vaulted the bridge railing and landed on the embankment slope. Out of view, he moved beneath the bridge and picked his way across the rocks piled up around the abutment, emerging into the dense foliage on the upstream side. Half a dozen feluccas were tied up along the bank, and further along the dark shape of what was once a tourist barge floated beam to shore, boarded up and derelict. Clay moved along the embankment wall until he came to a place where the masonry had crumbled away. Big sycamores sent shadows scattering through the yellow streetlight. He climbed towards the street, stopping just below the lip. The man was still there, still on the phone, but looking out across the street now, towards where Clay had been, swivelling his head left and right.

From where Clay crouched, still in shadow, he could hear the man's voice, the low murmur, but the words were lost. The man was close, a few strides away, his back turned.

Clay palmed the G21, checked the action. This was going to end here.

He emerged into the light, pushed into fractured shadow. The man was still looking away. He was right there. Clay closed, jabbed the G21 into the man's kidneys.

'Move and you die,' Clay said. 'Painfully.'

The man jumped, then froze. 'Okay,' he hissed. 'Shit.'

Clay took two steps back and disengaged. 'Turn around.'

The man complied, raising his hands in front of his chest as if to protect himself.

If Clay had had any doubt about the connection between whatever Rania was mixed up in and the AB's move to eliminate Crowbar – and, by association, him – it was gone in that instant. The man standing before him was Crowbar's contact from Kenya, the one who'd procured the Cessna for them; the Rhodesian Crowbar had only ever referred to as G.

'Give me the phone,' said Clay.

G held it out.

'Drop it.'

The phone clattered to the asphalt.

Clay crushed it under his boot.

'What are you doing here?'

'Take it easy, man.'

'Decided to take on Manheim's contract?' Clay said. 'Well he's dead.'

If anything, G looked even more malarial than when Clay had seen him in Mombasa. Sweat filmed his face, shone yellow in the lamplight. 'You can't kill the AB, man.'

'You here to kill me?'

'No. I swear.' G opened his arms wide. 'I don't work for the AB, man. Check. I ain't carrying. *Zut*, man. Nothing. If I was trying to kill you, don't you think I'd be packing a slayer?'

Clay had already scanned G's person for obvious signs of concealed weapons and had seen none. 'Why, then?'

'Looking for Crowbar. Need to talk to him, china.'

'Bullshit.'

'It's the truth, man.'

'Why not just ask me, then?'

G looked both ways. 'Fucking AB, man.'

'Make sense, G. And do it fast. You're running out of time, *broer*.'

'They're everywhere, man. Gotta be careful. They see me talking to you, like now…' G trailed off, glanced back towards the bridge. 'I was going to approach you yesterday, on the street. Was about to. But fuck, the way you came at me. Shit. I was scared, man. What people say about you.'

Clay pushed down a pang. 'How did you know I was here?'

'That place in Mombasa you made a call from. Got a friend to listen in. Called that number your woman gave you myself. Too easy.' G smiled, proud of himself.

Clay shook his head. *Too easy*.

'Figured sooner or later you'd show up there. I followed you from the guy's flat. The one you slayed.'

'I didn't kill him,' said Clay. 'He was dead when I got there.'

G smiled, nodded. 'Sure, man.'

'Asshole,' barked Clay. 'You took it on, didn't you?' Clay stepped back, tightened his finger on the trigger. 'Why else would you be here?'

G shrank back, trying to make himself small. 'Sure, man. I thought about it. The AB is offering a lot of money, especially now.'

'Now?'

'After what you and Crowbar did in Sudan.' G wiped the sweat from his forehead with the back of hand. 'But like I said, man. That's not why I'm here. I don't work for those assholes. And killing…' He looked down at Clay's weapon. 'Not my thing, man.'

'So why are you here?'

'Like I said, I need to talk to Crowbar. Got something to tell him.'

'Tell me.'

'I'd rather…'

Clay jabbed the gun into G's side.

'Easy, man. Easy. Okay.' G paused, breathed. 'There was a break-in at the company's office in Luanda, two days ago. They took files, hard drives, everything. Crowbar's business partner was killed.'

'Jesus.'

'I came to warn him. The AB is going after everyone in the company. He needs to disappear. Fast.'

'I'll tell him.'

G took a step back, swallowing hard. 'Where is he?'

'Disappeared.' Laid him in a hole and put a rifle across his chest and pushed sand down into those empty, Kalahari-sky-blue eyes.

G glared at him.

'I'll see him in a couple of days and tell him then.'

G glanced left then right, as if he were looking for someone. 'The AB are all over this, man. Couple of days may be too late.'

'Can you get in touch with them?'

'Who?'

'The AB.'

'I have contacts, sure.'

'Then tell them you killed me. Collect the reward.' Clay dangled the lure. It was worth a try. He didn't have a lot of options. 'I'll match whatever they're offering.'

G stared at him, wide-eyed. 'You're crazy. Not possible, man.'

'I'm serious.'

G was shaking his head now, shifting his weight from one foot to the other. 'They'll want proof.'

'Like what?'

'Something convincing. Photographs. DNA.'

'They have my DNA on file?'

'I expect.'

'Christ.'

'A finger, maybe.'

'I'm running out.' Clay raised his stump.

G grinned. 'Shit, yeah, sorry man. An ear would do.'

Clay shifted, looked into G's eyes, tried to see something there. 'So, you'll do it?'

'Look, man. Crowbar and me, we're friends. Went through a lot of shit together. I know you're a friend of his too. Still, I don't know, man. I've made it a rule to stay as far away from those assholes as possible. If the AB found out I was lying, I'd be a dead man.'

A couple, arm in arm, left the bridge pavement and turned towards where Clay and G were standing in the shadows. Clay shifted the Glock into his jacket pocket, but kept it pointed at G.

After the couple had passed, he said: 'Do it. Convince them I'm dead. Consider it a favour to Crowbar.'

'And if I don't?'

Clay jabbed the G21's muzzle hard into G's side. 'Then you're just as dead, *broer*. Only a lot sooner.'

G looked down at the bulge protruding from Clay's coat and shook his head. 'Shit, man. I was trying to do you guys a favour.'

'Do yourself one.'

G shifted his weight to his left foot and hung there a moment. It was as if by putting an extra inch between himself and the Glock's muzzle he might somehow avoid the danger it posed. 'You'd have to disappear, man. I mean, really fucking vanish. No trace. Can you do that?'

'Exactly what I intend to do, *broer*.'

'I said, can you *do* it?'

'All I need is a few days.'

'And how do I know you'll pay?'

'Because it's in my interest. If I don't do this, the AB will keep hunting me. And if you don't do this, I will kill you. Think of it as symbiosis.'

G looked down the street again, back over his shoulder. 'You got that kind of *kite*?'

'Don't worry about that. Just do it.'

G rubbed his chin, convincing himself. 'Okay, man. Okay. Deal. But make it fast. The AB have business here. They're watching me. And trying to find you. You and that pretty crow of yours.'

Lights pulsed inside Clay's head, blurred the peripheries of his vision.

'The AB is looking for your journalist friend, too, Straker. Even if I help you, they'll still want her.'

Clay drove the point of the Glock hard into G's kidney. 'You let me worry about that, G. Here's the way it will work. Whoever your AB contact is, tell them you're here looking for me. In two days, three at most, I'll come to your hotel. You'll get your DNA, and a down payment in cash. Then I disappear. When I know for sure that the AB thinks I'm dead, I'll wire you the rest of the money ... *Too easy.*'

'You're not giving me much choice.'

'There's always a choice.'

G rocked back and forth a moment, as if a sudden bout of vertigo had overtaken him. 'Sure,' he whispered. 'Sure.'

'Where are you staying?'

'Ritz Carlton, on the Nile. Ask for Grayson.'

'Business is good then.'

'Always.'

Clay lowered the gun and leaned in close. 'And G. You cross me, it will be the last thing you do.'

G tightened his mouth and forced a grin.

'Now piss off. And stay out of my way.' Clay turned and disappeared back the way he'd come, leaving G standing in the darkened street.

☾

It wasn't until next morning, as he woke to the smell of rising bread and the morning light streaming through the shutters, the sounds of traffic from the street below filling the room, that he realised how close he'd come to leading G to Atef's flat. Now he regretted not having killed G when he'd had the chance. He could have dumped the body in the Nile. No one would have ever known. Would the Rhodesian have come all this way simply to warn Crowbar? He doubted it. The guy was lying, of that he was sure. But about what? G's distress had been clear, his fear palpable. And yet, despite everything, Clay wanted to believe that there was hope, that there might be a future for him and Rania. Only by convincing the AB that he was dead – that they were *both* dead – could they live free of the gnawing fear that one day, somewhere, those faceless powers would catch up with them. At this point, G was his best shot.

Clay pushed himself up, pulled on his trousers, threw on the robe Atef had given him and went into the living room.

Atef waved him over from the kitchen. 'You slept.'

Clay nodded. 'Some.'

Atef bid him sit and pushed a plate of croissants and a cup of coffee in front of him.

Clay ate, drank. After a bit, he looked up. 'I have another favour to ask, Atef.' He could already feel the guilt pushing in on him, five fathoms of cold South Atlantic standing on his chest. When this was over, he would make it right somehow, bring things into balance. When it was over. He purged it all from his mind, killed the flutterings inside him. 'I need scissors, a razor, a shirt, trousers, and a light jacket.'

Atef smiled. 'You tire of being an Upper Egyptian.' He smiled big. 'Good. It does not suit you.'

Clay flicked the corner of a smile.

'The shower is there,' he said pointing to the far side of the room. 'Everything you need is in the cupboard. Go. My brother is a tailor. His shop is just below us. I will return in a moment.'

Twenty minutes later Clay emerged from the bathroom shorn and clean-shaven, wearing the dark canvas trousers and blue shirt that Atef had handed in to him. The Glock was tucked into his waistband at the small of his back and the dark jacket hid the pistol's bulk. With his stump thrust into the left pocket of the jacket, he looked almost normal, almost whole. 'Tourist?' he said.

'Not quite,' said Atef. 'But better than before.'

A woman and a young boy, perhaps eight or nine years old, emerged from another room. Atef gathered them under his arms. 'My family, Mr Clay.'

The woman and boy looked up at him. She was stout, plain-looking, with a lovely smile. The boy looked like his father.

Clay bowed, wished them peace.

'Now, go,' Atef said to his son. 'Work hard.'

His wife and son left.

'*Mash'allah*,' said Clay.

'I am blessed,' said Atef. He poured more coffee, sat opposite Clay and put the dead man's journal on the table.

'Did you read it?'

Atef nodded. 'As much as I could. Most of the Arabic is written in shorthand so it's difficult to know what it says. Some of it I could read. Parts only.' He opened the journal, flipped over a couple of pages and pointed to a sequence of hieroglyphs. 'This, not.'

'What can you tell me?'

'It is like a diary, in order of time.' Atef leafed back to the first page. 'It starts in July of last year. Something about his friend coming to him with evidence. It mentions a plan to go to the independent press.' He flipped forwards a few pages. 'Much is religious – praise for the old gods. Then, here, some ramblings about the coming revolution.' Atef closed the book. 'It is like this, Mr Clay. Pieces of things only. I think this person was *magnoon*.' He tapped his head. 'Crazy.'

'Any names?'

'Two: Yusuf Al-Gambal. He is the young man in the photograph, the one I recognised, the scientist. The other was Hamid Al-Farouk, a Lebanese Frenchman.'

A shiver strung its way from Clay's neck to his tailbone. 'A lawyer?'

'Yes, I think so.'

'Jesus.' Rania's husband. Somehow it made perfect sense. 'That photograph, in front of the courthouse. Him?'

'I do not know. I have never seen him.'

Clay flicked on the camera, scrolled to the photograph and zoomed in on Hamid's face. Prominent nose, dark, intense eyes, a shock of dark hair, mouth set flat, serious. The woman beside him, her face partially hidden.

'Also, Mr Clay, there was another name: *Al Assad.* The Lion. It is mentioned several times.'

'The Lion?'

'He is the leader of Al-Gama'a al Islamiyya, an Egyptian Islamist group. He has been in the news many times in the last weeks. They say he is fighting for the people, against the control of the Consortium. They have exploded bombs in Alexandria and also here in Cairo. So far no foreigners have been hurt, but this may change. The government calls them terrorists.'

'Was there anything else, Atef, about the court case?'

'I am sorry, Mr Clay. Too much of it I could not read. Perhaps someone who knows the old language.'

'Do you know anyone?'

'I can try.'

'Please, Atef. Try. It is important.' Clay reached into his waist belt, pulled out Crowbar's Jericho and placed the pistol on the table. 'I want you to have this.'

Atef's eyes widened. 'It is so bad?'

'Not yet, Atef. But if…'

Atef picked up the gun. '*Maafi mushkilla,*' he said. No problem. 'I understand.'

Clay stood. 'I have to go now. I will be back, *inshallah*, tonight.'

Atef thrust the gun into his pocket. 'God willing,' he said.

The Impermanence of Life

It was a big place.

Clay arrived early, stood in line with the other tourists and bought his ticket. It was the first time since arriving in Egypt that he hadn't felt conspicuous. The place teemed with Europeans, hundreds of them. A dozen languages collided, overlapped, cancelled. Not far away in the queue there were even a few Dutch guys – taller and fairer than he was. If indeed this was what Rania had meant when she'd made that half-second triangle with her two hands clasped close to her chest then it was a good choice.

Clay stood in the crowd, looking out across the sand and rubble towards the Sphinx, and beyond, the great pyramid of Cheops, and the smaller Chepren and Menkaure structures. He'd been here before, a couple of times, sat and marvelled at the dedication to the infinite embodied in these piles of rock. And yet everything he'd learned before and since only reinforced the complete impermanence of life. And now all of this was mere background. Less – irrelevance.

He searched the crowd. Would she come? Was this the place? And if it was, how would he find her? It was just gone one o'clock. The ramp to Cheops was crowded with sweating, harried, slow-moving tourists. Clay pulled his cap lower over his eyes and edged his way through the bodies. If she meant for him to meet her here, then he would go to the most obvious place – the biggest monument ever built to time and certainty in life after death.

Clay tracked along the side of the structure towards the south-west corner. He clambered up to the first tier of blocks. From here he could see back to the main entrance and across to the north-eastern side of Chepren. He looked out across the milling, camera-laden throng, and beyond to the encroaching blur of the city. Smoke drifted up from the streets, mingled with the exhaust of twenty million cars. Time passed. Clay sat, dangled his legs from the edge of the block and watched the crowd, looking for any sign of Rania, veiled or not.

At five minutes to two, a young woman with long black hair emerged from the main ticket barrier. She was wearing a summer dress that covered her knees but left her calves bare, a white cardigan thrown over her shoulders. At that distance, he could not make out her face. But there was something about the way she held herself, her build. His pulse jumped, hammered. It was her.

But then she stopped, turned back towards the barrier, held out her hands. Two young girls emerged from the doors, went to her and took her hands. They stood a moment like that, together, near the barrier. Clay watched as the woman engaged one of the white-uni-formed tourist police in conversation. Clay exhaled, calmed himself, closed his eyes, let it go. He could have sworn, just for a moment. Jesus Christ.

When he looked again, the woman and her daughters were gone, absorbed into the crowd. By twenty minutes after what he had assumed to be the appointed time, he decided to move. If she was here, she would have seen him by now. He jumped to the ground and rounded the south-west corner of the pyramid to the quieter, western side. A swath of green edged into view – the Oberoi golf course and the gardens of the Marriott hotel, stark against the sand monochrome of desert and city.

A veiled woman was standing up against the base of the structure, about a quarter of the way along from the corner. Her black burqa was patched with dust.

She looked at him, held his gaze.

Clay stood, transfixed. The woman reached into the folds of her robe, withdrew her hand, moved close to the stone so that she stood facing the big limestone blocks. Then she pushed something into a gap between them. Clay watched as she glanced up at him again, held his gaze for a moment, then turned and hurried off, moving north, away from the main entrance.

Clay sprinted across the sand until he came to the place where the woman had been standing. Wedged into a gap between two blocks was a paper coffee cup, crushed and stained. He reached in, pulled it out and opened it up. Inside was a folded piece of card. On it, someone had written, in plain block letters:

GARBAGE CITY. TONIGHT. COPTIC CHURCH IN THE CAVE. EVENING SERVICE. R.

Clay looked up. The woman was gone. He tightened the note in his fist and sprinted towards Cheops' north-western corner. Jesus, it was her. Again, so close. Right there. Materialising and then vanishing again like a dream, half reverie, half nightmare. His heart hammered. His legs felt like spongewood. He came to the corner, and looked out across the open ground. There she was. About a hundred metres away, hurrying towards the hotel green. But something was wrong. She stumbled, fell to the ground, picked herself up, kept going.

Clay started after her. He'd only managed five paces when two men appeared, moving across the open ground at pace, closing from the right. One was short, overweight, the other taller. The men he'd seen in the alley the day before, after Rania had disappeared. Cops. They called out. She stopped, looked in their direction a moment then kept going. They were closing on her fast, had almost reached her now. Clay pulled out the Glock, chambered a round. Rania stumbled again, tried to regain her balance, crashed to the ground. The cops were on her, pulling her to her feet. Clay raised his weapon, took aim. He was too far away, and he knew it.

Clay replaced the Glock in his waistband, moved back to the corner block of the Pyramid and watched the men lead Rania away. Plans started forming in his mind – counterattacks, improvisations many and varied. Free her, somehow. Get her back. He needed to follow. They were still too close. There was still too much open ground between them. He readied himself. Then the men stopped, as if suddenly they had realised something. Clay could see them look at each other and then at Rania. The tall one reached out and grabbed her headdress, yanking her head. She stumbled then righted herself. Clay took a step forwards, checked himself, anger pulsing inside him. The tall man pulled at Rania's headdress again. Her black veil fell to the ground. The men stood staring at her.

Clay snatched a breath. At first, he wasn't sure. It was a long way away. But no, the hair was wrong, thin and threaded through with lighter tones. A disguise? The face was round, not angular, and broader than it should be, the nose far more prominent, the lips slacker, without that distinctive arc and curve. Whoever the men had apprehended, it wasn't Rania.

12th November 1997. Cairo, Egypt. 18:30 hrs

We sit, the three of us, in the slowly filling amphitheatre of the appointed place. The evening service begins in an hour. The girls, so pretty in the new dresses we bought together this morning, sit quietly beside me, unsure about being in a Christian place of worship. I have told them that we will meet their mother here soon.

Eleana is so much better now than she was. She asked me just now if Christians believe Jesus is God. I explained to her that they believe he was the son of God, sent to spread God's message of love and peace. She asked me if this was true.

Dear God, what is the truth – about anything? I feel so adrift, so unsure. It is as if my life has lost all reference, and that all the ideas and beliefs that anchored me are eroding away like sand in the tide.

I looked into her eyes. So innocent still, despite everything she has endured. So trusting. In Islam, I said to her, we recognise Jesus as one of the most important of the Prophets of God. But we believe that he was a man like any other, not the son of God.

And then the inevitable question: but we and the Christians, is it the same God we worship?

Yes, I said. Of course it is.

Eleana smiled. She does not do it often, but she has a lovely smile. I like this, she said.

And to this God of ours, as I sit here and watch the Copts slowly trickle into this amazing place – an entire cathedral built into a cave in the Moqattam cliffs – I must entrust myself.

Today, just a few hours ago, I watched my friend, the mother of these two beautiful girls, risk herself for me. And then saw her taken away by the police. There was nothing I could do.

That is what I tell myself, but it is not true. At first she begged me not to go. She seemed convinced that something bad would happen. But once I had explained to her the reason I was here in Cairo, what had happened yesterday – I told her the truth – and that I had to go, she desisted. It was she who suggested that we switch places. In fact, she insisted. It seemed a good plan, and the chances that anyone could possibly have known about the rendezvous seemed so remote, I acquiesced. I flashed that signal to Claymore almost instinctively, once I knew that we were both being watched. It was not premeditated, and I did not tell anyone about it after.

Samira and I agreed that the girls and I would dress as tourists, and she would go ahead and seek out Claymore, dressed in my burqa. If, after making contact, everything seemed safe, I would come to them, and Samira would take the girls and leave. If there was a suggestion that we were being watched, she would get him a message to meet me here, then leave quickly. I should never have agreed to it.

Allah, most merciful, please protect my friend Samira.

I sit here and I realise that I have abandoned myself. If Samira tells the police we are meeting here, I am done. There is nowhere else to run. But what would become of these little girls?

Surely Samira will be able to claim innocence. I should have rehearsed it with her, as a contingency. I have forgotten my training. But I simply did not believe that anyone could possibly have known. I was sure we were not followed. Very soon after I arrived with the girls, I saw you there, Claymore. You were standing near the pyramid. You were alone. I saw no sign of the man who was following you yesterday – the pale, sickly one. I signalled to Samira and she started towards you. Then I saw them, the two policemen. I tried to signal to Samira, but by then she was too far away, lost in the crowd. There is no use pondering it, now. It is my fault, my failure. I pray that she is released unharmed. There is nothing left to do but wait and hope.

The service is about to begin. The place is almost full. I have watched each person enter the cathedral. Claymore, you are not here. Oh, God, will I ever see you again?

Wait. I see someone.

City of the Dead

He'd waited hours outside the cathedral as darkness fell, listening to the murmurs of the sermon and the rapt cheers of forty thousand worshippers. Now he watched them flow past – some purified, some uplifted and affirmed, others, perhaps, more confused than ever. How many, he wondered, simply felt satisfied in their conformity? Could you even call it conformity, here, where Coptic Christians were such a minority? They had done what was expected of them, at least, and now, warm in their piety, were heading back to the contradictions of their lives. Was his own atheism, his empty disbelief, in any way superior to their faith? Surely believing in something was better than having nothing, just the eons of infinite nothingness that filled the so-called heavens.

Clay swallowed, breathed in the foul, cancerous air and crushed these pointless musings. He'd learned long ago, Crowbar his teacher, that it was the only way to stay alive. Think too much and people got killed.

Clay stood inside the darkened shell of a disused workshop on the street leading from the cathedral's entrance down into Garbage City. After what he'd seen that afternoon, he was not taking any chances. Somehow those two cops he'd seen at Talaat Harb Square had known to be at the pyramids that afternoon. Whoever that woman had been, she'd risked a lot getting Clay that message. He had to assume that she knew what the message contained, and that when pressed by the cops, she'd talked. Everyone talks, eventually. It's only ever a matter of when.

People streamed by. He scanned each face as it appeared under the streetlights outside the cathedral, then let it go. After a while, the crowd thinned. Only the stragglers remained. The service had been over for more than half an hour and he'd seen no sign of her.

He waited, there among the scraps of plastic and the neatly stacked piles of cardboard, the sortings and huskings of a megacity's waste, unwilling to believe that after all they had been through, she hadn't come. Another ten minutes passed. The trickle of penitents slowed, then died. The lights inside the cathedral winked out, one by one. They were closing the place up.

He hung his head, sank back against the wall. Sweat ran cold from his temples. After seeing the woman taken away by the cops, he'd decided to wait outside the cathedral and catch Rania on the way in, rather than risk going inside. He'd arrived well before time, had watched carefully, but had not seen her enter. He'd checked for alternate entrances, but there appeared to be only one. And now, hours later, he convinced himself that maybe he'd just missed her. Maybe Rania was still in there, still waiting for him. He had to check.

He'd just emerged from the workshop when a woman appeared in the now-darkened cathedral entranceway. Two little girls in pretty dresses skipped after her, holding her by the hand. It was the woman he'd seen at the pyramids ticket gate that afternoon. They turned towards him, walking briskly. His heart jumped.

Jesus. It was her.

He waited until she was close, close enough that he could hear her talking to the girls in Arabic, something about seeing their mother soon. She was thinner than he remembered, her face more drawn, as if worry had pulled a decade from her in just two years. He stepped out onto the street.

She stopped, gathered the girls to her, stared back at him.

He started to speak but she raised her index finger to her lips, shook her head. 'We are being followed by two men,' she said. 'One is tall. The other…' She wiped her hand across her face. 'Like a moon. Please, Claymore. Stop them.'

'How will I find you?'

'Go to the main road outside Moqattam, at the bottom of the hill. I will find you.' And before he could answer, she was gone, hurrying away into the darkened streets of Garbage City.

Clay moved back into the shadows and waited. He scanned the street behind her, back towards the cathedral entrance, but saw no one. Glancing around again, he caught sight of Rania and the girls as they flashed through the blush of a solitary streetlight. They emerged a few seconds later in a place where the street was lined with bales of bundled plastic waste, stacked head high. The plastic glowed like phosphorescent algae in a dark ocean, absorbing and throwing back the light from the windows above the street, and it was as if he were watching them in negative, three dark figures moving across a back-lit city.

Another image flooded his brain, a small bundle disappearing into the depths – Grace and little Joseph, together, wrapped in white, that glowing phosphorescent trail as they sank. Clay closed his eyes, tried to push it away. He stumbled, reached out for the wall. They were almost to the end of the street now, moving through a well-lit intersection, Rania striding along, the girls running beside her. Her face caught the light as she turned and looked back towards him, and then she was gone, swallowed by the darkness.

If he fell any further back, he would risk losing her altogether. The cathedral entrance was quiet. There was no sign of Rania's pursuers. The last of the cathedral lights dimmed and faded. He stepped out of his hide, moved quickly along the dark side of the street, skirting the stains of light. He reached the phosphorescence, slowed, ducked into another of the dark, now-empty open workshops and looked back the way he'd come. Still no one. Perhaps Rania had been mistaken, or maybe whoever had been following her had decided to abandon the pursuit, for now.

He took a deep breath and was about to step back into the street when two figures emerged from behind one of the bundles of plastic that lined the opposite side of the road. They stopped a moment, looked in Rania's direction and pressed on. They were coming right towards him. The *okes* he'd seen at Talaat Harb Square, the ones who'd rushed past him as they chased Rania down the alley, the same cops who'd marched off that woman at the pyramids. They moved with intent, following Rania and the girls.

Clay waited until they were close, then stepped out into the street, blocking their way. '*Masa al khaeer,*' he said. Good evening. 'What's the hurry, gents?'

The cops stopped, looking past Clay to where Rania and the girls had been.

'*Ma'afi mushkilla,*' said the moonfaced one. No problem. He made to keep going, but Clay stepped in front of him, blocking his way.

The tall one stared at Clay, narrowing his eyes. 'You,' he said.

'Get out of the way,' said Moonface, taking a step towards Clay. 'Police.'

'It's him,' said Tall.

Moonface stood a moment, a look of realisation spreading across his face. '*Welad wesha'a,*' he growled. Son of a bitch – so much more stinging in this part of the world.

Tall, who until now had been hanging back, stepped forwards and whispered something into his partner's ear. Moonface's eyes widened as he stared at Clay.

'We know who you are,' said Tall. 'And why you are here.'

'*Mumtaz,*' said Clay. Excellent. 'Let's talk about it.'

'Leave Egypt,' said Tall. 'Take the woman with you. If you do it now, no one will get hurt.'

Moonface glared at his colleague.

'Nothing I want to do more,' said Clay.

Moonface turned side on, hiding his right side. Clay could see his shoulder rise, rotate back. Gun, most likely, or knife. 'Give us your weapon,' he said. He was close to Clay now, hiding whatever was in his hand. His gut spilled out over his belt, strained the buttons on his shirt.

Tall was still hanging back, hands on his hips. 'We know you are armed,' he said. 'Please cooperate, and no one will be hurt.'

'Why are you following her?' said Clay, stepping to within a pace of Moonface. Every second he kept them here put Rania further from danger.

'We're wasting time,' said Moonface, lowering his weight, pivoting his right shoulder back. He raised an automatic pistol, held it close to his chest in a two-handed grip. 'Give us your weapon,' he said.

Clay opened his palm, raised his stump. '*Tammam*,' he said. Okay. He reached slowly behind his back, pulled out the Glock. As it appeared, the two men took a half-step back.

Clay let the gun drop to the ground, moved a pace towards Moonface. The pistol's muzzle was now only inches from his sternum. 'So,' he said, 'how about the truth?'

'Truth?' said Moonface.

'Who are you working for?' said Clay.

Moonface glanced at his partner and laughed.

Clay knew he was out of time. Not just here, now, but more fundamentally. This was not a conscious thought, or even a distant echo. It came more as a side-effect, carried within the waves of adrenaline detonating in his system as he twisted his torso away from the pistol's mouth and clapped his open right palm down onto Moonface's gun hand, forcing the pistol side-on into his own chest, and driving the hard point of his stump into Moonface's throat. Moonface screamed as Clay wrenched the pistol from his hand, tearing the second knuckle of his trigger finger from its socket. Clay turned the gun back towards his attacker's face in a sharp jab, smashing the base of the pistol's grip into his forehead. Moonface slumped to his knees with a groan.

By now, Tall had started to react. He was fumbling behind his back, going for his gun. There was no way to close the distance in time. Clay flung Moonface's pistol at Tall's face. Instinctively, the cop turned his head, closed his eyes. The gun hit the side of his skull, jerked his head back, skidded away across the garbage-strewn tarmac. Tall stumbled back, fell to the ground. As he did, his own gun clattered to the pavement. Dazed, he raised his hand to his head, stared a moment at the blood on his fingers.

He looked up at Clay. 'Please…' he said. 'I…'

Clay crouched, reached for his Glock. He'd just taken hold of the grip when Tall scrambled to his feet and started to run.

By now Moonface had started to recover. Swaying on his knees, he reached towards his boot with his undamaged hand. Clay stepped left, balanced himself and let go a side-kick to Moonface's head. The cop toppled over, arms at his sides, unconscious.

Tall was already halfway to the corner. Clay sprinted after him.

It was dark, the lanes were narrow, and Tall was fast. Within thirty seconds, the cop had opened up a fifty-metre lead. He was heading downhill, towards the City of the Dead. Halfway down a long, curving street lined with parked trucks, Tall darted into a side street. By the time Clay reached the corner, Tall had disappeared.

Clay kept going, jogging now, breathing hard. He came to a row of small local restaurants with open air benches that encroached onto the street. People milled about the counters and wandered the lane. Faces stared out at him as he checked right and left. Tall was gone. He'd lost him.

Clay checked back the way he'd come. A man emerged from one of the restaurants and started off in the other direction at a walk. His back was turned, his head wrapped in a *keffiyeh*. In the half-light Clay couldn't make out his face, but the build looked right. Clay followed, closing the distance, keeping to the dark side of the street. At the next corner the man stopped. Clay watched as he looked left, right, then set off again at a quick walk.

If it was Tall, he showed no sign of knowing he was being followed, and with each passing minute his pace slowed. Soon he reached the City of the Dead, the first tombs, the first makeshift shelters, the dead and the living sharing the same ground. The man had just reached a particularly large and elaborate tomb, the resting place of some rich now-forgotten family, when he stopped. The lights of Cairo shone in the distance, yellow and diffuse through the smoke. Clay tucked in behind an adjacent tomb. Like the others, it was crumbling and derelict, and showed signs of recent occupation by squatters – scattered tins and bottles, rags spread over what appeared to be a cardboard sleeping place, a pile of shit in one corner, fetid and reeking.

The man hunched over, hands on knees, breathing heavily. After a while he straightened, lit a cigarette. He inhaled deeply, exhaled long. He was looking the other way, towards the city. The street was deserted. Clay emerged from his hide and started towards the man at a fast walk. He was three paces away when the man spun around.

'Stop,' said Tall, pulling a knife from under his jacket. 'Get back. You don't need to…'

But Clay didn't stop, didn't break stride. He hit Tall square in the chest with a straight kick, sending him staggering. Tall jabbed out with the blade, getting off a couple of quick underhand stabs before Clay's fist ploughed into his face. As the cop slumped back, Clay wrapped the man's knife arm tight at the elbow, stepped across his body, and flung him over his hip. Tall crashed to the ground.

Looking back, he should have stopped there. If he'd been a better man he might have. But he wasn't, and he didn't. It all happened so fast there wasn't time to pull away from it. Clay pushed his left shin down hard onto Tall's head, crushing it to the ground.

'Please,' whimpered Tall. 'I am trying—'

But before he could finish, Clay extended the cop's knife arm, straightening it back against the natural bend of the elbow, and drove it down hard across the top of his right knee. Tall screamed as the ligaments in his elbow and shoulder ruptured. But his cries were short-lived. Half a second later, Clay raised his boot and smashed his heel into Tall's face. The cop let out a gasp and went quiet.

Clay stood looking down at the man. Blood flowed from his shattered nose and the corner of his mouth. The knife lay in the dirt beside him, its blade glistening wet. Whoever he was, he was still breathing. Clay crouched beside him and went through his pockets. A wallet with a few thousand Egyptian pounds in it, a bank card, a faded photo of a young boy in a school uniform, another of the same boy with Tall and a plain-looking woman in a headscarf. An Egyptian police ID card. And in the front trouser pocket, a thick roll of cash – new US fifty-dollar bills, a lot of them. Payday? Not in US dollars. Not this kind of money. Cops, perhaps. But not normal ones.

Clay started towards the highway.

As the flood of adrenaline burned away and was replaced by the warm gush of dopamine, he knew that there was still time. Time to change this. All of it. Fractions of seconds, yes. Eons perhaps. Enough. All the time there ever was. And he also knew that the direction lay ahead. Down this street of tombs. Through the choking miasma of burning plastic and cadmium-thickened smoke. Past the stink of open sewers and makeshift tomb-homes and the bodies of rotting animals. Away from this place. Back, perhaps, to something he'd thought was lost.

He loped towards the main road. Had she waited? Or had she disappeared again, as she had so many times before? Dogs barked. Televisions droned, flickering blue from the windows of a thousand rooms. Somewhere behind him someone shouted into the night, called for help. Clay kept going. Could their destinies ever converge? Or was the evidence of three years a whole and blistering truth that he had wilfully ignored? And yet she had called him here. Called for his help. It did not matter why. He was blind. And he did not care.

He emerged from the City of the Dead onto the broad curve of the highway. The lights of the citadel and the Mohammed Ali mosque glowed in the distance. A black, starless sky weighed over the city. He started down the road, the first pain signals detonating in his brain. Cars sped by, a strobing countercurrent of white and red lights. The cops hadn't called in backup. They'd had no radios. Neither was carrying a phone. He knew now that they were working off-line, outside the system.

A taxi rolled up beside him. The driver gave him a couple of shots on the horn. Clay raised his hand to his chest, the sign for no thanks, kept his head down, kept walking. The taxi slowed. Clay stopped, faced the vehicle. The rear window was coming down. Clay stepped back, reached to the small of his back, palmed the Glock's handle.

A face appeared in the open window.

'Get in,' she said.

13th November 1997. Cairo, Egypt. 03:40 hrs

You lie, there on the floor, with your jacket spread over you. I watch your shoulders rise and fall, hear the steady sigh of your breathing as you sleep. In the light from the street I can see the fresh bandage pale on your left forearm, and the torn, blood-stained gash on your left trouser leg, just below your waist. Whenever I see you, mon amour, *you are like this — cut or bruised or shot. And I know that inside the damage is worse.*

Last night, when I asked you to intercept those policemen, I thought I might never see you again. Forgive me, Claymore, but I was ready to sacrifice you to save myself and Samira's daughters. I think back and I know this to be the truth. What am I becoming? Am I so obsessed that I would wish you dead? Or, perhaps, did I trust you to keep the policemen away? Knowing you as I do, should I be surprised at the state you are in? I know now that you would do anything for me. It is a terrible realisation, a hateful responsibility, one that I did not ask for. And yet, when the time came, I deployed you as one would a soldier in a battle, knowing what the consequences might be. And you obeyed.

And now you are here, sleeping so close to me.

I shiver and pull the bedclothes up around my neck. We share a room, but not a bed. A bond, but not a life.

The two girls are asleep in the lounge room, one on the settee, the other on cushions our hostess laid on the floor and fashioned into a mattress with a fitted bed sheet. They are good girls. Samira has raised them well, despite everything she has had to contend with. They did not complain once. I know that, after everything we have been through together, they trust me.

Yesterday, when you joined us in the taxi, you sat in the back seat, beside the girls. Your right hand was dark with blood and you kept it pushed down on your leg. Thank God it was night. You looked me in the eyes and told the taxi driver to go to Zamalek. *Your Arabic is as rough as ever.*

Hello, beautiful, you said in English, gazing into my eyes. I could see the pain there. The pain of your wounds, but also the damage I have done you over these past years.

I tried to respond, but something held me back. Was it the shock of having you so close again, of seeing your blood dripping to the floor of the taxi, the thought of all that we could have shared? Every time I thought I might speak, something held me back, so that the longer I remained silent, the more hollow anything I might say would sound. There was – there is – so much to say. And yet, as we drove through the night-lit city, I said nothing, until the echo of your two words filled the small space inside the car to rupturing.

I do not feel beautiful, Claymore. Quite the opposite. I sent you into a fight I knew might you cost your life. I feel dirty and befouled. I made a whore of myself. The widow-whore. How many of my sisters have been forced down this road of ugliness? And yet I chose it. My heart breaks. I have violated, and been violated. And worse, I have been made to betray my convictions. I am a murderer. And I know that, soon, I shall have to tell you all of this, and shatter your illusions of me. I am ugly.

But then, as we crossed the Nile into Zamalek, you reached out to me. You touched me on the shoulder with your stump. I reached up and put my hand over it, and you did not pull away. I sat in the darkness, not caring what the taxi driver might think, and ran my hands over the intimate, bloody topography of that calloused surface. Then I closed my eyes and traced my fingers along the big veins up the warm inside of your forearm and into the soft damp crook of your elbow. I know you could feel my hands quivering. *Do you know, Claymore? Do you understand?*

And then we arrived. You told the driver to stop in an alley behind a newish apartment building. I paid. We stood in the darkness and watched the taxi disappear. Then you led us through the streets of Zamalek. We walked another fifteen minutes. I could see you limping, cradling your arm. Finally we came to a crumbling, old pre-revolution apartment block. We climbed the stairs and came in here.

I remember you mentioning your friend Atef when we first met in Yemen, that time we walked out to the ocean side of the crater in Aden. You had brought a picnic dinner, which we ate on the rocks as we watched the sun go down over the Indian Ocean. It was very beautiful, and it seemed as if we were alone at the edge of the world. I complimented you on the food, and you told me that Atef, your friend, had made everything. I had only agreed to come with you because I needed information from you. But I know now that even then I loved you.

Atef's wife is a nurse at one of the local hospitals. She has cleaned your wounds, sewed you, bandaged you well. She gave you painkillers and a sedative, and you slept. Not before insisting that I take the bed, of course. Sometimes, chéri, your old-fashioned ways are ridiculous.

I resist the temptation to wake you. I have been lying here for more than an hour, watching you sleep. I know that tomorrow I will have to tell you everything. I also know that I will lie. I will say I am telling you everything. But I will not. How can I? I now know how difficult it has been for you, opening your past to me. I understand now, chéri. And I also know that you will want to take me away, and I will have to tell you that it is impossible for me to run.

And yet there is time, now, before the sun rises. I imagine myself creeping to your side, kissing your face, pulling you into bed, holding you tight and close and warm until the day comes. And yet I do not. My husband is not yet one month dead. Hours ago, a man forced himself inside me. And yet, dear God, I lie here in flames. Desire for you consumes me, eats away at everything I was taught to respect and believe, burns away my morals, as if it were not the greatest gift of God, but a vile disease over which I am powerless.

Allah, most merciful, if you are out there, guide me.

لي دليل الرحيم، الرحمن الله

All That Remained

When he woke, the bed was empty.

Memory sent a hit of adrenaline pulsing through him, pushing away the vestiges of sleep. Was she gone? He raised himself up, felt the pain flow through his arm and hip, and shuffled to the bedroom door. He grabbed the door handle and was about to turn it when he heard voices. Two women, talking. Atef's wife, and then, after a while, the other woman replying. Rania.

Clay exhaled long, let go the handle. She was still here. She hadn't run. And yet, after what had happened in the City of the Dead, he knew that they would have to leave Atef's place as soon as they could. If the two men he'd attacked had indeed been cops, then his description would already be circulating the city. They needed to return the girls to their mother and get out of Egypt as quickly as they could.

Clay shuffled to the bathroom and closed the door. He checked his bandages. Not too bad. He hadn't even realised he'd been cut until he was in the taxi. He knew the taller guy had hit him a couple of times, but they hadn't felt like strikes with a blade, just punches. Adrenaline did crazy things, warped your brain, tricked your pain centre. He lowered his face to the sink, splashed himself with cold water and looked into the mirror. A stranger gazed back out at him, hollow-eyed, dripping, unrecognisable. And then, the realisation: in a few minutes, he would walk out into that room and she would be there. But before he could begin the dangerous imagining that he knew was coming, he shut it all down, pushed it deep. Whatever she might still feel for him, and he for her, there was no room for any of it now. There was space, now, only for this: survive and get out.

Everything else was secondary. If you do it right, plenty of time after for all that other shit. If you don't, none.

When he emerged from the bedroom, Rania was sitting at the dining table with Atef and the two girls. Morning light streamed through the windows, cinder grey and diffuse. Four pairs of eyes gazed up at him.

Atef stood, reached out his hand. 'My good friend,' he said.

'*Sabah al kha'eer*,' said Clay. Good morning.

Atef glanced at his bandage. 'How are you?'

'It's nothing,' said Clay.

'It did not look as nothing last night, Mr Clay.'

Atef's wife came to her husband's side. He gathered her in under his big right arm. 'My wife is a good nurse.'

Clay bowed. 'Thank you,' he said.

She smiled. 'Tonight I will change the dressing. Please, no strenuous exercise for a few days. Especially here.' She pointed to his hip.

Clay nodded, looked to Rania. 'We must leave very soon,' he said. 'We must return these young ladies to their parents.'

The girls frowned and looked to Rania, but remained silent.

'To their mother, yes,' said Rania. 'But before we go, may I please use your telephone, Mr Atef? I need to call overseas. I can pay, of course.'

'Please,' said Atef, pointing to an old rotary telephone sitting on a side table in the lounge. 'You are among friends. Do not speak of money.'

Rania stood, touched Atef's arm. 'Of course, forgive me.'

Atef and his wife went to the kitchen. Clay sat with the girls, poured himself coffee and watched Rania sit on the divan as she picked up the telephone receiver and dialled. But for the eyes, she might have been a different person to the one he'd known in Yemen and Istanbul and Cyprus. Her cheekbones cut sharp ridges above hollowed-out cheeks, underscored deep sockets. The fullness of her body was gone too, the curve of hip and breast, as if her flesh had been flensed away and all that remained was bone and ligament. And yet, as she turned toward him, her eyes burned like the dark planets he remembered.

She was talking now, in French, a brief acknowledgement; then she listened. She scribbled something on a piece of paper, hung up the phone and looked at her watch.

Five minutes later, she picked up the phone again, dialled, waited. She glanced up at Clay and nodded. Clay tried a half-smile. He heard the line engage, a male voice on the other end. Rania spoke briefly, listened. She nodded once, again, glanced away and back towards Clay. She was listening intently now, staring into his eyes, right through him. Then she gasped, put her hand to her mouth, held it there. Tears welled in her eyes, poured across her cheeks. She lowered her head towards the floor, spoke a question, listened to the reply, and then looked back up at Clay as she put the receiver back into its cradle.

Clay went to her. She stood and folded herself into him. He wrapped his arms around her, felt the tremors run through her body as she sobbed. He held her a long time as she cried.

'What is it, Ra?' he asked after a while. 'What's happened?'

'God is great,' she whispered. 'Truly.'

'Tell me.'

'Eugène,' she gasped. 'My son.'

'Did they find something?'

'Yes.'

'What is it?'

She took a deep breath, held it, exhaled slowly, looked up at him. 'He is alive, Claymore. Alive.'

Part IV

13th November 1997. Cairo, Egypt. 09:15 hrs

Claymore is in the kitchen with Atef. Apparently Atef has a friend in customs at the airport. He is on the telephone to him now.

The conversation with my friend from the Directorate loops through my mind. I need to write it down. Before we go.

This was how it went:

Did you leave a message to call me? I asked.

Yes, my friend from the Directorate said.

How did you get the number?

From the hard drive.

Al-Gambal?

No. Another name.

How did you know? My voice trembled, wondering about the nature of the relationship between my husband and the Kemetic.

I guessed.

You have something for me?

Yes. Prepare yourself.

Vas-y. *By now my heart was pounding, my pulse rapid, my breath short.*

I have been going through the CCTV archives from all the airports, running face-recognition algorithms.

Yes.

I found something.

Me?

Yes. Geneva. So far, I have managed to bury it.

Thank you.

No need to thank me. We are even now.

We always were.

Now, yes.

How long do I have?

Days. A week perhaps. I will do my best. There are a lot of airports.

Thank you. Adieu. I made to end the call.

Wait. There is something else.

Yes?

The algorithm threw up another match. The day your husband and son disappeared. Charles de Gaulle airport. Air Egypt to Cairo. A woman. Almost you, but not you.

Mon Dieu, *I gasped.*

She was travelling with a little boy. You can see it clearly in the video. Dark, curly hair, toddler. She had him in one of those carriers you strap across the chest. His eyes are closed. He looks asleep.

What are you telling me?

It looks like Eugène.

I was quiet for a long moment, not believing what I was hearing. My God. Are you sure?

I can't be certain. Do you understand? But it looks like him, the last time I saw him. And didn't you say that a strange woman looking like you drove away with him that day?

Do you have a name?

I ran her picture through the airline's database.

I was crying now, shaking. Please, tell me.

The woman was travelling on an Egyptian passport issued to Jumoke Quarah.

My God.

There is one more thing.

Vas-y.

We have received reliable intelligence that Al-Gama'a al-Islamiyya is planning a major attack in Egypt. This man called The Lion has recently taken over as the leader and is pushing for action. We believe the attack is imminent. Days. We are going to share the information with the Egyptians tomorrow. This is why I had to contact you, why I took the risk.

Merci, mon ami.

Wait, do you understand? We will share all *of the information with the Egyptians.*

Compris.

My God, could it really be him? Am I fooling myself, allowing my desperation to kindle a faint hope into a blaze of self-deception? Is there any logic to it? Even if it was that woman my friend saw in the CCTV video, why would she have spared my Eugène, risked going through customs with an abducted child? And why take someone else's child? What could she possibly want with Eugène? No, it all seems too implausible. A set of random coincidences. My mind reels. Perhaps she…

Defy Gravity, Deny Time

They took Atef's car. Atef drove.

When they reached Giza, Clay told the girls to sink down in their seats and keep their heads below the windows. Rania directed Atef along the corniche and then west, south of and parallel to the market. It was midday and the streets were crowded.

Atef navigated his way through the swirling Cairo traffic. Clay pulled the cap Atef had given him down close over his eyes. The Kemetic's building was not far away.

'Turn here,' said Rania, pointing to a small side street.

Atef rolled the car to a stop beneath the red canopy of a flame tree.

Rania donned her burqa and stepped from the car. 'Wait here,' she said.

Clay jumped out of the car.

'Please, Claymore.'

'No chance, Ra,' he said, closing the door and moving to her. 'Not this time. We do this together.'

Rania shrugged, leaned into the car and said something to the girls. Then she turned and started down the street. Clay fell back, following at a distance. Rania moved quickly through the warren of back streets and alleys. He paced her, shadowing her twists and backtracks until he emerged into a lane flanked by a two-metre-high brick wall that ran all along one side. At the far end was what appeared to be the entrance to a parking area. Rania was halfway along the lane, standing near a clutch of browning palm trees and dust-covered sycamores. She looked back at him and then disappeared into the trees. When he came to the place, he saw that she'd climbed up onto a pile of rubble that had been pushed up against the wall and was crouching at the lip. The place was hidden from the lane by the trees, and someone had knocked out a notch in the top of the wall.

Clay joined her and looked out across a large area of vacant land. A few palm trees clung up against the wall, filmed over with that same dust that blanketed the city, those fine landed particulates that slurried the air. Piles of smoking rubbish hulked up along the edge of the canal, pimpled the open ground between where they stood and the far buildings, perhaps three hundred metres away.

'There,' she whispered, pointing to the far side of the lot.

But all he could see were wooden pallets, plastic bags, heaps of strewn and rotting peelings being picked over by a couple of goats, piles of broken masonry and twisted rebar. 'What am I looking for?' he said.

'Can you see those shelters, up against the wall?'

Same view, and now, a different meaning. 'Yes.'

'That is where the girls live. Where I lived.'

'Good place to hide.'

'Not so good, it turned out.'

'And your friend?'

'She helped me Clay. Without her I would never have been able to find you.'

'Yesterday, at the pyramids.'

Rania nodded. 'I think she's here.'

'That would depend on your two friends.'

She glanced at his bandaged arm, pushed her gaze deep into his. 'It was them you fought.'

'I had no choice.' Another truth hidden.

She closed her eyes a long moment. 'Did you…' she began, but stopped short.

'No, Rania. I didn't. They'll need some time to recover, but they'll live.'

'*Al hamdillulah.*'

Clay too gave thanks for this, but called on no divine power. 'They're cops, Rania, definitely. But they were carrying a lot of cash. Hard currency. They're on the take.'

'The Consortium,' said Rania. 'It has to be. I must speak to Samira, and we must return her daughters.'

'What if the police still have her?'

Rania shook her head, didn't answer.

'Do you trust her, Ra?'

'Yes, I do.'

'Are you sure? How did those cops know where you were going to be?'

'Of course I am. It was Samira's idea to dress in the burqa to make contact with you at Cheops. In case there were problems.'

'Then she also knew what you'd written in the note. Either they forced it out of her, or she told them freely.'

Rania shook her head from side to side. 'No, Claymore. No. She wouldn't.'

Clay reached up and touched Rania's face with his hand. 'How much does she know, Rania?'

Rania was quiet a moment, and then took Clay's hand in hers. 'I told her everything, Claymore. Almost everything. I...' she tailed off to a whisper. 'I shouldn't have.'

'Then we have to assume that by now, the police know everything she does.'

Rania hid her face in her hands.

'Everyone breaks, Rania. You know that.' Clay pulled out his field glasses and scanned the shelters. There appeared to be more than a dozen, ranked side by side like the Johannesburg township slum dwellings he'd glimpsed through the car window of his childhood. This, after all, was still Africa. 'Which one is yours?'

'Third from the far end. With the blue plastic roof.'

'And hers?'

'Next one to the right.'

He refocused. In front of the hovels was a small area of packed dirt. It had been freshly swept. Closer to the front of the shelter was a small brazier fashioned from the same dirt, moulded and dried into a horseshoe. A pile of ash smouldered within.

'She's there,' he said. 'Or has been recently.' He handed Rania the glasses.

She raised them to her face, twisted the focus knob and looked out a moment. Then she handed them back. 'I must go to her.'

Clay grabbed her by the shoulder, pulled her back down behind the wall. 'Don't, Rania.'

She twisted herself away from his grasp. 'Do not tell me what to do, Claymore.'

'Look, I'm sorry. But please, Ra, just wait. Think. If the police had her and let her go, they may be waiting for exactly this. We can bring the girls close. They can make their way home by themselves.'

'Home?' Rania hissed. 'You call that a home?'

Clay recoiled, surprised by the vehemence in her voice. 'I'm sorry,' he whispered.

'I cannot simply leave,' she said.

'We don't have time, Rania. Atef's friend in customs isn't going to wait for ever. We have to find your boy, if that was him.'

She stiffened. 'There is time.'

Clay filled his lungs, cycled through his breathing. He knew he wasn't going to win. 'Okay, Rania. Okay. But let's check out the area first. Do a recon.'

Rania turned to him, pushed away his hand. 'Please do not use that ridiculous language around me.' Scorn flashed in her eyes. 'Recon,' she spat.

Clay bit down on it, kept quiet, started scanning the area. If the cops were using the woman Samira as bait, they would be nearby, close enough to react, far enough away to be unobtrusive. One thing was sure, it wouldn't be Tall or Moonface.

Clay looked back up over his shoulder at the apartment block immediately behind them. A rooftop would be perfect. 'Will you wait here, Rania? Please?'

'Where are you going?'

He pointed to the top of the building. 'Up there.'

She nodded.

'I'll signal you: thumb up – go and be quick, meet back here; across the throat – danger, go back to the car, I'll meet you there.' As he said it, a car trundled down the lane below them, sending up a cloud of dust.

She closed her eyes, opened them. '*Oui.*'

He scrambled down to the lane and started towards the building. The back door was unlocked. He took the fire stairs and emerged onto the rubble-strewn rooftop. He was alone. Moving to the lane side he crouched behind the brick safety wall. From here he could see out across the whole neighbourhood, past the fetid bright green of the hyacinth-and-garbage-choked canal to the elevated freeway, the sea of rooftops covering the floodplain in every direction. In the distance, Cheops' frayed three-thousand-year-old crown pierced the brume, floating on the inversion as if trying to defy gravity, deny time.

If the cops were here, they could be anywhere. In any one of the cars parked along the road that paralleled the canal. On any of the nearby rooftops. In any of the hundreds of windows and doorways overlooking this small piece of ground in the middle of Cairo. He looked down. There was Rania, just visible in the little clutch of trees. She looked up at him, waved. He waved back. Something fizzed along his spine, echoed a moment in the big muscles of his legs. He raised the binoculars and started scanning, working outwards from the shelters in widening circles, the way he'd been taught. The way Crowbar had taught him. Be methodical. Be sure. There is time to do it right. Don't miss something that could get one of them killed.

He'd started his second, expanded, sweep, when he saw Rania wave. He lowered the glasses, looked down at her. She was pointing out towards the shelters. Clay looked up. A man had emerged from Samira's shelter, was standing with his back turned. The man turned his head left then right and started towards the canal, picking his way between the smouldering heaps of garbage. Clay followed him with the binoculars. The man was moving quickly, with purpose. He reached the canal road, stopped a moment, turned right. As he did, his face came into view. Clay's heart lurched. It was G.

Clay looked down towards the clutch of trees. Rania wasn't there. He looked left and right. Nothing. Then movement, beyond the wall. She had broken cover and was moving across the open ground towards the shelters.

Clay cursed, swung the glasses back towards G. He'd reached the road and had started along the canal road, walking at the same brisk pace. Seconds later he disappeared behind the nearest building. Clay jumped to his feet, sprinted to the stairwell, took the stairs half a flight at a time, vaulting from one landing to the next, pivoting around the railings. By the time he reached the trees and the wall, Rania was already more than halfway to the shelters. He jumped to the ground and started after her.

By the time he reached the shelters she had already disappeared inside. He pulled back the flap, peered into the half-lit darkness.

Rania was there, sitting on the floor. She looked up at him as he entered, but said nothing. Beside her, splayed out on the ground, staring up at the sagging plastic sheeting, was the woman he'd seen being dragged away from the pyramids. Samira.

Luxor. It is decided. We will leave as soon as we can arrange transport.

To find Eugène, we must find the woman, Jumoke Quarah. Customs records show her arriving in Cairo, just as my friend said, on 26th October, from Paris. With her, as an accompanied minor, was Said Qarrah, aged three years. There were no photographs or video from the airport, but Atef's friend gave us a printout of the two passport photo pages. I have them here in my hand now, as I write this.

It is him. My little boy. Eugène.

And she … The resemblance is remarkable. As if I had a twin sister.

According to Egyptian government records she obtained a visa to go to France in April of this year and travelled there in September. She went alone. Mon Dieu! *How did the authorities not pick that up? Atef's friend cross-referenced the name in the Egyptian government database, and confirmed that such a person is indeed registered in the Governorate of Luxor. He could provide no address or contact details, however.*

Is this the woman who murdered my husband? Was she sent by this group that everyone refers to as the Consortium? Could it even have been the AB? Is it something to do with the court case involving Yusuf Al-Gambal and the Kemetic? Can these things be related? And if so, what could they possibly want with Eugène? Has he become one more example of the ancient tradition of stealing the enemy's children and enslaving them – if not physically, then ideologically? If he is a hostage, then why have they not contacted me? Perhaps they have been trying, and by running from them I have missed the chance to barter for his life. It is me they want, surely. None of it makes any sense.

I am living a nightmare.

We are at Atef's apartment for another night. I know it worries you,

Claymore. You do not want to expose your friend, as I did not want to expose mine.

Earlier tonight you told me that Jean-Marie was dead. You would not tell me what happened, only that he died helping you. Mon Dieu, it does not seem possible. I wept for a long time. I wept for Hope and her unborn baby. I wept for you, mon amour, for the loss of your closest remaining friend. I cried for us all.

I lie here, unable to sleep, and I watch you as I write this. You are lying on the floor, as you did last night. You are on your side. Your head is crooked in your right arm. You are looking up at me. You have been that way since I started. You are silent. You do not interrupt me, just lie there caressing me with those smoke-grey eyes. I know you want so much more from me, Claymore. I can feel the power of your desire. But you let me write, allow me this time. You are a good man, despite everything, despite what you believe about yourself. You know I need time to come to terms with all that has happened.

I glance up at you now, and you smile at me. It is not a broad smile. I have never seen such a thing from you. It is partial, hesitant, half apology, half acknowledgment, as if you cannot allow yourself the full pleasure of the thing. And yet, for you, it is a smile, and the meaning of it warms me.

For I am cold. Despite the warm November, I shiver. I know I could go to you now and speak to you, instead of writing to you. But I do not. The future frightens me, Claymore, holds me back. And the glowing warmth of knowing that my son is alive – alive! – is replaced now by the chill of the knowledge that he is among strangers, far from home and those who love him. Where are they keeping him? Is he being cared for? Mon Dieu, he is only a little boy. Who could do such a thing? And to what end?

We are animals, Claymore. Base and vile creatures. It is the only explanation. Driven by lust and greed, the basest of instincts, the urge to kill nestles deep within us, encoded in our genes. I know this to be true, now. I would gladly kill again to get my son back, to keep him safe. Gladly. And yet, what is it that makes us human? Is it not our ability to rise above these forces, to aspire to a higher purpose? Is this not the word of Allah, brought to us through the writings of the prophet Mohamed? Is this not the real truth?

'What is the worldly life except the enjoyment of delusion?'

And so, I deny you your desire, as I deny my own. You will have to wait. I know not how long. Perhaps forever. Before God, I renounce myself to the delusions of this life. For Allah deprives as suddenly as he gives.

The girls are sleeping now, finally. I told them the truth – that their mother is dead. I did not tell them why she died, only than that it was the will of Allah, and that she was a good person, and long-suffering, and a true believer, and so she is now in paradise. They are young, but they seemed to understand this. And yet, something Ghada, the little one, said to me today haunts me. I cannot bear to think about it.

I ask God to look after these orphaned children. He has seen it necessary to take from them both of their parents. I cannot begin to understand the workings of God's wisdom. Samira is gone, and He has determined that it should be so. Atef and his wife have agreed to take her daughters in. Their kindness, surely, He has noticed and will reward and is perhaps in itself an indication of His grace. And while it was Allah who took Samira, it is you, Claymore, who have ensured that her daughters will be well looked-after for as long as they live. All that death money you got from Cyprus is being washed clean. There is justice in this, although whose I am unsure.

Tonight I called Hope in California. She was with her mother. I did not tell her about Eugène. Only that I was safe. I left it to you to tell her that Jean-Marie was dead. You told her that he had died helping us, that he died doing what he loved, that you were together at the end, and that you buried him as a warrior, with his eyes open. I watched you, Claymore, as you told her. Your face was set hard. Your voice did not waver, even as I wept openly. I saw not a hint of tears, of emotion of any kind. I know you would not have betrayed your friend's memory with such shows of weakness. Men like you and Crowbar foolishly think emotion is weakness. And yet I know that the things you have seen and done have not completely scoured away your ability to feel. That smile of moments ago is all the proof I need. And, perhaps, if we are allowed the time, I can help you heal, and then, if Allah wills it, you can love me. If these things can be done, maybe I, too, can find solace, and love you as I should. Inshallah.

After Hope had spoken to you, she told me that she had always known this time would arrive. That one day, she would get a telephone call, and that she would know he was dead. She has been preparing for it since before they were married, she said. I wish she were here now so I could hold her, and we could weep together. For I loved him, too, as I know you did, Claymore, in your way.

Better Than You Can Ever Know

Clay woke with morning's first grey intrusions. He turned on the floor, felt the dull hooks of pain tangle inside him. Rania was sitting up in the bed, wide awake, staring down at him. He pushed himself up and sat on the bed beside her.

'Did you sleep?' he said.

'A little,' she whispered.

'I need to get going,' he said.

She reached for his hand. 'When I reached the shelter, Samira was still alive,' she said. 'She looked up at me. She knew it was me.' Rania closed her eyes for a moment. 'I am sorry. That's what she said, Claymore. Her final words: "I am sorry."'

Clay said nothing.

'Last night, Ghada, Samira's daughter, told me she saw her mother take money from a man in the clinic. She said it was a white man, with yellow hair.'

Clay exhaled. 'The guy we saw leaving Samira's shelter was Rhodesian. He worked with *Koevoet*, but I'm pretty sure he also works for the AB – the people who are after me. And you.'

Rania took a sharp breath. 'Why would he…' She didn't finish the sentence, knew the answer.

'I should have killed the bastard when I had the chance.'

Rania closed her eyes, squeezed his hand. 'Please, Claymore. No more killing. Promise me.'

Clay pushed her hand away.

'I think he was after this,' said Rania, reaching to the floor for her bag. She reached inside and placed a thick printed file on Clay's lap and flicked on the bedside lamp.

He scanned the pages, the paper stained and battered, the columns of figures still legible. Concentrations in parts per million, particulate matter with diameters less than 2.5 microns, less than 10 microns. Lead, cadmium, oxides of sulphur and nitrogen, units in milligrams per cubic metre. The numbers were big, way above background. The values appeared to be attached to several different measuring stations.

Clay looked up at Rania. 'Where did you get this?'

'From my husband's encrypted hard drive.'

'Encrypted?'

Rania nodded. 'Do you know what it means?'

'Looking at the concentrations, the types of compounds, I'm pretty sure these are air-quality data.'

Rania was quiet a moment. 'Are you certain?'

'I've done this kind of work before, Ra. PM 2.5 and PM 10 are definitely air quality parameters. Lead and the other metals could be in water, but these units are definitely for air.' He flipped a couple of pages and pointed to another set of numbers. 'Look. Same measuring station. Could be a combined water effluent and air-monitoring station.'

'Where were the measurements taken?'

'I can't tell.' Clay ran his finger down one of the columns. They're not lat-long. Could be UTM coordinates, but I'm not sure.'

Over the next few minutes, as dawn came, Rania told Clay about her meeting with Yusuf Al-Gambal, his reaction to seeing this very file, his unwillingness to meet further. 'He sent me instead to a friend,' she said. 'A Kemetic – a follower of the ancient Egyptian religion.'

'*Ja*, I met him,' said Clay.

Rania glanced at him. 'You did?'

'He was dead.'

Rania closed her eyes.

'Someone cut his throat. He was cold by the time I got there.'
Clay reached into his pocket. 'I found this in his flat.' He placed the
camera on Rania's lap. On the screen was the photo of the dead man
and three friends.

She picked it up and sat looking at the screen.

'The dead guy is the one on the left. Atef said the one on the right
is Yusuf Al-Gambal. I don't know who the one in the middle is.'

Rania stared at him a long moment. 'It is Hamid,' she whispered.
'My husband.'

'Jesus,' said Clay.

She pointed at the screen. 'And this?' Her finger hovered over the
image of the woman.

'I don't know.'

Rania bit her lip. 'What else did you find?'

'Scroll back through the photos,' said Clay. She might as well
know.

Rania flicked through the photos, stopped. 'I've been here,' she
said. 'It was an industrial facility, a lead smelter in Hadayek-el-Koba,
here in Cairo. The address was on a card that Yusuf gave me.' And she
told him about the night she was chased out of the facility.

'Keep going.'

Rania flicked through a few more photos, then stopped dead. She
looked up at Clay, the colour rising in her face. '*Con*,' she hissed.
'*Louche.*'

Clay reached into his pocket and handed her the button. 'Yours?'

Rania took the button, turned it over in her fingers a moment,
but said nothing.

'Did he hurt you?' said Clay.

'I do not want to talk about it,' said Rania, looking away. 'Just
make sure you delete those photos.'

Clay pocketed the camera. 'Okay, Ra.' He handed her the journal.
'I found this, too. Most of the Arabic is in some kind of shorthand.'

Rania started leafing through the pages. She was quiet for a long
time.

'Can you read it?' asked Clay.

Rania nodded. 'Some.' She leaned across him and placed the open journal on top of the file, on his lap, then pointed to a string of Arabic characters. She was very close to him now; he could smell her hair and the sweet chemistry of her skin, feel the heat coming from her body. He closed his eyes. Despite everything, desire fizzed through him, jarred the ligaments of his joints, weakened the muscles of his legs. She was speaking to him now, her voice soft on swirling desert eddies.

'Claymore? Are you alright?'

He opened his eyes. She was looking right at him, gazing out from the infinite depth of those twinned constellations whose flecked and layered patterns he had long ago locked in his memory.

'Sorry. What did you say?'

'This word here,' she said. 'Blood.'

'And then more numbers,' he said, still swimming through.

'What does it mean?'

'I have no idea.' Clay stood, steadied himself. 'Keep looking through it, Rania.' He started dressing.

'What's wrong?'

'There is something I have to do. Back soon.'

☾

Clay arrived at the Ritz Carlton just as the main restaurant was opening for breakfast. He sat in one of the big armchairs in the lobby, his back to the front window, so he could see across the marble entranceway to the main desk and the bank of lifts beyond. The place was early-morning quiet – a few Western businessmen in suits waiting for associates or drivers; hotel staff carrying trays, arranging flowers. He pulled his cap down low, ordered a coffee and waited.

Rania had wanted to leave for Luxor immediately. Clay had called Mahmoud, asked him if he had any runs south from Cairo scheduled, and Mahmoud, as expected, had immediately laid on a trip.

They would meet him later that night and leave Cairo in the early hours of the morning, arriving in Luxor shortly after daybreak. As before, Mahmoud hadn't asked the purpose of Clay's trip, or the reasons for haste. He had behaved as might the oldest and most trusted of friends, without a moment's hesitation. And while the man's charity and trust were still a surprise to Clay, he nonetheless understood where such things were born, and had seen the power of these bonds between men. In comparison, the dark currents that seemed to buffet Rania were an unfathomable mystery. It was clear to him now that whatever they had once had – the love and physical intimacy they had shared for a time – was now gone. Like him, she seemed to know that such distractions could be fatal for them both. They had a job to do. That was all that mattered.

Clay's coffee came. He didn't have a room number and didn't want to alert G to his presence by calling the room. He would wait until G appeared. If he came down for breakfast, Clay would wait and follow him back up. If he went out, Clay would corner him somewhere in the city. Either way, he was going to get some answers. He had no doubt that G was still in Cairo. A man like him would not have come this far only to leave before the promised payoff.

Clay sipped his coffee and watched the lobby, scanning the faces of the people coming out of the lift.

The early hours crawled past. Nine o'clock came and slid away into history. Clay ordered a third coffee. A second wave of guests, the late risers, crowded the restaurant, ate, straggled away.

And then he was there, striding across the lobby. With his arm in the sling and the deep contusions around his eyes, Clay didn't recognise him at first. But then it was clear. That tall, lanky build. The asymmetric, stilted walk, as if someone had hobbled his legs with a metre of chain. It was the cop, Tall. And he was coming straight towards Clay.

Clay stood, palmed the Glock's handle.

Tall opened his free hand, palm out and up, slowed. 'Please,' he said in Arabic as he approached. 'Only to talk.'

Clay moved his hand away from the gun and indicated the chair opposite. Tall sat.

'Coffee?' said Clay, wondering just how this guy had found him, looking around the lobby for Tall's backup. An escape plan took shape. There was an emergency exit in the bar, just beyond the wall to his right, about five seconds away. Then out and double back towards Tahir Square, get lost in the crowds.

Tall nodded. Clay called over the waiter and Tall ordered.

'You don't look so good,' said Clay. It was worth reminding him.

Tall looked down at his arm. 'It was not necessary,' he said. 'I tried to tell you.'

Clay rolled up his sleeve, revealing the bandage. 'Neither was this.'

Tall pushed his lips into a flat line. 'I am sorry,' he said. 'After you followed me, I feared for my life.'

'And your buddy?'

'He is still in hospital. Still unconscious. You hit him hard.'

Clay twisted his cup on the glass tabletop and hardened his gaze. 'You said you wanted to talk. So talk.'

Tall glanced back towards the lobby, the main entrance, and leaned forwards. 'The man you are looking for, I know where he is.'

'And who am I looking for?'

'Yusuf Al-Gambal.'

Clay took a mouthful of coffee and swallowed it down, tasting nothing. 'I'm not looking for him.'

'Your friend is.' Tall placed a business card on the table and slid it towards Clay. 'And if she wants to speak with him, she should do it quickly.'

Clay glanced at the card then focused back on the man opposite. 'Suez.'

The waiter came with Tall's coffee. He took a sip, swallowed and waited a moment. 'He thinks he is safer there.'

'From what?'

'From us.'

'Why should I believe you?'

'I am helping you.' His busted nose made him sound as if he had a cold.

'Like last night.'

Tall closed his eyes, opened them again. The whites of his eyes were stained with blood. 'And the man you came to see is not here. He is down the road, at the Hilton, registered as Mr Leadbetter. Room 1506.'

Clay stared back at the guy.

'Your colleague from Africa.'

It was as if the world was reordering itself. 'Go on.'

'He arrived here five days ago. We were told to work with him. And no, he did not kill the woman. We did that.'

Clay could feel the fury gathering, a distillation of fifteen years' injustice and betrayal.

'Not me,' said Tall. 'My partner.'

'For fuck's sake, why?' It came out as a groan.

'She cooperated at the beginning, through Mr Leadbetter, but then she stopped.'

'After the pyramids.'

'She crossed us. My partner, he…' Tall tailed off, stared into his coffee cup. 'He has a serious temper. He doesn't like being crossed.'

There it was. The betrayal. But then, despite everything, Samira had found it within herself to fight back. And they'd killed her for it.

Clay leaned forwards so that his face was only inches from Tall's. 'Tell your partner, next time it won't be a hospital bed he ends up in, it'll be the morgue.'

Tall's index finger twitched against the handle of his mug.

'Who is paying you?' said Clay.

Tall shifted in his chair and lowered his eyes. 'I never see him. My partner does that. We do what he tells us.'

'He tells you to kill some poor woman with two kids to look after, living in a rubbish dump? And you fuckers go and do it? Allah will judge you harshly.'

Tall hung his head. 'I am trying.'

'Not hard enough, *broer*.'

'You don't understand,' whispered Tall, 'what these people can do.'

Clay said nothing. *I understand better than you can ever know,* he thought.

'Leadbetter was giving the woman money for information, passing it to us. At a price.'

'Information about what?'

'About your friend, Veronique Deschamps. Or should I say Lise Moulinbecq.'

Suddenly the room was as cold as a tomb.

'The people who pay us do not want her here. You must leave immediately. If they find her, they will kill her. I was trying to warn you, before.'

'What the hell has she done to them, whoever the fuck they are?'

Tall drained his coffee, stood. 'We are not told why. Only do.'

'But you know, don't you?'

Tall fumbled in his pocket, withdrew a packet of Marlboros and tried to shake one out of the opening. Three cigarettes fell to the floor. He cursed in Arabic, put the pack on the table and started picking them up one by one.

'Not so easy with one hand, is it?' said Clay.

Tall flashed what might have been a smile. He put one of the cigarettes between his lips, fished out his lighter, turned the wheel and lit it. After a few lungfulls, he exhaled and said: 'They are very frightened of her. She has a reputation.' He took another long draw and narrowed his eyes. 'It is for prevention. And revenge.'

'Revenge? For what?'

'For things she has written, and may write.' Tall stubbed the half-finished cigarette out in the ashtray, wincing as he adjusted his arm in its sling. 'I must leave now,' he said. 'Allah's blessing be upon you, non-believer. You have thirty-six hours. After that, I will no longer be able to delay putting out a city-wide alert and arrest order for you both. Go in peace.'

'Wait,' said Clay. 'Why are you doing this?'

Tall stared into his eyes. 'Yusuf Al-Gambal is not the only person who hopes for a better Egypt. I have children, Mr Straker.'

And then he turned and walked away, out the front door and into the Cairo traffic.

14th November 1997. Cairo, Egypt. 07:10 hrs

Atef's wife has just come to me and handed me a small black-and-white photograph. She found it in your clothes before she laundered them.

It is as if I am looking at a ghost. You stare out at me from the past, your face full of all of that wonderful round smoothness of youth, your eyes bright, the hint of a wry smile at the corner of your mouth, despite the hard stare you are putting on for the camera.

It is a military photograph, clearly. The collar and epaulettes of your uniform are visible. Your hair is cut brush-short. Am I looking back sixteen years, seventeen? How young you look! To see you like this, clean and fair and beautiful, like a child. I have only ever known you scarred, damaged, cut and shot and sewn and sliced through by bone and metal. But it is your eyes that hurt me most.

My heart swells, and then a deep sadness comes.

Keeps You Alive

The Hilton was only a short walk along the corniche. If it was a setup, it was overelaborate. He decided to trust Tall, take the chance and fight his way out if he had to.

Room 1506 was at the back of the hotel, halfway along a curved corridor, overlooking the Nile. Clay banged on the door.

After a moment a voice came. 'Who is it?'

'Open up, G,' said Clay. 'I've got your money.'

The sound of the chain being pulled back, the bolt sliding. G peered out from a darkened room. 'Fuck, Straker. Wait a minute, man.'

G made to close the door but Clay jammed his boot into the opening and pushed the door open.

G stumbled back. He was naked, blinking in the light from the hallway. 'Fuck me,' he gasped. 'I said wait, man.' Behind him a Nubian girl lay sprawled on her stomach, legs parted. She was naked. Her mahogany skin shone with perspiration.

Clay closed the door behind him, drew the G21 and levelled it at G's balls. 'I told you to back off.'

G covered his nakedness with his hands, stepped back and bumped into the corner of the bed. The girl gasped, flipped over onto her back, pulled the sheets up under her chin then lay staring at them open-mouthed.

'What're you talking about, Straker? I did what you said, man. The AB thinks I'm still hunting you down.'

'Get rid of her,' said Clay.

G turned to the girl. '*Yallah*,' he barked. 'Get out, stupid cunt.'

The girl slipped from the bed and started dressing. She looked very young, her breasts mere thimbles. She was speaking rapidly in Arabic, pointing at G.

'Pay her,' said Clay.

G sidled up to the desk, peeled off a couple of notes and tossed them on the bed. The girl grabbed the money, slipped a dress over her head and hurried to the door, shoes and purse dangling from her hands. She closed the door quietly behind her.

'The woman,' said Clay. 'In Giza.'

'Shit, man,' he hissed. 'I didn't do that.'

'I know you didn't. But you were using her to get to my friend.'

G smirked, but wiped it away.

Clay buffered his anger, held it back. 'Why were you there?'

'They want something. Some document. They're willing to pay for it. They think your *bokkie* has it. I thought she might have hidden it in the shack.'

'That's why you didn't lead the cops there yourself.'

'Gotta protect your sources, man.'

'So, you're working for these assholes from the Consortium, now.'

'Shit man, I don't know anything about any "consortium". It's the AB, Straker, like I said. They and the locals, they're working together. Common objectives, all that shit.' He ran one hand through his hair, kept the other over his cock and balls. 'Shit, man. I don't know what these fuckers get up to. As long as they pay, I do what they tell me.'

'A lot of that going around.'

'Keeps you alive, man.'

Clay breathed deeply, fought back a wave of vertigo. He was getting better at managing the episodes, hadn't been crippled by one for a while. 'You still want the deal?' he said. Perhaps G was venal enough. 'Or should I just blow your balls off?'

G's eyes widened, focused on the gun. He nodded. 'Calm down, man. You told me to wait. That's what I did.'

Clay stood, gun still aimed at G's groin.

'Say something, Straker. You're giving me the *bossies,* man.'

Clay caressed the trigger. 'Lying bastard.'

G shrank back. 'Look man, it's all set up, yeah? I contacted them, like you said. Told them I could get you. I couldn't just sit around for three days doing nothing. They'd know.'

Clay lowered his weapon.

'How about you put that away, yeah?'

Clay jammed the Glock into his waistband.

'You got the money?' said G.

Clay threw a wad of cash on the bed. 'Forty-eight hours. Then tell them.'

G's eyes lit up. 'And the proof?'

'We do it now.'

Clay reached under his shirt, unsheathed his neck knife in a reverse grip. Then he placed its tip inside the top of his right ear, pointing forwards. 'I'll know if you haven't told them.'

G nodded, staring at the blade.

Clay fixed G's stare and drew the blade in a smooth arc, down and back. The top of his ear fell to the carpet. Blood welled from the wound, ran across his jaw and neck.

G recoiled. 'Jesus Christ,' he muttered.

Clay resheathed the knife, the pain starting to come properly now. 'You got a camera?'

G pointed to his duffel bag, on the floor by the TV.

Clay pulled out the G21. 'Slow and careful.'

G stepped back, rummaged in his bag and produced a small instamatic.

Clay reached his stump up to his ear, smeared it in blood and dragged it across his chest. Then he lay on his back on the carpet and splayed his arms, the G21 still pointed at G. He opened his mouth, letting his eyes drift. 'Get going,' he said.

G hovered above him, fumbled with the camera and snapped off half a dozen shots.

After, Clay stood, backed away to the bathroom, grabbed a towel and held it up against his ear with his stump. 'Forty-eight hours,' he said.

'If I can get the file, I might be able to convince them that I killed your *bokkie*, too.'

Clay nodded. 'If in two weeks I'm clear, I'll tell you where you can get the file, and I'll wire you the rest of the money. Write down your bank details.'

G reached for a pencil, knocked it to the floor, stooped to pick it up then scribbled the details on a slip of hotel paper and handed it to Clay. His hand was shaking. 'Did you tell Crowbar?'

'*Ja*, definitely.'

'What'd he say?'

'He said thanks.'

G's face twisted into a gapped smile.

'He also said that if you sell us out, he's coming for you, *broer*. You know what that means.'

The smile was gone. G grabbed the cash, started flipping through the notes.

'Got it?' said Clay, wiping the blood from his face and neck.

'Sure, man. Got it,' said G. 'Just disappear good, okay?'

It has been more than four hours now since you left, and still you have not returned. I did not want you to go alone, but you insisted. We argued. I know that Atef and his family heard us, though we closed the bedroom door. You want to protect me, and part of me loves you for it. You are a man. This is your purpose. This behaviour is programmed into you. I know this. But you are wrong when you say that you can do these things better alone. No one is better alone, ever, in anything. Nothing is stronger than a team. I told you: for us to be together, we must learn to trust each other. I know that you do not trust me.

We leave for Luxor tonight. The hours between now and then stretch almost to infinity before me. Eugène, my sweet little boy, what has become of you? Are you even in Luxor, even in Egypt? All we have is one name, a partial address in a database. It is not enough. If I were this woman, Jumoke – and it seems that I almost am, or she me – I would go anywhere but the place recorded as my address. Unless of course she feels invulnerable, protected somehow. And of course, if she was acting for the Consortium, that is exactly how she would feel. It seems even the Directorate is not immune to the Consortium's reach.

The girls are disconsolate. They have been weeping all morning. Grief cannot be denied. It can only be surrendered to. Claymore, you must also learn this, if you are ever to be whole again. As must I.

Atef and his wife are at work now, their son at school, and I am alone with the two girls. I considered taking them to the mosque so that we could pray together, but I do not know the area, and we must stay hidden. Instead, we knelt together on the carpet in the lounge room, faced Mecca and prayed together to Allah.

I miss Samira already. If she had never met me, if she had never offered me friendship when I needed it most, she would still be alive.

Her daughters would not be here, in a stranger's house, as orphans, if not for me.

They Can't Own You

Clay disinfected and bandaged his ear, cleaned himself up as best he could then donned the Nubian headdress and *thaub* that Mahmoud had given him. When he left the room, G was sitting in the chair by the window counting out the cash Clay had given him, laying the bills out in fanned piles of ten, a thousand US dollars to a pile. He didn't even look up as Clay left.

On the road outside the hotel Clay flagged down a taxi and showed the driver the address that Tall had written on the card. He was pretty sure now that it wasn't a trap. Tall's information about G had proved good. He had taken a big chance speaking to Clay as he had. What had been his motivation? He'd said he had kids. Was he one of the people Mahmoud and Atef had spoken about – one of the many Egyptians longing for change, secretly working to undermine the power structure that had run the country since 1954? Was this his own small act of rebellion?

Clay looked at his watch. Suez was more than a hundred kilometres away, but there was still plenty of time until the RV with Mahmoud. He knew it was a long shot, going to Luxor. But it was all they had. And Rania was going nowhere without finding out what happened to her son. Every day they delayed leaving Egypt put them in further peril. Not just him and Rania, but all of them – Atef, Mahmoud, their wives and children, Samira's girls even. If the Consortium and the AB were working together, as now appeared certain, then the danger was multiplied. These were not people who compromised, or forgot. He had to make Rania see this. She was acting out of desperation, holding fast to the thinnest of probabilities, a blurry CCTV image of an infant, a picture she hadn't even seen herself. A passport photo that could have been obtained anywhere. Her son was dead. He had to make her see this. Perhaps whatever this Al-Gambal knew would help her understand. Maybe. Maybe not. Either way, he had to try.

Outside, the work morning traffic lay stalled along the banks of the Nile, gasping under a blanket of ethylated lead and partially combusted hydrocarbons that thickened the air into vapour. Clay pushed the tail of his *jelabia* over his nose and mouth, shallowed his breathing. Finally leaving the corniche, the taxi driver turned east, towards New Cairo City and Suez. The Moqattam cliffs loomed above the haze-shrouded minarets of the citadel then faded in the distance. Forty minutes later the taxi was speeding east through a desert of construction waste, miles and miles of it, spread like a pox in millions of individual truckloads across the sand plains. Cairo's buildings faded in the rear window, swallowed in an inversion of brown smog.

By the time they reached Suez it was just gone eleven in the morning. The driver, unfamiliar with the area, stopped several times to ask for directions, was sent this way and that. Finally they arrived at a low-rent apartment complex, a half-dozen identical five-storey buildings set around two opposing semi-circular roads. Crumbling pavements spilled sand onto the tarmac. A few dead palm trees, withered and bent, perhaps planted at the grand opening years ago, lay slumped and toppled in a field of smashed brick and rubble. The driver stopped the taxi and pointed at a building. Half the windows were boarded up with plywood. Arabic graffiti snaked across the walls of the entranceway.

'Are you sure?' said the driver.

Clay gave him half the fare. 'Wait here,' he said, stepping out of the car.

Clay climbed the stairs to the fourth floor. Apartment forty-seven was at the end of the hall, towards the back of the building. He stood outside the door, listened a moment but heard nothing. He knocked, waited. After a minute, he knocked again, louder this time. Nothing. He raised his hand to try one last time when the door opposite cracked open against its chain. An unshaven face peered out from the darkness.

'Upstairs,' came a voice. 'On the roof.'

Clay mumbled his thanks and started back to the stairs.

Yusuf Al-Gambal was sitting in a canvas director's chair facing the Gulf of Suez, smoking a cigarette. He was bare-chested and wore tinted Vuarnet sunglasses. A can of Coke swung hinged between the thumb and index finger of his other hand. He turned as Clay approached, ran his gaze over Clay's face and frowned. 'What took you so long?' he said.

Clay stopped a few paces away but said nothing.

Al-Gambal took a puff of his cigarette, raised his chin and blew the smoke skywards in a slow, steady, exhalation. 'If my father were alive, all you bastards would be behind bars.'

Still Clay didn't reply.

'Do what you have to do,' said the young man. 'I don't care anymore.' He flicked the smoking butt of his cigarette over the lip of the roof. 'Burn in hell.'

'I probably will,' said Clay, his Arabic so much better now than it had been just three weeks earlier. 'But I'm not who you think I am.'

Al-Gambal set down his Coke, pushed himself out of the chair and stood staring at Clay through his reflective lenses. Clay looked back at a dual image of himself, the sky warped dark blue and vanadium behind him.

'You're bleeding,' said Al-Gambal, in English.

Clay reached up to his neck. His fingers came away stained bright red.

'Who are you?' said Al-Gambal

'A friend.'

'I don't have many of those left.'

'Neither do I,' said Clay, stepping closer. 'I'm a friend of Madame Al-Farouk, Hamid's wife.'

Al-Gambal took off his sunglasses, narrowing his eyes against the sun.

'She's here in Egypt,' Clay continued, 'and she's trying to find out what happened to her husband.'

Al-Gambal nodded slowly. 'I met a woman a few days ago. She said she was Hamid's private secretary. She said her name was Veronique Deschamps. I didn't believe her.'

'I don't know about that,' said Clay.

'Hamid was murdered,' said Al-Gambal.

'Why?'

'Because he challenged the system. Because of how close we came to exposing them.' Al-Gambal replaced his glasses. 'I always knew they would come after us.'

'Was it the court case?'

Al-Gambal turned away, walked to the edge of the roof and looked out across the water. A freighter appeared from behind the breakwater that marked the entrance to the canal.

'Yusuf,' said Clay. 'Please. I don't have a lot of time.'

'I am not able to discuss any matters associated with the case,' he said, still staring out to sea.

'I can protect you. Get you out.'

Al-Gambal laughed. 'You don't understand, do you?' he said, his voice wavering. 'I'm already dead.'

'Your choice, *broer*. Then it won't matter. So tell me.'

Al-Gambal glanced at Clay, looked back out across the Gulf. The freighter had moved away from the breakwater now and was plying south towards the Red Sea, trailing a long plume of black smoke against a flawless sky. 'I suppose I could...' he began, but let it go.

Clay reached into his pocket, pulled out the dead Kemetic's camera and showed Al-Gambal the photo of the three men and the woman in front of the court buildings.

'Where did you get this?' said Al-Gambal.

'That doesn't matter now,' said Clay. 'What were you being tried for?'

'High treason,' replied Al-Gambal. 'The prosecution was asking for the death penalty. A little ironic, don't you think?'

'But you won.'

'We didn't win. But we made it difficult enough for them that the attorney general offered us a deal: our silence, and in return they drop the charges, and we go free.'

'And you took it.'

'I didn't want to. I wanted to fight. So did Ali.'

'Ali?'

'My colleague from the project. The official story is that he hanged himself in prison. It happened the day after we were offered the deal.'

'Jesus.'

'He was twenty-four.' Al-Gambal flicked the end of another smoke off the roof. 'It was his first job.'

'I'm sorry,' said Clay, meant it. He'd seen far too many young guys die before they'd had a chance to learn how to live.

Al-Gambal inclined his head. 'We thought Hamid wanted to fight, too. He was very, very good at what he did. Very passionate, very skilful. But then Ali died, and something else happened...' Again he stopped short, let his sentence trail off.

'So you made the deal.'

'Yes. But then, when I heard on the news that Hamid and his son had been killed in Paris, I knew. They killed Mehmet a few days ago. I'm next.'

'Mehmet?'

Al-Gambal pointed to the third man in the photo, the one Clay had found dead in his flat. 'My oldest friend.'

'Jesus,' said Clay. 'What happened to change Hamid's mind?'

Al-Gambal placed his hand on his bare chest, covering the place where his heart was. 'Me. It was my fault.'

'Tell me.'

Over the next fifteen minutes, Yusuf Al-Gambal told his story. Whether he wanted someone to hear his version of events before he died, or just needed to get it straight in his own head, he let it all come out.

He'd been working as a scientist on a new project funded by the Canadian foreign aid agency, looking at air pollution in Cairo and how to improve air quality. He and Ali spent over a year installing monitoring stations across the city, collecting and compiling data. And what they found was far more disturbing than anyone had expected. Of course, you could see the smog. Everyone knew that air quality was poor, especially in the summer months when big inversions would lock the city in a gas chamber of its own making. But as they analysed the data and started to model toxicity, it became apparent that the air was far more poisonous, in considerably more ways and far more often, than anyone had imagined when the project had been set up.

Yusuf lit another cigarette. 'Lead,' he said, smoke pouring from his nostrils. 'That was the big one.'

Yusuf and Ali ran some preliminary calculations on human toxicity, focusing on lead. Then they got permission from the project manager to do some blood testing on selected children, working with a few local schools in the worst-affected areas. It wasn't in the original project budget, but the project manager told them that if they could find savings in their other monitoring work, he would allow them to apply it to the blood testing. They collected samples from thirty-two children in the end.

Over the coming months, they put it all together: the air quality data, the blood lead levels, the toxicity and dispersion modelling. Their work showed that children growing up in the worst areas, breathing this air for the first five to ten years of their lives, were not only far more likely to contract respiratory illnesses, but would suffer significant declines in cognitive skills, learning and language ability, and IQ. And the effects would be permanent.

'It blew us away,' Yusuf said, taking a long draw on his cigarette.

A preliminary report was prepared, and the Canadian project manager presented it to the EEAA – the Egyptian Environmental

Affairs Agency – and the Ministry of Health. Al-Gambal was in attendance. Two days after the presentation, the project manager was removed from his position and sent back to Canada. The report and the slides used in the presentation were removed from the office and a new manager was installed. Over the coming weeks, the terms of reference of the project were rewritten, radically scaled back. Staff were ordered to hand in any and all copies of data they had on their hard drives, or backed up on disc, and any hard copies of information they may have had. Shocked by the speed and ferociousness of the coverup, Al-Gambal and Ali decided to save as much of the original data as they could.

'We didn't keep much,' he said, speaking rapidly now. 'But it was enough.'

Al-Gambal's father had been a famous high-court judge, and Yusuf knew enough about the law to realise that he had a case. He went to one of his father's old associates, and presented him with the information. The next day, the police came to his flat and arrested him. After two weeks of detention, he was charged with high treason. It was Mehmet who sought out Hamid Al-Farouk and asked him to take on Yusuf's defence. Al-Farouk had successfully defended a number of other high-profile cases in Egypt over the previous few years and had a reputation for brilliance. They met, and he agreed to take on the case.

Al-Gambal paused long enough to light another cigarette using the burning end of his last, and continued. 'Hamid was fantastic. It was beautiful to see him work.'

'But something went wrong,' said Clay.

Al-Gambal nodded, inhaled, let the smoke drift from his mouth as he spoke. 'I offended him.'

'That's it?'

'Over the course of the case, we watched him change.'

'How?'

'He became increasingly zealous and intolerant. His behaviour was more and more erratic. He started invoking God and fate, and quoting the Koran out of context.' Al-Gambal stared up at the sky. 'And yet I loved him.'

Clay waited for him continue.

'I finally worked up the courage to tell him how I felt. Despite everything that was happening, it was all I could think about. I knew he was married, had a son. But I didn't care. It was madness. I was completely and madly in love with him. I have never felt like this about anyone before.' Al-Gambal grabbed the lip of the wall, leaned out so that his head and shoulders extended into the void. 'I know I will never feel that way again, about anyone.'

'But he rejected you.'

'And I was jealous. That woman. She followed him around like a dark shadow.'

'The woman in the photograph?'

Al-Gambal stared at the screen a moment and nodded. 'Ali's cousin, Fatimah. Her father died when she was young, and she was sent to live with her uncle, in Lebanon. She and Ali grew up together. Fatimah helped organise the children for the blood testing in Hadayek el-Koba.'

'The lead smelter.' The one Rania had told him she'd broken into that night.

Yusuf lit another smoke, closed his eyes. 'It was the neighbourhood she grew up in, before she was sent away.'

'Jesus.'

'Exactly,' said Yusuf. 'These kids were her relatives, the children of her friends.'

'And they were being poisoned. No wonder Hamid took the case.'

'Perhaps,' said Al-Gambal. 'But by then, it didn't matter.'

Not only did Hamid reject his advances, he viciously attacked him, accusing him of blasphemy and impiety, questioning his faith in Islam, deriding him and his kind as abominations, freaks, servants of Satan. After that, Hamid rapidly lost interest in the case. They knew that without Hamid, they were lost. They decided to take the deal.

But before they could inform the prosecutor of their decision, Ali was found dead in detention. 'It was a warning,' Yusuf said. 'We all knew it.'

All information about the case was sequestered, and Yusuf was sworn to secrecy. It was made very clear that if he broke the agreement, he would be in prison for the rest of his life. 'That was when I knew,' he said. 'We could never win. The project was closed down, the information buried. And nothing was going to change. Those smelters would go on polluting and children would continue growing up stunted and stupid. It was Hamid who convinced me, finally. He said to me: "The law isn't enough. Not when it's *their* law. You can't fight this from the inside." That's what he said. I knew then it was over.'

'He was wrong,' said Clay. 'Hamid kept some of the data. I've seen it. He must have been planning something, some kind of fightback. And Mehmet's journal. A lot of it is in some kind of code. It's your blood toxicity analysis, isn't it?'

Al-Gambal nodded. 'Mehmet was a very brave man, and a great friend. He cared very deeply about this country and what is happening to it. We all did.'

'I know someone who can get this to the press in Europe.'

Al-Gambal pushed back from the wall, faced Clay.

'Come with me,' said Clay. 'We can be out of Egypt in forty-eight hours.' What he'd just heard would surely be enough for Rania. Hamid had simply gotten involved in the wrong case. Someone must have found out that he'd managed to keep some of the incriminating evidence. That would explain the encryption of his hard drive. All Clay had to do now was convince Rania that Eugène, too, was dead. The woman who'd last been seen with Rania's husband and son was undoubtedly the assassin, sent by the Consortium. Framing Rania for the murders was the perfect coda.

Al-Gambal stared at him through his polarised lenses. Then he slumped his shoulders and lowered himself back into his chair. 'Against people like these, you can never win,' he said. 'We don't even know who they are. All we ever see are the functionaries – the crooked policemen, the paid-off judges, the cowed bureaucrats, the captured politicians. They make the laws, and they pass the sentences. But the people who really run the country – them we never see.'

Clay stood and looked out across the Gulf, the shifting currents of aquamarine and slate grey, the buff, heat-traced headlands on the far side of the canal. He thought about Crowbar, there in his desert tomb with the Galil across his chest. Where, he wondered, can people of conscience exist? How, in a world governed by the raw calculus of money and power, can individuals find justice? How can you fight something you cannot see? There were no targets, nothing physical to attack. Just an amorphous juggernaut of companies and ever-shifting capital. These were not enemies that he was trained to fight. If someone like Hamid, an expert in the law, in human rights, could be so easily undone, what hope was there for people like Yusuf Al-Gambal, like Rania, like him?

'And this idiot, The Lion,' Al-Gambal spat, 'with his warped view of Islam, blowing things up, killing innocent people while claiming to fight for them. Doesn't he realise that every time he commits an act of terrorism, the government can justify more repression? Brainless fool.'

'Fuck 'em,' said Clay, finally. 'You don't have to live by their rules. Get out. Live on your own terms. Don't participate. It's the ultimate rebellion. If you don't comply, they can't own you.' He meant it. Every word. 'Come with me.'

But he could see the resignation in Al-Gambal's slouch, in the calm way he lit yet another cigarette and filled his lungs. He was waiting for the end. He'd prepared himself, made his peace. Clay had seen it so many times before, in so many places, that easy departure.

Clay put out his hand. Al-Gambal took it. They shook.

'Peace be upon you,' said Clay. Then he turned towards the stairs and the waiting taxi and Cairo.

14th November 1997. Cairo, Egypt. 11:50 hrs

Claymore, you still have not returned. The minutes coalesce, accreting seconds like slowly dripping water builds a stalactite in a mountain cave, a centimetre in a thousand years.

I remember visiting such a place in France, once, when I was a little girl. Coloured lights had been installed in the cave, and although it was beautiful, I remember very clearly being terrified, clutching my father's hand as we went further and further into the mountain. The guide had told us that some of the stalactites were more than fifty thousand years old. I was doing calculations in my head. I knew my father was thirty-six at the time – I had just made him a birthday card. Suddenly, I realised that he was going to die and that these delicate constructions would remain, slowly growing, for long after. By the time we emerged back into the daylight, I was crying.

I could never have imagined how quickly his death did come, in the end, or its manner.

Mon Dieu, I should never have agreed to stay here and let you go alone. After everything that has happened, I could not bear to be separated from you again. I would rather die.

I have just reread this last paragraph. I blanch imagining that you might ever read this. I will never allow it, of course. Am I being hysterical? Would I, literally, rather be killed than live on without you? It is a cowardly thing to admit. In thinking such things, I blaspheme. I exist to worship God, not to indulge my own frivolities. I must be strong. Eugène is depending on me.

16:25 hrs

My friend from the Directorate just called me, here at Atef's apartment.

We used our usual code. I am his sister. He told me Mother was feeling ill, which meant we needed to speak urgently, and we arranged another line. Five minutes later I called him on the prearranged number. He is taking a big risk every time he speaks to me.

The woman, Jumoke Quarrah, I ran her photo through our database, he said.

And?

The name is an alias.

Who is she?

Her real name is Fatimah Salawi, a Lebanese national.

Mon Dieu.

She was originally from Egypt, a place called Hadayek el-Koba, a suburb of Cairo. Her father was killed when she was a child, under mysterious circumstances. Seems he may have been murdered, but the crime was never solved. He was a union leader in the factory he worked in. After his death, she was sent to live with her uncle in Lebanon.

A lead smelter, I said, feeling faint.

I do not know. But you must be very careful. Fatimah Salawi is a known member of Al-Gama'a al-Islamiyya.

Are you sure? I gasped.

Egypt is not my area. I must be very careful. I cannot dig too far. But from what I am told, the source is rated as highly credible.

Thank you. Thank you.

One last thing.

Please.

The Directorate expects Al-Gama'a Islamiyya to launch a major attack, directed against Westerners, within the next forty-eight hours. And they believe that it will occur somewhere in the vicinity of Luxor.

Luxor. Are you sure?

The intelligence is rated as highly credible.

Luxor. We must hurry.

It Could Never Be Any Other Way

By the time Clay returned from Suez it was dark and the scheduled rendezvous with Mahmoud was less than an hour away. He made his way back to Atef's apartment in Zamalek, ensuring as best he could that he was not being tracked.

When he arrived, Rania was jumpy, withdrawn. She looked as if she'd been crying and hadn't slept in days. But she noticed his wound right away, insisting that Atef's wife examine him. As the bandage he'd applied came off, she gasped, muttered some invocation in Arabic under her breath.

As Atef's wife sewed, Clay told Rania about his encounter with Tall at the hotel – what he'd said about Samira and G.

Rania listened in silence, watching the needle moving across what remained of Clay's ear. He knew it hurt her to hear of her friend's betrayal, of Samira's guilt and final attempt at redemption – all things he knew well. By the time he finished telling it, Atef's wife was finishing up, and Rania's eyes were spilling silent tears.

'She defied them, in the end,' said Clay. 'That probably saved you, those extra few minutes she held out.'

Rania said nothing, just stood gazing out through her tears.

Then Clay told her about meeting Yusuf Al-Gambal in Suez, about the details of the case and her husband's involvement, the unrequited love, and finally, Al-Gambal's unwillingness to continue the fight, to run even, his seeming resignation in the face of imprisonment or death.

'I don't understand it,' Clay said, shaking his head. 'It's as if he just wants it all to be over.'

Rania watched as Atef's wife finished bandaging his ear, cleaned him up.

'We have a decision to make,' he said, once Atef's wife had left them alone. 'We can go to Luxor, as planned, or we can head straight for the Red Sea, now. Mahmoud knows someone who can get us passage on a freighter heading south. We can be out of Egypt and on our way in twelve hours.' What they needed now was clarity. Certainty. Logic. They needed to think it through well, all of it. If they didn't, they were not going to leave this place.

Rania stared at him as if he'd just proposed that they turn themselves in to the authorities. But instead of the rebuke he expected, she said: 'I have managed to make some sense of the Kemetic's journal.' She handed him a card. 'Yusuf Al-Gambal gave me this, the one time I met him.'

It was a business card. Clay turned it to the light.

'It's a big industrial plant. A lead smelter. The one I told you about. The same place, the same name, is mentioned here.' She pointed to a symbol on the open page of the Kemetic's journal. 'You see, it is the company logo.'

'The place in the photograph.'

Rania nodded.

'One of the Consortium's companies?'

'According to the journal, yes. Majority-owned.' Rania traced her finger along the string of Arabic shorthand. 'And you see here? SRD Holdings. The minority partner. I did some checking, while you were away. SRD is registered in South Africa.'

'The AB.'

'It must be.'

Clay told Rania about the blood data the Kemetic had encoded in his journal, that Ali had a cousin who organised the testing of the neighbourhood children. 'They were starting to trace the link back to the actual sources of pollution.'

'And when they got too close, the Consortium hit back.'

'That's why those cops were so interested in the file you got from your husband's computer. Can you imagine if this got out?'

'That is why they killed my husband,' said Rania. 'It is logical. Yusuf Al-Gambal, the Kemetic, and my husband. Together, taking on the Consortium in the courts. About this.' She stabbed the document with her finger. 'Pollution from their factories. Samira mentioned the same thing.'

'And now, Yusuf and Ali's cousin are the only ones left.'

'Ali's cousin?'

'Fatimah. She was the one who organised the blood testing.'

Rania gasped, held her breath a moment then grabbed Clay's arm. 'Of course,' she said. 'The one in the photograph, standing next to Hamid. She knew him, worked with him on the case. It all fits. Fatimah Salawi is Ali's cousin.'

'Hold on. Who is Fatimah Salawi?'

Rania told Clay about her conversation with her friend, about the warning of an imminent attack by GI. 'That's why we have to go to Luxor. Because Fatimah Salawi is the woman who killed my husband and who kidnapped my son. She is a member of Al-Gama'a al-Islamiyya, and she's on her way to Luxor right now to do something terrible.'

☾

An hour and a half later the southern outskirts of Giza were fading into the distance. The Western Desert Road unspooled before them in the yellow myopia of the headlights. Mahmoud had brought the big twenty-two-wheeler and had arranged to carry a container of electronic goods bound for Aswan. He'd greeted Clay as he might an old friend, with a bear hug and scratchy kisses on each cheek. To Rania he offered a bow of the head and a smile, bid her welcome.

'Your very good friend,' he said to Clay, pushing out a big smile. 'You found her.'

'Thanks to you.'

'And now? Luxor or the coast?'

'Luxor. We must find her son.'

'God willing.'

'Yes. *Inshallah.*'

'And then?'

'To the coast, as planned. Out of Egypt.'

Mahmoud ran his fingers through his beard, considering this. 'I will arrange it.'

Clay and Rania sat up front, ready to disappear into the cab's rear sleeping compartment if they encountered roadblocks.

As the kilometres wound by, Rania leafed through the pages of the Kemetic's diary. Clay could feel her there next to him, her hip warm against his, her right elbow moving against his side every time she turned a page. Her smell filled his senses, that same elixir he'd first breathed in Yemen three years ago now – the smell of wildflowers and honey that would always remind him of their time together at her aunt's chalet in the Alps, after he'd been reported killed and somehow found her again. He counted the times they'd been together. Once in Yemen, desperate and frightened, before she'd vanished into the night. Then Switzerland, three weeks that in his memory occupied a space equivalent to all of his life before meeting her. London, on the run from Medved and his thugs. And then, much later, those few days in Istanbul when they'd come as close as any time before or since, after which he'd lost her in the maelstrom of time and distance and events, chaotic and uncertain. Twenty-seven nights, or parts of them. That was it.

And yet, in everything she'd told him, everything he'd learned from Yusuf Al-Gambal, there was something that didn't fit. 'Al-Gama'a al-Islamiyya,' he said. 'Who are they fighting against?'

'The regime,' she said, her voice almost lost among the sounds of the road.

'And who is the regime?'

'According to The Lion, to Samira, to the Kemetic, it is the Consortium.'

'Right. And Yusuf Al-Gambal told me he was sure that Hamid and the Kemetic had been murdered by the Consortium. So, if this woman, Fatimah Salawi, really is a member of Al-Gama'a al-Islami-yya, working with Hamid and her cousin to help expose one of the Consortium's companies, then why would she murder Hamid? And why take your son? It makes absolutely no sense.'

Rania was silent for a long time. Clay let her ponder.

After a while, she said: 'Perhaps she was using Al-Gama'a al-Islamiyya as a cover, as misdirection. Maybe she does work for the Consortium. Maybe she was the one who blew the cover on what Yusuf and Ali were doing.'

'A mole? Working against her own cousin?'

'Maybe. Perhaps she always intended to murder all three of us. When I didn't come home on time that day, maybe she decided to kill Hamid and take Eugène, framing me for their murders. What better way to ensure my silence than to kidnap my son?'

'Then your friends in the DGSE have their facts wrong.'

'Quite possibly,' she said.

'But if she isn't with the Consortium, then she is exactly who your contacts in DGSE say she is – an Islamic terrorist – and most likely your son is dead. And if she is with the Consortium, mole or not, then she isn't going to Luxor.' He felt as if he was stepping into a minefield. 'Your son is dead, Rania. Face facts. We should leave. Now. Get out while we can.'

Rania stared at him, her hair haloed in the phosphorescence of the truck's instrument panel, her face in darkness. Time passed. Miles of darkened desert. The slow turning of stars. The drone of the truck's big diesel engine. Clay let her alone. Mahmoud too, knowing this was a silence that should not be broken.

The lights of Beni Suef were well behind them when she said: 'I need to be sure, Claymore.' Then she reached for his hand, took it in her own. He could feel her calloused finger tracing the big vein from his second knuckle to the point of his wrist.

'Please understand, *chéri*. This is the best chance we have of finding out what happened to my son. I need to do this. And I need your help. After, I release you from any obligation you may feel you hold.'

Clay let her words wash over him. 'Okay, Ra. We make sure. Whatever it takes.' It could never be any other way.

The Greatest and Truest
Means of Your Salvation

Over the next two hours they shared their plight with Mahmoud. They'd talked it over and agreed they had no other choice.

If he hadn't already, Tall would soon issue a nationwide police bulletin for their arrest. If the DGSE was right, and some kind of attack by Al-Gama'a al-Islamiyya was imminent, and if indeed the woman, Fatimah Salawi, aka Jumoke Quarrah, was somehow involved, and was either in or on her way to Luxor, and if Eugène was with her, they had perhaps a day to find the boy. There were a lot of unknowns, far too many ifs, and no leads other than a partial address and two conflicting theories. They needed help, the help of locals, people who knew the area and its inhabitants. People like Mahmoud.

Rania described the woman. 'She looks like me,' she said. 'But she is Lebanese, we think, a foreigner. She would have arrived here no more than two weeks ago, perhaps less. She will either be very pious, or pretending to be so.'

'And your son will be with her?' said Mahmoud, leaning over the steering wheel. Perhaps in deference to Rania, he hadn't yet produced a bottle.

'I think so. Perhaps.' Rania passed Mahmoud a photograph of Eugène.

'*Mashallah*,' said Mahmoud.

Rania repeated the invocation.

'My wife is from a very old Luxor family,' said Mahmoud. 'She knows everyone. Her father is imam of the largest mosque in the city.

It is best if she makes enquiries, while the two of you stay hidden. If this woman can be found, my wife will do it.'

'Please,' said Rania. 'Tell her to be careful. This woman is extremely dangerous.'

❨

By the time they arrived at Mahmoud's house, the sun was up and the heat was coming off the hills in incandescent sheets. A hot wind blew in from the desert, sending dust devils spinning down the narrow lane.

Mahmoud led them to the house, a simple two-storey building set at the back of the garden, shaded by a pair of towering sycamores. He showed Clay to a small room on the ground floor.

'Rest, now,' he said. 'There is clean water.' He made as if to pour a bucket over his head. 'Lunch is at two o'clock.' And then to Rania: 'Come. I will introduce you to my wife. You can trust her. Tell her everything. She will start looking for the woman right away. If Fatimah Salawi is in Luxor, we will find her.'

Clay tried to catch Rania's gaze but she had already turned away. He watched her as she followed Mahmoud down the corridor. Her gait was compressed, stilted somehow, stress there in every move-ment. Would she be able to do as Mahmoud had counselled, and stay put, trust their new friends to find the woman? And when they came up with nothing – no woman called Fatimah, and no little boy called Eugène – would she finally see reason and allow him to take her away? In twenty-four hours, with any luck, and if G was as venal as Clay thought him, the AB would be notified of Clay's death. The window for escape would open, just. But it wouldn't last long.

Clay pulled off his *jelabia*, unwrapped his headscarf and dropped his pack on the floor. He stripped off his clothes, closed the shutters, switched on the ceiling fan and locked the bedroom door. He took the G21 from his pack, checked the action, and set it on the table next to the bed. Then he lay on the bed and closed his eyes.

Women's voices drifted up from the courtyard, the sounds of children playing. Coloured lights flashed in the distance, from some other part of the room, perhaps. He was standing in front of a bar, a beer in hand. It was very cold. He hadn't had a beer in a long time. There were others in the place, figures in dark clothing, men and women. Some of the women were bound, their wrists tied behind their backs. As they approached, he could see that their skirts were very short and their naked breasts quivered as they walked. Some were chained, dragged heavy weights across the floor, hunks of metal, large stones. They strained against their bonds. One of the women approached him. She too was bound, partially naked. She looked at him. For a moment, he thought it was Rania. It looked like her, but it wasn't. The eyes were wrong, the lips, the build. She turned away and bent slightly at the waist, revealing smooth labia and a glistening cleft. And then she was gone and Crowbar was there, at the far end of the bar. Crowbar smiled, raised a glass, but then he turned and started towards the lights. Clay made to follow, but his feet were rooted to the floor. He pushed out one foot, felt it scrape heavy across what was now thick sand. The lights came into focus for a moment and there was a flash of blue sky, a sun-browned savannah, a green empire of scattered trees, and he knew it as the Africa of his wartime – scarred and murdered and beautiful. Crowbar stopped there, on the threshold, looked back at him, urged him on. Clay called out, but Crowbar turned and was gone.

Clay woke gasping, bathed in sweat, painfully erect. He reached for the G21, dropped the mag, checked the breech, worked the action. The last time he'd fired it, it had ended Manheim's life. The images from his dream came to him, clear and troubling. He wanted Rania. It was all he could do to stop himself going to her now. He imagined her here, now, in the bed beside him, trying to push him away, turning her face away at first then yielding as he overpowered her.

Clay swung his feet from the bed, set down the weapon, combed his fingers through his hair and tried to calm himself. He stood, stretched. Slowly, the images faded.

He began field-stripping the Glock. He dry-fired the weapon, placed the handle between his knees, pushed in the takedown lever, eased the slide forwards and detached the slide, barrel and recoil assembly. He was about to remove the recoil spring when there was a knock at the door. Clay set down the Glock, rose, wrapped a towel around his waist, and opened the door.

It was Mahmoud. 'We have found something,' he said, glancing at the parts laid out on the bed.

Parveen, Mahmoud's wife, was seated in the garden under a vine-covered trellis. Her broad face was framed by a severely drawn headscarf, but she smiled with strong yellow teeth as he approached, indicating with her hand where Clay was to sit.

Rania was seated on Parveen's left. Clay bowed, sat on the cushion to Parveen's right. Mahmoud sat across from his wife. Parveen's youngest son brought tea. Parveen poured. The tea was black and sweet. They drank in silence. Clay paced himself, matching Mahmoud. Second cups were poured.

'We are very pleased that you have been reunited,' said Parveen, smiling at Rania and then at Clay. 'It is God's will.'

'Thank you,' said Rania, glancing at Clay.

'And now,' said Parveen, 'we have news of the woman in the passport.' She paused. 'Jumoke Quarrah was born here in Luxor over thirty years ago. At first I was not sure that it was her. It was a long time ago.' The matriarch waved to the kitchen, called for more tea. 'I had almost forgotten her. It was a very sad story. Her father died two months before she was born – drowned in the Nile when the boat he was working on overturned. Her mother, a widow, died in childbirth. The girl was claimed by her aunt, who took her to live in Edfu. We never saw her again.'

Rania glanced at Clay. 'Could this be her?'

Mahmoud's son came with fresh glasses of tea, offered them from a polished copper tray.

'I made enquiries with friends from Edfu,' said Parveen. 'Jumoke died when she was eight years old, poor girl. The aunt not long after.'

She sipped her tea. 'Tragedy has a way of following some families,' she said. 'God is great.'

'*Allah'u akbar*,' repeated Mahmoud and Rania almost in unison.

'If this Lebanese woman you have described has taken poor Jumoke's identity,' said Parveen, 'there is no surviving family to expose her.'

Rania covered her face with her hands. 'What about Eugène?' she said after a moment. 'Have you heard anything about a little boy?'

The matriarch closed her eyes. 'Not yet, my dear. Not yet. But do not lose hope. My eldest son is out now, making enquiries. My husband will take me to the mosque immediately and I will speak with my father.'

'Please,' said Rania, 'may I come with you?'

Parveen smiled, took Rania's hands in her own. 'Please, dear, stay here where it is safe. If you are with us, it will only arouse suspicion. Allow us to do this good work for you, in our own way.'

Rania inclined her head and kissed the older woman's hands.

'But before we continue, I must speak with you both.' Parveen closed her eyes a moment. 'My husband is a very trusting man,' she said. 'Sometimes too trusting.'

Clay looked over at Mahmoud. He showed no sign of being displeased.

'And you understand that I must protect my family.' Parveen looked at her husband. Her face was drawn now, the earlier warmth gone.

'Yes,' said Clay. 'I am sorry for…'

The matriarch raised her hand and turned the full power of her gaze on Clay. 'My husband has told me of your first meeting. He tells me you are a traveller, an engineer.'

Clay glanced at Mahmoud, replied that yes, this was true.

'Do not be surprised, young man. We tell each other everything,' said the woman. 'I am my husband's only wife. I have borne him five sons.'

Clay nodded.

'He told me that you came from the desert, wounded by bullets.' Parveen glanced at Rania, frowned. 'Are you Israeli, young man? Tell me, truthfully.'

'South African.'

The matriarch nodded, considered this. 'I have heard of your apartheid. Are you racist?'

Clay looked inside himself. 'I was brought up that way. But now, I am not.'

She blinked twice. 'Changing one's views is a sign of intelligence and open-mindedness. Do you believe in God, young man?'

Clay did not hesitate. Perhaps he should have. 'No, ma'am.'

Parveen sat quietly a moment. 'No matter,' she said, taking Clay's hand in her own so that Clay and Rania were now linked by her touch. 'This woman has faith enough for you both. Do you love her?' She turned her gaze to meet his. 'Answer me truthfully.'

Clay began, stumbled, stopped. 'I'm sorry,' he said. 'My Arabic is not sufficient.' He might have said, had he been able, that he could still not understand the binary nature of this thing that seemed to exist only as yes or no. And if there were degrees of it, then it was not absolute; and if it was not absolute then surely it could not exist at all. Or that he had insufficient experience of it to know if this raging, sex-fuelled, physical longing was a betrayal of the thing, or its truest expression. That all the other emotions at war inside him were beyond his understanding, and even, on most days, his contempla-tion; and that for a long time it had been a matter of pure survival that these things be buried, annihilated. But he could say none of it, and instead sat mute, staring at the tightly woven geometries of the carpet.

The older woman closed her eyes. Rania looked away.

'There will be time for this, *inshallah,*' said Parveen after a time, patting Rania's hand. 'For now, it is Allah's will that you are here. He has chosen this for you and for us. It is our task to discern his purpose, and to be faithful to it.'

'*Inshallah*,' said Rania.

'Do you understand, young man?' said Parveen.

'I will try,' said Clay. 'But in these things…' He stopped, looked up. 'It is difficult.'

'Allah will guide you,' said Parveen, getting to her feet, still holding Rania's hand.

Mahmoud and Clay stood.

'Now, come daughter. We will talk more of this woman we must find.' Rania followed Parveen into the house.

'She is very direct,' said Mahmoud. 'But she is a good woman, and wise. She is very glad you found your friend, that you have managed to protect her from the danger she faces, and that you have brought her here to stay with us.'

Clay grabbed Mahmoud's wrist. 'We don't have time for this, Mahmoud. The danger is close. We need to leave Egypt now.'

'You are safe here,' said Mahmoud, looking down at Clay's hand. He moved his free arm in an arc around the garden. 'All around, all of these houses, this whole neighbourhood, are my family. You are safe.'

'No one is safe.' Clay released Mahmoud's wrist, looked into his eyes. 'Her boy is dead, Mahmoud. She will not accept it.'

He nodded. 'Women can be this way. They are much stronger than we in these things.'

'Please, ask your wife to speak with her. We need to go. I cannot put you in danger any longer.'

'I will talk to her, my friend. But right now, you must allow us to do this. If this woman is here, if your friend's son is here, we will find them.'

'Understand me, please. I am speaking of hours, not days.'

Mahmoud put his hand on Clay's shoulder. 'I understand,' said Mahmoud. 'I will tell her.'

'We are very grateful,' said Clay. 'More than I can say.'

'I am pleased that Allah saw fit to put you in my path. It is I who am grateful.'

Clay bowed his head.

'Allah, though you do not believe in him yet, favours those who are truthful, and those who fight for what is just.'

Clay said nothing, did not attempt to articulate the turmoil boiling within him. For he had no such certainty of right or truth. He was acting out of pure selfishness. Whatever higher purpose he had ever felt or acted upon had come not from within himself, but from Eben. It had been his friend's philosophy, his burning sense of justice, that had set him on his life's course, back then during the war when they had made the conscious decision to reject apartheid and all that it stood for, all that they had been raised to believe. And after Eben had been wounded, put into a decade-long coma, living but not, it was Crowbar who had taken carriage of Clay's soul, taken it in another direction entirely. And now that both were gone, he knew it was time for him to find his own way.

'What do you think of this man who calls himself The Lion,' said Clay. 'Is he fighting for what is just and right?'

Mahmoud ran his fingers through his beard. 'My other brother runs a company that charters boats for tourists wishing to see the Nile,' he said. 'He calls this man a terrorist. Every attack he makes, no matter where in Egypt, means fewer tourists come. His business is already half of what it was before.'

'And you, Mahmoud?'

'I understand my brother's view. But I also know, as he does, that our government and those that control it are deeply corrupt and do not care about the people. Many Muslims feel this and are convinced that things cannot continue in this way. The Lion is expressing this discontent. But he does it in a way that is not good.'

'Right fight, wrong method?'

'Perhaps, my friend, it could be put this way.'

Clay grabbed Mahmood's forearm. 'Tell your family to be very careful.'

Mahmoud looked at him through narrowed eyes.

'Just tell them to be extra safe in the next few days. There is talk of an attack in Luxor. Stay away from tourists. Tell them now, Mahmoud.'

Mahmoud nodded. 'I will do as you say. And now, my friend, you must prepare to leave, and despite the difficulty in doing so, you must wait. But most difficult of all, you must search inside yourself. The greatest and truest means of your salvation is right in front of you.'

16th November 1997. Luxor, Egypt. 16:30 hrs

We waited all the rest of yesterday, and through the day today.

Mahmoud's eldest son scoured the east bank with his grandfather, speaking to dozens of people. No one had seen anyone fitting the descriptions. His mother, Parveen, the one who calls me daughter, has said that I should not give up hope, but I feel my reserves of belief slipping away. If the woman, Fatimah Salawi, is not here in Luxor, how can we possibly hope to find her? If my friend from the Directorate is right and a terrorist attack is coming, somewhere here, then surely Eugène is in even greater danger. Terrible possibilities begin to form in my mind and I pretend that I have not glimpsed them; I force myself to think of other things.

My God, what if you are right, Claymore, about Eugène? Am I deluding myself?

I have been going through the Kemetic's diary, the one that you took from his apartment. I have decided never to tell you about what happened that day. Even though you may suspect something, you have not asked me about it. If you ever do, I will reveal nothing. What you already know is enough.

Much of what is written in the diary is in hieroglyphs, or in demotic – a simplified ancient Egyptian script. This material is impenetrable. But he also used a shorthand of his own devising, which I am starting to understand. There are also many passages in plain Arabic, which are relatively complete. In one, he writes:

> *We had a big argument tonight with H. He is very angry, and has been for several days now, ever since Y declared himself. My heart aches for my poor friend, trapped in a physical body that desires love from men, as mine craves the love of women. We are both miserable creatures, but we believe we are fighting a just cause. Perhaps it will*

absolve us both in the eyes of Allah. The Consortium is a cancer, eating away at our society from within. H has begun to express sympathy with the extremists. Tonight he said he agrees with GI, and that there is no other way to defeat and remove the Consortium. Fatimah has begun to influence him. She is beguiling and beautiful, and I do not trust her. It is wrong to invoke the name of our God in such a mission.

I reread the words, ensuring I have not made an error. If this can be believed – and why would I not believe it? – the Kemetic was a Muslim. The ancient religion must have been a hobby, or an affectation, or perhaps camouflage. It also corroborates what Yusuf told you – that Hamid rejected his advances, and that this led to a breakdown in the professional relationship. Hamid never expressed to me, in the time we were married, any revulsion towards homosexuals. He was always very liberal about such matters whenever we discussed them, very modern. He reminded me so much of my father.

I looked for a date for the entry, but could not find one. Looking at the other entries, it was probably written sometime between July and September of this year, well before the acquittal. It is clear, now, that Fatimah knew my husband for some time before then. Did she lure him in, use sex to get close, disguise her real intentions?

This is another passage I was able to decipher, a more recent entry:

The lady who calls herself Veronique came to see me today. Y sent her to me. She is seeking information about H, about the case. She seems to know a lot already. I want to help her, but I am afraid of myself. She is beautiful. Uncommonly so. I promised myself, after the last time, that it would be the end of it. I swore, made a promise to God.

After the last time! Those photographs. He had done it before. Perhaps with Fatimah? My God! That there are such depraved people in this world. And yet, I can see that he was a good man, fighting a terrible injustice as best he could, with grace and perseverance. We are all flawed, all suspect, hiding our secrets, struggling against our baser selves.

22:15 hrs

Claymore, you just knocked on my door. We spoke only briefly.

The distance between us opened up like a cold sea. After our conversation with Parveen, I know that you do not love me. This is clear to me now. You act only from some deep sense of loyalty. Perhaps, God help you, it is simply that you have no one else. Your ignorance is shocking. I pity you. You know nothing.

You came to tell me that you had just spoken to Atef on the telephone. The girls are fine. Yusuf was found yesterday in an industrial landfill site outside Suez. He had been shot in the head.

Strength

When Mahmoud woke him, it was still dark.

Whatever nightmare Clay had been inhabiting faded as the urgency in his friend's voice doubled his heart rate. Clay pulled on his shirt, checked his weapon, secured his ammunition and grenades in his waist pouch, and then threw on the *jelabia*.

'My father-in-law just called,' whispered Mahmoud. 'They think they have found her. A neighbour from Al Alqalta came to him late last night. She told him that a strange woman – a foreigner – arrived a week ago. At first, she paid it no attention. Then, over the next few days, she began to notice other men, also strangers, arriving and staying in the same flat. It is not far from here, on the west bank. The foreign woman goes to the nearby mosque every morning for the *fajr*, the dawn prayer, and again in the evening.'

'That's it?' said Clay.

Mahmoud nodded.

'Not much to go on.'

'My father-in-law showed the neighbour Rania's passport photo. She said it was her.'

'Jesus.'

'We must hurry.'

Rania was waiting by the car with Parveen. They embraced and Rania sat in the back. Mahmoud drove. Soon they were speeding south along the dark canal road towards Al Alqalta.

'This is why it took us some time to find her,' said Parveen. 'We started in the town, the big places.'

Mahmoud slowed the car and turned right onto a small, unpaved road. Dawn was still an hour or so away, just a hint on the eastern horizon. After a few hundred metres he switched off the lights and rolled the car to a stop under a giant sycamore.

'There,' whispered Parveen. 'At the end of the street, on the left. She is in the second-floor apartment facing the road. Where the balcony is.'

The place was dark, shuttered. Clay pulled out his binoculars, scanned the front.

Minutes passed.

'Maybe she has already left for the mosque,' whispered Rania.

'It is still early. The mosque is very close. Walking distance.' Parveen pointed. 'Over there.'

A single minaret poked above the scattered buildings, bathed in a wan green light.

'I am going to look,' said Rania. And before anyone could respond she was out and moving away in the darkness.

'Shit,' said Clay. They'd just made their first mistake.

A light came on in the flat, then another. Clay and Mahmoud sat motionless. A minute or so later, the lights were extinguished. Clay checked his watch: just before five o'clock, the sky greying now in the east. A dark figure emerged from a side alley, got into a small van parked nearby, started the engine and drove it around to the front of the building. The front door opened. A man stepped out, looked both ways, walked to the van, opened the sliding door and got in.

'Look,' said Mahmoud.

Five more men filed out of the building and jumped into the van. Each carried a duffel bag. The door closed and the van moved away.

'What should we do?' said Mahmoud. 'Follow?'

'No, wait,' said Clay.

A dark figure emerged from the same alley and hurried across the narrow street. A woman in a black *burqa*. She was carrying a small backpack. She turned left, in the direction of the mosque, and disappeared down a side street.

'Follow her,' said Clay.

Mahmoud waited a few seconds, started the engine and backed the car away, keeping the lights off. At the end of the street he turned left. The call to prayer echoed out across the sleeping town. They trundled along the rutted, potholed road for a minute or so then Mahmoud stopped the car.

The mosque was perhaps fifty metres away. From where they sat they could clearly see the entrance, a house built close to its walls on the left, and to the right, the fields and palms of the flood plain. People began straggling into the mosque in ones and twos – men mostly, wrapped against the morning chill. There was no sign of the woman or Rania.

'We must wait,' said Parveen. 'The woman we spoke to says she leaves after *fajr*.'

Clay scanned the street and the adjacent buildings. Rania wasn't thinking straight. This woman – if it was her – was dangerous. Rania was unarmed, and they had no way of staying in contact. They should have established a rendezvous point. He had to hope that if they became separated, she would find her way back to Mahmoud's. More mistakes.

Five minutes passed, ten. Clay and Mahmoud and Parveen sat in the car and watched the sky lighten. Worshippers began leaving the mosque, the same people they'd seen going in, the men hunched, wrapped against the chill, matrons in their dark burqas, neither the woman nor Rania among them.

Minutes passed. They waited.

A quarter of an hour later the lights on the minaret flickered out. 'Jesus,' said Clay. 'They're gone, both of them.'

Mahmoud pressed his fingertips together. Patience. But this was a commodity that Clay had long since husked away to the slimmest of cores. Any moment now, the call might be going out to the AB, the evidence perhaps already on its way, and then the window would open, at least for him. Whatever grace Tall had promised was already gone. They needed to go, now, not be scurrying around the back-streets of some shithole town in rural Egypt. And yet her strength beguiled him. It was one of the things that had first attracted him to her, all those days and months ago. But this seemingly blind, sometimes ugly stubbornness also frightened him, so beyond their control did it seem. He reached for the door handle.

'Wait,' said Mahmoud. 'Look, there.'

A woman was leaving the mosque. Her face was veiled. She carried a small backpack on one shoulder and in the other arm, slung on her hip, a child.

Clay held his breath.

'Is it her?' said Mahmoud.

'I can't tell.' Clay raised his binoculars and tried to focus on the child, but its face was turned towards the woman.

She stepped out onto the road, looked to her left. A car emerged from the darkness, rolled towards her. The car stopped, a bearded man behind the wheel. She opened the front door, got in. The car moved off in the direction of the canal road. Seconds later, it was out of sight.

Mahmoud made to follow.

'There,' said Clay.

Another woman was leaving the mosque. She stopped, looked both ways, flung off her headscarf. It was Rania.

Mahmoud gunned the engine. They pulled up in front of her moments later.

Rania jumped in the back. 'Did you see?' she said, breathless.

'Was it her?' said Parveen.

'Yes. And she has my son.'

Echo and Die

'There they are,' said Mahmoud, turning the car onto the canal road.

The early-morning traffic had started to build. Cars with head-lights still burning, a few long-haul trucks trundling along the two-lane trunk road. Up ahead, the car they'd seen the woman leave the mosque in, a white Nissan sedan, ubiquitous here, kept a steady pace, heading north.

'Where are they going?' said Rania, desperation in her voice.

Mahmoud was keeping well back, behind a big lorry, occasionally inching out as if thinking of passing. 'Perhaps the Western Desert Road.'

Clay told Rania about the men they'd seen getting into the van. 'Do you think they're together?'

'If the Directorate's information is correct, yes.'

Soon they were approaching West Luxor. Hatshepsut's temple glowed on the hillside, bathed in the sun's first blush. Cut into the mountain rock, it looked, even from this distance, impossibly huge. The car containing Eugène and the woman approached the turnoff for the temple, then kept going north towards the highway.

'Not a sightseeing trip, then,' said Clay.

Rania shot him a stare. 'Perhaps they are going back to Cairo.'

As she said it, the car made a sharp turn to the left and started along an unpaved road that led away west into the hills, trailing a cloud of sun-shot dust.

Mahmoud slowed and pulled to the side of the paved road. 'Not Cairo.'

'Where does this road go?' said Clay.

'Into the desert,' said Mahmoud. 'It follows the valley into the hills and eventually to the plateau and then into the desert.' He pointed further north. 'Up there, over that ridge, is the Valley of the Kings. But here, there is nothing. Some old quarries. A few archaeological sites, but nothing of importance.'

'We must follow them,' said Rania.

Mahmoud eased the car onto the gravel and started up the valley. The road was poorly maintained and the car groaned through pot-holes and rattled over the washboard as it wound its way up into the hills. Mahmoud was very careful, backing off at corners, using the other car's dust trail as a gauge of separation. After about ten minutes, Mahmoud slowed the car and rolled it to a stop.

'Look at the dust,' he said. 'They have stopped, around this next bend.'

Clay jumped out of the car and started up the hill on foot. Rania followed. He crouched as he approached the lip of a crumbled ridge of weathered sandstone. From here he could see up along the length of the next bend in the valley. The rear of the white Nissan was just visible, tucked into a notch in the rock on the south side of the road. He went prone, pulled out his binoculars.

'What are they doing?' whispered Rania. He could feel the warmth of her breath on his neck.

'He's opening the boot,' said Clay. 'Jesus.'

'What?'

'He's got an AK.' Clay watched the man heft a pack onto his back, sling the weapon, then throw a cloak over his shoulders, covering it over. The woman strapped the child across her chest and the pair started off into the hills, moving south, back towards the temple. He handed Rania the glasses. She followed the pair until they disappeared over a ridge.

'Looks like they're planning to be out here a while,' said Clay. 'That's a big pack he's carrying.'

'Come on,' said Rania, starting down the hill towards the car.

'Wait,' said Clay. 'We have to tell Mahmoud and Parveen.'

'You go.'

Clay grabbed her by the elbow. 'No Rania, wait. Whatever they are doing out here, it isn't good.'

Rania said nothing, stood staring in the direction of her son.

Clay started pulling her back to where Mahmoud was waiting. Rania tried to wrench herself away, but could not break his grip. 'Let me go,' she hissed. 'You wanted to leave him.'

Clay released her arm. 'Please, Rania. I'm sorry. You were right.'

She glared at him.

'Please, wait here. I'll only be a minute.'

Rania said nothing, stood staring towards the hills.

Clay breathed in and started scrambling back down the hill. When he reached the car, Mahmoud was waiting for him, standing by the open driver's-side door. Clay looked back. Rania was gone.

'Go, Mahmoud,' said Clay. 'As fast as you can. Call the police. Tell them about those men in the van. Do you have a pen?'

Mahmoud fumbled in the glove box, produced an old pencil and the owner's manual. Clay thought back, visualised the van's registration plate, the Arabic characters. Mahmoud scribbled as Clay recited the numbers.

'They need to find that van. Tell the police you think they might be terrorists. Tourists will be the target.'

Mahmoud nodded and clasped Clay's hand. 'God be with you, my friend. I will return and wait for you here.'

Clay clapped Mahmoud on the shoulder. 'But please, my friend. No police here. We must handle this ourselves.'

'I understand.'

Clay started back up the hill at a sprint. When he reached the lip, he could see that Rania had reached the car and was already starting up into the hills, tracking her son's captors. Clay set off, loping down the hill. When he reached the road he doubled his pace, aware that if they were spotted, they would be easy pickings for a good shot. The AK's effective range meant that his handgun would be useless unless they could get close.

Rania was moving fast, matching the pair's pace. By the time he caught up, she was almost at the top of a second ridge. He crouched beside her, breathing hard.

'Look,' she said.

The pair had stopped and installed themselves in a hollow near the top of the next ridge. They were at least two hundred metres away, maybe more, and appeared to be arranging themselves to look down into the next valley. Were they overlooking Djesr-djeseru – the temple of Hatshepsut? Was that the plan? To fire down at targets below? If so, why bring the woman and the child? He'd seen only one weapon. It made no sense. Unless, of course, he was carrying something else in the pack.

'Come on,' said Rania, up and moving again.

Clay followed, keeping low as they skirted the edge of a saddle. They emerged another seventy-five metres closer, looking up at the pair now from directly behind their position. Clay checked his watch. Eight-forty in the morning. Half an hour since they'd left Mahmoud. Hopefully, he'd alerted the police by now, and they would be looking for the van.

'Eugène was living there,' whispered Rania. 'In the mosque.'

'How do you know?'

'I heard her speaking to someone. He'd been there for some time.'

'Did she see you?'

'Yes. But I was veiled. She did not recognise me.'

'I hope you're right.'

'What are they doing?' said Rania.

Clay focused the glasses. The man was staring intently down into the next valley. His elbows were raised to shoulder level. 'He's got binoculars. He's scanning whatever is over that ridge.'

A pair of shots, closely spaced but distant, cut the stillness, echoed back across the hills, became four, then eight. The distinctive crack of a Kalashnikov. Something crawled up Clay's neck, fluttered its wings inside his feet and hands, that old chill.

The man stood, his own AK still slung over his shoulder, focused his binoculars.

'It's coming from somewhere down the valley,' said Clay.

Before he could finish another flurry of shots reverberated through the hills. The woman was standing, too, looking down into the valley. The man made to start down in the direction of the shots but the woman reached out and grabbed his arm, held him fast. From here they could hear her voice, high-pitched, insistent. She was shouting at him.

Rania was up now, moving quickly across the barren ground. Clay drew his G21, chambered a round, followed. With every step closer, their chances got better. Rania knew this. The pair was fixed on whatever was happening below in the valley, and seemed unaware of their approach.

Clay and Rania were fifty metres away, crossing open ground, when the firing started again. This time it was intense and sustained, dozens of detonations echoing and dying among the rocks. The man shrugged off the woman's hold, stepped to the lip of the hollow and raised his AK in one hand above his head. Then he started shouting. He waved his arms above his head, back and forth. The shooting lulled a moment, then intensified, filling the valley. The man pointed his AK skywards, let go a burst. Spent cartridges spilled around him. They were close enough now that they could hear him.

'Brothers,' he screamed, almost hoarse now. 'Brothers, stop. What are you doing? Brothers, no.'

Clay stopped, went down on one knee, raised his weapon, steadied it on his forearm. Rania was ahead of him, off to one side. The man and the woman were still looking down into the valley, their backs turned. He had a clear shot. Thirty-five metres. He sighted, took a deep breath.

Just then the woman turned, faced them. She screamed. The man pivoted, started bringing his AK down and around.

F = M(dv/dt)

Time slowed. Seconds spun out into eternity.

Clay could see the man's hand tense around the AK's pistol grip, the tendons starting to flex, the woman's shriek hanging there in the terse viscosity of the stilled air, the blood creeping winter-slow in his own veins, everything mountain-clear and definitive.

Clay tightened his finger down on the Glock's trigger.

That was all it took. This smallest of movements. The force required miniscule – insufficient to lift a pen. Three times, one-fifth of a second apart.

The first round clipped the man's shoulder. The second hit his right leg just above the knee. A spray of red mist erupted from high on his chest as the third bullet hit. The man toppled back to the ground, the AK cartwheeling over the stones.

The woman shouted something, darted towards the weapon. Clay fired again, hit the AK where it lay. The woman's outstretched hand jerked back as two more rounds sent shattered stone whirring around her. Rania screamed for him to stop, sprinted forwards until she was steps away from the woman.

Below, the shooting had lulled, took on a cadenced rhythm, slow and methodical. Muffled screams filled the silence between detonations. Clay reached the edge of the ridge, looked down into the valley. The air was so clear he could see every detail. The sunlight shining on the fractured sandstone slopes. The broad valley opening up onto the deep green of the Nile valley. Hatshetsup's temple, its ranked gods and carved pillars set in perfect geometry. Near the top of the first stairway he could see a cluster of people, three of them, lying motionless. Cameras, bags and hats littered the ground around them. Dark stains haloed the bodies, deep red against the near-white sandstone. His heart tripped, shuddered. Further up, near the first bank of pillars, a woman sat propped up against a column, looking out towards the Nile. Her face and the front of her dress were lit by the morning sun. Inside the temple, tourists were running in every direction. A collective scream surged across the hills.

Clay could see that there was no escape. The tourists were hemmed in by the high walls of the temple. A man in a black police uniform and wearing a red bandana around his head stood at the only exit, brandishing an AK47. Inside, four other men, similarly dressed, walked among the screaming tourists, shooting them one by one. The police were nowhere to be seen.

Clay stood on the ridge, waved his arms above his head and shouted down into the valley. He raised his gun, fired off three quick rounds. If the attackers could see him or hear him, they paid no attention. The killing continued, slow and methodical. Clay counted at least thirty bodies now. From here he could see at least as many tourists running or hiding in various parts of the temple. Unless the police arrived soon, they had no chance.

Clay looked down at the wounded man. He was pushing himself along the ground with his undamaged leg.

'Brothers, no, please,' the man whispered. He looked up at the woman: 'You bitch. What have you done?'

The woman paid him no attention, backed away from Rania. Before Clay could react, she drew a long-bladed knife and put it to the boy's throat. 'Get back, both of you,' she screamed.

Rania gasped, held her ground. 'Please,' she said. 'I only want my son back. I don't care what you do. Just give me my son.' From where she stood, Rania could not see what was unfolding in the temple.

The man's eyes widened. 'Fatimah, what are you doing?' he shouted at the woman. 'Put that down.'

Rania swung her head towards the man, stood there staring, open mouthed. 'How could you?' she said. 'For God's sake, why?'

Below, another tourist fell, hit in the legs. He screamed, started using his arms to push himself towards one of the pillars. A smear of bright-red blood painted the tiles behind him. The gunman moved on, picked a new target.

Clay glanced at Rania, levelled the G21 at the man. 'What the fuck is going on?'

'I … I did it for you,' the man blurted. 'It wasn't supposed to be this way.' He turned towards the valley. 'Brothers,' he screamed, vocal chords rupturing. 'No. No. What have you done?'

'Fool,' said the woman. 'Did you really think that hostages would be enough? Nothing can be achieved peacefully. The blood of the *kuffar* is the only way.' Her resemblance to Rania was unsettling.

The boy was crying now, his wails loud against the screams from the temple, the slow, methodical, *crack-crack* of the AKs.

'Bitch,' yelled the man. 'Put down that knife.'

The woman backed away, again touched the blade to the boy's neck.

Rania took a step forwards, stopped dead. 'Please,' she said, hands raised before her. 'Whatever you want, we can help you. Anything. Just give me my son.'

The woman took another step back. As she did, her foot caught a loose slate. She stumbled, opened her arms to catch her balance. Just then, the man reached into the fold of his cloak, drew out a handgun, started pivoting it towards the woman.

'No!' screamed Rania.

Clay fired just as the man raised his arm for a shot. The big .45 calibre slug blew the man's face apart. Bone and brain and blood-matted hair splattered the ground.

'Hamid!' screamed Rania.

Clay turned and faced the woman. She was about the same distance away, side on. The boy was strapped to her chest, facing out, the knife across his throat. Clay raised the Glock, pointed it at the woman's head. 'Drop that knife, or the same thing happens to you.'

'Why?' said Rania, closing the distance between them. Tears

welled in her eyes, poured across her face. Deep sobs shook her body. 'Why did you do it?'

'For Islam,' she said, raising her eyes to the sky. 'For justice. They murdered my father, poisoned my family.'

Below, the firing had died down. The occasional shot rang out across the hills, the attackers finishing off the wounded, searching out the last victims.

Rania dropped to her knees, put her hands together. 'He is only a child. Innocent and pure. You speak of justice. Show it now. I beg you.'

The woman was smiling now, looking down at Rania, queen to slave, goddess to supplicant. But it was not a smile of benevolence. Her mouth was etched in cruelty. She tightened down on the blade. She was going to do it.

Clay filled his lungs, blanked his mind. He put away the sounds of shooting still coming from the valley. He closed off Rania's sobs, the cries of her son, the echoes of the dead and the dying, both real and remembered. He stilled all the tremors and ruptures of his soul. Then he exhaled, long and slow as he'd been taught, and pulled the trigger.

Force equals mass times acceleration. $F = ma$. Basic physics. The stuff you learn in high school. At that range, it took the fifteen-gram bullet less than eighteen one-thousandths of a second to reach its target, impacting the woman's skull at a velocity of almost a thousand kilometres an hour.

The woman's forehead disintegrated. Her body pitched over and sandbagged into the ground, the baby beneath her.

In the valley, the shooting had stopped. For a moment, silence came. The armed men were running back across the open ground towards the parking area.

Rania screamed, scrambled over to where the woman lay. The bullet had taken the top of her head away, scattered it over the crushed and powdered sandstone. Rania rolled the body over, tore at the carrier straps, wailing in desperation. Finally, she pulled her son free, cradled him to her breast.

Clay stood contemplating his work, the shattered bodies motion-less but for the bloodstained clothing flapping in the breeze. He stepped over to where the woman lay and dropped his G21 and the two extra magazines to the ground next to her outstretched hand. Next to the dead man, he placed his two grenades. He stood, unarmed, looking out across the temple and the scattered bodies, these murders they had been unable to prevent. It was just gone nine-thirty. Forty-five minutes since the shooting had started, and still no police.

After a time, Rania's sobs subsided and silence returned to the hills and the valley, this intended but long-since defiled resting place of kings.

Part V

17th November 1997. Luxor, Egypt. 23:10 hrs

I am not sure I can write. And yet I must.

Today I was reunited with my son. Today I was widowed, again.

Today I saw you, the man I love, reveal yourself for what you are: a brutal, clinical killer.

Today I was witness to a horrific massacre that will remain etched on the cracked-china surface of my consciousness until I die.

And yet Eugène lies here beside me, sleeping quietly. He has changed since I saw him last. His face is fuller, his arms and legs longer. His eyes are different, larger somehow, the colours of his irises more intense, deeply patterned. He looks so much like his father, may his soul rest in peace, despite what he has done. Even with all that has happened, what I feel now is joy. Deep, uninhibited joy. My son is alive, and he is home. الله أكبر

The events of the last days now seem as a continuum. Our journey here, following that hateful woman into the mosque, pretending to pray in the corner, seeing her emerge from one of the back rooms with Eugène, whisper her thanks to the imam. Following her into the hills, and then, seemingly centuries later, walking back across those same barren ridges with you beside me, silent and so far away. And then Mahmoud driving us north, across the river and back into Luxor, explaining that when he'd gone to the police, they would not believe him, had paid no attention to his warnings.

This evening, back at Mahmoud's house, we heard on the television news that the terrorists fled the temple on foot and were found a few hours later in a cave in the hills, dead by their own hand. Leaflets were found at the scene of the 'accident' as it is already being called on national television, some thrust inside the wounds of the dead, proclaiming this the work of Al-Gama'a al-Islamiyya. God help us all.

As expected, all hell is breaking loose. The president himself is coming to Luxor tomorrow to visit the site – the same president who is now grooming his son to take over from him when he retires. The security services have been put on high alert across the country, and tourists are fleeing in droves, cutting short their holidays and going home. We saw them this evening, streaming from hotels into buses for the airport. The same is happening across the country. Mahmoud's brother, who works in tourism, is despondent. It seems that, initially at least, GI has achieved its goal.

Tonight, after dinner, I spoke with Parveen. We were alone. She is very worried. Mahmoud speaks of nothing except a conspiracy within the police, their refusal to even consider his warnings, their complete absence from the temple as the massacre unfolded. She has tried to caution him, counsel prudence, but he is furious. We have put this lovely family into real danger, I know. I assured her that we were only here to retrieve my son, that we had nothing to do with the massacre, and quite the contrary, had tried to stop it. I did not tell her that, in my heart, I know we could have done more.

Now that we have Eugène, we will leave. Mahmoud is arranging this now. I pray to God to please look after these good people, protect and guide them.

And yet these murderers have killed and died in Allah's name. How can this be? How could He have allowed this? Such hate must dwell in their souls, to do such a thing.

The future lies before me as a dark and unknown sea, vast and deep.

Panamax

The first roadblock had been thrown up on the outskirts of Luxor, not far from the airport. The road was clogged with dozens of buses packed with angry, scared tourists. It took them nearly an hour, inching along behind a queue of at least twenty buses, to reach the checkpoint. The police were searching each vehicle. Dazed tourists milled about the roadside, clutching cases, bags and each other. Mahmoud slowed the big truck as they approached the barrier.

Clay and Rania had decided to dress as Westerners, to blend in with the flood of outgoing tourists. Gone were the *burqa* and *jelabia*. Clay wore the shirt and trousers Atef had bought for him, Rania a floor-length dress and padded jacket: husband and wife with young son, quitting Egypt like everyone else. They had decided to head for Safaq on the Red Sea coast, just over 150 kilometres away. Airports were too dangerous, and they did not want to go north. They each had passports issued in different names, and by different countries. Explaining why they were travelling with a child named Al-Farouk would be difficult. Instead, Mahmoud had telephoned a friend who worked in a shipping company and secured them a place on a freighter from Suez bound for Maputo via Djibouti, Mogadishu and Mombasa. Ten thousand US dollars for the three of them. No names, no questions asked. The ship would berth in Safaq tomorrow to take on cargo and was leaving the next day.

The black-uniformed policeman raised his hand to his eyes, flashed his torch.

Mahmoud made to stop. Torchlight lit his face. 'Say nothing,' he said, leaning his head out of the side window.

The cop with the torch started towards them. He'd got halfway to the cab when he stopped and smiled. Then he stepped back and away, and called to his colleague to raise the barrier. As they passed, he waved to Mahmoud and speared him off a salute.

Mahmoud thrust his big, hairy forearm through the open window and returned the wave. 'These, I know. I am sure they are good,' he said, gearing up. '*Al hamdillulah.*' He sounded as if he was trying to reassure himself.

Once past the airport, the road emptied. They ploughed on into an uncertain night. It wasn't long until they encountered the next roadblock, on the highway coming into Qus.

'It will be like this all the way to Safaqa,' said Mahmoud, air-braking the truck, gearing down. They were flagged to a halt. A policeman wearing the same uniform that Clay had seen the terrorists wearing at the temple – black with sliver buttons and epaulettes – clambered onto the cab's running board and waved a light into their eyes. Two similarly uniformed men stood in front of the truck, their weapons illuminated in the headlights, AK47s with double-taped magazines and folding stocks.

'Destination?' asked the policeman.

'Safaqa,' said Mahmoud, pointing back to the trailer. 'Dates and vegetables.'

The cop ran the light over Clay's face, held it a while on Rania. 'And these?'

'Friends,' said Mahmoud. 'Canadian and Swiss.'

'Passports,' said the cop.

Clay handed over his: Mark Edwards, born in Vancouver. Rania passed over hers: Veronique Deschamps.

The cop opened each passport in turn, directed the beam of his torch onto the photograph pages. 'You are leaving Egypt?' he said in Arabic, looking up at Clay.

Clay feigned not understanding.

Mahmoud shrugged. 'All the foreigners are leaving now.'

'Of course,' said the cop, handing back the passports. 'Safe journey. *Ma'a salaama.*'

As they drew away, Clay pursed his lips, exhaled long. The feeling of being defenceless, unarmed, welled up inside him. What dangers might they face between here and wherever fate would take them? He raised his hand and felt for the neck knife under his shirt, resting in the hollow between his pectoral muscles, and pushed its plastic sheath flat into the hard bone of his sternum.

He looked across at Mahmoud, there in the darkness, Rania between them, little Eugène sleeping in her arms. This man who'd spent his life plying the roads of Egypt from as far as Alexandria to the border with Somalia and south, who'd raised a family, built a life with his wife of thirty-one years, had done it in peace, had lived without ever having to kill, without having to suffer the true and insistent accusations of murdered souls. Rania, too, was, in this sense, pure. Despite all the danger she'd faced, she'd always found a way to do it without killing. Something that felt like awe coalesced within him, threatened to fill some of the emptiness.

By the time they reached Safaq, Rigel had passed its apogee and was falling towards the still-dark horizon. The docks were quiet, night-lit. Mahmoud parked the truck outside one of the loading terminals and turned off the engine. The place was deserted.

'Now we wait,' he said, pointing to a door in the side of the terminal building. 'Use the toilet, there. Then sleep.' He motioned behind him. 'Please, use the bed.'

Rania changed Eugène, fed him and retired to the sleeping compartment. She'd spoken little since leaving Luxor, and Clay left her to her silence. Clay and Mahmoud sat up front, sipping Mahmoud's whisky. Dawn came, lit a blue, cloud-strung horizon. Slowly, the docks came to life. More trucks came, big eighteen- and twenty-two-wheelers, loading and unloading cargo. Cranes swung, catching the sunlight on their tube frames. Mid-morning, a freighter rounded the northern point of the harbour and slipped into a berth.

'That's it,' said Mahmoud. '*Sirius Star*.' He opened the cab door. 'Stay here.'

Half an hour later Mahmoud returned. Rania was still in the back.

'Time to go,' he said.

Clay nodded, called back. 'Let's go, Ra.'

Rania emerged a few minutes later, carrying Eugène. His cheeks were red. He'd been crying. Tears covered her face.

'What's wrong?' said Clay.

'He does not remember me,' she said in Arabic, wiping her face with her free hand.

'It will take time,' said Mahmoud. 'Come, we must go.'

They crossed the open concrete apron to the quay. The ship was there – big and grey against the hazy white of the horizon. Cranes swung containers into the hold. After the desert, the smell of the sea was strong, the air thick and humid, laden with iodine and chlorine. Rania pulled a blanket close over Eugène's head and reached for Clay's hand as they approached the aft gangplank.

A man was waiting on the quay. As they approached he moved towards them. He was short and powerfully built. Tattoos veined his closely shaved head, snaked down both sides of his neck. He and Mahmoud shook hands.

'The payment,' said Mahmoud over his shoulder.

Clay passed him the cash. The man stood and counted through each bill. Then he did it again. He glanced at Clay, passed his gaze to Rania, held it there a moment. Then he nodded. 'Follow,' he said.

Clay shook Mahmoud's hand and looked into his eyes – this man he now called friend. 'Please, look after yourself,' said Clay in Arabic.

'And your family,' said Rania, defying convention and going up on her toes to kiss his cheek.

'Go with God,' said Mahmoud.

They followed the man up and onto the big Liberian-registered Panamax, and down three levels to a small starboard-side cabin. There were two bunk beds, a head, a small washbasin and mirror.

'Galley is this level, aft,' said the man. 'Meals for you at six, thirteen, and nineteen. Same food as rest of us.' His accent was vaguely Slavic, or Nordic, perhaps.

Clay nodded.

'How far you go?'

'Mombasa,' said Clay.

'Five days,' said the man. 'You can go topside during day. Not at night. Stay away from cargo holds. Stay aft.' Then he turned and was gone.

Rania sat on the bed, lay Eugène next to her. She looked up at Clay. Her face was drawn, 'Do you think…' she began, but stopped herself short.

'What?' said Clay.

Rania shook her head.

Clay looked out of the porthole. Mahmoud was there on the quayside, looking up at the ship. He was still there three hours later when the big freighter pulled away from the dock and churned its way out into the hazy expanse of the Red Sea.

19th November 1997. Somewhere off the
coast of East Africa. 09:30 hrs

Eugène is sleeping now, finally. My joy at finding him again is tempered by the knowledge that he is changed, that he seems, still, not to know me. He does not cry, does not respond as a child should. He is withdrawn, silent. What did they do to him? What traumas has he endured?

You are up on the deck somewhere, chéri, exercising or staring out to sea. Last night I lay in bed and watched you change. You turned away from me. Only the small light over the sink was on, but I could see the thickness in your shoulders, the heavy slabs of your shoulder blades flexing as you pulled off your shirt. You carry no fat around your waist, unlike Hamid. The muscles of your legs are very big, almost too big for your derriere, which is compact and angled. Everything about your body is edged, hardened, familiar. The damage is there quite plainly, also: the new welted scarring across your side and those other traumas you have suffered. Your ear is healing quickly, but with the old scar across your cheek and the smaller gun welts from the farm in Cyprus, it is only your pale eyes and the cut of your jaw and the stubble of fair hair that keep you from being ugly.

As I watch you, the man who killed the father of my son, confusion and regret surge through me. I have simply no idea what I should feel, how I should behave, what I should do in the face of everything that has happened. Only with Eugène, caring for him, hoping that he may begin to respond to me again, do I find solace, some measure of meaning.

What was Hamid doing there, on that mountainside, looking down as that horrible massacre unfolded? I can only conclude that he, too, was a member of GI. It is clear to me now that it happened over the course of his many work trips to Egypt. The woman, Fatimah, must have played a key role in radicalising him, in bringing him to make such a monumental decision. Did he love her? I know from the way she spoke to him on the mountainside that she did not love him. How long had they been planning it? Hamid said, there on the mountainside, that he had done it for me. What can that possibly mean? The knowledge that he betrayed me this way – taking our son and framing me for murder; the lengths to which they went – the planted emails on my computer, the DNA in the incinerator, the teeth, the clothing, all of it – makes me shudder. My violation is now complete.

And yet the irony seems like the work of Greek gods, toying with us for their fancy. The four of them – Yusuf, Hamid, the Kemetic, and yes, even her *– fighting a terrible evil, not just the pollution and the poisoning of innocents, but the systematic exploitation of an entire nation, an entire people. And each of them reaching a different conclusion on what means were justified, each finding in the response of their enemy the limits of their own conviction, and eventually, coming to the same end.*

That this end should come as it did! How could this have happened? The only man I have ever loved kills my husband. I kill my husband's friend, one of the few men brave enough to stand up to this scourge, this legal crime. Samira is killed for getting too close to me. And, if I had told you, Claymore, there in Garbage City, to kill those two crooked policemen, you surely would have, and perhaps Samira would be alive now, and her girls would have a mother now instead of a foster family.

And for all of it, nothing has changed. As Mahmoud said, this last atrocity will only allow the government and the people that control it to further restrict freedoms, to redouble their efforts to eliminate dissent, to rule this country and its people purely and solely in their own interest. I am crying inside. The waste.

For the first time in my life, I doubt God.

The days pass. The coast of Africa slips by, sometimes obscured in haze,
sometimes close, barren and deserted, without a trace of green. My slide
into nihilism continues.

Claymore, my love, we have not exchanged a single word since we
left Egypt. You tried, at first, but I have steadfastly rejected all your
advances, verbal and physical. We go together to the meals – I do not
want to go alone and have all those men stare at me. When I am with
you, their stares become furtive glances. Most do not look at all. I know
you frighten them. They look at you and I can feel their fear. We eat,
but we do not speak. We return to our cabin and you go up on deck,
returning only to take me to the next meal. At night, you climb into
the top bunk and read for a while and then turn out the light. In the
darkness, your voice comes, deep and sure: Goodnight, Ra, you say. And
each night, I do not answer.

I can feel myself turning inwards. Only Eugène matters to me now. I
have not prayed for three days. I can no longer feel God.

When I was just a girl, after the men had come to our house in
Algiers and murdered my father as I watched, my mother told me that
it was Allah's will, that there was purpose and meaning to everything.
My mother's faith was strong, and it nurtured mine, so that as the years
passed I began to see indications of God's purpose. I came to believe that
my father had been taken from me so that I could see the value of life, of
the limited time we are given, and that like him, it was my purpose to
resist the forces of extremism that were corrupting Islam. That was why
I joined the Directorate. Then, when I met you, and you helped me see
the error we were about to make in Yemen, I again saw God's purpose
revealed. For without the events so entrained, I would never have met

you, the love of my life. And then, finally, Eugène. It was complete. And in a way, I was happy.

And now, I have lost you both.

I read my Koran, searching for direction. But the words are empty to me.

There is no God.

It Was Something

24th November, 1997
Latitude 02°, 29' N, Longitude 46°, 47' E
Off the Coast of Somalia

Clay stood on the starboard aft deck and looked out across the grey early-morning chop towards Africa. He'd risen while it was still dark and come above deck to breathe and think. The journey had been uneventful, so far, reassuring in its monotony, the routine of life at sea.

The day before, he'd picked up a newspaper in the galley, a copy of the *Al-Ahram* weekly, in English. The Luxor accident was front-page news. There was a photograph of the dead insurgents, laid out in front of the cave where they were found. Exiled members of Al-Gama'a al-Islamiyya were already blaming the massacre on foreign radicals who they said had taken control of the organisation. In particular, they blamed the new leader of GI for what they called a grave miscalculation. At the bottom of the page was a recent photograph of Rania's husband, clean shaven, in shirt and tie. The caption identified him as Hamid Al-Farouk, also known as The Lion. There was no mention of bodies in the hills above the temple.

Rania was still locked in a prison of her own devising. Other than her interactions with Eugène she had maintained a strict isolation, neither acknowledging Clay's attempts at conversation, nor allowing eye contact with any person other than her son. After what she'd just been through, he didn't blame her. After his first firefight, he'd huddled in his hole all night without saying a single word to anyone, Eben included. For days after, he'd felt bruised inside, dulled somehow, as if some essential part of his psyche had been torn out and replaced dead. All she needed was time. He hadn't shown her the newspaper.

Each day since they'd boarded *Sirius Star*, he'd watched her, sometimes for hours, as she wrote in her diary or pored over her Koran – the copy her father had given her. Mostly she would read silently, her lips moving but making no sound. But occasionally she would whisper a sura to Eugène. At least she had her faith to support her. For a long time now he'd had nothing, just a vague, far-off hope that maybe, one day, he would find some meaning in it all. The clemency he thought he might find by going back to South Africa to testify to the Truth and Reconciliation Commission turned out as the false hope Crowbar had warned him it would be. Instead, he got the AB and its assassins. And because of it, Crowbar was dead. His only hope now was that G would keep his word, that the promised additional fifty thousand dollars would be enough to buy his silence.

In a few hours they'd arrive in Mogadishu, unload cargo, and then continue south. No one wanted to stay in Somalia any longer than absolutely necessary. A day later, they'd be in Mombasa. If *Flame* was still where he'd left her, hidden in the mangroves, they had a way out. The world was a big place.

☾

Mogadishu, once called the white pearl of the Indian Ocean for its Italian and Arabic architecture and stunning setting, lay stunned and bruised under a mid-afternoon sun. Burned-out vehicles hulked among decapitated palms and the rebar-and-concrete skeletons of smashed buildings. A blanket of soot and dust had settled over the city as if it had recently been witness to a huge conflagration. Great slabs of masonry peeled from the walls and turrets of the old town, revealing flesh-coloured stone beneath the once-brilliant whitewash.

Bullet holes riddled the quayside warehouses. Only the water seemed to have retained its vibrancy. The sea here was clear, the shoals and reefs reflecting in shimmering waves of ultramarine, shifting banks of oyster shell and pearl.

As the freighter approached, crowds began to gather on the quay. Clay watched from the porthole as they drew close. A vehicle parted the throng, a Toyota *bakkie* with a mounted heavy machine gun manned by a Somalian irregular in mismatched camouflage and reflective sunnies. Soon the freighter had tied up alongside and the onboard cranes swung into action, setting containers onto the quay. Even in the midst of chaos and civil war, the business of commerce continued.

Clay stood back from the porthole and watched Rania playing with Eugène on the lower bunk. She had fashioned little shapes out of some paper she'd found in the galley and was helping the boy arrange them on the blanket. The little guy had been good, sleeping long parts of the night and napping frequently, rocked to sleep by the slow rhythms of the ocean and the vibration of the ship's engines. Although he knew little of such things, she seemed a good mother, attentive and affectionate.

'Mogadishu,' Clay said. 'Want to look?'

Rania looked up at him. It was the first time she'd made eye contact in days. She gazed right into him, held it, said nothing. For a second he thought she might speak, share something with him, some of what he knew was torturing her, but she looked away, went back to playing with Eugène.

It was something. Progress. In a few more days they would be aboard *Flame*, and then everything would be different. They would have to work together to survive, to ensure Eugène's safety. They would have to communicate, cooperate. There would be much to do: navigate, provision, cook and clean, pilot and sail. She would have no choice but to focus. Unless of course, she decided to go her own way. She had money, wherewithal. She had never said that she would go with him after, only that she needed his help to her find her son.

Clay was about to turn back to the porthole when there was a knock at the cabin door.

Rania looked up at him. He shrugged, stepped to the door, put his hand inside his shirt and grabbed the handle of his neck knife. 'Who is it?'

'It's me.' It was the tattooed skinhead who acted as their official shipboard liaison.

'What do you want?'

'Need to talk.'

Clay opened the door.

'You have visitor,' said the skinhead. There was someone standing behind him, off to one side, obscured by the bulkhead.

Clay blinked. 'I don't...' That was as far as he got. The man pivoted past the skinhead and let go a powerful front kick, catching Clay full in the solar plexus, sending him toppling back against the bulkhead.

Rania screamed. The man stepped into the cabin and closed the door behind him. He raised a pistol, aiming it at Clay's face. Rania snatched up Eugène and held him to her. Clay looked up. The face before him was almost unbelievably hideous. The jaw misshapen, wired shut. Both cheeks sunken, caved, covered over by patches of weeping, bruised skin, horribly grafted. Only the eyes seemed undamaged.

It couldn't be. But it was. Manheim.

Soliloquy for the Fallen

'Don't look so surprised, Straker,' said Manheim in Afrikaans through clenched jaw.

Clay stared down the barrel of the silenced automatic. He couldn't see the head of the bullet waiting in the breech, but he knew it was there.

'You really thought we couldn't track you?' said Manheim.

'Just leave her alone,' said Clay.

Manheim's face twisted into what may have been a smile. 'Aren't you going to ask me, Straker?'

'Go ahead. Tell me.'

Manheim turned his head. 'Bullet went through both cheeks. All I lost was a couple of teeth and part of my jaw.'

'Should have made sure.'

'*Ja, ja,*' said Manheim. 'Hindsight.' He pulled aside his shirt, revealed a custom-fitted ballistic Kevlar vest. 'Never go anywhere without it.'

Clay glanced at Rania. She was staring right at him, terror in her eyes. He shook his head, opened his hand palm out to her.

'She's safe as long as she doesn't try anything,' said Manheim, switching to English. 'Understand *bokkie*?'

Rania nodded and moved Eugène so that her body was shielding him.

'Where's Crowbar?' said Manheim.

'Dead.'

Manheim's eyes narrowed. 'Bullshit.'

'You were there.'

'Sudan?'

Clay nodded.

'Shit.' Manheim glanced at the porthole. 'I wanted to ask him something. I tried to tell you, back at the airstrip.'

'Maybe it was the way you opened the conversation.'

Manheim ignored this. 'He and I, we—'

'He saved your sister's life, and you fucking hunt him down and kill him. He was right, you have no honour.'

Manheim swallowed hard. 'What did you say?'

'He saved your sister. During the break-in at your parent's farm. That's what he told me. They killed your parents, but he got them all before they could touch your sister.'

Manheim took a step back, lowered the gun a few inches so that it was now pointing at Clay's knees. '*Fok* me.' He raised the gun again. 'No, it can't be. She never told me.'

'Maybe she didn't want her big brother to know that she was screwing one of his army buddies.'

Manheim seemed to wither again, shifted his weight from one foot to the other and back. He was thinking about it.

Clay looked for an opening. 'He thought you knew. Ask her.'

Manheim took three more steps back, leaned against the cabin door and lowered the pistol so that it was pointing at the floor. '*Fokken moeder van God*,' he said. 'I always thought...' he began, but cut himself short. 'What did you do, anyway, to get the AB so pissed at you?'

'They didn't tell you?'

Manheim forced a smile. 'They don't tell us shit.'

'Operation Coast. Our nation's secret biological and chemical warfare programme. I helped tell the world what they were doing.'

Manheim considered this a moment. 'That's all over now.'

'Tell them that.'

Manheim made little circles with the pistol's barrel, as if he was aiming to hit the circumference of a target painted on the floor. 'To think that old bastard was working from the inside, all that time,' he said. 'The AB knew for years they had a leak, a Torch Commando mole, but they could never pin him down.'

Clay had first become aware of Torch – the underground movement dedicated to the creation of a free, liberal, multi-racial South Africa – and the bravery of its mostly white members, back in 1981. He cycled through a few deep lungfulls of air, tried to push the memories away.

'It wasn't just you, Straker. He helped dozens of people escape, tipped them off, helped them get out of the country. Killed at least five AB assassins in the process. We had a name for him: *Rooikat*. The Caracal.' Manheim wasn't speaking to Clay or Rania, now. He was speaking to himself, a soliloquy for the fallen. 'He was a good friend, and a *fok* of a good fighter.'

'He said the same about you.'

'When I came looking for whoever was tipping you off, I never believed for one second that it would be him.' Manheim stared at the floor for a long time.

'Crowbar said that you fell out. What happened?'

'Let's just say we grew to have opposing views of the world.'

'You joined the AWB.'

'That's right.'

'Then why the hell are you working for the AB?' Clay had slowly gathered himself, put himself into position for a last desperate lunge. With Manheim on the other side of the cabin now, it would be a long shot. But he wasn't going to go down without a fight.

Manheim nodded slowly. 'We're not so different – you, me, Crowbar, even her.' Manheim pointed the gun at Rania.

'*Fok jou*,' said Clay. 'We're nothing like you.'

Manheim swung the gun back towards Clay. 'You don't see it, do you Straker? We're all fighting the same enemy. Each in our own way.'

'That's not the way it looks to me.'

'I don't give a damn what you think, Straker. I really don't give a shit.'

'The innocents you killed on Zanzibar?' said Clay, barely holding himself back. 'Were they the enemy?'

'You know I didn't kill that woman and her kid, Straker. I told those two *kaffirs* to keep it clean.' Manheim lowered the gun a moment. 'That was unnecessary.'

'Well so is this.' Clay opened his arms wide. 'We're done fighting. We're leaving. Leave us be. You don't need to do this.'

Manheim ran his free hand across his face, thumb on one cheek, fingers on the other, entry and exit wounds. 'My sister. She's married now. Has three kids.'

Clay tensed, readied to charge. Next time Manheim looked away, he would go.

'Claymore, *chéri*. Please, do not.'

Both men looked at Rania. Clay unwound.

'Please, *monsieur*,' she continued, setting her gaze on Manheim now. 'I knew your friend, Jean-Marie. His wife is my friend. She is pregnant with their first child. He saved your sister. Be the honourable man your friend thought you to be.'

Manheim stared at her as if she were an oracle come to presage his destiny.

'There has been enough killing,' she said.

Manheim stood there for a long time, drawing those little circles with his handgun. And then he sighed, breathed in and out slowly, and lowered the pistol. He glared at Clay, as if to warn him against a sudden attack, shoved the pistol into his waistband and covered it over with his shirt.

'G told me everything,' he said. 'Gave me the photos and the ear. Wire me the money you promised him within three days. Here are the account details.' He placed a card on the table near the door. 'And then go. I'll look after the AB. You ever surface again, you're dead. You hear me, Straker? Both of you. No more fucking Operation COASTs, no more goddamned bleeding-heart court cases trying to right the world's wrongs.' He glanced at Rania. 'Raise that kid of yours. Hell, have a few more for all I care. Just don't ever show up on anyone's radar again.' He cracked the cabin door, stepped over the threshold.

'And that goes for your little girlfriend in Zanzibar, too,' said Manheim, leaning back in. 'Consider my debt to Crowbar repaid. We're even.' And then he was gone.

3rd December 1997. Long 00°, 42' S; Lat 46°,
42' E. The Indian Ocean. 10:35 hrs

This morning I took my first star sight, calculated my first position. You have been teaching me how to use the sextant, how to navigate by the stars. You say I need to know how to do it, in case you cannot.

Looking up into the infinite, seeing order in seeming chaos, I find myself regaining a measure of faith. In what, exactly, I am not yet sure. Perhaps, as I watch you go about your tasks on our little home, securing the sails, working the tiller, rigging the self-steering (all these terms I am only just starting learn!), it is faith in you. In us. In our ability to make a life for ourselves, on our own terms. To take all that we have seen and learned, and forge it into something new, something lasting and true.

Eleven days ago, we found Flame *among the mangroves, where you had left her. Seeing this little boat for the first time, there in her hiding place, was like glimpsing part of your life without me. And now that I am here, I marvel that after everything I have done and said, you came for me, as true and constant as the compass that guides us.*

As the days have passed, we have had time to talk. You have recounted to me the events on Zanzibar, your flight across East Africa, the terrible ambush in Sudan the day Jean-Marie was killed. I, too, have shared some of what I have been through.

Yesterday, for the first time, Eugène laughed and smiled at me. He is getting better. Each day I feel him coming closer to me, remembering, or perhaps just building new trust in me. The resilience of children is amazing.

Before we left Mombasa, at your urging, I called Inspector Marchand in Paris. To say she was surprised to hear from me is a gross understatement. I told her that Eugène was in my arms. That my husband was dead, killed in Egypt only a few days before. She asked if I was coming back to clear my name. I told her I had no intention of returning. Then she wished me good luck. It was very human of her.

I also called Hope. She is strong and seems to be managing alone. The baby is due soon. I told her we were safe, but that we would be disappearing for a while. I could hear her crying. I know she wishes she could be with us. Somehow that would seem right. Her son is yours. Her new baby is Jean-Marie's. We all love each other. That will have to be enough, for now.

From Mombasa I posted everything we have on Yusuf's case to my editor at AFP in Paris. The parcel I sent contained the data dossier, the Kemetic's diary with my transcriptions, and the memory card from his camera with most of the photographs. He may do with it as he wishes. The Directorate have now been informed, via my friend, of the death of Fatimah Salawi at Luxor, and the fact that Hamid Al-Farouk, a French citizen, was almost certainly the militant who called himself 'The Lion'. I told him to tell them not to try to find me. That I needed time, and peace.

I try not to speculate on Hamid's motives, on what led him to do what he did. We can never really know another person, what drives them. Perhaps he simply lost faith in the law, in the concept of justice as he'd practised it. It is clear to me now that Hamid knew that the Consortium would come after him. And so he decided to pre-empt them, fake his own death, and take the fight to them. Whether it was his idea or hers, I will never know. But the thought that he would sacrifice me to achieve this, make me out to be a murderer, hurts me more deeply than I can express. I cannot help wondering: if I had not been late coming home that day, would they have killed me? Had they argued, perhaps? She wanting to kill me, he opting for framing me. Did he anticipate, perhaps, that the Consortium would come after me, too, and devised the framing to protect me from its assassins? He would have known that, behind bars, I would be safe. Is that perhaps what he meant when he said he had done it for me? I must resign myself to the fact that I will never know.

The degree to which Fatimah Salawi influenced Hamid I can only guess. Love is a powerful thing. So is hate. I know that I will find it within myself to forgive him one day. I doubt the families of the Luxor victims ever will.

It is clear to me now that once the Consortium had determined to eliminate Hamid, the direction of events was set. Knowing my association with you, and our role in exposing Operation COAST, the AB and the Consortium decided, together, that it was time to get rid of us both. We are dangerous.

Last night we sat in the cockpit together. It was cold. Your put your arms around me and pointed up to a small cluster of stars. Those, you said, are the Pleiades, the daughters of Pleione, the seven sisters. At first, I saw only five stars. But then you gave me the binoculars and I realised that there were nine. You named them each. The parents, Atlas and Pleione, hand in hand, so close together that to my naked eye they had been one. And then the seven daughters: Alcyone, the brightest, Merope, Electra, and Maia, and the three smaller stars I had not seen at first: Cleano, Taygeta and Stereope, the smallest. In any monolith there are cracks – places where the light shines through.

After leaving the estuary where you had hidden Flame, we set sail for Zanzibar's northernmost island, Pemba. We visited the daughter of the woman Manheim murdered. Zuz is living with her grandmother and great-aunt now, in this most remote place. We stayed three nights only, long enough to provision for our voyage.

Zuz's mother must have been very beautiful. I could see from the way she looked at you, Claymore, that she is in love with you, in her own adolescent way. It made me smile to see the two of you together – you fatherly and stern, she mature beyond her years, twisting you this way and that. The two of you work on different planes, and yet there is a bond there, a deep respect. You told me about Grace and Joseph.

Flame is small but sturdy. The weather has been fine, and the winds fair. Nights, you sleep in the cockpit, allowing Eugène and me the forward berth.

The ocean is beautiful, so powerful. There is peace here in the endless blue horizons, the shifting of weather and clouds, the deep currents. We are making steady progress north along the coast. There is something deeply satisfying about watching the daily position fixes as they move across the map. Soon we will start east across the Arabian Sea, as the north-east monsoon builds. I have always wanted to see India.

As each day goes by, I can see something growing in you, my love. You are healing, physically. Your ear is fully mended, the wound in your side also. You are tanned and strong. Your hair is bleached by sun and salt. You smile at me from the cockpit, standing with the tiller under your arm. There is, for the first time since I have known you, no pain in your eyes, no deep, lurking terror. It is as if something has left you, a shadow of some kind – a dark umbra; and in its place I can see glimpses of something you may have been once, traces of a boyish innocence.

Last night, for the first time in years, we made love. Eugène was asleep in the forward cabin. Stars filled the sky to bursting. The ocean surged beneath us. The air was so pure in our lungs. I cannot describe it. I love you. And for the first time, I am sure that you love me.

And yet in my happiness, I think of all of those we have left behind – some dead, others locked in a hell of their own making, others surviving as best as they can, trying to stay sane in an insane world. You say that we have done our fighting, you and I. That it is time to live for ourselves now. Life is fleeting. I do not know how long this can continue, but right now, I do not ever want it to end.

Absolution for the Living

Clay stands, tiller in hand, and looks up into the night sky. Time spreads out before him, a universe of stars. He feels the deep vibrations of the rudder, the finer harmonics of the hull folding back the water. The boat is alive with the soft inhalations of its occupants. And all around him are the flowing currents and deep, living rhythms of the planet.

It is all there, pulsing inside him like some distant quasar – each death, every mercy. He thinks again of all those who time has eclipsed. He thinks of Grace and Joseph, now part of this same limitless ocean. Of Eben and Kingfisher and Bluey, and so many more, sacrificed for a lie. Of Vivian, whom he might have loved, in another, saner, world. He remembers Crowbar, lying in his desert grave, weapon at his breast, as the first grains of sand cover him over. And he decides that this will be the last time. He raises his voice and speaks aloud to the universe their names, each in turn, and asks them for absolution. Then he says goodbye.

He lashes the tiller amidships, loosens the jib and with Capella steady off the starboard bow, goes below. Rania is asleep in the forward berth with Eugène. In the starlight, he can just see the curve of her hip under the light blanket. He lights the alcohol stove, pumps some water into the kettle and settles it onto the gimbals.

Landfall is still seven or eight days away if the winds hold. He wonders what she will do, after they reach India. He hasn't asked what her plans are, and she has not offered. On past evidence, he must assume that she will again disappear and leave him to navigate these meridians on his own.

He spoons instant coffee and sugar into a mug, pours in hot water, stirs it with a knife, and sits at the table. There, before him, is Rania's diary, the one he has seen her writing in ever since they were reunited in Cairo. He sips the coffee, stares at the black leather cover, the elastic strap. Never before has he seen it anywhere except in her hands.

He contemplates it for a long time as he finishes his coffee. Then he reaches out and opens the front cover.

His own eyes look up at him from the past. He looks at the photograph a moment, and then reads:

25th October, 1997. Paris, France. 02:50 hrs

Chéri, mon amour:
My husband has disappeared. And so has my son.

Historical Note

On 17th November, 1997, at approximately 08:45, six men entered the Temple of Hatshepsut in Luxor, southern Egypt, dressed as police. They were carrying AK47 assault rifles and knives. After killing the two policemen stationed at the parking area entrance, they moved into the temple, trapping almost a hundred tourists inside. Over the next forty-five minutes, moving methodically through the columned courtyards, they killed sixty-two tourists and wounded twenty-six others. Many of the victims were shot in the legs and then dispatched later at close range. Several, mainly women, were mutilated with knives. The dead included four Japanese couples on honeymoon, almost all of a Swiss tour group, and a five-year old boy. The terrorists subsequently hijacked a bus, apparently intending to continue their rampage at the nearby Valley of the Kings. But the bus driver took them in the opposite direction. When stopped at a police roadblock, the gunmen fled into the hills, and were found later, dead, in a cave. They had committed suicide. Notes were found on the bodies claiming: '*We shall take revenge for our brothers who have died on the gallows. The depths of the earth are better for us than the surface since we have seen our brothers squatting in their prisons, and our brothers and families tortured in their jails.*'

The massacre, termed an 'accident' by the Egyptian government, destroyed the Egyptian tourism industry for the next two years. Egyptians were outraged. Sensing that they had badly miscalculated, organisers and supporters of Al-Gama'a al-Islamiyya quickly distanced themselves from the attack. Some claimed it was the work of the Israelis, others that it had been planned and executed by the police to justify further repression and restrictions of personal freedom.

(

During the 1990s and early parts of the following decade, several major scientific studies of air quality in Cairo were conducted by different organisations. They revealed the immense economic and human health costs of some of the worst urban air pollution on the planet. Several of the studies pointed clearly to the severe effects on children in particular, including a significant lowering of IQ. The reports were never released to the public.

Air quality in Cairo is now much improved, thanks to a number of foreign-aid funded initiatives. When I was there in May of 2017, doing some additional research for this book and visiting old friends, you could actually see more than a couple of hundred metres. And yet, a few days later, not far from where I was travelling in the Western Desert, a busload of Coptic Christians were stopped at the side of the road by men dressed as police. They boarded the bus and opened fire, killing all aboard, including children. The Copts had been on a pilgrimage to the monastery of Saint Samuel the Confessor. Islamic State claimed responsibility.

Since the revolution of 1952, which deposed King Farouk and the monarchy, Egypt has been ruled as a dictatorship by three presidents: Gamal Abdel Nasser until his death in 1970, Anwar Sadat from 1971 until his assassination in 1981, and Hosni Mubarak until his resignation in the face of the 2011 popular revolution. All were ex-army, supported by a cadre of loyal officers and extremely wealthy businessmen. At the time of publication in 2018, the army was back in control, having ousted the only democratically elected president in Egyptian history, the Islamist, Mohamed Morsi.

(

After years of civil war costing over 1.5 million lives, Sudan was divided in two in 2011. The conflict continues, in part driven by the struggle to control oil revenues. At last reckoning, over a million people have been displaced from Darfur, and more than two hundred thousand are dead.

❨

In 2017, the Lancet Commission on Pollution and Health estimated that over nine million people die prematurely every year because of air pollution, more than from war, smoking, and AIDS combined. Meanwhile, in the same year, the world's eight richest people, all men, controlled as much wealth as the poorest thirty percent on the planet. And inequality is growing.

Tens of thousands of people now live permanently on the high seas, out of the reach of governments, moving with the winds and currents from place to place, living on their own terms. The choices are ours to make. Only the past is written. We control the future.

Acknowledgements

I finished the final edits of this novel in one of my favourite places in the world, a little hideaway in the south-west of Western Australia, where we camp and swim in the river and walk the deserted coastline. To have such places to visit and spend time in, I am truly grateful. To paraphrase one of my favourite authors, the world is a beautiful place, and worth fighting for. This small contribution to that fight is made inestimably better by the efforts and insights of my fabulous publisher Karen, my editor, James, my agent, Broo, and Heidi, my wife of thirty years, to whom this book is dedicated. I couldn't do it, any of it, without you. And thanks, finally and most importantly, to you, the reader. It is because of you, and the hope that this collection of words may, in some small way, connect with something special within you, that I write.